KT-484-430

What Lucy's fans say . . .

'Wonderful characters and the stories are
always great, with twists and turns'
Gemma

'Lucy's books are as snuggly as a blanket, as warm
as a cup of tea and as welcoming as family'
Cheryl

'Full of friendship, family and how when life throws
something at you, you have to fight back!'
Emily

'A skilful writer with the ability to
place herself in anyone's shoes'
Sue

'Lucy's books make me smile, cry and give me
happiness, a little bit of escapism from everyday life.
Page-turners I just can't put down!'
Mandy

BY THE SAME AUTHOR

Novels

Any Way You Want Me

Over You

Hens Reunited

Sweet Temptation

The Beach Café

Summer with My Sister

Me and Mr Jones

One Night in Italy

The Year of Taking Chances

Summer at Shell Cottage

The Secrets of Happiness

The House of New Beginnings

On a Beautiful Day

Novellas

A Baby at the Beach Café

Ebook novellas

Christmas at the Beach Café

Christmas Gifts at the Beach Café

Lucy Diamond

Something to Tell You

MACMILLAN

First published 2019 by Macmillan
an imprint of Pan Macmillan
20 New Wharf Road, London N1 9RR
Associated companies throughout the world
www.panmacmillan.com

ISBN 978-1-5098-5109-6

Copyright © Lucy Diamond 2019

The right of Lucy Diamond to be identified as the
author of this work has been asserted by her in accordance
with the Copyright, Designs and Patents Act 1988.

All rights reserved. No part of this publication may be reproduced,
stored in a retrieval system, or transmitted, in any form, or by any means
(electronic, mechanical, photocopying, recording or otherwise)
without the prior written permission of the publisher.

Pan Macmillan does not have any control over, or any responsibility for,
any author or third-party websites referred to in or on this book.

1 3 5 7 9 8 6 4 2

A CIP catalogue record for this book is available from the British Library.

Typeset in 11.25/16 pt Dante MT Std by Jouve (UK), Milton Keynes
Printed and bound by CPI Group (UK) Ltd, Croydon, CR0 4YY

This book is sold subject to the condition that it shall not, by way of
trade or otherwise, be lent, hired out, or otherwise circulated without
the publisher's prior consent in any form of binding or cover other than
that in which it is published and without a similar condition including
this condition being imposed on the subsequent purchaser.

Visit **www.panmacmillan.com** to read more about all our books
and to buy them. You will also find features, author interviews and
news of any author events, and you can sign up for e-newsletters
so that you're always first to hear about our new releases.

For my family, with love

Chapter One

The door was painted white, with a smart brass letterbox and matching knocker. Standing there, trying to summon up some courage, Frankie Carlyle could smell the sweet fragrance of the pale velvety roses that rambled up the side of the house, and felt the warmth of the midsummer sun on her bare head. Behind her, shouts and laughter from a nearby sports field were carried on the breeze, as well as the faint rumble of the ring-road in the distance. Come on, then, she said to herself. This is your moment. The one you've been thinking about for the last six months. Are you going to knock or what?

She'd set off that morning feeling determined, feeling ready. Had driven all the way here – up the tarmacked spine of the country, through the Midlands and into Yorkshire, gripping the steering wheel so doggedly that her hands had stiffened with cramps the second she'd pulled on the handbrake. Craig had suggested taking the train – it was so much faster, he'd said, clicking at his phone to look up the timetable for her – but Frankie preferred to travel under her own steam. Not least in case she needed to make a quick getaway again.

The miles of motorway, the service stations and traffic were all behind her now, though, the northward slog already dimming in her mind compared to the surreal situation of standing there, outside his house. But what if he no longer lived here? Or, worse, didn't want to know?

Well, there was only one way to find out.

After a final smoothing down of her tousled dark hair, and an apprehensive lick of her lips, she swallowed back her trepidation and rapped the knocker once, twice. The sound was almost as loud as the thumping of her heart. For a hysterical moment she was seized by the urge to turn and run, to get back in the car and drive away, give up on the whole ridiculous idea. Then she imagined Craig's astonished face if she went home and told him this – 'What, you didn't even wait for him to answer the *door*?' – and managed to hold her nerve instead, folding her arms across her chest and doing her best to compose herself. Deep breaths. This encounter didn't have to be combative or upsetting. She would be pleasant, friendly, calm. If he ever opened the door, that was. If he ever appeared!

A car chugged past behind her, but otherwise the street was quiet. The house was still, unresponsive, and she began to feel her adrenalin leaking away, disappointment edging into its place. She knocked again. Perhaps he was out in the garden, tending to a vegetable plot. Perhaps he was snoozing in a deckchair, the morning's newspaper half-read on his knee. Perhaps he was deaf. Perhaps he was dead.

'You all right there, love?' came a voice just then and Frankie turned to see a woman emerging from the neighbouring house, unlocking the small blue Micra on her drive in a businesslike manner. She looked to be in her fifties and was giving Frankie a beady once-over, as if she could smell trouble.

'Oh,' said Frankie. 'Yes. I was looking for Harry Mortimer.' It felt peculiar to actually say his name aloud after all this time; to speak of him in terms of being a real person, rather than as a shadowy concept. A mystery. 'Does he still live here?'

'Harry? He certainly does. Although you've missed him today; they'll be down at the village hall for hours yet.' She eyed Frankie with barely disguised interest. 'I'll be there myself later, if you want me to pass on a message?'

Yeah, right. Like that wouldn't be the most inappropriate thing ever. 'It's okay, I'll . . . The village hall, did you say?'

'Yes, darling, it's over on Main Street, opposite the Co-op.' She jerked a thumb up the road. 'Left at the top there, you can walk it in a few minutes.' Then she hesitated, one hand on her car door as if she wanted to ask something else.

'Thanks,' said Frankie quickly, just as the woman's mouth

was opening again, a question no doubt forming on her lips. 'Thanks very much.'

Still alive then, and at the village hall. Right you are, she thought, striding off to find him, before her courage could drain completely away.

'Let me begin,' said John Mortimer, 'by welcoming you all here this afternoon. It's great to see so many friends and family members together, and it's a testament to Mum and Dad that virtually everyone who was invited today was able to join us in celebrating their Golden Wedding anniversary. Thank you very much for being a part of it, and for sharing this special day.'

A crowd of faces beamed back at him, some more flushed than others, thanks to the free bar. There were four grown-up Mortimer children, four grandchildren, countless cousins, Harry's pals from the bowling club and Jeanie's entire knitting circle (eighteen opinionated women, plus one snake-hipped young man whom they all mothered shamelessly). There were babes in arms, old school friends, various people who'd been taught piano by Jeanie over the last four decades (even if nowadays many of them wouldn't know a semi-quaver if it bit them), a clutch of Harry's old colleagues from the High School, and, in a grubby changing room behind the scenes, a stout man wearing a lot of fake tan was stripped to the waist, gluing on a chest wig.

'Now, as legend has it,' John said, 'Mum and Dad met at a dance in this very room. According to Mum, Dad asked her to dance because of some bet or other with his mates.' He paused to acknowledge the smattering of laughter that followed. 'And according to Dad, Mum only said yes because all his friends were sniggering behind his back and she felt sorry for him. So it wasn't exactly your traditional love-at-first-sight scenario.'

There was more good-humoured laughter at this, not least from Harry and Jeanie themselves, hand-in-hand, leaning against one another companionably.

'Whoever would have thought,' John continued, 'that, more than half a century on from this bet, Mum and Dad would be looking forward to their second honeymoon together – not to mention celebrating fifty years of wedded bliss?' Somebody cheered and John grinned out at the throng. He was a confident public speaker, poised and assured; years of working as a university lecturer meant that he knew how to work the room, keep the interest of those listening and deliver a well-timed punchline.

The sun was slanting through the window and falling around him as if it had been directed specifically there. He'd begun the party in a suit and tie, but his jacket was now slung over the back of a chair somewhere, with his tie stuffed in a pocket, his shirt sleeves rolled up and his top button undone. He still looked good, though, his wife

Robyn assessed, watching him from the other side of the room. Forty-four years old and he cut the same fine figure he always had: charming and witty, tall and handsome, with the audience in the palm of his hand. Look at all those women twinkling at him, in fact. Everyone loved John.

'And so today is really all about love and friendship, and the joy that they bring,' John went on. 'Fifty fantastic years of marriage, sticking together, come what may. There have been highs – I'm guessing the birth of their first and best child is up there as a highlight.' He paused to preen himself jokingly. 'Although to be saddled with Paula, Dave and Stephen afterwards . . . Well, let's just say there have been tough times for Mum and Dad as well. Disappointments.' He grinned, shrugging as some protesting heckles came from his siblings. 'Anyway, Mum and Dad have been great parents, great friends, great members of the community, and we all think the world of them. So will you please do me the honour now of raising your glasses and joining me in a toast. To Jeanie and Harry.'

'JEANIE AND HARRY,' the crowd cheered as one, before John gave a salute and sauntered down from the stage, where one of his brothers pretended to punch him and another got him in a headlock. Meanwhile Paula, their sister, was making *I-see-you* gestures at her teenage sons, who were minesweeping random abandoned glasses of alcohol (please God, let them make it through the party without throwing up). Stephen's partner, Eddie, was surreptitiously checking eBay on his phone (the Mortimers en masse always drove him to reckless spending). And Bunny, Dave's girlfriend, had decided it was time to slather on another coat of Frosted Raspberry lipstick, if only to stop her eating anything else from the buffet. Diet-tip number 376, she thought to herself, heels clicking as she tottered across the parquet floor.

They knew how to throw a good party, did the Mortimers. Birthdays, Christmas, Halloween: you name it, they'd be there with their dance-floor playlists and groaning buffet tables, everyone in their finery and up for a good time. Sometimes there would be a theme – Hollywood Glamour, for example, or Guilty Pleasures – when the more imaginative family members would go to town with elaborate costumes and wigs, and props and decor would be sourced weeks in advance. There would be dancing. Drunkenness. Cake. Nostalgia. Only very occasionally a fight.

Two and a half hours into this particular do and things were starting to hot up, a feeling of looseness in the warm air, the casting aside of inhibitions. The cask of Black Sheep best bitter had already run out, the gallons of home-brew that Harry had brought along reduced to their last cloudy dregs, and all that remained of the buffet were a few dried-up sandwiches curling at the corners on a plate.

The tables had been shunted to the sides of the hall, and now they had the Tom Jones impersonator giving it his pleather-trousered, open-shirted all up on stage, while a throng of dancers joined in with complete abandon below. Everyone was happy, everyone was enjoying themselves, and a deep feeling of contentment swept over Robyn as she cleared egg-mayonnaise-smeared paper plates into a bin bag and neatly stacked the empty platters. This was where she belonged – to this family, this tribe. Growing up as the only child of a single parent, enduring quiet Christmases and lonely holidays when she'd been too shy to strike up any friendships at the campsite kiddies' clubs, she still sometimes felt like pinching herself that she was a part of the noisy, gregarious Mortimer clan.

'WHY, WHY, WHHYYYYYY, De-LI-LAH!' roared the crowd as 'Tom' tipped his head back for the chorus, the microphone angled above his fleshy pink lips. A medallion bounced in the rug of his chest hair with each pelvic gyr-ation, and Robyn's lips twitched in amusement as she saw Dave throwing a brotherly arm around John and Stephen, the three of them swaying and bellowing along together. Nearby, Eddie was stepping out of their way with a roll of his eyes, and Robyn couldn't help feeling kinship with him. In her opinion, the world was divided into two types: those who Joined In, whether it was singing along with a song, clapping enthusiastically to music during a show or shouting out the catchphrases in a pantomime ('He's behind you!'); and then there were those who were just a bit too awkward and self-conscious to really let themselves go in the same way. She, unfortunately, had always been a member of the latter camp; the sort of person, in fact, who would take it upon herself to clear up a buffet table so that she didn't inadvertently get hauled onto the dance floor. The Mortimer siblings, needless to say, were all most definitely in the former.

Still, it was good to see John looking so relaxed after a tough few weeks at work, she thought. He always found the summer term stressful – exam pressure wasn't solely for the students – but this year there had been a suicide on campus within his department, as well as some kind of cheating scandal. It had taken its toll on his sleep recently, and he'd been distracted and withdrawn. For all that he could make eloquent speeches at parties or give interesting lectures on civil engineering to his undergraduate classes, he had never been the most communicative person when it came to the subject of his own feelings, plunging into a silent sort of gloom if things became particularly difficult. She hoped he might be coming out of this most recent episode at last.

Meanwhile there was their son Sam, eleven and awkwardly tall, hunched over his phone on the sidelines, while his older cousins gathered with their friends in a huddle elsewhere. *Go and talk to them,* she'd urged him earlier, but he had given her one of his *As-if* looks and slouched away. He seemed to have hit adolescent self-consciousness early, all elbows and lanky legs, his gaze dropping to his feet whenever anyone tried to speak to him. Conversely, Daisy, his nine-year-old sister who didn't have a shy bone in her body, was in the thick of it near the cake table, gesticulating and bossing around a group of little ones, organizing some game or other involving balloons. Any minute now, though, Robyn suspected, Daisy would start regaling them earnestly with information about insects – her current fascination – which might be of less interest to the others. Not that *that* usually stopped her.

'My, my, MYYYY De-LI-LAH!' the crowd howled along with the strutting Tom Jones-alike. 'Why, why, WHYYY, De-LI-LAH!'

'"Why" is the bloody question,' said Paula just then, appearing beside Robyn with a glass of red wine. Robyn sometimes felt a bit plain beside the dramatic looks of her sister-in-law, who had glossy dark hair in a long, straight bob, complete with millimetre-perfect fringe and excellent eyebrows. Paula worked as an estate agent in the city centre and was always smartly turned out, in satiny blouses and tight skirts plus heels that would hobble Robyn within five minutes. Today, she wore a dark-pink dress with some complicated ruching at the waist, plus a silver feather necklace. 'Why-why-why the hell did Mum and Dad book this orange-faced twerp – and why does he think it's a good idea to sing about a man murdering a woman at an anniversary party, for crying out loud? I mean: inappropriate, much?'

'Valid point,' Robyn laughed. 'It's not your average smoocher, let's face it.'

'Worse, he'll do "Sex Bomb" any minute, and then they'll all be going for it with the thrusting, and one of the oldies will put their back out,' Paula went on with comic exasperation, rolling her brown eyes up into their sockets.

'I'd say the odds are pretty high right now on that person being your Aunty Pen,' Robyn replied and they both paused to giggle at the woman in question, who had one plump hand clasped to her wobbling cleavage and the other flung out in the air as she sang along. 'She'll give someone a black eye, with all that gesturing and pointing, any minute, you wait.'

Paula snorted, but then her eyes narrowed as she caught sight of one of her sons apparently filming their boogying great-aunt on his phone. 'Busted,' she said, getting to her feet. 'You wait, the little sods will be planning to put this on YouTube . . . Hey!' she called, hurrying over to them, her hair catching flashes of the neon disco lights. 'Oh no, you don't.'

Robyn watched her go, smiling to herself as Paula clamped a hand on the culprit's shoulder, like a police officer making an arrest. Turning back to her bin-bag duties, she had just decided that yes, she probably *should* polish off the last mini sausage roll rather than condemn it to the depths of the dustbin, when she noticed a new arrival to the party, someone she didn't recognize. The woman in question had slipped in through the entrance hall and was gazing around warily from the doorway. There was something familiar about her heart-shaped face, wide-set eyes and snub nose that gave Robyn pause. She must be some friend of the family, although . . . Well, Robyn had known the Mortimers for a long time. She thought she'd met all of the friends and neighbours by now.

Plus, was it her imagination or was the woman even in the right place? Rather than striding forward, gift in hand, scouring the room for Jeanie and Harry like everyone else, she was staring around as if she didn't recognize anyone. A gatecrasher? Robyn wondered with a frown. A wrong turn?

Tying the top of the bin bag, Robyn watched in interest as the newcomer's expression suddenly changed, a muscle twitching in her jaw. Turning to see what had caught her eye, Robyn's gaze fell upon Harry, holding court amidst a group of bowling-club cronies. He was laughing and moving his hands expressively, telling one of his tall stories, no doubt. Glancing back, Robyn saw that the woman, still staring, had begun walking swiftly in his direction.

Robyn felt her skin prickling, a portent of doom. Growing up, she'd had a Jack Russell, which would always stand rigid and bark whenever a thunderstorm was about to roll in, as if he could feel the electrical charge in the air. She could almost hear him barking now in her head, warning that the wind was changing.

Feeling unnerved, she watched the woman cross the floor towards Harry. And then she saw Harry's face freeze. His smile falter. He stared at the woman, eyes bulging as if he'd seen a ghost. Paling and seeming to forget about the punch-line to his story, he stepped through his friends to approach her. The two of them then moved to one side of the room together, while Jeanie stared after them in what looked like confusion. Robyn similarly couldn't tear her eyes away, certain that something very important was happening.

'All right!' yelled the Tom Jones singer just then. 'Anyone feeling sexy? This one's for you!' And the band launched into the opening chords of 'Sex Bomb', which prompted an immediate scream of joy from the bevy of aunts, as well as a whooping conga line of Jeanie's knitting group as they flooded onto the dance floor.

'What did I tell you?' laughed Paula, reappearing and grabbing Robyn's arm in the next moment. 'Come on, let's stun the crowd with our moves.'

'Embarrass our kids, more like,' Robyn said, already predicting her son's expression of horror when he saw her awkward attempts at dancing, but she overcame her reluctance, allowing her sister-in-law to tow her onto the dance floor nonetheless.

A short while later, when she next glanced across the room to see what had happened to Harry and the stranger who'd appeared, Robyn noticed they had gone. So too had Jeanie. Perhaps it was nothing, she told herself, putting them out of her head.

Except it wasn't.

Chapter Two

Traffic was horrendous on the journey back to London, the motorway reduced to one slow-churning, bad-tempered lane somewhere in Northants, as the result of an overturned lorry. Closer to home, the outskirts of the city snarled with bottleneck after bottleneck, and Frankie felt gritty-eyed and numb as she changed from first gear to second and then back again, in a seemingly endless stop–start queue of cars.

Back when she'd decided to make the trip to York, she'd had vague thoughts of making a weekend of it – wandering around the Minster and visiting The Shambles, enjoying imagining her mum walking those same streets once upon a time, young and carefree. She'd even daydreamed about returning, in some rose-tinted future, with Craig and Fergus to introduce them to Harry, tentatively joining her two worlds together in a family Venn diagram. But oh, such things seemed impossible now. Even the idea was laughable.

Of all the many outcomes she'd considered for the weekend – that she was too late and Harry had died; that he wasn't interested and told her to leave; that he denied all knowledge of her mother and wouldn't so much as look her in the eye – it was safe to say that the scenario where she accidentally blundered into his Golden Wedding anniversary celebrations had never once occurred to her.

Her mouth dry, her palms clammy, she had stood there in a panic at the edge of the room, feeling paralysed, as if all her power had been taken from her. Craig had suggested from the outset that she write a letter first, introduce herself at a distance in order to give the man some time to digest the situation in private. And sure, Frankie knew he'd had a point, but then Craig made his living as a writer, he'd have found that sort of thing easy, whereas she . . . didn't. Far better to knock on a door, she'd thought: say hello in person, begin a dialogue right there and then. At least you'd know where you stood.

Although look where she'd ended up: in a packed, steamy village hall, where a prancing tight-trousered singer was giving it his best Tom Jones on a stage, with flashing disco lights, inebriated dancers and a huge gold-foiled banner strung across the room: CONGRATULATIONS HARRY AND JEANIE! 50 HAPPY YEARS! She'd gone looking for a father, but she'd managed to stumble into his whole family. For so many reasons, this was most definitely not the place to launch into a delicate conversation about dads and daughters and decades-old secrets.

And yet she'd driven all that way, she kept thinking in dismay. And Craig had rearranged his workload specifically so that he could spend the weekend with Fergus. And she'd already spent so much on petrol and the budget-hotel room, and it wasn't as if she could afford to waste such a sum. But what was the alternative? Ruin Harry Mortimer's anniversary party, just because she wanted to get her money's worth out of the trip?

Disappointment had coursed through her, weighting her feet to the floor. Wrong time, wrong place. This was what you got for being hot-headed, for making it all about you, she told herself despairingly. But then, just as she was about to sidle out of there again, leave them to it, she noticed a man across the crowd and a spear of recognition stabbed her. Tall, pink-faced, a white thatch of hair, laughing brown eyes . . . was it him? Was it really him? Impulse took hold, propelling her across the floor before she could stop herself and then, as he saw her, she caught his double-take of wide-eyed surprise. He'd made a beeline through the knots of people towards her. 'Do I . . . have we met?' he asked in a hoarse, almost tremulous voice, a haunted look on his face.

This was her moment. The one she'd been wondering about for so long. And yet now that it had arrived, she felt as if there was static in her head, a huge lump in her throat, a too-bright spotlight dazzling her eyes. 'I . . . no, we haven't met,' she replied honestly. She couldn't stop staring at his face, seeing her own nose reflected back at her, the similar jawline. Here he was, this man in a beige linen jacket and polished leather shoes, still clutching his half-pint glass, a faint waft of lime cologne reaching her. This was him, the mystery revealed: a real person who was responsible for roughly half the genes in her body. She swallowed hard and forced out the rest of her reply. 'But I think you knew my mother.'

He nodded slowly, as if he'd already guessed. 'Kathy,' he said and his mouth buckled for a moment, emotions playing across his face. 'You've got the same eyes as her. I always wondered what—'

'She's dead,' Frankie interrupted quickly, just to get it out there. 'She died last year.' Her hands flapped uselessly by her side; she hated thinking about those final days in the hospice, followed by the funeral and then the wasteland in her own heart afterwards. 'Anyway,' she went on, just as he said, 'I'm so sorry.' There was a moment of intensely charged silence and then he spoke again.

'Katherine Hallows,' he said faintly, as if the memories were filling with colour inside his head. 'She just vanished at the end of that summer. I never heard from her again.' He stared at her, drinking her in. 'And you . . .'

'And I was the reason for that disappearance, yes,' Frankie replied. Stating the bleeding obvious, as Craig would say.

'Look,' she went on apologetically, 'I realize this is not exactly the best day for us to be meeting, so—'

'Everything all right, Harry?' There was a woman by his side suddenly, with bobbed silvery hair and a mint-green dress, placing a proprietorial hand on his jacket sleeve. Her quick, flashing glance tick-tocked between Frankie and Harry, and the air seemed to crackle with suspicion.

'So it can absolutely wait for another time,' Frankie said quickly, guessing that this was his wife – the Jeanie of the fluttering foiled banner – who presumably knew nothing about what her husband had been up to thirty-five years ago. 'Don't worry about it.'

Harry hesitated. 'I don't even know your name,' he said quietly, his eyes kind and friendly. 'Will you tell me your name?'

'Harry, they want us to cut the cake after this song,' his wife interrupted, tugging at his arm. Her face had gone very tight and pink, and she was no longer looking at Frankie. Had she guessed? Frankie wondered with a gulp.

Guilt twisted her insides. Starting a family ruck had really not been her game-plan. 'It's Frankie,' she replied as the woman began hustling Harry away.

He looked back over his shoulder at her. 'Frankie,' he repeated earnestly and they stared at one another for a final moment. 'Well, then. Another time. I promise.' Then his wife steered him firmly across the room, and that had been that.

With a wave of hot shame at her own impetuous blundering, Frankie had slunk out of the hall and scuttled, head-down, back along the road to her car. Her hands shook as she clicked in her seatbelt, and she felt very much like leaning her head on the steering wheel and crying. It was only the vision of the nosy neighbour rapping on the window – 'Everything all right, love?' – and asking prying questions that compelled her to turn the key in the ignition and drive away.

Once in the anodyne safety of her hotel bedroom, she had sunk onto the bed in a daze, her head seething and whirling with what had just happened. She had *met* him. She had *spoken* to him. He was *real*. He had looked at her and seen her mother's eyes in hers and they had recognized something in one another, blood signalling to blood. *Kathy*, she kept hearing him say, with that catch in his voice.

But then her mind would snag on the memory of the stiff expression of his wife, who, after one lightning assessment of her husband's disquiet, seemed to have jumped to a damning conclusion, possibly even the truth. Frankie cringed as she remembered the way the woman had tightened her grip possessively on her husband's arm, how desperate she'd been to wrench him away.

'Well, I'm sorry, Jeanie,' Frankie said aloud now, as the

traffic crawled to yet another standstill. 'I didn't mean to upset anyone. But I do exist. I am a real person. And like it or not, that's partly down to your beloved husband.'

'So he'd put his foot down, telling her, "No, it's too late, we're over", and she was absolutely gutted, begging him, pleading with him to change his mind – but he was so angry, you could see the hatred in his eyes, and he pushed past her, really roughly, to get out of the house.'

'God,' said Robyn, shelling peas at her mum's kitchen table.

'And then she lost her balance and fell over right there in the hallway, banging her head on the radiator as she went down. So she's lying there, not moving, and you can see on his face, he's thinking: Oh, shit, have I killed her? What have I done? – and then it was the *end*. So we won't find out if she's dead or alive until next *week*!' Alison's eyes glittered with the thrill of it all as she peeled carrots; she was a lifelong fan of *Casualty* and never missed an episode. *I can't possibly come out,* she would say if invited anywhere on a Saturday night. Sometimes with an incredulous laugh in her voice, as if the question was absurd. *Not when my favourite programme's on!*

Robyn wouldn't have minded so much if her mum didn't have a similar must-watch show for every single night of the week, which meant she effectively never went out socially these days. And no, don't be silly, of *course* she didn't want to watch anything later, on catch-up. It wasn't the same! She was part of some telly-lovers' Internet forum where they'd all chat excitedly to one another online during a programme; dissecting plot threads, speculating on potential twists the story might take, aiming to spot 'whodunnit' from the outset. Alison had recently been asked to become one of the forum moderators, which meant she felt obliged to spend each evening keeping an eye on the unfolding discussions. 'Stops me getting into mischief,' she would say, but Robyn was starting to wish her mum would actually indulge in *more* mischief, not less.

'Sounds very dramatic,' she commented now, running her thumbnail along another peapod and glancing through the open back doors to check on Sam (silent and unmoving in the hammock) and Daisy (crouched in concentration, painstakingly building an obstacle course for woodlice down by the shed). The day was overcast but whenever the breeze did occasionally stir, it would waft in scent from the frothing white gardenias and bee-sodden lilies outside, reminding you that it was actually midsummer. This red-brick Harrogate house was where Robyn had spent the second half of her childhood after the big move; if she shut her eyes, she could be fifteen and doing her science homework at this very table, humming distractedly to Radio 1 in the background.

A pea skidded between her fingers, bouncing down onto the floor, and Robyn bent to retrieve it just as her mum asked, 'So John's okay, is he, apart from being called in for this mysterious family meeting? What's all that about, anyway?'

Good question. 'I'm not sure,' Robyn replied. There had been a phone call from Harry first thing, requesting that John join the rest of the Mortimers at his and Jeanie's house for a 'family war cabinet', and Robyn had been a bit taken aback at the urgency in her father-in-law's voice. She hoped everything was all right. 'It's probably a post-mortem of the party, but I can't see why that would be so important,' she went on. 'Especially as Harry and Jeanie are off on this second honeymoon of theirs this afternoon. Sorry,' she added, with a glance over at her mum, hoping she hadn't taken John's absence as too much of a snub. 'Hopefully, he can still join us, if they sort whatever it is out quickly. Other-wise . . .'

Alison waved a hand to signal that she would survive the disappointment. 'And how was the party? Was it a good one?' she asked. She had been invited, of course, but Robyn had had to pass on her apologies as usual. ('Is everything all right with your mum?' Jeanie had asked in concern. 'She never comes along to any of our get-togethers. I haven't seen her for . . . goodness, it must be two years!')

'Well,' said Robyn, trying to conceal her irritation as she remembered how awkward she'd felt at that moment, 'you could have seen for yourself, if you hadn't been too busy watching the telly. You know –' she hesitated, trying to find the right words – 'I think Jeanie was a tiny bit offended that you didn't come, Mum.'

'Offended? Give over. She'd have had that many guests, she wouldn't have paid me a second thought. Probably glad to have one less mouth to feed,' Alison replied, peeling faster than ever and with a certain amount of huffiness. 'I'm very happy for them to have been married fifty years – how lovely for them – but I don't see why I should have to trog all the way up the A59, to some village hall, in order to say that. For a glass of lukewarm wine in a room full of people I don't even know!'

Her voice was rising. 'All right, all right,' Robyn said, backtracking. 'I only meant—'

'Your dad was the party-goer, not me,' Alison said defensively. 'And I had a whole bridal party to do yesterday morning anyway: seven-thirty start, barely time for a cup of coffee, and I didn't get away again until nearly two. After that, I just felt like putting my feet up and catching my breath. You can't deny me that, surely.'

'Okay, I'm not criticizing,' Robyn said, even though she had been, in her head. She prised open another peapod and there was silence for a moment. 'I don't remember that about Dad – him being a party animal,' she added humbly. Her mum barely mentioned Rich, Robyn's father, who'd died of a sudden heart attack when Robyn was just eight years old. Younger than Daisy. One day he'd been there, as normal, and then the next morning Robyn had woken to find her mother catatonic with grief and her grandmother in the house, stuffing clean pants and socks into a bag, saying that Robyn was going to have a little holiday with her for a few days. He was just thirty-five – so bloody young – and she had been paranoid for years that the same fate awaited her. 'Does my heart sound okay?' she always asked anxiously at the doctor's, braced for history to repeat itself.

'Well, in the early days he was,' Alison said vaguely, her eyes misting over. 'But anyway.'

Robyn wanted to ask more, greedy for any new nuggets of detail about her father that might illuminate her own paltry memories, but sensed her mum closing down the conversation, as she so often did when he was the topic. 'How are things with you?' she asked instead. 'What's the latest news?'

Alison was a mobile hairdresser, zipping between appointments in her pastel-blue Honda Jazz, her concerned, listening face every bit as important as her skill with a comb and scissors. It was amazing what people confessed to her while she was snipping away behind them, she often said. Perhaps it was having experienced her own share of tragedy that made her a good confidante; perhaps it was her general air of non-judgemental kindness; for whatever reason, Alison knew *everything* there was to know within the community. If there was a story, she'd be the first to sniff it out.

In another life she might have been an investigative journalist, following her nose to one juicy scoop after another.

Robyn went on shelling peas as her mum detailed tussles between neighbours regarding gigantic garden-shading Leylandii, Rita Daly's plans for her retirement party over at The Bridge, and Josie Simpson's new baby having been born on a pile of tea-towels on her kitchen floor, could she believe, with Anil Singh, a local delivery lad, fainting clean away when he looked through the window to see what all the shouting was about. 'Right there by the front door!' Alison chuckled, enjoying the story. 'He's had a bit of ribbing about that, by all accounts, soft idiot.'

Robyn laughed too, but she'd been pierced by a sudden flash of memory that her mind had churned up unexpectedly: of running towards her father's legs as he came home from work, the evening sun golden behind him as he stood in the doorway, then being swung up into the air, aloft in his strong arms. 'Daddy, my daddy!' she had cried. 'Robyn, my Robyn!' he'd replied with a laugh.

You got to Robyn's age – the wrong side of forty – and childhood memories were so much fuzzier. Had the moment really happened or was it just her imagination, hopefully proffering a fictional scene in order to appease her hunger for him? Soon after her dad had died, they'd moved out of their old house in Wolverhampton and up here to Yorkshire, but she still carried around small moments of having lived there: could remember, for example, how it felt to lie on the brown, tufty living-room carpet, how you could never get the Playmobil people to stand up properly on its uneven surface. There was that lozenge of glass in the front door with the large, rounded bobble that made people's faces distort; she remembered bursting into tears when her grandpa had peered through it one day, because he looked all wrong. The fake coals in the fireplace – how she'd puzzled over Father Christmas being able to come down the chimney because it didn't look like the pictures in books.

Meanwhile Alison was still talking about the unexpected delivery. 'She was fine anyway. Little girl, seven pounds ten ounces,' she said, briskly sweeping the carrot peelings into an empty margarine tub, destined for next door's guinea pigs. 'They've called her Tallulah – very sweet.' She took a knife to the bare carrots, fast and efficient, the round wet slices toppling like pennies.

'Ta-dah!' came a triumphant cheer from outside just then and they looked out to see Daisy, with dusty knees and a streak of dirt across one cheek, beaming at the newly built woodlice-house before her. 'They love it!' she cried. 'Come and see.'

Out Alison went immediately, exclaiming over Daisy's cleverness and laughing at the sight of the pale-grey woodlice that, with surprising cooperation, now trundled up and down the twiggy walkways constructed for their benefit.

27

'My goodness, and you made all of this yourself?' Alison cried, and Robyn smiled to see how pleased Daisy looked, her thick red hair falling around her face as she regaled her grandma with a series of new facts.

'Did you know woodlice have their skeletons on the outside of their bodies, Grandma? It's called an exoskeleton. They are terrestrial isopod crustaceans,' she said, stumbling a little over the long words, 'and—'

'And they are very, very boring,' came the disembodied voice of her brother from the hammock. 'Nearly as boring as you.'

'They're *not* boring! Grandma, tell him!'

Robyn went on shelling peas as her mother sorted out the squabble. Despite her earlier grumbles, in some ways she was glad Alison hadn't come to the party, she found herself thinking, not least because of how much John had drunk. Robyn had barely been able to manhandle him into the taxi afterwards. This morning his face had been as pale and crumpled as an old paper bag, and he'd seemed very subdued. Was it the hangover causing this quietness or was he brooding about something? Robyn really needed to find a moment to talk to him, try and get to the bottom of whatever was on his mind.

'The thing I love most about my children,' Jeanie had once confided in Robyn, 'is that they're all so different. John's the ambitious one. Paula's loyal. David's always content. As for Stephen, well, he was a surprise baby and he's never failed to surprise me since!'

At the time, Robyn had been pleased with the label assigned to her husband – that of ambition. But with ambition came restlessness, she had come to realize; a dissatisfaction with the status quo that sent a person pushing on, endlessly trying to achieve more. Wasn't it better to be contented, like Dave; to simply enjoy what you had?

'MUM! I said come and see the *house*,' shouted Daisy just then, and Robyn blinked her worries away, before dutifully going out into the sunshine.

They all made their houses, didn't they, she thought, crouching down to admire her daughter's efforts. Real or imagined or woodlouse-sized, they all worked so hard to build and create, to configure walls and doors, to call a place a home, as if that was enough to keep out the bad things. Robyn's mind flicked back to their own warm, comfortable house on its quiet little cul-de-sac, with their Christmas china in the cupboard and their toothbrushes lined up in the bathroom, and the sofas, gone spongy from the children's bouncing. That life she and John had put together for themselves, piece by piece, year after year, memory upon memory. She thought of her husband's late nights out recently, his black moods. She hoped their cosy little world wasn't in any danger of crashing down. Was it?

Chapter Three

Paula Brent had always been able to put a good spin on things. At work, she didn't bat an eyelid when calling a small, damp-ridden fleahole an 'exciting investment opportunity'. As the mother of two teenage boys, she had learned to unearth a silver lining where nobody else could see one, including the time she'd replied, 'Well, at least he can *spell* "vagina",' when called in to see the head teacher about her eldest son's graffiti last term. And God help her, she'd been married to Matt Brent for seventeen years, and still found it amusing when letters arrived addressed to 'Mr and Mrs Bent'. But today, here in her parents' lounge, the same room where she'd sprawled on the sofa to watch cartoons on telly as a child, where they'd had the Christmas tree in the back corner every single year, everything she thought she knew was being unravelled. Because it turned out there were some occasions when a good spin was actually not possible at all.

'I'm very sorry to have to admit to you all that I had an affair some years ago,' her dad's opening gambit had been, and the words spattered like shrapnel into her brain. Paula had to clutch the armrest of the sofa, because it felt like the ground was tilting beneath her, as if they were all on board a capsizing ship. Wait – *what?* Dad had cheated on *Mum?* Dad, the soppiest man alive, had done the dirty on kind, lovely Mum? No. No *way.*

It had to be some sort of wind-up, she reassured herself; one of her dad's daft pranks. Because her parents were supposed to be going off on their second honeymoon today, for goodness' sake! Their hotly anticipated week in Madeira, all sunbathing and sherry; new swimming costumes packed in the cases. He was kidding them, right?

But when Paula turned to her mum beside her for confirmation, a chill travelled the length of her spine. Jeanie's mouth was trembling, like she wanted to cry. Her eyes were bloodshot and bruised-looking. And her body was held rigid, arms tightly folded about her own waist as if it was all that kept her from crumbling to pieces. Even an optimist like Paula had to admit that the signs did not appear promising.

Her brothers appeared every bit as dumbstruck as Paula. 'For real?' Stephen asked dazedly, but their dad was still talking. There was more. There was *worse.*

'And I found out yesterday . . .' Harry looked down at his hands, briefly clenching them in his lap, before detonating a second explosive, 'there's a daughter. A half-sister to you all.'

'What the—' cried John, rising in his seat. His eyes bulged as he swung round towards Jeanie, desperate for one parent to start talking sense. 'Mum, is this true? It's not, is it?'

Jeanie pressed her lips together very tightly, and Paula felt her heart fracture at the pain on her mother's face. 'It's true,' Jeanie confirmed, her chin wobbling.

'Oh, Mum,' Paula said immediately, putting an arm around her as if trying to protect her from the blow. Jeanie was never usually one to wear her heart on her sleeve like this. A piano teacher for years and years, she'd get a bad mood or disappointment out of her system by playing certain thunderous pieces, chords crashing until she felt better. Rachmaninov's Prelude in C-sharp Minor for your average annoyance. Chopin's 'Revolutionary Etude' for the rare occasions when she was truly cross. And yet now look at her, so completely devastated she seemed beyond the point of playing a single note.

'Look, I'm very sorry, of course I am,' Harry went on, looking wretched. 'I'm *so* sorry. But I had absolutely no idea this girl – this woman, rather – even *existed* until yesterday.'

'Well, who is she?' Paula blurted out, rounding on him. 'And how come she's just turned up now? On your anniversary, of all days?'

'She came to the party,' Jeanie said, her voice catching.

'To the *party*? What, you invited her, Dad?' Even Dave,

usually the most mild-mannered and laidback of the siblings, sounded incredulous.

'No! She came here first, apparently, and Lynne next door told her we were in the hall . . .' Harry was a picture of agitation, shifting in his seat as if he'd rather be anywhere else. 'It was all very unexpected. To be fair, I think she felt pretty bad about the circumstances—'

Stephen snorted. 'Clearly not that bad, if she turned up anyway. To your *anniversary party*. God!'

Paula said nothing, reeling from a secondary wave of shock as the reality sank through her. Dad with another woman. Dad with another child. When the Mortimers had always previously seemed so unassailable, so tight, so solid. When her parents had been such role models, the greatest advertisements for happy marriage! It was like finding out Father Christmas wasn't real all over again, only worse – a million times worse.

'It was unfortunate timing; she had no idea . . .' her dad was saying in a weak, apologetic voice, so unlike his usual cheery confidence.

Paula didn't care about timing or what this other woman thought, when Jeanie was sitting there, so broken and hurt. She couldn't even look at her own dad any more, she felt so stunned.

'Fuck,' John said, shaking his head. It didn't even earn a 'Language!' from Jeanie, as it normally would have done, that was how dire things were. 'Does she want money or something? Is that why she's come here now?'

'What if she's lying?' Stephen put in, sounding suspicious. The youngest of the Mortimer siblings, he'd become a lawyer and now worked in very grand office premises near the Theatre Royal; his childhood years of being wrestled and sat on and pillow-whacked making him an excellent advocate for those treated unjustly by others.

'I don't think she's after money,' Harry replied. 'At least she didn't mention it. And she's definitely not lying. I knew as soon as I looked at her that she was . . . that she was mine. I'm sorry, love,' he added as Jeanie gave a wounded sniff and blew her nose. 'But why would she lie anyway? Why would anyone make up something like that?' He sighed. 'It was all so out of the blue.'

'You're telling me,' Paula snapped, anger flaring inside her. She'd never had a bad word to say about her dad before, never. He'd been her hero her entire life, rescuing her from outside nightclubs when she was young and the last bus had gone; walking her up the aisle on her wedding day; speeding her to the maternity unit when she went into labour early and Matt was working out near Leeds. As the only daughter, she'd always felt so special, so beloved, the apple of her father's eye. But now, as it turned out, there was a rival apple. Suddenly she was quite a lot less special than she'd imagined.

'But even if she *did* want money,' Harry went on, sounding braver all of a sudden, 'then yes, of course I would give her that, if she asked me for it.' He gazed around at them in turn, defying anyone to interrupt. 'Because the bottom line is: I *am* her father and we've all got to get used to that fact. I'm sorry if you don't like me saying so, but there we are. I've apologized to your mother, I've apologized to the four of you. I don't know what else you want me to say.' He cleared his throat. 'Her name is Frankie, by the way. And that's all I know about her, except that she must be about thirty-four.'

About thirty-four. Nobody said anything for a moment, and Paula guessed they were all quickly working out the maths. Stephen was thirty-eight. Had their dad really been so shallow as to have an affair while their mum was doing her best to cope with four young children under the age of ten? Paula herself must only have been about seven, she calculated. Seven, and preoccupied with horses and dogs, gymnastics club and Brownies. Bile rose in her throat at the thought of her dad carrying on behind everyone's back. Sneaking off to his bit on the side, then coming home to be daddy and read adventure stories to them at bedtime. It was repulsive. Repugnant. It was unthinkable!

'Clearly this is a bit of a shock, to all of us,' said Dave, the erstwhile peacekeeper, while the others sat in horrified silence. 'Dad included, if you had no idea about this . . . this

Frankie person.' He said the word as if it tasted strange in his mouth, as if worried that by mentioning the woman's name it might conjure her up in front of them. 'But you two are still going on holiday, right?' he went on, addressing his parents. 'Maybe a break is what you need: get away from it all, have some space.'

What – and sweep the whole sorry saga under the carpet, like it never happened? Paula thought in disbelief. How was that going to work? If it had been her and Matt in this situation, a holiday would be the last thing on her mind. She'd have been more inclined to shove him off the nearest cliff.

Her brothers disagreed with her, apparently. 'Yes, absolutely,' John was saying in a similarly bracing Keep Calm and Carry On manner.

'Bit of sunshine, a chance to talk . . .' Stephen added encouragingly.

Paula squeezed her mum's hand, not wanting to insult her by joining in with them. 'So, er . . . How did you leave things, Dad?' she asked when a strained silence fell. 'I mean – I take it we're going to meet her, are we?' She felt a weird shuddery sensation at her own question. Growing up with three brothers, she'd always longed for a sister in whom she could find an ally and confidante, but not a sister like this, thrust upon them without warning. 'Is she . . . local?' she added, not entirely sure what she wanted the answer to be.

Harry gave an uncomfortable shrug. 'Well, that's the

problem,' he confessed. 'Everything happened so fast, we didn't really get to say much more than hello to each other. I've no idea where she lives, I'm afraid.'

Jeanie's eyes were like gimlets suddenly. 'We needed to cut the cake,' she said, a dangerous edge creeping into her voice. She wasn't just upset, Paula realized with a jolt of alarm, she was boiling over with anger and humiliation.

'But you've got a phone number for her, haven't you, Dad?' John put in. 'Some contact details?'

Harry shook his head regretfully. 'She'd gone before I could ask her,' he admitted. 'I don't even know her last name. We're just going to have to hope that she gets in touch with me. Otherwise . . .' He spread his hands wide. 'Otherwise we might never see her again.'

'Well, good. Because I don't want you to see her again,' Jeanie said suddenly and they all turned to look at her. She was sitting up a little straighter now – regally even, you could say – and her chin was positively pointy with rage. 'Do you hear me? I don't want to hear so much as her *name* mentioned in this house again. Because it's her or me, Harry Mortimer. Understand? It's her or me.'

Chapter Four

The west-London flat where Frankie lived was on the fourth floor and the lift, as so often seemed to be the case when she was particularly tired, was out of order today. By the time she'd tramped up the stairs with her overnight bag, there was sweat beading on her forehead and her hair weighed hot and heavy on the back of her neck. The air was humid, the clouds huddled ominously above; you could feel the storm just waiting there on the horizon for its big, dramatic entrance.

'Hello,' she called, trudging through the front door and dropping her bag by her feet. She heard an excited yelp from Fergus, followed by an answering 'Hi!' from Craig. He'd rung her last night, but she hadn't felt like discussing the awkward reunion on the phone with him, instead sending the call to voicemail and texting as a stopgap message: *Knackered! Will tell you all tomorrow.*

'Mumma!' yelled Fergus, bursting from the living room and barrelling towards her. He threw his arms around her legs, pressing his face against her jeans, and she reached down to stroke his curly head, comforted by his presence. Four years old, Fergus was a chunky little thing, with his stocky barrel-chest and the most squeezable thighs of any small person, plus a mop of black ringlety hair that framed his beaming, chubby face.

'Help! Don't pull me over,' she cried, laughing and almost losing her balance as she bent down to hug him. Her dear little boy with his naughty, gurgling chuckle and tight-gripping arms now clasped around her neck, it was exactly what she needed. 'I missed you,' she told him, snuggling against him.

'A lot? A big lot?'

'Oh, a big, big lot. The biggest, most enormous lot there ever ever was!'

Seeming satisfied with this answer he gave her a wet kiss on the cheek, wiggled out of her grasp, then charged back down the hall. 'Daddy! It's Mumma,' he proclaimed joyfully just as Craig emerged from the room.

'Hey,' he said, eyes scanning her expression, trying to read her mood. 'Welcome home. Are you okay? How did it go?'

She leaned against him as he embraced her. They'd been together three years and he was kind, good and solid, every-thing that your loved one should be. 'I'm okay,' she replied. That much at least was true. She was alive, breathing, still in one piece. Then she sighed, because he was waiting for the rest of the story and it was going to be painful to get it out. 'It wasn't exactly what I was hoping for,' she admitted eventually.

'Oh, love,' he said, stroking her hair, just as she'd stroked Fergus's.

'I just . . . I think I blew it. You were right, I shouldn't have gone steaming in there unannounced. I picked pretty much the worst possible time, as it happens.' There was a lump in her throat. Craig was only ever going to be on her side, but it was hard to confess to anyone that you'd been rejected. That you'd made a fool of yourself.

'I set up the TRAINS, Mumma. I set up the TRAINS!' Fergus was back, seizing her hand triumphantly, trying to pull her along the hall to their small living room, which, at any given time, felt like it was eighty per cent train set.

'Cool!' Frankie cried, allowing herself to be hauled forward to bear witness to his latest feat of engineering. Fergus was big on trains. Also dinosaurs, space, zoo animals, the dustbin lorry, squirrels and water pistols, but his heart beat with most passion when it came to trains.

'Tell me about it later,' Craig said from behind her and she nodded. 'Listen, I . . .' He hesitated, and she turned back to look at him. 'Now that you're back, would you mind if I catch up on some work? Just for an hour or so? Then I'll make us something to eat. Is that okay?'

'That's fine,' said Frankie, because she was too tired to

do anything else and, actually, the thought of playing trains, making bridges and stations, pantomiming dismay at Fergus's eager, ghoulish engine crashes . . . it all sounded kind of soothing. Anything to distract her. Besides, this was how it went, when you had two self-employed people and one small hullaballoo of a child; you had to seize an hour here, twenty minutes there, to get anything done.

Craig was a journalist. Frankie had actually read about him and Fergus before she met either of them, in Craig's 'Dad About the House' column in a Sunday newspaper. By turns light-hearted and deeply moving, the column was started by Craig as a means of detailing the highs and lows of being a single dad, and one who was facing a series of challenges at that. Fergus had not had the easiest of starts to life. He'd been born with a cleft lip and been plagued with ear infections for the first few months, as well as difficulties feeding, and he'd been in and out of hospital for surgery and follow-up appointments. Understandably, this had all come as shattering and unexpected news to Craig and his then-partner Julia, and she'd become depressed, blaming herself for Fergus's problems, not feeling as if she could bond with her child. Despite Craig's best attempts to keep things going, she'd vanished when Fergus was barely six weeks old, leaving a note to say that she couldn't manage and was bailing out.

Left to pick up the pieces, sleep-deprived and consumed

by worries for the future of his son, Craig had struggled and stumbled through those early months: the surgery, the pitfalls and problems, as well as the moments of sheer fatherly delight. Writing about it helped him deal with the complicated mess of emotions that he experienced, and when he ran the idea of a weekly article past his editor, the column was duly commissioned. By sheer serendipity, Frankie, a freelance illustrator, was asked to provide the artwork for his page each week and so their relationship began – as words and pictures initially, two people doing their jobs. But quickly, and like millions of other women around the country, Frankie found herself falling for funny, capable, wonderful Craig and his devotion to his boy, looking forward to receiving his new instalment every week, and cheering him on from the sidelines as she illustrated each piece. They'd met at the newspaper's Christmas party and had sought each other out, exclaiming, 'I love your work!' in drunken sincerity, before ending up, much later on, knocking back whisky in a nearby bar and telling one another their life stories. She'd moved into Craig's flat six months later, and when Fergus had started talking and called her 'Mumma', neither of them had stopped him. It was, all things considered, the happiest of happy endings.

And it was enough, Frankie thought now, as she sat down on the carpet and Fergus talked through his elaborate new track layout with her, and chose which engine she was allowed to have (the worst one with the wonky wheels, obviously). Forget Harry Mortimer and his shocked expression, forget his dagger-eyed wife – to hell with the lot of them, Frankie told herself fiercely. This small lovely family of hers right here was enough. This was *plenty*.

Back in Yorkshire, the Mortimers were all struggling to come to terms with the shockwaves caused by Harry's announcement. Stephen was driving his parents to the airport, a freezing silence splintering the atmosphere inside the car, despite his Herculean efforts to make conversation. Whenever he glanced across at his dad in the passenger seat, it was like looking at a stranger. How could he have done that to Mum?

Meanwhile, Paula was peeling potatoes for a roast dinner, her head in a spin. A sister, she kept thinking. A half-sister who'd existed all this time, completely unknown to the rest of the family. What was her agenda? Had she grown up feeling resentful of Dad? What did she even *look* like? Her fingers shook and a wet potato slid from her hand, bouncing to the floor, where Oscar, her wire-haired dachshund, made an immediate dash for it. 'No!' Paula admonished him, but her voice cracked on the word and she found herself sliding to a kneeling position on the lino and bursting into tears. She didn't want this to be happening! She wanted it all to be unsaid, undone, for life to go back to the way it was before today. 'Oh, Oscar,' she wept, as he lost interest in the potato and pushed his nose against her arm in a show of canine sympathy. 'What are we going to do?'

On the other side of town, Dave kept staring into space, seemingly miles away, occasionally raking a bewildered hand through his hair. 'I can't believe it,' he murmured now and then. 'I just can't believe it.' Bunny knew what a person in trauma looked like. She steered him to the sofa, tuned the radio to the soothing burble of cricket commentary and found him a beer. 'Don't worry,' she kept saying in her calmest voice. 'Everyone will get over this. Everything will work itself out.'

John, too, was struggling with the situation. Once Robyn and the children had returned from her mum's, he'd given her the bare bones of the story, but then closed down under questioning, telling her he didn't want to talk about it any more. His phone kept ringing, but he sent the calls to voicemail, his face locked in an unreadable expression. It was like having a wounded lion pacing about the house, snapping at the children for bickering with each other, snarling at any attempted small talk. Robyn couldn't help a disloyal sigh of relief when he eventually took himself off for a long run.

It was only once he'd gone that Robyn realized just how shocked and upset she was herself by the whole drama. Harry and Jeanie were the central dynamo of the Mortimer engine, solid and dependable, powering everyone else. With their relationship now seizing and faltering, what would it mean for the rest of the family?

Over at the airport, having said goodbye to Stephen and thanked him for dropping them off – he was a good lad, he really was – Jeanie wheeled her suitcase up to the check-in desk without a backward glance. Dramatic chords rumbled in her head, an ominous crescendo building as she came to a decision. 'There's been a change of plan, I'm afraid,' she said crisply to the man behind the check-in counter, showing him her boarding pass. 'My husband is no longer able to come with me.'

Harry gasped. 'I . . . Jeanie!' he cried in dismay.

The man behind the counter looked from Jeanie to her husband. 'Um . . .'

'Yes, it's a real shame,' Jeanie went on. 'But he's going back to our house now, to think about what he's done. And I'll be taking the holiday alone.' Harry opened his mouth, but she rounded on him with unexpected ferocity. 'Don't you dare say a word,' she warned, poking a finger at him. 'Not a *word*.'

Once again the man behind the counter looked from Jeanie to Harry, doubt writ large on his face. 'Right,' he said after an agonized moment. 'So it's just the one case to check in today then, is it?'

'Yes, that's right, just the one.' Jeanie presented her passport, then turned back to her husband. 'I'll see you in a week,' she said coldly. 'If I decide to come back, that is.'

'Jeanie,' protested Harry. 'Please. We need to talk. This is our second honeymoon!'

His wife stared him down. 'It's not our second honeymoon any more,' she told him. 'It's my holiday now. And if you want me ever to forgive you, then you can jolly well bugger off home and leave me to get my flight. Without you. Because you're not welcome.'

The check-in assistant's eyes boggled. He glanced at Harry worriedly, seeming unsure what to say. A few silent seconds passed. 'Um . . . So if you could put your case on the scale please,' he said timidly to Jeanie.

'No problem,' she replied, just as Harry stepped forward to help her. She shooed him away as if he were an irritating bluebottle. 'I can manage, thank you. Please go now. I'll see you in a week.'

Harry and the check-in assistant looked at one another again. The fearful shrug from the younger man seemed to say, *There's no arguing with this one, mate.* Harry bit his lip, trying not to think about the turquoise hotel pool they'd admired in the brochure, the dark-blue trunks he'd bought especially, the new World War II thriller he'd been planning to read on the plane. He knew when he was beaten. He recognized that determined set to his wife's shoulders, that

Just-you-try-it look in her eye, that pointy finger. *Game over,* his grandchildren would say.

He swallowed. 'Are you sure you'll be all right on your own?' he asked in a low voice, as the check-in guy sent Jeanie's case trundling off on the conveyor belt.

Jeanie scoffed. 'Will I be all right on my own? he says. Well, let's hope so, eh. Seeing as I might have to get used to that.' Turning angrily away from him, she fixed her attention back on the dazed-looking man behind the counter, lavishing him with her most dazzling smile. 'You've been *very* helpful, love. Thank you.'

'You're welcome. Enjoy your flight,' said the man, with a final anguished eye-flick over towards Harry.

'I'm sure I will,' said Jeanie and then off she went without a backward glance, hearing the barnstorming finale of the 1812 Overture start up in her head, cannons and all, as she marched towards the Departures sign.

Harry meanwhile stood there dumbfounded, watching her go, until the people who were waiting to check in next began making polite Excuse Me noises behind him and he had to step aside. The wheels of his case squeaked plaintively as he trudged in the opposite direction to his wife. Then he stopped outside the WH Smith as a thought occurred to him, and he reached inside his jacket for his phone.

'Stephen? You haven't left yet, have you?' he asked when

his son answered. The airport seemed to seethe around him, a mass of busy, laughing people pushing trolleys and talking excitedly, while he stood there in the centre of them: a hunched, forlorn figure with his suitcase and nowhere to go. 'Ahh. It's just that there's been a slight change of plan.'

Chapter Five

The heat seemed to weigh down oppressively on Robyn as she hurried along the pavement towards Sam and Daisy's primary school on Monday afternoon. Well, that had been a rubbish day at work yet again, she thought crossly, checking her watch and hoping she wasn't going to be late. She was supposed to finish at two o'clock, which in theory gave her plenty of time to drive home and have a cup of tea before walking up to meet the children, but as usual she'd been waylaid by extra tasks.

Back in the day, Robyn had worked at the university, like John, as a lecturer in the Biochemistry Faculty, but these days she was mostly a dogsbody. ('Robyn? She used to be this, like, real high-flier' she had once heard John's tactless Aunty Pen telling some new boyfriend or other, unaware that she could hear, 'but these days she . . . well, I don't know what she does with herself, to be honest. Pushes the Hoover round? Makes cakes?') A dogsbody who did all the housework and went out three days a week to be a part-time lab technician at a secondary school across town: that was her. Sure, it wasn't the most taxing job for someone of her scientific background, but the hours fitted in with her own children's school day, and it got her out of the house – further than the supermarket at least. Except that every now and then there'd be some supply teacher in, like today, who'd talk down to her patronizingly, as if Robyn was completely thick and didn't know her beakers from her Bunsen burners. Or there had been the day last week when two of the naughtier boys in one class had surreptitiously 'liberated' the classroom stick insects from their glass box, and it had been Robyn's job to recapture them all afterwards. She had crawled around on the floor trying to catch the little buggers, thinking ruefully of her Masters degree and the respect she'd once been afforded by her peers.

Sometimes she just missed being 'somebody', that was all.

Dashing through the primary-school gates now, she felt frazzled as she joined the sea of waiting parents gathered in the playground, where the sweet, piping voices of infants singing 'You Are My Sunshine' came wafting through a nearby window. Phew, made it, she thought, ferreting in a pocket for a tissue, in the hope that she could dab her sweaty brow before anyone noticed how shiny she was. It was so muggy, and she'd been in the middle lab at school where the windows didn't open properly; the heat had sent the classes stir-crazy all day.

Just as she was mid-dab – embarrassing! – she realized that one of the mums nearby was addressing her and turned apologetically, crumpling the tissue within a fist, to see that Beth Broadwood, PTA superstar and mother of four clever, sporty daughters, was gazing expectantly at her, presumably waiting for her reply. 'Sorry, I was miles away,' Robyn confessed. 'What was that?'

Beth was giving her a strange sort of smile, one Robyn couldn't quite interpret. 'I said, I was sorry to hear the news. I hope you're all okay.'

Robyn stared blankly at her. 'The news?' she repeated, then guessed the other woman must be talking about John's parents. Oh, goodness! Had word spread that far already? 'You mean . . . about Harry and Jeanie?' she asked warily. Was Beth referring to the airport drama, or the revelation about Harry's other daughter? she wondered. She couldn't help feeling disloyal for even entering into a conversation about it, when John had been so reluctant to tell her, his own wife, the full story yesterday. She was sure he wouldn't want the whole playground gossiping. And how come Beth Broadwood thought it was any of her business anyway?

'Oh!' said Beth, looking confused herself. 'No, I meant about John. Losing his job,' she added, a moment later when Robyn didn't respond. She turned red. 'Sorry – I'm not being nosy. It was just something Paul said . . . Maybe

I've got it wrong. Probably. I just wanted to say I hope you're okay anyway.'

Robyn's brain was working very fast, but she didn't seem to be making sense of this conversation. What the hell was Beth on about – John losing his job? 'We're fine, thanks,' she managed to say, her mind still spinning. Beth's husband Paul worked at the university too, she remembered now.

'Right. Of course you are! Anyway, I'll . . .' Beth's teeth were bared in an awkward grimace. 'Here come the kids,' she said in the next moment, sounding relieved.

The singing inside the school had come to a close and the first children were emerging from the building, some hand-in-hand and deep in conversation, others practically bouncing with the release of freedom, one dreamy-eyed boy running a thoughtful hand along the railings. Beth melted into the crowd as she spotted one of her blonde, pigtailed daughters, and Robyn was left standing there in a daze. Beth had to be mistaken, surely? John would have told her if he'd lost his job! Except . . . She remembered how strangely he had been acting lately, how distracted he'd seemed. He *would* tell her news like that, wouldn't he?

Here came Sam amidst the throng anyway, head and shoulders above the others, however hard he tried to fold himself into a smaller size; and Robyn waved a hand in the air, trying to stop thinking about her husband. Sam's dark hair was sticking up at the front, she noticed, probably where he'd wiped a sweaty hand through it earlier, and there was a grass stain on his shirt. With his brown eyes, the mud-splat of freckles and his broad shoulders, Sam was Mortimer through and through: John's mini-me. It pleased her, on a very deep level, that her boy was cast from the same mould as his antecedents, unmistakably the latest in the line. Today, though, she looked at him and saw her husband's closed face. What happened, John? Why are you keeping secrets from me?

Ah, and here came Daisy too, talking earnestly to another girl – about mosquito larvae probably, or the life-cycle of a cockroach, judging by the bewildered look on her companion's face. Robyn felt a pang for her daughter, who always seemed so unaware that other children found her behaviour strange. 'She is so *weird*,' Robyn had once heard a group of girls sniggering to one another, and it had taken all her restraint not to grab them by the throats and tear into them. With her gorgeous red hair and big wonky smile, sensitive Daisy was desperate for a best friend, but found herself excluded from cliques and party invitations with painful frequency. 'Hello, darling,' said Robyn, as Daisy, engrossed in conversation, appeared on the verge of walking right past her.

'Oh!' Daisy blinked in surprise and then beamed. 'Mum, did you know that a ladybird might eat five thousand insects in its lifetime? Five THOUSAND, Mum!'

'Wow!' Robyn cried, hugging her and Sam, then delved in her bag to find some cheesy crackers, which they fell upon like starving hyenas. Across the playground she noticed that Beth was gazing at her again, with that same strange look in her eyes. Robyn turned away hurriedly, but not before she realized what lay beneath the woman's expression.

Pity, that was it. Beth Broadwood was gazing at her in pity.

Bunny had felt bad for leaving Dave on Monday evening when he still seemed so dumbfounded with shock about his parents, but she'd had the Willowdene meeting booked for two months, and the lady organizing it had phoned three times in the last week with parking information and a checklist of Bunny's requirements. A microphone? A Power-Point display? Snacks? 'Or shouldn't I ask?' she'd tittered conspiratorially. No, it would be impossible to back out now.

'Go round and keep your dad company,' she instructed her boyfriend as she grabbed her car keys, then fluffed up her hair in the hall mirror. 'Take him for a pint and a game of darts, distract him with your best small talk. Better still, why not see if he wants to stay with us for a few days? It can't be very nice for him, being stuck at home on his own.'

'Good idea. What would I do without you?' Dave said gratefully as she kissed him goodbye.

'You'd probably still be lying in the road with your bike wheels spinning,' she said, as she always did to that question.

'Almost certainly,' he agreed. It had been an unusual way to meet the love of your life, after all. Bunny had been on her way to work one morning a year or so ago when she'd seen a Vauxhall clip a cyclist on Micklegate right in front of her, sending him flying. She'd been feeling pretty good that day, what with all the weight she'd lost, not to mention the atrocious husband she'd lost too, and she'd promptly stopped the traffic, called an ambulance and put the unconscious Dave in the recovery position. Once he'd been whisked off to A&E, she had carried on towards work for a few minutes before an impulse made her turn and catch a bus to the hospital instead, in order to track down the (admittedly rather handsome) cyclist.

Later on, when Dave came round, woozy on painkillers and concussed, he'd gazed up at Bunny's kind face, haloed with her blonde hair, then blinked and mumbled, 'Are you an angel?' (His brothers never tired of guffawing about that particular detail of the story; in hindsight, perhaps it had been a mistake to tell them.) Bunny had smiled down at his lovely battered face and replied, 'It's your lucky day.' And so it had proved, for them both.

Bunny slowed now as she approached the village of Willowdene and then, moments later, parked with practised aplomb, whipping skilfully into a tight spot outside the Parish Church Hall. People were always surprised at what an excellent driver she was, particularly men, as if they expected someone who liked false eyelashes, short skirts and frosted pink gel-nails to be useless at any practical skills. 'Full of surprises, me,' she would say if anyone made a comment. She enjoyed being able to confound people's expectations, to keep them guessing. 'Don't judge *this* book by its cover.'

Glancing into her rear-view mirror, she exchanged a look with the cardboard replica of herself propped in the back seat. 'Here we are, kid,' she said. 'Let's get ready to wow the weight-watchers all over again.' Ever since she'd won SlimmerYou's 'Slimmer of the Year', she'd been doing these inspirational talks to dieting groups around the North, standing beside her double-chinned cardboard self and enjoying the way people looked with genuine respect from the old version of her to the current svelte incarnation. You did it, their eyes said, and you could see the longing on their faces, not to mention the admiration and – quite often – the envy.

SlimmerYou paid her a small fee plus travel expenses, but it wasn't something you would do for the money alone. Nevertheless, Bunny had discovered that there was a certain catharsis about telling her story again and again, through Yorkshire and Lancashire and Merseyside. It was unexpectedly affirming, too. With every musty church hall, with every rapt listening face in the rows of seats, she found herself surprised anew at her own dogged determination as she detailed her route to success. *I really did that,* she would sometimes marvel, smiling graciously as the audience applauded her afterwards.

She leaned across to the passenger footwell, retrieved the pink sash that SlimmerYou had requested she wore, then got out, opening the back door to haul out her enormous cardboard self from the rear seats. 'Let's be having you then, my darling,' she said, tucking the figure under her arm. Despite having hated her nineteen-stone bulk at the time, these days Bunny felt nothing but compassion towards her cardboard doppelgänger; that woman who had been so downtrodden and meek and scared, yet who had discovered a seam of unexpected gutsiness. Who had finally found the courage to say, *No. Enough.*

Her throat tightened, as it always did whenever she thought about the bad old days. But they were all behind her, she reminded herself. She was Bunny Halliday now, and she could handle anything.

Right then. There was a room full of slimmers who were waiting for inspiration. For her. Briskly locking the car, she held her head high and marched towards the church-hall entrance.

Was there anything lovelier than walking through your own front door, after a busy day's work, and knowing that your favourite TV programmes awaited, along with a very nice microwave Meal-for-One and an even nicer bottle of wine? No, thought Alison, sliding the bolt across, then kicking off her shoes. No, there was not. She knew how to have a fun night, all right. Whatever her daughter might think.

'Aren't you lonely, though? Do come and join us, if you want some company,' Robyn would offer regularly, approximately nine million times in the last year alone. It was the 'us' that hurt Alison the most. The 'us' that meant Robyn and the rest of the Mortimers as a combined unit, with Alison on the sidelines. Oh, she was sure her daughter's in-laws were very nice people; Robyn certainly adored them all. But this only made Alison feel inadequate in comparison, as if the Mortimers were a *proper* family, giving Robyn what Alison had never been able to provide for her. Giving Sam and Daisy cousins and aunts and uncles and party-throwing grandparents too, none of which they had when they came round to her place.

She should have known it would be like this, right from Robyn and John's wedding, when the Mortimer side of the church was stuffed so full of relatives and friends that they'd had to edge into Robyn's side, which consisted merely of Alison plus a handful of university friends. Even then, the balance had been there for all to see. Worse, Jeanie had made some comment to Alison a few years ago, out of misguided sympathy – 'It must be hard, being on your own sometimes, Alison', or something similar. Yes, okay, so no doubt the words had been meant with kindness, but all the same they had jabbed into Alison like little barbs. The other woman's pity. The other woman's condescension. How dreadfully *hard* it must be for Alison, with no husband and no huge family get-togethers and no flock of doting children!

Er, no actually. More like, how patronizing could you get? Because it wasn't hard, and she wasn't lonely, thank you very much. How could anyone be lonely when they worked as a mobile hairdresser and spent every day in different houses, cutting hair and listening to clients' stories? Besides, she had all her pals on the Telly Addicts forum, some of whom had become dear friends over the years. She had her pride too, which was why she had said, 'No thank you' to Jeanie Mortimer's invitations ever since. Because life was too short to have your nose rubbed in it, in Alison's opinion. Count her out.

Twenty minutes later she had her feet up in front of the TV, a plate of microwaved lasagne on her knee, a glass of chilled wine on the coffee table and the laptop open at her side. The muggy weather had burst at last, and rain was pelting against the windows, leaving long wet streaks. There was even a rumble of thunder overhead. Good. Alison loved a thunderstorm when you were warm and cosy inside. *And* she'd just remembered there was one last Crunchie ice-cream bar in the freezer for afters. Heaven, right there.

Evening all, she typed between mouthfuls, once she'd

logged into the forum. *How's everyone doing tonight? I see we have a few new members with us – welcome! We're a very friendly bunch here and looking forward to talking telly with you! Now for the big question: what's everyone watching tonight?*

She flicked on the TV, humming to herself as she went through that evening's programme guide. There was a detective drama on at nine, the first episode of which she'd enjoyed very much last week. Before then, the tennis was on BBC2, which was quite soothing; one of the sounds of summer, she always thought – the clop and swish of racquet hitting ball. Plus, of course, there was no small amount of pleasure to be had from watching those very athletic young men in their nice white shorts; always an enjoyable way to while away the hours. What else? Well, good old *Coronation Street*, obviously, and—

BOOM! Crack!

Thunder crashed outside, lightning flashed and then there was a violent bang directly overhead, followed by the television making an alarming fizzling noise and going completely blank. 'Oh!' gulped Alison aloud, spluttering on her wine in shock. For a second she sat there frozen, hunched over with fright, as if the ceiling was about to come down on her in a shower of plaster, before she unfolded herself again with a wary glance around. Unfortunately the television remained silent and apparently dead. 'Oh . . . bugger,' she added unhappily. She pressed the remote, trying to switch the thing back on, but nothing happened. 'You're kidding me,' she groaned, stabbing repeatedly at the button with no success. 'Please. No!'

Well, she'd gone right off thunderstorms, that was for sure. Had lightning struck the satellite dish? she wondered anxiously. Were all the electrics in the house now trashed? She thought with a pang of her Crunchie ice-cream awaiting her in the freezer and jumped to her feet. No, the lights were still working at least, she realized, flipping them on and off. And when she went into the kitchen, the fridge was purring obediently, the clock on the cooker displaying the correct time.

Rain continued to slap against the windows as she returned to the sofa and ate another mouthful of lasagne. Okay, so she would have to watch her programmes on the laptop, she supposed, just until she could get someone round to figure out what was wrong with the TV. One of her clients, Becky, had an electrician husband who might be able to fix it for her, she comforted herself. But when she tried to refresh her laptop screen, she was faced with an error message instead of her home page. *No internet connection can be detected*, it said unhelpfully and she let out a growl of frustration. 'Oh come *on*!' Had the lightning frazzled her broadband as well? Her grasp of electricity and circuits – of technology in general, let's face it – was flaky at the best of times, but she was not feeling hopeful.

She munched glumly on the lasagne before pushing the plate away, her mood souring. No telly. No Internet. She had her phone, and the mobile data on that at least . . . but who wanted to watch a programme on a tiny screen? It would give her a headache within two minutes, even with her reading glasses on. So what was she supposed to do now?

It was at times like this – few and far between, admittedly – that she found herself missing Rich. Thirty-three years had ticked by since he'd died, but he still sometimes appeared in her head, frozen in time with his favourite checked shirt and corduroy trousers, his tufty brown hair and that calm way he had of dealing with a problem. 'Let's see what we can do here then,' he would have said, had he been with her now. Give him a screwdriver, tuck a pencil behind his ear and he'd be away, whistling cheerfully between his teeth as he tackled whatever new practical test lay ahead. Alison was quite sure that many of his shelves and bookcases would still be standing, back in their old house in Wolverhampton; ditto the shed he'd put together one Sunday afternoon, lengths of wood all over the lawn like a gigantic timber jigsaw. That huge workbench he'd built in the garage, too: sturdy as anything. It would take a meteorite to blast through the roof to destroy that. The evenings he'd spent there, happily tinkering with his beloved vintage car – a red Jensen Interceptor that he was doing up – it had been his idea of bliss, quite frankly.

Not that Alison liked to think about the garage at their old house for long, obviously. You couldn't dwell on these things. But the memory poked insidiously at her, regardless: how she'd woken up on that still, soundless Sunday morning to find his half of the bed empty; how she'd felt that throat-tightening impulse of dread, strong enough to send her tiptoeing past Robyn's bedroom and downstairs. Rich had lost his job as foreman of a building site three months earlier, after being wrongly accused of theft, and he hadn't been the same since. Down she'd padded to the kitchen, where a note lay propped up beside the kettle: *I'm sorry.* And she'd seen the door ajar between the utility room and the garage, and she'd dashed through uselessly to find . . .

The bitter smell of turps. The soft speckles of sawdust on the workbench. And that grotesque creaking of a rope, twisting slightly from the rafter as her husband's body dangled, limp and unresponsive. She had staggered away as if punch-drunk, knocking over a box of Rawlplugs, her mouth open in a silent scream of horror. *No. No!*

Decades later, in the safety of her quiet Harrogate living room, Alison gave a violent shudder and tipped back the rest of her wine in a single gulp, trying to block out the image, to shut the door on it, just as she had done in real life. She'd closed that door tight, locked it, put the key in her dressing-gown pocket, because there were some things in life that a child should not see, should not have to deal with, should never be told about even. Then, with the same numb composure, she'd called her mum – 'I need you to come and get Robyn for me. Please. As soon as possible' – before screwing up the note Rich had left ('Why's he sorry? Did he break something?' Robyn, a child brimming with questions, would ask, if she saw it) and burying it deep in the kitchen bin, beneath the teabags and potato peelings and eggshells.

A sudden heart attack, she'd told Robyn a few days later, when it was safe for her to come home, all evidence of her father's true death discreetly removed by a pair of kind policemen; a packet of prescription sleeping tablets newly arrived on Alison's bedside table, the only thing that could knock her out at night. Was it wrong to rewrite history, to blur a few lines, when it was your own child you were protecting? Whatever – she had stuck to the story ever since, moving to a new house, a new area, just as soon as she could, to escape any gossip that might be lingering.

'Oh, for God's sake, stop it,' Alison said viciously to herself now, standing up suddenly and walking quickly into the kitchen, as if trying to shake off these dark memories with the movement. 'What is the *point*? Stop brooding, you stupid woman.' She poured out more wine and drank the glass straight down while she was standing there at the kitchen worktop, the alcohol puckering her mouth like medicine, the thunder still booming and rumbling outside.

In the next moment, as the thunder rolled away, she

heard a voice from the other room, a male voice speaking urgently, and for a second she thought she was going mad, that she had somehow conjured up her long-dead husband. Mad? Or drunk? She rushed back to the living room, only to see – oh, thank heavens! – the television back on again and a newsreader speaking solemnly about the latest refugee crisis, at which point she collapsed heavily into the sofa, a sob escaping her throat.

'Thank you,' she croaked to the television.

A power surge? A loose connection? Who knew, but there was her laptop busily refreshing itself as well, all back to normal. Panic over.

She wiped her eyes, then blew her nose, trembling with relief. 'Pull yourself together,' she scolded herself. 'Daft old bat, getting in a state like that.' She put a hand to her chest, feeling her heart pumping too fast. 'It's all right now. Come on, you're okay. You're okay.'

Chapter Six

In stressful times there was something about having a young, inquisitive child that was very grounding, Frankie thought over the next few days. Like all four-year-olds, Fergus lived completely in the now: exuberant one moment, asking a string of complicated questions in the next, and then completely ignoring the answers in order to squat down and examine a crawling beetle or an interestingly shaped puddle a second later. He demanded attention in such a sweet and innocent way, Frankie was happy to give it to him. As a result, by the middle of the week she was almost starting to feel as if the disastrous Yorkshire trip was a strange dream rather than something that had actually happened. Flashes of the experience would come back to her – Harry Mortimer's stunned expression as their eyes met, his unexpected height, the disbelieving way he'd said her mother's name . . . all with a rowdy version of a Tom Jones song in the background. None of it seemed quite real any more.

'What will you do now?' Craig asked gently when two days had passed and she hadn't revisited the subject of her father. 'Are you going to try again? Write him a letter or something?'

'I don't know,' she'd replied, wrinkling her nose. 'Maybe. I probably should. But then again, what would I say? I don't want to make everything worse for him.'

'How could someone as glorious and delightful as you make things worse for anyone?' Craig had asked.

Frankie wasn't convinced she wanted to answer that. While she appreciated his cheerleading support, she was pretty sure her surprise appearance hadn't exactly made things better for Harry's wife. Or Harry himself, judging by the look on the other woman's face.

She would do what she always did, she supposed. Nothing. Let the whole situation drift to a distant horizon, allow it to become sidelined by the real and more pressing matters of everyday life. Who needed a biological father anyway? Her mum had married Gareth Carlyle when Frankie was twelve – amiable, easy-going Gareth who'd been a good enough substitute dad, even though he had jetted off for a sunny retirement in Palma earlier this year; his way of coping with widowerhood, Frankie guessed. Perhaps at some point in the future she'd feel like trying again with Harry, but for now she would plump for denial and not dwell on it.

On Thursday, she dropped Fergus at playgroup for his morning session as usual, exchanged pleasantries about the sunny weather with a couple of the other mums, then stopped on the way home at the deli, to pick up two cappuccinos for her and Craig as a surprise treat. At some point in the future – maybe even in the autumn when Fergus started school – they were hoping to rent some decent office space in which to work (Frankie dreamed of a light-filled attic studio with huge windows). Until then, though, they'd have to carry on making do at opposite ends of their kitchen table, taking it in turns to look after Fergus, make lunch, chase up unpaid invoices and bung on a load of laundry in between.

'Your own cottage industry, how charming!' various friends had commented over the years, as if the two of them lived and worked in a beautiful stone farmhouse, with chickens scratching around in a yard outside and a dog thumping its plumy tail on a flagstone floor. One journalist had even interviewed them for a feature on 'Love in the Workplace' and, on reading the finished article, Frankie had to admit she'd made their working set-up sound cosily idyllic. In reality, they were squeezed into Craig's fourth-floor ex-council flat on the seamier side of Ladbroke Grove, with a view of the Westway from the window. But it was home.

Once back at their block, Frankie climbed the stairs, wondering if she should have bought iced coolers rather than steamy hot drinks. There was about one day a year when their flat felt like the perfect temperature, but the rest of the time it was either airless and sweltering, like today, or absolutely freezing, when they'd be forced to work wearing coats and woolly hats like a couple of students.

'Bloody hell,' she moaned, letting herself back in, feeling unpleasantly clammy. 'It's roasting out there.' And then she stopped because she could hear voices, and she frowned, trying to make out who they were. Craig was fiercely protective of his work time, guarding the scant Fergus-free hours they had as a chance to crack on single-mindedly with a column. Sometimes he wouldn't even answer the phone to a friend, so determined was he not to be tempted by offers of skiving or distraction.

'Hello?' Frankie called, wandering through to the kitchen. 'Oh,' she said in surprise, seeing an unfamiliar woman at the table. Her brain simultaneously registered two separate facts – one, that the woman looked very relaxed there, leaning expansively against the radiator with her legs crossed at the ankles. The second fact was how much the woman looked like Fergus: the exact same dark curly hair, the same olive skin, the same pretty Cupid's-bow mouth. And then Frankie's blood ran quite cold because she knew, without question, that this was surely Julia, Craig's ex-girlfriend, back from the unknown. 'Hi,' she said, her mouth dry, as the visitor gave her an appraising look.

'Hi,' the woman replied, and for a horrible moment it felt to Frankie as if *she* were the guest in the situation, that this was still Julia's flat, and she merely an interloper. No wonder Craig's ex looked so at home here, lounging against the radiator in that way, when she'd lived here herself for years, long before Frankie had arrived on the scene.

'Um,' said Craig, who looked similarly discomfited, 'Frankie, this is Julia. Julia, Frankie.'

'I guessed,' Frankie blurted out. 'Fergus looks so like you.'

At the mention of his name, Julia's face lit up. 'I gather he's at playgroup,' she said.

'Yes,' said Frankie, trying not to stare too nakedly at her. *So here you are.* Then her nerves got the better of her and she started babbling whatever came into her head. 'He always has a great time there. The staff are brilliant and he's got this fab best friend called Preena, who he loves playing Lego with, and—' She broke off, struck by the strangeness of this conversation: the unlikely fact that she was having to tell this woman details about her own son. All the countless things Frankie knew about Fergus, yet Julia didn't. All the cuddles and conversations and silly jokes that Frankie had enjoyed and Julia hadn't.

'So how often does he go there, then?' Julia asked.

Was it Frankie's imagination or did Julia sound a bit critical, as if she thought they were outsourcing Fergus's childcare because they couldn't be bothered to look after him themselves? 'Three mornings a week,' Craig replied tersely. *Not that it's any of your business*, his expression added.

'It's good for his social skills,' Frankie said, in a bright TV-presenter sort of voice that didn't sound like her at all. 'He's made lots of friends. And with school coming up, we thought . . .' Craig shot her a look and she trailed off, biting her lip. 'Yeah,' she mumbled. Craig was right, she told herself, they didn't need to explain their decisions to Julia, not when she'd abandoned Fergus just when he needed her most. They didn't owe her anything. So why did Frankie feel as if she was the one being judged here?

'Great!' said Julia, clapping her hands together. 'Well, I'll have to get the details from you sometime.' She smiled widely. She was an attractive woman, toned and healthy-looking, wearing a turquoise kaftan-style top, spotless white cut-off jeans and sparkly silver flip-flops. In the past Craig had told Frankie that Julia was depressive and unpredictable – 'unhinged' was a word he'd used – but she looked completely normal to Frankie. Radiant, even. But what did she mean, about getting the playgroup details from them? Surely she wasn't saying . . . ?

Frankie swung questioningly towards Craig, who was scowling and shaking his head at his ex. 'Julia – no,' he said. 'You can't just walk in here and—'

'Oh, but I can,' she said, and suddenly her smile was as

71

toothy and gleaming as a crocodile's. 'Because I'm his mother.' Her eyes glittered and the temperature in the room seemed to plunge. 'You've had him for four years. I think it's my turn now, don't you?'

'What?' cried Frankie in anguish, just as Craig said, '*Julia*—' again, in a tone of voice that Frankie had never heard before, one so stern and terrible that it chilled her to the marrow.

A whimper escaped from Frankie's throat because, deep down, there was a part of her that had always known this day would come: that Fergus's real mother would return, seeking some kind of reparation, and stake a claim. *He's mine. Not yours.* And even though Frankie loved every last inch of that little boy, she couldn't escape the fact that he wasn't hers. Not properly. Not according to the paperwork. She'd only ever had him on loan. And if Julia wanted to be back in Fergus's life, get to know him anew, then how could Frankie deny her that privilege?

She stared fearfully at Julia, wondering how Fergus would feel about all this. He would be confused. He thought *she* was his mummy. How would they explain it to him? And was it selfish and pathetic of Frankie to be worrying already that he would love Julia more than her?

'I've had a lovely chat with the people at the Citizens Advice Bureau,' Julia was saying, and Frankie jolted back to the room, 'and they told me: a mother's rights are *sacred*. A mother's rights have more weight than a father's rights. And while I couldn't cope before, that was because I was ill. I had some problems. But I'm better now, and I'm ready to pick up where I left off.'

'You're *ready*?' Craig repeated with such blistering sarcasm that Frankie half-expected the paint to start peeling from the walls. 'You're *ready* to pick up where you left off.' He shook his head, incredulous, before rounding on her. 'You can't do that with a child, Julia. It doesn't work like that, you can't just press pause and then play when you feel like it. Because, tell me: where were you when he was having surgery, when he was teething, when he was ill, tired, upset, scared? On his birthday, at Christmas, when he took his first steps? Why weren't you ready for your own son four years ago?'

Frankie flinched at the bitter fury in his voice. His words came out so fluently, so vehemently, she had the feeling they had been rehearsed many times in his head before. Craig had always been rather tight-lipped about Julia in the past, intimating that he had cut her completely out of his thoughts, detaching her from his life like a broken old piece of furniture. Frankie hadn't realized just how much hurt and rage were still seething volcanically away inside. 'Craig,' she said timidly, because she couldn't bear to see him like this. And actually if Julia *had* been ill and suffered some kind of breakdown, then he should cut her some slack. You could hardly blame a person for that.

'What?' he retorted, his face contorted with anger. 'She wants to take Fergus away. What part of that don't you understand?'

The words were like a slap. 'Take him *away*?' Frankie repeated in horror, turning to Julia. 'But I thought . . .' She'd assumed – perhaps naively – that Julia merely wanted to spend a bit of time with him. Start a new relationship. Maybe have him for the occasional afternoon here or there, building up to a night. A weekend. That would be all right, wouldn't it? Seeing as she was his mother and all? Nobody could deny her that much, surely. But to take Fergus completely *away* – to rip him from Frankie and Craig, from this flat, their bedtime routines and favourite play parks and silly family jokes – no. No. This could not possibly be an option. No!

'He's my son,' said Julia, playing her trump card. The card that could not be denied or beaten; not by Frankie anyway, she thought helplessly.

Shock and fear flooded her system. Her heart contracted painfully, as if there was too much to process; it felt hard to breathe. Was this what happened when you meddled with other people's families – that someone turned up, days later, to meddle in yours? It was as if, by going up to York to investigate her own parentage, she'd somehow let loose some celestial mischief that was now set to wreak havoc in Frankie's own small world, to put in jeopardy everything she loved.

'What's his favourite story, then? What's his favourite food? You don't even *know* him,' Craig said. His nostrils flared, his hands gripped the side of the table, his whole body seemed braced to spring into action, as if adrenalin was pumping through him by the gallon. 'Go on, get out. We don't want you here.'

'Craig, wait,' said Julia, and Frankie wanted to echo the same words. *Craig, wait, you're making this worse. Craig, wait, don't attack her, listen to what she has to say. Craig, wait, there has to be a sensible way around this.* He hated Julia, though, she realized uneasily. He really, really hated her.

'You heard me,' he snarled, bristling like a wild animal. 'Kindly leave.'

Julia stuck out her chin in defiance. 'I didn't come here for an argument,' she said, eyeballing him right back. Then she scribbled down her number on a piece of paper and pushed it across the table. 'Here are my details. Ring me when you're ready to discuss this like an adult.' Her chin jutted. 'But you need to know that I've got a solicitor. I've got people who will help me. And I have every right to see my son!' Her composure suddenly crumbling, a sob swallowed up her voice. 'Because he's *my* son too, and don't you forget it.'

She banged the table as she got to her feet, and Frankie

quailed as the woman's angry gaze swung between Craig and then her, before she slammed her way out of the flat. The silence that followed her departure seemed deafeningly loud, filling the small room. Everything in there was the same as it had been an hour ago – the cheerful yellow walls, Fergus's paintings Blu-tacked on the doors of the cabinets, two spotty mugs upside down in the draining rack, the photos of happy days stuck on the fridge, along with a load of Thomas the Tank Engine magnets. And yet Julia's appearance seemed to have cast a spell over the place, so that the window now looked small and grimy and Frankie couldn't help but notice the dust balls in one corner of the floor, a teabag splash on the counter, the cupboard door that hung wonkily where the hinge had been broken for months.

Feeling as if her heart had become a gigantic painful rock, she set one of the lukewarm cappuccinos in front of Craig and sank into a chair with the other. 'What are we going to do?' she asked, her voice a fearful bleat. 'What are we going to do, Craig?'

Chapter Seven

'This is a nice surprise,' Alison said as Robyn sat down opposite her at the beer-garden table. It was Friday, Robyn's day off, and she'd originally planned to spend the afternoon getting the house in order for the weekend: catching up on the laundry, with a quick whip around the supermarket if she had time. As it turned out, what she really wanted was to see a friendly face. *Don't suppose you're free for lunch today? The White Horse?* she had texted her mum hopefully.

It must have been serendipity because, not ten minutes earlier, Alison had just had a cancellation and so here they were now, at a pub equidistant from them both. Alison was being her usual comforting self, handing over a menu and saying knowledgeably that the home-made pasties were very good here, before she lifted up her sunglasses to peer more closely at her daughter. 'Is everything all right, love?'

Robyn smiled wanly. What was it about mums that meant they had a built-in worry detector? 'Not really,' she replied with a sigh, turning the laminated menu over in her hands. 'John's lost his job.'

'Oh no.' Alison's jaw dropped, mirroring the shock Robyn had experienced on hearing the news. 'He hasn't!'

'He has. Redundancies across the department, apparently,' Robyn said, grimacing. John had worked at the university for eighteen years; a job for life, or so he'd thought. He was the main breadwinner of the family, the mortgage payer, the holiday provider, the man with the golden credit card. More than that: he prided himself on his ability to provide for them, and was old-fashioned in the sense that he thought this was what a husband should do. But then two days ago, when Beth Broadwood had approached Robyn with her attempted solidarity – *I was sorry to hear the news* – it turned out that John's job, and all that it meant for the family, had fractured and collapsed to the ground while she had been looking the other way.

'I was going to tell you,' John said glumly, when she'd built up to asking him if it was true. 'I was just . . . trying to find the right moment.'

He looked ashamed, poor man; he looked broken by his confession. He'd hardly been able to look Robyn in the eye as he revealed the facts in a weary, defeated voice. 'I'm so sorry,' she cried passionately in response. 'What a nightmare.' She took his hand and squeezed it, wishing she could make things better for him. John's job defined him; it was all he'd ever done. He was the sort of person who became restless during the long vacations; he much preferred being at work and getting on with the job. 'Are they scrapping the course, or what? Is everyone going?'

He'd shrugged. 'Dunno.' He opened his mouth as if he was about to elaborate, then seemed to change his mind. 'Anyway. Now you know,' he continued, heaviness in his voice. 'I'm sorry. I feel as if I've let you all down.'

'John, no!' she'd exclaimed. 'Of course you haven't. You haven't let anyone down – it's not your fault. It's just bad luck, that's all. Really rotten luck.'

'He's gutted,' she went on to her mum now, remembering John's glum face. No doubt the redundancy was the cause of all those dark moods of his, the excessive drinking, the silent withdrawal from her. He hadn't wanted to burden her, clearly. Somehow this made her feel even worse.

'Oh dear. That *is* bad news,' Alison replied. 'Will you be all right for money? I mean, he's been there a while, hasn't he? They do have to give you a decent pay-off at least when you're made redundant – employment law and all that.'

'He didn't seem to know what they'd give him,' Robyn said. 'I'm sure he'll find something else, but . . . It's such a shock. He seems so crushed.'

'Poor John. It's a blow to his manly pride. Your dad was—' Alison broke off, the words hanging mid-sentence between them.

'What?' Robyn asked. That was two mentions of her dad in the space of a week; unheard of. 'Did Dad get made redundant?' she asked, wondering if it had affected his health, contributed to the heart attack that had ultimately felled him. Maybe she wouldn't have a fattening home-made pasty for lunch after all, she decided, picturing her own heart keeping time inside her ribcage.

'It was a long time ago,' Alison said dismissively, before changing the subject back again. 'Anyway, no offence, but I'm guessing your job doesn't pay all that much,' she went on. 'So if you're stuck, let me know, because I've got some savings put aside, remember. Or maybe . . .' She cocked her head and considered her daughter. 'Well, you said yourself not so long ago that you might look for a more interesting job again, didn't you? So—'

'Yes, but . . .' *Whoa*, thought Robyn. They were leaping all over the place here. She'd hardly been able to digest John's redundancy news yet, let alone start making plans for her own career revival.

'So this could be your chance. You know what they say – when life gives you lemons, and all that. The kiddies are old enough now not to mind, aren't they? You could contact your old department, I'm sure they'd welcome you back with open arms. Lemonade all round!' Alison had perked right up, with the brilliance of her idea, and was leaning forward, eyes alight with excitement. Oh, but she had been the proudest mum in the world when Robyn had passed her degree ('The first in our family!'), and then her Masters ('I don't know *where* she gets her brains from'), and then worked as a postgrad at the university, before rising through the departmental ranks.

How Robyn had loved working there, though! She'd felt interested and challenged every single day; almost able to hear the synapses in her brain fizzing and buzzing from the stimulation. She relished being surrounded by highly intelligent people, everyone keen to learn, foraging for discoveries and information. And of course she'd met John there on a rainy night too, at an open lecture on the 'Unknown Universe', when Fate persuaded them both through the door in the first place, and then sat them next to each other. ('And about time, and all!' Alison had cried in relief, when Robyn told her she was seeing a new bloke. 'I was starting to think I'd have to dust off a space for you on the Old Maids' shelf soon, next to me.')

All of this felt like such a long time ago now, of course. When Sam had been born, Robyn had taken maternity leave, fully intending to return to her job, but he'd been a sickly baby, plagued by eczema, and when it had come to the crunch, she hadn't felt able to leave him. Then Daisy had arrived; a clingy little thing who roared with sorrow and outrage if anyone but Robyn dared try to hold her. It had been eleven years since Robyn had considered herself any kind of career woman, in short.

Had she left it too long now to return? she wondered. She did her best to keep up with *New Scientist* magazine when time permitted, but was surely out of the loop in terms of the minutiae of the latest developments in her field. Besides, she had lost confidence in her own abilities. Once upon a time she had been able to stand in front of hundreds of students in lecture halls and talk to them enthusiastically about genetic engineering and molecular biology. Nowadays the thought made her feel kind of terrified. She could actually feel her top lip starting to sweat with nerves as she pictured herself there again.

'Mum, no, it's fine. I'll keep you posted, I'm sure everything will work out,' she said after a moment.

'I'm sure it will too,' Alison replied. 'But honestly, why do these things all happen at once? It's been one of those weeks, hasn't it? Did you have a massive storm on Monday as well? My electrics went and everything for a while, it was a right pain in the neck. And then there was John's mum and dad having their bust-up, too . . . Crikey. Must be something in the air. Anyway –' she grabbed her menu theatrically – 'we should order, because I've got Elizabeth Perry's highlights to do at two-fifteen and she doesn't half get narky if I'm late. What do you fancy? I'm going for the pasty and some potato wedges. Sod it, it's Friday after all.'

Robyn studied the menu. It might be Friday, but she was going to have to watch the pennies from now on, she reminded herself, at least until John found a new job. 'Salad and a diet Coke,' she replied, reluctantly.

It was Saturday morning, and Jeanie Mortimer stirred sleepily in the double bed, the enormous ceiling fan whirring lazily above her head. One more day of paradise, she thought, opening an eye to see bright sunshine already streaming through the gaps in the shutters. One more day, before she was due to pack up her swimming costume and floaty dresses and return to the real world. Despite the rocky start to her holiday, she'd gone on to have a very nice stay here.

She'd spent the first day in tears, mind, replaying over and over again the moment when she'd seen the young woman – Frankie – staring at Harry, frozen to the spot, and some dreadful sixth sense had sent the hairs prickling on the back of her neck, a descending scale of notes playing ominously in her head. Was there such a thing as female intuition? Whatever, Jeanie had just *known*.

Kathy Hallows's daughter, Harry had confirmed to her miserably later on. 'Me and Kathy, we—'

'I guessed as much,' Jeanie had replied before he could get any further. She hadn't even felt a twinge of surprise. Instead, decades-old memories had flashed up instantly in her consciousness. The school sports day that summer, when she'd been passing the playing field, with Stephen in the pushchair, and they'd stopped to wave to Harry. There had been this very pretty young woman with long chestnut hair and even longer tanned legs, jumping up and down at the sidelines of a race, cheering on the sprinting kids, and Jeanie remembered asking Harry, 'Who's that?'

'That's Kathy,' he'd replied, and there was something about the way he said it, something about the softness of his smile that made her shiver as they both turned and looked at her. The memory of this made her feel sick now, obviously. *That's Kathy. The woman I'm actually having an affair with,* was what he *hadn't* said back then, of course. *And believe it or not, in thirty-five years' time, we'll have a right old surprise when her daughter – and mine! – turns up unexpectedly at our anniversary party.*

There was more. Another flickering film-reel that had emerged from the depths of her brain: the drinks at the end of term that July, in the Bricklayers' Arms, for the teachers and their other halves. Jeanie hadn't thought she'd be able to make it, what with Stephen coming down with a tummy bug and John having just cracked one of his teeth at the cricket club, but her mum had offered to babysit at the last minute and Jeanie had decided that popping out for an hour wouldn't hurt. She'd changed her top and brushed her hair out from its ponytail, she'd even dabbed some rouge on her cheeks and put on lipstick, for good measure. It had been a lovely evening, she remembered it still, because in those days it was such a novelty to be walking along the sunny street on her own, and she actually felt quite uplifted to be out like this for once, going to meet her husband for a social event. And then she'd got to the pub and she'd seen Harry sitting next to her – that Kathy girl – their heads close together, their bodies turned towards one another, and she'd heard a warning bell jangling in her head. A wife noticed these things.

'I didn't think you were coming!' Harry cried, springing up away from the girl as soon as he saw Jeanie there, and the warning bell went on with its discordant jangle as Kathy glanced over at her and moved swiftly to another table.

Jeanie had kept her suspicions to herself – she had enough on her plate, with four young children occupying her time – but had breathed a private sigh of relief on hearing from another teacher friend that Miss Hallows had left town and was no longer at the school the following autumn. So that was that, she'd thought.

Except it wasn't quite the end of the matter, after all, was it? Because here she was now, without her husband on their so-called second honeymoon, as a result. Oh, life could play cruel tricks on a person sometimes.

For the whole of her first miserable day in Madeira, Jeanie had been convinced she had made the most dreadful mistake, jetting off by herself in a trembling fit of rage and hurt; but after that, she'd jolly well pulled her socks up and done her best to distract herself from the anguish. Had she been bored? Had she heck. She'd swum in the pool every day, read four excellent books and seen her skin turn a perfect bronze.

Had she been lonely? Not a bit. She'd met a couple of very friendly women from Pembrokeshire who were holidaying together, and they'd invited her to join them for cocktails and dinner several times. Plus the staff had been unfailingly kind, bringing her drinks at the sun-lounger, encouraging her to try the cabaret evening, leaving the most beautiful tropical flowers on her pillow whenever they turned down her bed in the evening. She'd even had a bit of a dance at the Sixties Music Disco, shimmying around to Martha and the Vandellas as if she were twenty again. Obviously her case was already loaded up with all kinds of silly souvenirs for her beloved grandchildren, which she hadn't been able to resist in the gift shop. It was one of the greatest joys in her life, being a grandma, and just the thought of her grandchildren's dear smiling faces was enough to bring her tiny crumbs of comfort through her darkest moments.

Jeanie's life had always been so *busy*, until now. As well as bringing up four children and working for twenty-five years as a piano teacher, it had still been *her* putting all those dinners on the table, and organizing the shopping and housework. Even when the children had grown up and flown the nest, she'd kept herself active, doing shifts as a volunteer in the local charity shop and helping with the little ones at a playgroup nearby. She'd maintained an open house for all the Mortimers, when it came to Sunday dinner – everyone welcome! – and always laid on a special party tea for family members on their birthdays: a proper Yorkshire cream tea with home-made scones as well as the cake of their choice. She was never happier than when she had her complete flock around her, all safely gathered in, when she could see them enjoying her dinners and cakes, when she could marvel at what wonderful people her children had grown up to be.

'I don't know how you do it,' Harry's sisters would cry. 'How do you find the energy?' This was from the three of them, mind, who'd serve you shop-bought Battenberg if you went round to their houses, a Wagon Wheel if your luck was in.

Well, Jeanie found the energy because she loved looking after her family – that was the simple answer, even if, truth be told, the get-togethers took their toll on her these days, wiping her out afterwards with the exhaustion of all that shopping and baking and hosting. Not that she would ever admit it to anyone other than Harry, of course. No, because it was always worth it.

Oh, Harry, she thought unhappily, turning over in the

huge bed and hugging one of the spare pillows to herself. His infidelity, his betrayal seemed to have severed her from all of that now. Whatever had possessed him to jeopardize the family in such a terrible way? Why had he gone looking elsewhere for attention, into the arms of this other woman, when she, Jeanie, had always loved him so completely? He had quite broken her heart. He had broken the family too. How could she go back and face them all when her marriage was in ruins, when the future seemed so fraught with uncertainty? Would the family ever be able to enjoy a party or Sunday dinner together in the same way, after this revelation? She and Harry had been a twosome for so long, had weathered so many storms between them, but this – this felt like a hurricane. One of those awful ones you saw on the news that wrecked everything in its path: trees, houses, lives, all tossed aside.

She was dreading tomorrow when the holiday would be over. Being here had been like escaping into a brightly lit bubble of temporary pleasures, far from the pain and embarrassment left behind at home. A bubble where she was looked after and cosseted, where she was protected from the pain of real life. But tomorrow, it ended. Tomorrow, she'd have to pack her bags, hand back the key to her room and then catch the bus to the airport, where she would wait, drearily, resignedly, for her flight home. She'd have to face Harry's grovelling apologies, maybe even at the

Arrivals gate at the other end, if he was really desperate to creep back into her good books. And then, once home, she'd have the prospect of being confronted with every last gossip on the street, their faces lighting up as they spotted her, flocking in like iron filings to a magnet. Oh, you wait – the news would already have whipped between the neighbours like wildfire, Chinese whispers from house to house. (*Have you heard? He's got a secret love-child. Yes, Harry Mortimer. Who would have thought? She left him at the airport, you know. She did!*)

Worst of all, at some point, when they couldn't put it off any longer, she and Harry would have to have The Conversation, make some decisions. Harry would tell her what he wanted to do about Her, and Jeanie would have to put her own feelings on the table in response. *It's her or me,* she had proclaimed a week earlier, and she was not a woman to go back on her word. What if Harry chose her, this new daughter? What if he said he'd preferred Kathy all along? Their marriage might never recover from this hit.

Doom-laden minor chords played in her head at the prospect. It was all too terrible for words.

Rolling over in bed and nestling into the soft, comfortable pillows, she shut her eyes, not wanting to think about Harry or his betrayal any more. If only she could stay here instead, she thought longingly. Stay here and never go back . . .

Chapter Eight

The radio silence from her mother over the last week had been very odd, thought Paula as she parked at the airport on Sunday. The two of them had always been close, speaking on the phone or texting pretty much every day, if not catching up in person. When Paula had first become a mum, Jeanie had been like a guiding star through the early weeks of parenthood, pushing colicky baby Luke around the streets in his pram for hours at a time so that Paula could try and sleep. She had always loved her mum, of course, but it wasn't until she saw the tender, patient way Jeanie engaged with Paula's own children that it really struck her how strong family bonds could be, and how deeply love could run between generations. But for the last seven days there had been no cheery text message or phone call, no funny photos on the family WhatsApp group. A hole had opened up in Paula's life without Jeanie there.

It wasn't just Paula she'd gone quiet on; nobody had heard from Jeanie. Paula had sent her various supportive messages and voicemails with no reply, before becoming worried that her mum had somehow gone AWOL in transit – or worse. After two days she'd actually called the hotel in a panic, caught up in a terrible *What if . . . ?* loop of doom. If something had happened to Mum and she'd been on her own, Paula would kill Dad for it. Kill him with her own bare hands, just see if she didn't. But – 'Your mother is here and says she is perfectly fine,' the manager had assured her, in charming broken English. 'She is having a lovely holiday, but doesn't wish to speak to anyone.'

So that had been that. And it was understandable, after all, if Jeanie wanted to switch off from the real world for a bit, Paula supposed. Only . . . well, her mum was a proud sort of woman, and going off alone was completely out of character. For all Paula knew, Jeanie might be sobbing into her pristine hotel pillow each night, desperately lonely and feeling awkward too, about having to do everything on her own. 'Tell them I'm fine,' Paula imagined her sniffling, blotchy-faced, when the manager came knocking. (What must the hotel staff *think* of the Mortimer family, for letting this happen? Harry should have flown straight out to Madeira after Jeanie, begging her forgiveness, in Paula's opinion. Instead he'd meekly come back to York and had gone to stay at Dave's house in Clementhorpe because he couldn't face being alone. Should have thought of that, shouldn't you, before you went and cheated on Mum? she'd mused crossly.)

'I'll take Dad to the airport,' she'd offered Dave, when she rang him the night before. The middle brother, he was closest in age to Paula and her favourite of them all, due to his kind, earnest nature. As eldest, John had always been keen to shoot ahead and do everything first. Stephen, the youngest, had been the rebel, involved in all kinds of naughtiness. Dave and Paula were the easy-going middle ones, who held the balance. 'I just want to see Mum for myself, do you know what I mean? I've really missed her.'

'Me too,' said Dave, then lowered his voice. 'As for Dad . . . honestly, he's lost without her. He doesn't know what to do with himself. He hasn't made himself lunch once this week while Bunny and I have been at work. Says he doesn't want to take liberties.'

'Doesn't know how to work the toaster, more like,' Paula replied, rolling her eyes. Her dad was a total old-school man's man, who considered the kitchen and everything within it his wife's territory. You'd have thought he'd at least have *tried* to make himself something to eat, though, rather than going starving hungry all day, she thought in exasperation.

Anyway, here they were now, she and Harry, striding through the airport terminal together, both looking forward to welcoming Jeanie home. 'Arrivals this way,' said Paula, pointing ahead. 'So, how are you feeling about seeing Mum again?' she asked, remembering with a pang the way Jeanie's lip had quivered the last time they'd all been together. 'Have you worked out what you're going to say?'

Harry looked at the ground as they walked along and she wondered if he was reliving the scene here the week before, and Jeanie's acrimonious departure. 'Well, I've already said it a million times,' he replied. 'That I'm sorry, and that I love her. And I hope she can forgive me.' A hang-dog expression came over his face. 'But I'll say all of those things again when she gets here, if that's what it takes. And I'll just have to keep on saying them until she accepts my apology.'

'How about Frankie, have you heard from her?' Paula asked, feeling peculiar, as she always did, when she thought of this unknown sibling of hers, the mystery guest at the party. Paula hadn't even got to look at her, but kept picturing an angry young woman bursting through the doors, out for vengeance. 'Have you managed to track her down or anything?'

'Track her down?' They had stopped in front of a bank of screens detailing flight departures and arrivals, and Harry stared blankly at them. 'Oh. I hadn't thought to . . . I mean . . .'

'You could look for her on Facebook, or just Google her, if you've got her surname,' Paula went on, unsure why she was being quite so helpful when she didn't even know if she wanted this new half-sister in the first place.

'Facebook,' Harry repeated, as if it was some country he'd heard of, but had never visited in person. 'I guess I could try. If you think it's a good idea,' he added uncertainly. Then his face lit up and he pointed at one of the screens. 'The plane's landed!' he cried. 'She's back. She's back!'

He looked so childishly excited and yet so nervous and vulnerable that, for the first time, Paula actually felt a bit sorry for him. Dad was hopeless without Mum, he really was. If it hadn't been for Dave and Bunny taking him in, he probably wouldn't have eaten properly all week. Paula had gone round to the house with him that morning and had been dismayed to discover that the post was still in a pile on the mat, the plants were drooping and the butter, left out in its dish since the previous weekend, had turned completely rancid. 'Dad, you can't let her come home to this,' she'd scolded, opening the fridge door and finding it almost empty inside. She'd sent him out to buy groceries while she cleaned and tidied, shaking her head over his cluelessness. No wonder he wanted things to go back to the way they were. Maybe he'd appreciate Jeanie a bit more after this.

'It'll be a while yet, Dad, she'll have to collect her case and go through passport control,' she pointed out now, but Harry was already hurrying expectantly to the Arrivals doors.

Paula followed him and they waited together. The trickle of arrivals soon turned into an outpouring; a river of tanned people looking cheerful and healthy after their Madeiran holiday. Duty-free bags clinked. Bulging cases trundled. This family heading for the car park. That family being greeted by awaiting friends. The couple over there looking hungover in his-and-hers matching sunglasses, holding hands and smiling at each other. Through they all came, one after another: not Jeanie, not Jeanie, not Jeanie. Still not Jeanie.

Half an hour after the plane had landed, an elderly man with a walking frame shuffled slowly through the doors, and they closed behind him with a certain finality. You could almost hear Harry's anticipation fizzling out to nothing as the doors remained shut for several minutes afterwards. He frowned and wet his lips. 'That's strange,' he said. 'I wonder where she is?'

'She might be in the Ladies, touching up her lippy,' Paula suggested. Jeanie had been known to put on mascara to do the gardening, after all – plus she liked to make an entrance. If Paula herself ever had the massive kind of bust-up with her husband that saw her jetting off on holiday alone in a fury, she'd damn well stake out the Ladies for a full hair and make-up check before she emerged through the Arrivals door. Wouldn't most women?

'Maybe they're still loading on some of the luggage,' Harry said, checking his watch. 'They batch them up, don't they, in those big trolleys? You never know, one of the trolleys might have got stuck or . . .' His voice petered out again.

'She'll be here in a minute,' Paula said bracingly, although as that same minute ticked by, followed by another and then another, the two of them found themselves beginning to doubt these words.

Everything all right, Mum? Paula texted as Harry trudged disconsolately towards the information desk in the hope of discovering his wife's whereabouts. A few moments later, Paula's phone pinged with an incoming message and she let out a gasp. 'Um . . . Dad?' she called after him, blinking and checking the words again, just in case she'd gone mad. 'You might want to come and read this . . .'

'No *way!*' breathed Robyn, open-mouthed, when John got Paula's update with the no-Jeanie bombshell. 'She wasn't on the *plane?*'

'Is she all right?' asked Bunny in alarm, when Dave told her the same piece of news. 'Well . . . when *will* she be back?'

WTF??? texted Stephen. *Do we need to stage an intervention?*

'Bloody hell,' spluttered Matt, sitting up straight in his deckchair on the patio, as Paula came home, still pop-eyed with shock, and told him the latest. 'So what happens now?'

Paula sank into the chair next to him, still hardly able to believe the text that had arrived from her mum. *I've decided to stay here a bit longer,* it had said, verging on brutal in its simplicity. *Having a lovely time. Not sure when I'll be back.*

'What happens now,' Paula replied, massaging her temple where the first stab of a headache was setting in, 'is that Dad has to convince her to come home. Somehow or other. Otherwise . . .' She shrugged, grim-faced, and shook her head. 'Otherwise, your guess is as good as mine.'

Chapter Nine

I know you said you didn't want to know, Frankie's mum Kathy
had written at some undetermined point in the past, *but just
in case you ever change your mind, these are the facts.* The letter
had been tucked in an album of baby photos that Gareth
had put in a box for her when he'd cleared out the family
home, after Kathy had died. Frankie might not have discovered the missive for years and years, perhaps never, if
Fergus hadn't disputed the fact that she and Craig had ever
been babies themselves, back on a sleety winter's day. 'No,'
he had decreed firmly, dark curls bouncing as he shook his
head. 'You are my mumma and daddy. Not babies.' Laughingly, Craig had found an old photo of himself as a newborn,
as the blinking, wobbly-headed proof, and Frankie had been
requisitioned to find one of her, too. The letter had slipped
out of the photo album, still smelling faintly of her mum's
perfume, and with a deafening crack Pandora's box had shat-
tered clean open.

A letter? For me? Of course she had opened it at once,

photos forgotten, tearing through the envelope with a bubble of joy swelling in her chest. One last surprise from her mother, one final letter that she hadn't been expecting! What a gift, what a blessing, she had thought, delighted. But then of course she had read those opening warning sentences and had reared back immediately, joy replaced by apprehension, her heart giving a hard, worried gallop. She had looked away, troubled, but felt her attention dragged back, like a driver compelled to stare at a traffic pile-up on the other side of the motorway. Don't want to look. Want to see. Don't want to know. But how bad *is* it?

She had sat there, the letter in her lap, and gazed up in anguish at the bedroom window as if seeking guidance. *You were right the first time, Mum: I didn't want to know. I was happy with you, and then with you and Gareth, and that was enough for me.*

But how could anyone ignore the very last letter from their mother? How could anyone fail to be bewitched by the chance to see that sloping handwriting one last time, hear the words spoken in her mum's own voice? Her eyes fell helplessly down to the paper again and she read on, knowing that to do so would mean there'd be no turning back:

Well, he was handsome and I was young – prettier then, too! – and he was kind and funny and . . . Oh, you know. That old chestnut: I fell for him. Yes, I knew he was married.

Does that make me a bad person? Probably, Frank, but it was too late by then. And besides, how can it have been a bad decision, when you were the delightful consequences of our affair?!

He doesn't know about you, I'm afraid. He already had four children and, when I discovered I was pregnant, I knew he wasn't about to leave them and his wife for me. It was the end of term and my job at the school had come to an end, so I did a flit before things got even more complicated. I've never seen him since.

Sod it, I thought. I can manage alone. I wanted you, see – I wanted you very much. 'We'll be all right,' I said to myself (and you), hitching a ride back to London with my last pay packet rustling in my pocket. I spent the money on the most beautiful white-painted cot for you and a new winter coat for me, and then turned up on your grandma's doorstep, asking if she'd help me out. And we did manage, didn't we? We never had much to spare, but you never went without. You certainly never went without my love, Frankie, I hope you always felt it around you, like your very own strong, shining force-field, because I did my best to surround you with it every single day.

Anyway, my darling, his name is Harry Mortimer and he lives just outside York. He may have moved on long ago, he may be dead, he may be onto his seventeenth wife by now, who knows, but if you did have an inkling to meet him, then his address is 12 Penny Street in Bishopthorpe, which is about five miles out of the city. Even if he's gone, those four kids of his will be grown-up – your sort of age! – so you could meet them. Siblings at last! You always wanted a brother or a sister, didn't you? I'm sorry I couldn't give you one myself.

I'm sorry, too, if all this is shocking. I'm sure it is. I can picture you reading it, becoming very still as you try to digest everything, and my heart breaks a bit that I'm not there to put an arm around you, to apologize for the body-blow this must feel like. You know I would rather have told you myself, in person, just the two of us having one of our good old chinwags. I'm sorry if you hate me for telling you like this. It's just I thought: I can't die and not say anything. I can't pop my clogs and leave her with nothing; no clue, not so much as a name. So now you know. You do look like him, by the way. Better-looking, obviously – but that's thanks to me.

Favourite girl, loveliest person, please know that this was written in love. And whenever you read this, I'll be blowing kisses from afar, wishing you all the best things and all the happiness in the world.

Love Mum x

One letter, one single sheet of paper, and it had totally pulled the rug out from under Frankie's feet. She'd felt angry at first – tricked into being told something she had insisted all along that she didn't want to know. Then she'd felt sad, bereft for the loss of her beloved mother, whose voice and humour and love rang so clear and true through the handwritten words. Finally – eventually – she had felt maddened with curiosity, overwhelmed by the revelations. Those four half-siblings, for one thing. The fact that she looked like her father. Even, stupidly, the fact that she knew his *name*!

One letter, and it had been as explosive as a stick of dyna-mite. How could she write to this Harry Mortimer bloke, she had thought at the time, and her own letter not feel like a similar weapon? Hence the whole doomed northern road-trip, which had only served to convince her that a letter probably *would* have been a better introduction, after all. She would try again, she had decided now, make a better fist of things this time, apologize if she'd wrecked his party. And if he didn't respond, then so be it. At least she would have given it a go.

And yet each time she set out to write the perfect letter, she found it impossible to find the right tone, worrying about the way she was presenting herself. She wanted to give a good first impression – second impression, rather – but it wasn't easy. Her first attempt was too stiff and defensive. The next try tipped the balance the other way and was apologetic and timid. The third was over-friendly, shar-ing far too much detail about her life. The fourth sounded desperate – pleading almost. The fifth was a cringeworthy mixture of all its predecessors. In the end, she chucked the pen and paper to one side in defeat. The perfect letter didn't exist, simple as that.

It wasn't only her poor writing skills that were stressing her out. Ever since the unpleasant and unplanned-for visit of Julia the previous Thursday, a subdued sort of atmosphere had settled upon the flat, as if they were all biding their time, waiting for the next dramatic episode to unfold. Frankie felt helpless in the face of the other woman – and in the eyes of the law, too. Previously she'd nursed a private hope that in time she might be able to adopt Fergus as her own child, or at least apply for parental responsibility, but she and Craig had only been together three years; she hadn't wanted to jump the gun by broaching the subject too soon. Now she wished she'd been a bit more proactive because, as things stood, Julia held a lot more power than she did in the situation.

'Don't worry,' Craig assured her. 'All that guff she was spouting about a mother's rights being sacred . . . it's not really like that any more. Whatever they told her at the Citizens Advice place – if she even went in there – I bet she didn't give them the full story. Because nobody in their right mind would think her rights to Fergus outweighed mine.'

'We should probably give her a chance, though,' Frankie ventured reluctantly in reply. Not because she particularly liked Julia or anything, but because this seemed to her the only decent course of action. Julia had given birth to Fergus after all; he had grown inside her body. Not to mention the fact that Julia's abandonment of motherhood had been Frankie's joyful gain. She owed her one, really.

'It won't be good for Fergus,' Craig had said flatly. 'Julia's chaotic, all over the place. She doesn't even know him.'

'But she did say she felt better,' Frankie had reminded him, to which he merely snorted.

'She's all talk,' he'd muttered. 'This will be a whim, you wait. I know her, remember.'

That wasn't much consolation. Because Frankie *didn't* know her, and didn't know what she was capable of, either. And so, even though she wanted to be fair to Julia and not completely write her off, Frankie found herself sticking close to Fergus when he went to his friend Preena's soft-play party at the weekend. Usually she'd nurse a coffee in a nearby café, far from the seething ball-pit of frenzied small children – but not today. 'The things we mums put up with, eh?' one of the other women had laughed to her, when the two of them ended up scrambling through a shiny red tunnel to haul out a stuck toddler, and the words had stabbed at Frankie like daggers. If Julia took Fergus, Frankie wouldn't *be* a mum any more, she realized bleakly. This whole world would become closed to her overnight, the metal shutters abruptly dropping, sealing her off. The thought was unbearable. Fergus had been like the most wonderful gift, the bonus package that came with Craig. She had fallen in love with them both at the same time, and had adored learning how to be Fergus's mummy. 'Do you think you two might have a kid together one day? Another kid, I mean?' friends had asked now and then, and Frankie always felt torn when it came to answering. Yes, of course she'd love to have a baby with Craig – but then she already adored Fergus so absolutely. Was there even room in her heart for anyone else?

She had taken it for granted that he would forever be her child and she his mummy, that was the thing. But she *wasn't* really his mummy, was she? She had been acting the part all this time. And now she was in danger of having Fergus – and motherhood – snatched away from under her nose.

'Aren't we the lucky ones?' she replied to the mum who'd spoken to her, forcing a laugh. Inside, though, she felt like clutching at Fergus and never letting him go. Sometimes you didn't know how lucky you'd been until you were in danger of losing it all.

Monday came around and, having dropped Fergus at play-group first thing, Frankie was able to turn her thoughts to the work she had planned for the next few hours. She'd been in touch with a possible new client, the head of art at a decent-sized greetings-card company, and had been asked to pitch ideas for new designs. She was currently mulling over the concept of a range of cards featuring a family of dragons, and had been making quick doodles in her notebook over the weekend: of scaly tails and rounded ribbed bellies, magnificent wings and fiery nostrils. Everyone loved dragons, right? Especially the fat, funny ones of her imaginings. Now she needed to translate her thoughts into some preliminary sketches, bold and bright, in the hope that the client would be keen.

The postman must have called while she was out, because there was an envelope on the mat, addressed to Craig. There was something about the thickness of it, the classy starched feel of the paper, that made her glance at it again as she walked through to the kitchen. The postmark bore a north-London code and there was a company name she didn't recognize franked alongside: Hargreaves and Winter. It sounded like a law firm, she thought worriedly, dropping the letter down by Craig. 'One for you,' she said.

He was already at the table, frowning at his laptop as he tussled with the opening sentences of a book review for the newspaper's Culture section. 'Ta,' he mumbled, considering his screen for a moment and then resuming typing again, eyes narrowed.

Frankie hesitated. Her big sketchpad and coloured pencils were calling her, but she couldn't help flicking another glance at that envelope, about which she suddenly had a bad feeling. 'Maybe you should open that,' she said. 'It looks important. I can't help worrying—' She broke off, not wanting to tempt fate by saying the words out loud. She was probably over-thinking things, leaping to the wrong conclusion, after all. Wasn't she?

Craig glanced across at her in surprise, but did as she suggested, ripping open the seal and unfolding the paper inside. Scanning the contents was enough to prompt a sharp intake of breath. 'I don't bloody think so,' he said, his face darkening. He tossed the letter across to her so that she could read it, and made a growling noise in his throat. 'Shit. I might have guessed she'd try a stunt like this.'

Frankie's intuition had been right. The letter was from a solicitor's office, brief and to the point: due to a change of circumstances, their client, Ms Julia Athanas, was seeking a child arrangement order regarding living arrangements for her son, Fergus Jacobs, initially as shared care, with a view to eventually having him on a full-time basis. They hoped Mr Jacobs would be amenable to this, otherwise they would advise mediation sessions to resolve the situation.

The words danced about mockingly on the page and Frankie heard herself give a moan of pain, as if someone had physically hurt her. 'Living arrangements,' she read aloud in dismay. Her arms twitched uselessly, for wanting to hug Fergus's squirming warm body right then and there, to nuzzle her face into his curly hair and breathe in his delightful good-ness. Hadn't she known? Hadn't she been right to fear this?

'She wants to have him,' said Craig grimly. 'Have him, when he doesn't even *know* her. Well, over my dead body. That's not going to happen.'

Frankie's heart was thumping, hard and painful in her ribs, at the terrible, unbearable prospect of Fergus not living with them any more. Of not tucking him into bed at night, of not gazing at his beautiful sleeping face, of not hearing his chuckles and songs and train noises . . . oh my God. No. It was too awful to think about. 'They can't . . . I mean, nobody could think that was best for Fergus,' she said, aghast. 'He lives here, with us. We're his family!'

It all came back to family, she thought numbly, as Craig strode around, denouncing his ex. Did the family you belonged to have to be tied together with blood and genet-ics, in order to have merit? Because this little family of three, which she had come to be a part of, had been built through love – and yet it seemed horribly precarious all of a sudden. Having grown up an only child, with her mum now dead and her stepfather an expat, Craig and Fergus were the only family Frankie had, unless you counted Harry Mortimer and his clan, that was, which she didn't. It seemed ridiculous that technically, biologically, Harry and those other four children of his could be deemed more of a family to Frankie than the two people she adored most in the world.

'We will fight for him,' Craig was saying, jaw clenched. 'We will take this all the way, if we have to. And she will not win. Absolutely no way. Julia will not take him from us.'

'She will not,' Frankie agreed, wishing she could feel quite so sure.

Bunny turned off the engine and unclipped her seatbelt, trying to dredge up some energy after the long drive. Back at the weekend, when it looked as if they might have to put Harry up for another week, she'd been glad that Margaret, the SlimmerYou PR woman, had talked her into coming all the way down to Gloucestershire for this talk – a chance to get away on her own for an evening, she'd thought. Harry was a very nice man, of course, and he was, understandably, in a state over the falling-out with Jeanie, but . . . Well, without wanting to sound mean, he *was* quite irritating to live with. He complained about her dinners: not enough meat, too few potatoes, he was suspicious of couscous and avocado ('They didn't have them in my day') and couldn't cope with anything spicy. He never thought to pick up after himself or do the washing up. Plus he sometimes treated Bunny like an idiot – advising her on the upkeep of the flowerbeds in the tiny back garden, and insisting on attempting to explain the rules of cricket to her, several times over, when the simple fact of the matter was: she really did not care.

Bunny was *not* an idiot. Moreover she was allergic to

anyone, particularly men, making assumptions about her and treating her as if she was. Her first husband had been domineering and a bully, and look how that had turned out.

Still, she had kept her temper, she had bitten her tongue, she had listened patiently to Harry every time he bored on about leg before wicket and the length of an innings, reminding herself that he was probably missing Jeanie very badly and that perhaps he thought he was redeeming himself in some way by being helpful. But now – hallelujah – he had moved on to stay with John and Robyn, so he wasn't Bunny's problem any more. In fact, now that he'd packed up his bag and left them, she half-wished she hadn't agreed to schlep all the way down here to this small Cotswold town, when she'd far rather be cocooned with Dave at home, enjoying the peace and quiet.

'I know you didn't want to go further south than Birmingham, but the organizer has offered to bring three groups together for the occasion, and they're willing to pay a bit extra to have you visit,' Margaret had wheedled. 'Plus you were born round there, weren't you? Well, then – they love a local success story. Perfect!'

'Ahh,' Bunny had replied apprehensively. 'The thing is, I'd rather not advertise the fact that I was born round there, to be honest. Just because . . .' She hesitated, remembering how the local newspapers had printed pictures of her, retelling her story with unnecessary salacious details. 'Because of . . . privacy issues.'

'But you'll do it?' Margaret had pushed. 'I can say yes to them?'

Margaret wasn't an easy person to argue with and so, after some toing and froing, Bunny had eventually caved in and said, 'Okay, just this once.' But that was it. She would sneak back into the county for one single night, she had decided, do her thing and then slink away again, as if she'd never been there at all. Having deliberately cut her ties with the area, the last thing she wanted was to find herself getting tangled up in any loose threads now.

But in the meantime here she was, parked up outside a secondary school where the slimmers' meeting was due to take place, a mere fifteen miles down the road from where she'd spent the most miserable, frightening years of her life. It was a part of her past that she deliberately tried to shut down whenever her mind flickered in that direction, and now that she was here, so close to the area, she felt besieged by ambushes of memory that kept bursting through. The small terraced house. The smell of her ex-husband's aftershave. The moment she'd woken up in hospital, bewildered and disorientated . . .

She shuddered there in the driver's seat, feeling small and sad and vulnerable. Remembering how broken she'd been for a while, how she hadn't been able to imagine a way through the darkness. Oh, help, this *had* been a mistake, she shouldn't have let herself get talked into coming this far, she thought despairingly. Why had she allowed Margaret to bulldoze her into it, rather than listen to her own instincts?

She put her hand on the key, wondering if she should just turn it again, restart the engine, bail out with some excuse. She could blame a flat tyre, a sudden stomach bug that had erupted on the motorway; she remembered, from all the times she'd phoned in sick in the past, that if you went into enough graphic detail, people just said, 'Okay, don't worry about it', simply to shut you up.

But then a smartly dressed woman walked through the car park, carrying a large bag as she headed for the school door, and Bunny knew this would be Sally Coles, her contact, who'd be leading the slimmers' group; and – yes, right on cue – just as she was thinking this, the woman turned round, spotted her skulking in the car and changed direction. 'Hello. You must be Bunny!' she cried, as Bunny rolled down her window. 'Excellent, you found us all right, then? We're so looking forward to your talk. You're an inspiration!'

No turning back now. Bunny hoped her bright smile of reply was enough to cover up the inner clenching of her heart, the dismay she felt at being there. 'Great,' she said. 'I'll be five minutes. I just need to make a quick call,' she added, which wasn't actually true, but would at least mean that this woman wouldn't stand there and wait for her.

'Absolutely,' said Sally. 'Well, we're very easy to find – straight through the double doors and into the main hall. I'll be setting up for the next twenty minutes, so you just come on in when you're ready.' She beamed, showing neat white teeth. 'You're really going to motivate our group. Thank you so much for coming.'

'Thank you for having me!' said Bunny in the most enthusiastic voice she could manage. *You're an inspiration,* she repeated sternly to herself as Sally trotted away and unlocked the school doors. She had lost over half her own body weight since she lived in this area, she was happier and more confident than she'd ever been. Nobody pushed Bunny around or made her feel worthless any more. 'You've got this,' she told her reflection as she dusted powder onto her nose and sprayed on an encouraging blast of perfume. 'Don't look so scared. It'll be over in an hour. Think of everything you've been through to get here. You're a survivor.'

She glanced over her shoulder at her broad cardboard doppelgänger, propped faithfully in the back seat as ever, and cringed a little at that wide, fake printed smile, the smile that had never quite reached her eyes back then. In hindsight, it was a smile that said: I'm lost in this big old body, I'm hiding here and hoping things will get better for me. But in the meantime, I'm going to self-medicate with chips and wine until I feel I can cope.

Oh, Rach. Poor old big, fat Rachel.

'You're not her any more,' she reminded herself under her breath as she got out of the car, then opened the passenger door and reached in for her old unhappy self, her arms circling the wide cardboard waist like an embrace. 'You're Bunny, and you can do this.'

Her mother had started the nickname, back when she was about seven. With a fuzz of fluffy blonde hair, round blue eyes and – yes, okay – endearingly protruding front teeth, the affectionate 'My little bunny' soon became 'Bunny' or 'Bun'. Little Rachel would twitch her nose obligingly, just like a real rabbit, and it made her mum laugh and ruffle her hair. Bunnies were so cute! Who wouldn't want to be called that, anyway? The pet name stuck, for years and years, until she was a self-conscious teenager and suddenly would rather die than stand out from the crowd in any way, let alone with a seriously uncool name. And so 'Bunny' went, along with the goofy teeth (thanks to the local orthodontist) and she was Rachel again, ordinary Rachel with spots and a tendency to blush; Rachel who was good at netball and swimming, popular with both girls and boys. She had breezed through school and college and her first couple of jobs, until . . .

Well. There was no need to go into how she'd fallen for charming Mark Roberts and how everything ended up going wrong. Especially not now, when she was standing in front of a room full of people waiting for her to begin.

She tapped the microphone, took a deep breath and then gave them all her best and brightest smile. One more time, with feeling. 'Good evening, everyone. My name is Bunny Halliday, and I'm delighted to say that nine months ago I was voted SlimmerYou's 'Slimmer of the Year', having lost almost ten stone!'

Cue a generously thunderous round of applause.

'This was me, three years ago,' she said, gesturing to her portly cardboard twin, propped up beside her. 'There I am, with that big old smile on my face. Doesn't she look happy? you might be thinking. But no. Deep down inside, I was not happy. I was bingeing on ice-cream and biscuits. I would think nothing of eating a family-size pizza all to myself for dinner, along with chips, onion rings, chicken wings . . . the lot. Side orders don't count, right?'

A few smiles of acknowledgement greeted this comment, and she went on, emboldened.

'So no, I was not happy. I slept badly and had very little energy. The thought of doing any exercise was just so embarrassing, I couldn't face it. Swimming at the local pool, where I'd have to wobble along, thighs quaking, to the edge of the water? Forget it. Go jogging around my local streets to be smirked at by teenagers or, worse, overtaken by pensioners on mobility scooters? No, thanks. It was all I could do to wheeze my way into the kitchen for another snack and then back to the sofa to watch telly. Even that felt like an effort.'

She paused, trying not to think about how Mark's voice would become dangerously soft sometimes when he came in at night and saw her there. *Fat fucking bitch. Look at the state of you.* 'The irony was,' she went on, trying to push him out of her thoughts, 'that I had reached this size and all I wanted to do was shrink away, where nobody could see me.' She cocked her head, a self-deprecating expression on her face. 'You'd think I might have twigged that there was a better way of achieving *that* than getting even bigger, right?'

Rueful laughter, several people nodding. They knew her. They were with her.

'According to my doctor, I was morbidly obese and in danger of becoming diabetic,' she went on. 'My blood pressure was high, I was at greater risk of having a heart attack, a stroke – all kinds of alarming conditions. I felt pretty miserable, I can tell you. Pretty defeated. I made excuses not to socialize because I could feel people judging me. I could hardly look at myself in the mirror any more, because I was so ashamed of what I'd become. I felt like a bad person, basically. And yet . . .'

This was always the part when she could feel the audience shift in their seats and lean forward hopefully. Because here, right down at the depths of despair, came the turning point, the moment of change.

'And yet, there was one small kernel within me that held out,' she went on slowly. She always felt her fists clench when she reached this bit of the story, that same old determination taking hold of her. 'One small shred of me that still had some dignity. Which said: Something's gone wrong here. This is not the person I thought I would be. And do you know what? The only one who can fix the situation is me.'

You're very good, Margaret had said, the first time she saw Bunny give one of her talks. *Very sincere. I'll see if I can get you some TV coverage, they'll love you.* ('No,' Bunny had said immediately. 'No TV. I want to be as low-profile as possible. If it's all the same to you.')

A man in the audience had his hand up and she gave him a quick, pleasant smile. 'I'll take any questions at the end, by the way,' she said as an aside, before continuing down her well-worn path. 'So I decided I would make a change. To hell with what other people thought. I was going to get fit – but not because the doctor said I should. Not because of those kids shouting "Fatty!" at me in the street. Not because I felt bullied into it by all the many, many unkind remarks I'd heard made about me, either to my face or behind my back. No.' She let her pause hang in the air for effect. *Work it, girl,* said Margaret in her head. 'I was going to get fit and lose weight because *I* wanted to. Because *I* wanted to change.'

More nods from the audience. Some people already had that glassy-eyed look of reverence as they listened, although the man with his hand up was still trying to get her attention, she noticed with a flicker of irritation. 'Excuse me,' he called, waggling his fingers.

Bunny ignored him. 'It's not easy, though, is it? Making that decision and then sticking to your guns,' she went on. 'All of you, I can see, have taken up a similar challenge. Just by coming here, you've made a commitment, you're on your own journeys. So you'll understand when I say that for the first few weeks I found myself wondering if—'

'*Excuse* me,' the man said again, louder this time. He was actually waving his hand from side to side now.

Bunny broke off, losing her thread, glancing round to try and catch the eye of the group leader, Sally, who'd introduced her. Wouldn't somebody help her out and shut this man up? But nobody was coming to her rescue, so she smiled at him tightly. 'If you don't mind, I'd like to save questions for the—' she began, but he was already talking over her.

'Is it true you stabbed your husband?' he called out.

A ripple of astonishment spread through the audience like a Mexican wave, while Bunny stood there, stunned. 'I . . .' she stuttered, the ground seeming to rise and tilt beneath her feet. 'What? I . . .'

'I never forget a face. It *was* you, wasn't it? Married to that Mark Roberts fella? My uncle lived next door to the pair of youse. Bakerfield Road, right?'

Bunny was going hot and cold all over. She swallowed hard, her mouth dry, her mind in freefall. 'No,' she did her best to say. 'You're mistaken.' She could feel the audience eyeing her differently all of a sudden; there was a chilliness in the air, a terrible stillness, as every single person began recalibrating their impression of her.

Maybe she's not one of us, after all.

Did she really do that?

And she's got the nerve to stand up there and lecture us!

Sally had hurried over to the man and had a hand on his arm, leaning close to him. The spell was broken, noisy chatter bursting out like gunfire amidst the hall. Every survival instinct in Bunny's body was telling her to run, to get away, forget the rest of her talk and escape in her car, as fast as she could, back up the motorway. 'Did you really stab him?' a woman called out from the crowd, with a mix of horror and fascination, and Bunny felt her face turn scarlet, hot and humiliated – the feeling of being unmasked, a disguise ripped off her, leaving her stranded there vulnerable and afraid.

'I'm sorry about this, everyone,' Sally said, wringing her hands as a large bloke hauled the man out of the room.

'I was only asking a question,' he protested, twisting in his captor's grip and glaring back at Bunny. 'Get off! This is assault, this is. Get your hands off me!'

Bunny's heart was pounding. She was trembling all over. Fight or flight, fight or flight, her body said, adrenalin going berserk through her veins. And then a cool, determined voice in her head said, *Fight. Fight on. Keep talking. You were just getting to the good bit of the story. Big smile and keep going. Don't let that bastard beat you.*

So she gave it her best shot. Even though she felt very much like crying, even though she was shaken and unnerved, and sweat was drenching the back of her top, she stood there and rolled her eyes comically and said, 'Do you know, I must have got one of those faces; it's a nightmare. Because *everyone* thinks they know me! This happens wherever I go – someone thinks I am their niece's friend, or that I used to work in their local pub, or that I was at school with them. Mind you, the response I've just had tonight was a *bit* more dramatic, granted.' She even managed a tinkling laugh and the audience, God love them, laughed along with her, their faith in her seemingly restored a little bit.

Keep going. Keep breathing. 'But just in case you were wondering, let me assure you right here and now: my other half is very much alive and uninjured, and is probably sitting at home with his feet up on the coffee table, watching Sky Sport as I speak.' She arched an eyebrow. 'Well, that's what he told me earlier, anyway . . .' More laughter. Thank goodness. She'd turned the sinking ship around, no matter that she was talking about Dave rather than her ex. 'Now, where was I? Ah yes. Those difficult early weeks.' She pulled another funny face. 'The weeks from hell. My goodness, I'm not going to forget *them* in a hurry . . .'

On she went, her speech salvaged, her composure just about recovered. Outwardly, at least. Because inside she was on fire with the terror and mortification of what had just happened; she had gone hurtling straight back to the bad old days, to the bleep and whirr of the hospital machines, to the policeman taking notes and asking her to sign a statement, to the stony-faced jury in the courtroom.

Somehow she was still talking on automatic pilot, she was saying all the right things in the right order, she had drawn her audience back so that they were rapt, hanging on her every word. But oh boy, this was it – she was done, she thought to herself as she paused for breath. Just as soon as this was over, just as soon as she was allowed to leave, she was driving back home to Dave and safe anonymity. And whatever Margaret said, however coaxingly she pleaded, Bunny was never doing this again, *never*, and that was that.

Chapter Ten

Something strange had happened to Alison since the night of the thunderstorm. She couldn't put her finger on the exact moment things changed, it was more that there had been a gradual dimming of her usual ebullience, as if her happiness dial had been turned down low. After finishing work on Monday, she found herself driving the long way home and stopping for petrol, even though she still had half a tankful. She paused to chat to the lad at the cash desk, until she realized he was glancing behind her apologetically to the customers waiting their turn, at which point she turned bright red and stuffed her purse back in her bag.

'Some of us do actually want to get home tonight, you know,' somebody muttered unkindly as she scuttled past.

It was only when she was sitting at the wheel of her car again, key slotted in the ignition, that the words resonated fully. Because unlike the grumpy woman in the queue, Alison didn't feel her normal enthusiasm for going home. In fact, when she thought about walking in there and sitting down in her usual spot in the living room, she realized with a start that she felt almost . . . well, *depressed*, at the prospect.

Depressed, she scoffed to herself in the next moment, starting the engine and driving away, rolling her eyes at her own melodrama. Her, depressed! It was ridiculous. Of course she wasn't depressed.

But then when she was inside and the front door was closed behind her, the feeling descended upon her again, this sort of gloom, settling like soft, chilly snowflakes in her hair, on her shoulders. She'd always thought of her house as cosy, her little refuge from the rest of the world, but tonight the walls seemed to be closing in. The very air seemed to be smothering her. Knowing it was irrational, knowing that she was overreacting, she found herself walking straight through to the kitchen and out of the back door, where she sank down onto the doorstep, breathing heavily.

Daft woman. What had got into her, carrying on like this? Maybe the lightning had zapped a few of her brain cells when it frazzled her telly. Elbows on knees, she put her head in her hands, waiting for the feeling to pass, listening to the sounds of people having a barbecue in the garden behind hers. She could hear Lois next door laughing with her little daughter, and a couple of kids singing in another garden as they bounced up and down on a trampoline, and even though these were all happy noises of people enjoying themselves, for some reason tonight they just made Alison feel like crying.

It was bewildering, frankly. Discombobulating. She never usually felt this way. She'd always cherished her evenings at home, looking forward all day to that moment when she walked in and closed the door behind her, leaving the rest of the world behind. Telly and a TV dinner – that suited her; you couldn't beat telly and a TV dinner, she'd always said. Only all of a sudden, it didn't feel quite so enticing. It didn't feel enough any more.

It must be hard being on your own sometimes, Alison, Jeanie Mortimer said in her head, with that cloying sympathy, and Alison felt her hackles rise. Because she was *fine*. She was absolutely fine!

And yet . . . She kept spooling back to the moment her TV screen had blanked, the horror she'd felt at the prospect of an evening without it. You'd think she was some kind of an addict, the way she'd panicked at being cut off from her drug, terrified of having to face her own solitude.

She stared unseeingly out at the garden, absent-mindedly listening to the shrieks and squeals coming from next door, where Lois's daughter was splashing about in the paddling pool. Music started up from somewhere – the barbecuers' house perhaps – and she found herself getting up and turning away, unable to bear the sounds of other people's enjoyment any longer. Then, crossing the kitchen, some impulse compelled her to unlock the door to the garage where Rich's beloved old car sat, the red Jensen Interceptor, his pride and joy. When he'd died, she'd given away or sold a lot of his possessions, but she hadn't quite been able to bring herself to part with his car. Not after he'd spent so many happy hours 'tinkering', as he called it.

'You've still got that old thing?' Robyn said periodically in a disapproving sort of way. 'And you don't even drive it?', as if her mother was soft in the head, far too sentimental for her own good. 'You should flog it, Mum, I bet it's worth a fortune!'

Yes, I've still got this old thing, Alison thought, opening the car door and sliding into the front seat (tan fake-leather; you'd never get that now). She folded her arms against the steering wheel and rested her head there. *Oh, Rich. Why did you have to leave me?* she thought, as she always did, tears leaking out of her eyes. *Why couldn't you just talk to me about how desperate you must have been feeling?*

The wetness against her forearms was enough for her to sit back after a few moments and pull herself together. 'Sorry,' she said aloud. 'Don't want to get mascara all over your car.' Then she blew her nose and grimaced at herself for talking to thin air.

She leaned against the seat, trying to breathe in any last scent of his aftershave that might be clinging to the fabric of the vehicle, but it was no good – all traces of Rich had long since evaporated. These days the car merely smelled a bit damp and old. ('Yes,' said Robyn, exasperated, in her head, 'because you never drive it anywhere! Because you never use it, other than for taking up space – in your garage, and in your head, Mum!')

Alison took a tissue from her pocket and tenderly wiped some of the dust from the dashboard. She cupped her hand around the knob of the gearstick for a moment, ran a finger along the indicator and adjusted the rear-view mirror a fraction. Rationally, Alison was able to appreciate that her daughter had a point, but today she was grateful for the comfort of the Jensen; for the link it still held to happier times. Maybe at the weekend she'd give it a proper clean; sponge off the cobwebs that festooned the wheel arches, give the bonnet a good old waxing. Just in case Rich happened to glance her way from wherever he was now. Just so he'd know that she still thought about him.

'We'll be all right,' she told herself after a moment, in the bravest voice she could muster up. 'We'll be all right, won't we? Of course we will.'

And then, feeling marginally better, the magic of the Jensen having done its work, she stepped out, gently closed the door and locked up the garage once more. Now then: dinner. Something really delicious, she decided. And maybe a good old box-set binge to take her mind off everything. Perfect.

★

'Matt, is that you?' called Paula, hearing the front door. 'Come and have a look at this.' She was perched at the kitchen table, laptop open, staring at the screen. Rewind, play. Rewind, play. 'Matt, are you there?'

'What is it?' Matt walked into the kitchen, wet-haired, and chucked a pair of trunks and a damp towel down by the washing machine. He was a tree surgeon and had been working out near Castle Howard, taking the chance for a post-work dip in the lake there. Give her husband a stretch of water and he'd strip off and dive in like an enthusiastic spaniel, whatever the weather.

'This,' said Paula, her eyes still glued to the laptop screen. 'Come and see.'

She hadn't thought anything much of the email from the photographer when it arrived that day, with a zip file attached. It was her and Matt's anniversary present to her parents, having a set of photos professionally taken of the party and compiled in a nice album. When she'd made the booking, though, the photographer had been running a special offer whereby, for only a small amount more, you could have photography *and* video footage of your special event, courtesy of his nephew, who was doing an apprenticeship with him and was very keen. Paula had always wished they'd shelled out for someone to compile a video of her own wedding day and was deeply envious of friends who could watch their happy celebrations again and again. 'Go on then,' she'd said to the photographer, giving him her debit-card details.

He'd emailed her today, asking her to check the photos and rule out any that she didn't want in the album. The edited video footage would be arriving separately, on a DVD and bespoke memory stick, he said, although his nephew had made a mini-highlights film, which he had attached, too. Paula had a few minutes to kill before she needed to start making dinner, so she'd sat down with the laptop, meaning to have a quick scroll through, out of interest – only to have one photograph stop her short. It was a perfectly nice picture of her cousin Lisa, beaming into the camera, and Paula herself was captured in the background with her dad. But then she looked again. Because she'd definitely been wearing a sleeveless pink dress for the party, and yet the woman behind Lisa was wearing a pale-blue shirt and jeans. So that was weird.

Frowning, Paula zoomed in for a closer look, realizing that it wasn't her after all. This woman, although she had the same dark hair and beaky nose as Paula, was younger and didn't have a fringe. And then she noticed the way the woman and her dad were looking so intently at one another, and it hit her like a shovel: oh my goodness. Was this *her* then: Frankie, the mystery half-sister? Surely it had to be!

'Frankie,' she breathed aloud, staring intently at the

screen and drinking her in. So here she was: Paula's little sister, right there at the party.

Obviously that was dinner forgotten about. Paula had gone clicking through all the other photos like a madwoman, searching desperately for another glimpse of her. Her efforts led her to one more image where you could just see the interloper entering the hall, her dark eyes wide and uncertain as she looked around; but that was it, the full extent of the evidence. 'Oh. My. God,' she murmured to herself, flicking from one picture to the other. Before and after, before and after. And indeed, you could see a certain strain on her parents' faces in the later photographs, once Frankie had made her brief surprise appearance and had churned up an old secret. Captured by the lens, her mum's mouth looked wobbly, her dad's jaw taut, presumably as they tried to process what had just happened. Bloody hell. Blink and you'd miss it.

Paula had felt so unseated by her dad's revelation; upset with him, with this Frankie person, with the whole world, frankly, for playing such a joke on her. And yet just look at this little sister of hers, sidling into the hall in that second picture, where she looked almost scared. That wasn't the face of a family-wrecker, marching in, hell-bent on trouble, not at all. In fact she looked very much as if she was standing there, thinking: *Oh shit.*

It was at this moment that Paula remembered the video

footage. The photographer's nephew was twenty-one, straight out of college and clearly had some artistic notions, because he had edited the highlights package as if it were a Hollywood trailer. There was the bunting going up. The cake arriving. The flowers and buffet being arranged and set out. Here came Jeanie and Harry, happy and excited to see the gold-foil banner fluttering, the beautifully decorated hall. Here were the guests, hugs and handshakes, joyful exclamations. Brief excerpts from the speeches, some dance-floor action – oh God, just look at Paula's Aunty Pen, what was she like? – and then . . . Paula paused the film. And then there she was again, visible at the edge of the dance-floor shot, just edging into view. Frankie, all nervous and doubtful, those big, dark eyes sliding around the place.

Paula pressed Pause, watched it again. But there was more, because here came her dad in the background, the strangest expression on his face, as if Frankie were some otherworldly apparition. He had his arms stretched out towards her, his mouth open and marvelling. *How can this be?* his eyes were saying. *Is it really you?*

Then, almost immediately, Jeanie was in shot – and just look at her, puffing up like a defensive cat, grabbing hold of Harry's arm, possessive and commanding, practically dragging him away. You could just glimpse the shocked expression, the agony of Frankie's face, before the camera angle changed again, this time to show Bunny dancing with

Dave, the two of them laughing as she tried to teach him a routine. Rewind, play. Rewind, play.

'See?' she said to Matt, showing him. 'Look! It's her – it's Frankie.'

'Bloody hell,' he said leaning over and peering at the screen. 'She doesn't half look like you.'

'I know!' Rewind, play. She couldn't help watching it all over again, a mini saga dramatized in a few short frames: hope, recognition, rejection. Rewind, play. Her *sister.*

Matt had wandered over to the fridge and was peering forlornly inside. 'What were you thinking for dinner?' he asked. 'Only I said I'd meet Gav at seven-thirty for a drink. Want me to start peeling anything? Chopping anything? Searching out a takeaway menu?'

He was always starving after a day's work, Matt. Doubly starving if he'd been swimming as well. Reminded of this, Paula felt as if she'd been awoken from an enchantment and finally dragged her eyes away from the screen. 'Oh. Yeah, sorry. Um . . .' She'd been planning to bake some haddock fillets with lemon and black pepper, roast a tray of baby Jersey Royals, and dish it all up with green salad and garlicky tomatoes. Clearly none of that had happened, though. 'Is it outrageous to get a takeaway on a Monday night?' she asked apologetically.

'Hell, no,' said Matt, amiable as ever. 'I'll go up the

chippy. Boys?' he yelled, leaving the room. 'What do you want from the chippy?'

Paula was left alone with her laptop, the screen frozen on that last frame of her sister. Her *sister*. All of a sudden, Frankie had become real in Paula's mind, no longer a shadowy threatening figure, but an actual person with a shy smile and a hopeful, questioning look in her eye. But over a week had now passed since the day of the party and, as far as Paula was aware, Frankie hadn't made a second attempt to get in touch with the Mortimers. Had Jeanie scared her away? Was this minute or so of footage the only thing she would have of her brand-new sister? Because all of a sudden, to Paula's surprise, she realized she wanted more.

The front door banged as Matt set off again, and Paula's fingers flew over the keyboard as she composed a quick email to her brothers. *Hi all,* she typed:

So this is a bit weird. Pics – and a video!! – of our half-sister attached. No denying the family resemblance! I can't help feeling intrigued; how about you guys?

Still no word from Mum, I take it. No news here. She didn't even reply when Luke texted her a pic of the pie he made in Food Tech, which is so unlike her, I actually rang the hotel again to check she was okay. She's fine apparently, but still doesn't want to talk to anyone. Poor Mum. Feel so bad for her. I've arranged to meet Dad for lunch in town tomorrow, so will chat to him about it then.

Hope to see you all soon. John, are you still okay to drop the boys at cricket club on Sat? Give my love to your other halves,

P xxx

Chapter Eleven

Until Robyn met John she had never really held down a very long or enjoyable relationship. She was quite shy and awkward, 'backward about coming forward', as her mother put it, and never felt as if she was getting the whole boyfriend-thing quite right. Clearly she wasn't, because men kept finishing with her after about six weeks – and to make matters worse, they almost always said the same sort of thing: *Robyn, you're a lovely person and you'll make someone a great wife one day, but right now I just want to have fun.* Implying, in other words, that she was no fun at all. Which didn't exactly fill a girl with confidence.

The day she ended up sitting beside John at the 'Unknown Universe' lecture had been a pivotal one. At the end of the lecture she'd realized that her wet umbrella had been leaning against his bag and was terribly embarrassed, apologizing for her clumsiness, but to her relief, he'd laughed it off. 'These things happen,' he'd said, and she'd noticed what nice brown eyes he had, what an open, friendly face. 'I suppose I could forgive you, for a glass of wine . . .'

Oh! Was he flirting with her? she'd wondered in surprise. *Be fun,* she reminded herself hurriedly. *Not wifely – fun!* She found herself thinking of Michelle Crossley, the most outrageous girl in Robyn's sixth form, who'd gone off to work as a croupier in Las Vegas after A-levels and was still living the American high life, according to Facebook. *Be more Michelle.* 'I thought you would never ask!' she cried, laughing and trying to make her eyes go sparkly (she'd been practising in front of the mirror, for this very reason). 'Hey, let's go wild and make it a bottle.'

Goodness, but it was quite hard work being fun, she had decided after three weeks of dating John, when she'd drunk far more than she usually did, and her feet ached from dancing in wine bars along Swinegate. She and John seemed to be getting on brilliantly, but secretly she was starting to wonder if there was such a thing as too *much* fun. Maybe he was out of her league and she should stop pretending, and admit that she was actually quite a lot more sensible and boring than she'd made out. But then, a few weeks before Christmas, she met the Mortimers and changed her mind.

'It's our Paula's birthday on Saturday,' John had said, looking sheepish. 'And Mum's insisting I bring you along for one of her party teas. Do you mind? They're a bit full-on, my family, so if you don't fancy it, I won't blame you . . .'

Robyn had been intrigued. More to the point, she'd always found meeting people's parents a lot easier than necking cocktails and trying to dance in a sexy way. 'Sounds good to me,' she'd said cheerfully.

John had not been exaggerating about his family being 'full-on'. Robyn had been overwhelmed initially by the hot crush of parents and siblings and their partners crammed into a flock-wallpapered living room in Bishopthorpe, all talking in loud voices and taking the mick out of each other, hooting with laughter at old shared jokes and reminiscences. This was a proper family, she had thought, feeling an ache of envy that she'd never had this herself, growing up. But then in the next minute, Paula, John's sister, was making introductions and exclaiming in delight as Robyn shyly pressed a pot of winter jasmine into her hands, wishing her a happy birthday. 'Aren't you lovely? Thank you, it's gorgeous!' And then John's mum, Jeanie, had bustled over with the pot of tea, urging a scone on her ('Just out of the oven!') and they were all so nice, so friendly and welcoming, that Robyn felt herself unfurling amidst their easy warmth.

She'd seen another side of John too: the loving son, giving his mum a squeeze and helping clear away the dishes; the big brother, asking after his siblings; the kind, attentive host, who made sure Robyn had a good time and kept the conversation flowing. 'They loved you!' he had said afterwards, back in his car, as they drove away, and she'd felt happiness soar inside her, as if she'd passed some crucial test. Maybe John wasn't out of her league after all. Maybe being herself was going to be okay, if it meant his family liked her.

The weeks of dating had turned into months, and Robyn felt as if the colours and sounds in her world had been turned up, brighter and noisier; experiencing and appreciating life with more exuberance and intensity than ever before. The Mortimers were big on spending time together, she had quickly realized, and it had been a summer of barbecues and parties, day-trips to the Dales and the coast, meeting John's cousins and aunts and uncles, with all of them telling her: Oh, it was about time John settled down, and Oh, what a lovely couple they made, and teasing John about how he should hurry up and get a ring on her finger quick, she was far too good for the likes of him. Robyn blossomed with the compliments and jokes, had been flattered when Paula asked her along to her hen night, had been faint with relief when she'd cooked a roast dinner for John's parents and Jeanie had pronounced it 'Not bad at all'.

And then, in September, it was Robyn's birthday and John had said, again with that slight air of sheepishness, 'Um, Mum wants to do a party tea for you sometime this weekend. Family tradition. Is that okay?'

Was that *okay*? Hell, yeah! she had thought with a rush of pleasure. *Family tradition* – and she was now part of it! For

Robyn, it was like being giving the keys to the kingdom, her acceptance and belonging officially confirmed. For the first time in her life, she felt as if she was part of something bigger than just her and her mum; she'd been welcomed into this clan of fun, friendly people, initiated with a plate of scones and jam. And then the following Christmas, when John had given her an engagement ring and asked her to marry him, almost the first thought that had whistled through her head – other than YES! – was that she was going to be a Mortimer too. For better or worse. Better, of course!

Was it wrong that she'd felt the same stunned delight at becoming a Mortimer as she'd felt at the prospect of being John's wife? Would she have agreed so quickly to his proposal if he'd been an only child like her, from a small, quiet family?

Robyn thought about this now as she picked up Harry's *Gardeners' World* magazine from the sofa, plus Harry's glasses case from the bottom of the stairs and then Harry's breakfast things, which had been left, along with those of her husband, on the kitchen table all morning while Robyn had been at work. She hadn't just married John, she'd effectively married the entire family – which she had been thrilled about! – and part of that involved rallying round when someone was in trouble. Right now that someone was Harry, who couldn't bear to be home without Jeanie, following her no-show at the airport. Reading between the lines, Bunny had been less than ecstatic at the prospect of having her father-in-law to stay for a second week, and so John had stepped in with the offer of their spare room before Robyn had been able to say, 'Of course I don't mind.'

She *didn't* mind, not really. She was extremely fond of Harry, who'd been the next best thing to having her own dad, with his kindness and steadiness, and his ability to come to the rescue at the drop of a hat. In the circumstances, Robyn felt it was the least she could do, to make up the spare bed and set an extra place at the table, in the hope of propping up the listing Mortimer ship. Not to mention pick up after him constantly and deal with his laundry, and try not to complain when he and John vanished for hours on end at their favourite fishing spots.

All the same, this was not the greatest time for a houseguest, when John had just lost his job and everything about the future seemed newly precarious. 'Don't tell Dad about it, yeah, he's got enough on his plate and will only worry,' he'd warned her – which was fair enough, but then he didn't even want to talk about the redundancy with her, his wife, either, when she still had so many questions.

No, he wasn't sure how many other members of staff had been laid off.

No, he didn't know when the compensation package would be paid out.

No, the department hadn't tried to help him find a

replacement post – for crying out loud, Robyn, what's with the Spanish Inquisition here? Give a bloke a break, won't you?

Robyn couldn't help feeling rejected. Couldn't help harking back to their early days of romance and tenderness, when he'd seemed so delighted to be with her. When she was pregnant with Sam, for instance, you could not have found a more doting husband than John. He'd gone to every scan and midwives' appointment, he'd cooked her wholesome dinners and rubbed her feet when she was tired in the evening; and then, when Sam was born and they'd brought him home from hospital, he'd actually had tears in his eyes as they held hands and peered at him sleeping in the Moses basket. 'You gave me a son,' he had said, his voice cracking. 'Our son. You are the most amazing woman.'

Robyn had felt that they were such a team together – that was what she couldn't help remembering now. That it had been the two of them standing side by side in this marriage, facing down every obstacle between them. John might not show his emotions all that much, preferring to hide his feelings in his bluff, gruff practical manner, but those feelings were there, and she alone was privy to that secret vulnerable side of him. And yet recently it was as if he was shutting her out of this particular problem. He wouldn't talk to her about money, about how they were going to pay the mortgage and bills next month. The grim picture of a future where they depended on her meagre part-time salary kept sliding around her mind. Was it too late to get the deposit back on their summer holiday? Should they sell one of the cars? She could try to up her hours at the school next term, she supposed, or do what her mum had suggested and brave a look at returning to the university herself. Or would that be rubbing salt in John's wound, effectively stealing his place as Breadwinner Numero Uno?

Robyn wiped down the table and then twisted the wedding ring on her finger, round and round, as she wondered what, if anything, she should do. Hurt pride, her mum had said the other day – and John *was* hurting, that much was obvious. Maybe it was hard for him to go cap in hand and ask how much he would be given in the redundancy package. So why didn't she do that for him, spare him the indignity? At least it would be a start, she figured.

Feeling pleased with her own thoughtfulness, she grabbed her phone – no time like the present – and dialled the number of Gabrielle, John's secretary. Former secretary, rather. Gabrielle had worked in the department for years and knew everything. She was trustworthy, efficient and organized, with her calm manner and that steady gaze behind small steel-rimmed spectacles. If anyone could advise Robyn on departmental workings, it was this woman.

'Good afternoon, Gabrielle Patterson speaking, how may I help you?' came her reassuring tones over the audible patter of typing. Robyn could picture her sitting there in her neat shift-dress at the reception desk, earpiece and microphone in place, and instantly felt better.

'Hi! Gabby, it's Robyn Mortimer here,' she said thankfully. 'How are you?'

'Oh!' said Gabrielle. The peck-peck of typing stopped. 'Er . . . hi. How can I help you?'

'It's about John,' Robyn said, feeling a surge of matrimonial loyalty for poor, wounded John. 'About him losing his job.'

There was a delicate pause. 'Ahh,' said Gabrielle. 'Yes?'

Was it Robyn's imagination or did she sound uncharacteristically flustered? Usually she was brisk and businesslike, all 'No problem' and 'Leave that with me'. Robyn ploughed on regardless. 'I gather the redundancy package hasn't been announced yet and – look, he'd kill me for phoning up like this, but the thing is, Gabby, we really need to know what John's actually going to get, financially, because—'

'Um,' said Gabrielle awkwardly. 'Can I just stop you there?' She cleared her throat, before adding in an apologetic sort of way, 'I think there must have been a misunderstanding.'

'A misunderstanding?' Robyn's heart swelled with immediate hope. Oh my God! Maybe John had got the wrong end of the stick. Had she been panicking over nothing? 'Do you mean . . . ?'

Gabrielle sounded agonized. 'I mean . . . Well, there haven't actually *been* any redundancies in the department.'

Robyn felt confused. 'Oh,' she said, frowning. 'So what are you saying? He's still got a job? I don't understand.' This was good news, surely. So why was Gabby sounding so cagey and weird?

'Um,' said Gabrielle again. 'Look, I'm not sure I should really be having this conversation with—'

'But he's not been made redundant,' Robyn confirmed, interrupting her. 'Well, that's great! Oh my goodness, that's such a load off my mind.' She found herself laughing out loud like an idiot. 'I've been so worried, I can't tell you.'

'No, Robyn, the thing is—' Gabrielle broke off, as if it was hard to get the words out. 'The thing is, he *has* lost his job,' she said eventually.

What? Robyn couldn't keep up. First he was redundant and then he wasn't, and now . . . Suddenly it dawned on her what Gabrielle was trying to convey, in her polite, embarrassed way, and her stomach gave a lurch. 'Wait – are you telling me John was *sacked*? Is that what you mean?'

'Er,' said Gabrielle, clearly wishing she had never picked up the phone. 'Well, um . . .' A small sigh came down the line. 'Yes, actually, Robyn. I'm sorry.'

Robyn swallowed, her mouth dry. 'Are you sure?' she asked faintly. 'Are you absolutely sure?' Sacked, she kept thinking. There was no fat pay-off when you were sacked, was there? There was nothing, not even a good reference, she realized, turning cold. What had he *done* to get sacked?

'I'm sorry,' Gabrielle said again and, give her credit, she did sound very apologetic. It was almost as if she could see Robyn leaning like a dead weight against the kitchen counter with her legs on the verge of giving way.

'Can I . . . can I ask why?' Robyn whimpered after a moment. John, sacked. *Yes, actually, Robyn.* She still couldn't believe it. He was so good! He was so clever and competent! His students had done really well in their exams, he'd been positively jubilant when the results were posted. This didn't make sense!

'I'm afraid I can't tell you that,' Gabrielle replied after an awkward pause. 'Listen, I've got calls backing up here. Do you want me to transfer you to anybody else or . . . ?'

'No,' Robyn said, gulping back a sob. 'No. Thank you. You've been very helpful. Goodbye.' She clicked off the call and stayed frozen there, in the middle of her lovely kitchen, surrounded by their wedding crockery and nicest wine glasses, and the cookery books on the shelf. They'd built this life together, she and John, ever since that first fortuitous meeting in a lecture theatre. But what was the next line in their story? Where did they go from here?

She shut her eyes, scared and worried. Alarmed by the fact that John hadn't told her the truth, that he had been keeping secret upon secret from her. And then she remembered Beth Broadwood's face – that look of pity as she spoke to Robyn in the playground. Pity because of the redundancy, she'd thought before. But now she couldn't help wondering what, exactly, the other woman knew.

Chapter Twelve

'May I fetch you some lunch?'

'Would you like me to move the parasol?'

'Please – an aperitif, on the house, Miss Jeanie. Enjoy!'

Enjoy? Oh my word, she was enjoying herself all right, thought Jeanie, thanking the smart, handsome waiter and accepting the orange-pink Negroni, which clinked pleasingly with ice cubes. (Daisy would love that little cocktail umbrella, she noted, removing it from the glass and putting it on the side to keep for her.) What was not to enjoy? The hotel staff had been positively delighted when she'd ventured down to the polished mahogany reception desk in the lobby last Sunday and explained her position: that she was supposed to be flying back home today, but had come to the conclusion that she would actually much rather stay on here. Would that be possible?

She was rather embarrassed about asking – after all, there was nothing to be proud of: her 'being a wuss', as her grandchildren would say, hiding away at the hotel rather than going home and facing the music. However Bernardo, the manager, had reacted as if she were some kind of hero. 'But of course!' he had cried, clicking the mouse energetically so as to shuffle around the allotted bedrooms on the hotel system. He was smartly dressed, with a pristine white shirt and comb-marks visible in his neat dark hair; the sort of man you could tell had been brought up nicely. 'Do you need me to change your flight? When do you think you will return?'

'Well, that's the thing,' she'd told him, with a little shrug. 'I have absolutely no idea. I'm having such a wonderful time, I might never go home again!'

This last had been a joke, it had come out of nowhere – of course she *would* go home again at some point – but it was clear that Bernardo loved her reply. He'd actually clapped his hands together with delight. 'You never want to go home! My dear, then you shall be our guest for as long as you like,' he declared. 'We are honoured to have your company.'

Goodness, Jeanie thought, as she gave him her credit card for the deposit and he suggested that she might like to book a treatment at the spa, with his compliments, and could he do anything else for her? So this was what it felt like to be a daring person, to go about breaking the rules and behaving impulsively. Usually she would be holidaying with Harry, and he would make all the arrangements: signing the two of them in, dealing with keys and bills, organizing the day-trips and nights out. *Leave it to me,* he would tell her. As a result, she barely received a second glance in places like this; she would stand there by his side, the dutiful wife, and people's gazes would slide right over her. Nothing to see here, only the little woman. The *boring* little woman, they probably thought.

Not any more, though. Now she was the darling of the Hotel Amarilla. The bold, impetuous woman who had turned up alone and defiant, having shucked off her husband like an unwanted jacket at the airport. Not only that, but she'd paid the Amarilla the ultimate compliment by changing her mind about leaving, by prolonging her stay. They could not do enough for her in return, and it was, quite simply, heavenly. Field calls from her family, telling them that she was fine, but didn't want to talk to any of them right now? Not a problem. Save her favourite sun-lounger for her in the morning until she was ready to take her position there? Absolutely. Shower her with little treats – a cool drink here, a bowl of plump chilled grapes there, a bunch of flowers in her room? Nothing seemed like too much trouble.

Of course she wasn't completely made of stone. She did keep panicking about what she had done by postponing her return – and what that might mean for her marriage. When she had turned her phone on, to tell Paula she wasn't on the plane home, it had buzzed and chirped with so many messages and missed calls that she had panicked and switched it off again, just as soon as her text was sent. She missed her children and grandchildren terribly, it was killing her not being able to pop round and chat away with them as she usually did, and if she started reading their messages, she might have second thoughts about staying. She missed her friends in the knitting group, too – she loved those women (and their token man) – and despite everything, she found herself missing Harry as well, whenever she forgot to be angry with him, that was. But soon enough she'd remember his betrayal – his other *daughter*! – and she'd feel her heart frost over and harden towards him once more. No. She wasn't ready to forgive Harry just yet.

In the meantime, there were plenty of other things with which to distract herself. Was it naughty of her to include a certain member of staff as one of them? Luis, his name was: softly spoken and broad-shouldered, with soulful chocolate-brown eyes and a smile that revealed perfect white teeth. He worked in the pool bar and she would often find her gaze drifting over admiringly to him, watching from behind her sunglasses as he theatrically mixed cocktails, both hands on the glinting silver shaker, joking with the customers so that their laughter carried across the water to her. Sometimes he would catch her watching and give her a cheeky little salute as if to say *I see you*, and then she'd blush like a schoolgirl.

Jeanie Mortimer, now you just behave, she would scold herself, but really, honestly, if she was thirty years younger and single, she knew she'd be feeling pretty tempted right now. 'Miss Jeanie' he called her every time he brought her a drink, and it made her feel girlish again, and a tiny bit trembly, as those dark, melty eyes lingered mischievously on hers for a second too long.

Heavens! She was starting to sound like Harry's sister, Penelope, who had already burned through four different husbands and always seemed to have a new boyfriend on the go, even though she was seventy-two years young, in her words. Jeanie had always felt faintly disapproving of Pen's waywardness, but she was starting to see the attraction of such behaviour. Because being out here on her own was the closest she'd come in decades to feeling carefree and heady again, to feeling *young*. She had strolled to the beach the other day and picked up a hot pink maxi-dress from one of the boutiques there, along with a pair of matching flip-flops with huge plastic flowers on them, just because. Some people would call them trashy and they were – oh, they were – but that was the point! They were tacky and silly and would probably fall to bits before the week was out, but so what? She was on holiday! She was having the time of her life, and if she wanted to wear naff flip-flops and a dress that was slit all the way up the thigh, then by God she was going to do those things and enjoy every minute.

She sipped her Negroni appreciatively, enjoying the gentle splashing sounds of the pool nearby, appreciating the smell of the evening buffet that was just starting to waft out from the dining hall. She'd had an aromatherapy massage in the spa earlier and her skin was still soft and fragranced. Afterwards, the charming masseuse had talked her into a special promotion they were running, where you could have a half-price cut and colour done in their salon next door. Jeanie had been feeling so floaty from the massage that she'd promptly booked herself in for tomorrow. A make-over, she kept thinking excitedly, wondering if she should take the plunge and go for some honey-coloured highlights, just to take the edge off all that grey. She'd grown up think-ing vanity was frivolity, but maybe she'd been wrong. It was only a bit of fun! And why not reflect the new carefree Jeanie with a new carefree look?

Another day in paradise, she thought happily, turning the page of her book. She had a cocktail at hand, the sun was still shining and she was blissfully relaxed. Best of all, there'd be a day just the same as this tomorrow. The day after, too. And after that . . . well, who could say?

'Dad,' Paula began, as they sat opposite one another at the Formica-topped table. She'd suggested lunch in his favourite café in town, the one run by an old teaching pal of his, where the staff called him Hazza and slipped him an extra fried egg with his all-day breakfast. Now that they were here, though, with the coffee machine hissing behind them and the smell of sizzling bacon in the air, the words she wanted to say were surprisingly hard to extricate.

'Yes, love,' he said, sawing through his jumbo sausage. 'Everything all right?'

'I just wanted to know about Frankie, Dad.' She turned her fork through her gluey orange baked beans, too churned up with anticipation to feel very hungry. 'If you've heard any more from her. And about what happened with her mum.'

Harry put his cutlery down. 'Ah,' he said, the smile sliding from his face. 'No,' he admitted. 'I haven't heard from her. She must have my address – Lynne next door said she was knocking at our place the day of the party, before Lynne sent her on to the hall, thinking she was a guest. But I don't know where she lives. I don't even know her second name,' he confessed. 'Kathy's surname was Hallows back then, but for all we know, she might have married and changed it, or Frankie could be married and have changed it herself, of course.' He speared a fried mushroom-half, looking glum. 'I feel bad, because I'd like to meet her again – properly, you know. Without your mum breathing down our necks, shooing her away. Because she *is* my daughter.'

'Yeah,' Paula said, sipping her stewed tea and wondering if she'd ever get used to hearing her dad say 'my daughter' and not meaning her.

'I looked her up online, like you suggested, to see if I could find her,' he went on. 'I typed in "Frankie Hallows", but there was no one with that name who looked like her.' He slopped brown sauce onto his plate and dipped a chunk of sausage into it. 'I'll pop back to our place to see Lynne next door, just in case she picked up any other clue that would help us find her. It's a long shot, granted, but I'm not sure what else to do.'

'Knowing Lynne, she's got a secret CCTV camera set up somewhere,' Paula commented, attempting a joke. 'She'll be able to give you Frankie's car registration plate, her shoe size, her height . . .'

Harry shot her a worried look. 'You don't mind, do you?' he asked. 'Me looking for her, I mean. It's just that she went to all the effort of tracking me down, only for me to . . . not push her away, exactly, but, you know. It wasn't the best moment to chat. So . . .'

'I don't mind you looking for her,' Paula told him, and then a knotty silence descended, when they both munched and wondered what to say next. 'What was Kathy like, then?' she asked after a moment. 'How come you and her . . . ?' Unsure how to finish the question, she left it dangling, and her dad grimaced, his voice gruff when he eventually replied.

'She was fun, Kathy. She was temping in the school office for the summer term one year, bit of a wild one, bit of a daredevil. At the time I was – not *dissatisfied* with life, exactly, but maybe feeling a bit restless. Feeling as if I was a bit stuck, as if the world had got very small around me, whereas Kathy seemed to represent something different. An escape.'

Paula bit her lip, trying to get her head round this version of her dad. He'd always seemed perfectly content to live in the same house for years on end, happy within the boundaries of that so-called small world. Clearly not.

He glanced across at her when she didn't reply, looking awkward. 'Sorry,' he mumbled after a pause, then a thought seemed to strike him. 'You're not just asking because your mum put you up to it, are you?'

'No,' Paula replied. 'I haven't heard a thing from Mum. Not for want of trying. I don't even know when she's coming home again, do you? I mean, I looked online, and the flights are every Sunday, so I'm hoping she'll be back at the weekend, but . . .' Her voice petered out, as she saw her dad shrugging.

'I don't know, either,' he replied, his eyes mournful. 'She's never going to let me forget this, is she?' he added after a moment.

'Probably not,' Paula agreed. 'But then again . . .' Her own hurt feelings lay like a tight bandage around her chest. 'I dunno, Dad. I feel kind of sad about it myself,' she confessed. 'I mean, I've always looked up to you and Mum as, like, the happy-ever-after to aspire to. And now . . .'

He flinched but didn't look away. 'I'm sorry, love,' he said. 'I'm really, truly sorry. I was a selfish young idiot – there's no excuse. I never did it again, though.' His voice shook. 'Because I love your mother. I absolutely worship that woman. And as soon as Kathy left town, it was like the scales dropped from my eyes. I looked around me and realized how lucky I was, with your mum and you kiddies, and I realized, too, just what I stood to lose. *You bloody fool*, I thought. *You stupid, stupid man.*' He buttered another piece of toast and shook his head. 'It taught me not to take anything for granted. And from that day on, I devoted myself to Jeanie and the family. I swear.'

Paula nodded, believing him. He was a good man at heart, she knew that, and this whole saga seemed to have aged him, to have ground him down. He looked tired and defeated, a fuzz of stubble on his jawline, an ink smudge on his shirt. Sometimes you forgot that your parents were fallible human beings too, especially when they'd previously seemed so adept at life. 'So what happens now?' she asked. 'I mean, Mum was pretty clear that she wanted nothing to do with Frankie. So what will you do if she turns up again, and Mum gives you an *It's-me-or-her* ultimatum again? Who will you choose?'

Harry poked a triangle of toast into his fried egg and bit off the corner. 'I'm not going to be had by any ultimatums,' he replied, munching. 'I'll choose them both, of course.

And if your mother has ever loved me, then she'll know she can't ask that of me. I can't turn away my own daughter.'

'Good,' said Paula, remembering the alarmed face of her half-sister on the few seconds of video she had. Remembering too how strong a pull she, Paula, had felt inside, at the sight of her. *That woman is my sister. My actual, real sister.* 'Then I'll stand by you,' she promised her dad. 'Because I want to meet her too. Whatever Mum says.'

'Whee! You're flying! You're a bird! You're an eagle!'

'I'm flying!' Fergus yelled in agreement, as the swing soared up into the air. Craig had gone to meet an old magazine contact who wanted to discuss some possible feature ideas, and Frankie had taken Fergus down to the local playground where, joy of joys, they'd been able to get on his favourite swing without even having to wait.

'Kick your feet out in front when you go up, that's it,' Frankie reminded him and pushed again. 'Whee! You're a rocket, shooting into space – you're whizzing up to Mars!'

'ROCKET!' bellowed Fergus gleefully. 'Harder, Mumma. Harder!'

Another push. 'Wow! You're a seagull zooming over the sea, hunting for fish!' she cried.

'I'm a PTERODACTYL!' he replied, spreading his arms out wide as the swing arced up again. They'd just borrowed a library book about dinosaurs and it was his current bedtime reading favourite. They were both rapidly becoming experts on the subject.

'Hold on tight, pterodactyl,' Frankie warned as he wobbled within the sturdy safety bars of the swing, his chest banging against the front. She grabbed hold of the swing and put her hand on his little round tummy. 'Ow. Are you okay, poppet? Do you want to stop?'

Fergus bucked in the seat, trying to make himself swing once more. 'Again, Mumma. Don't want to stop.'

'Okay,' Frankie said. 'Get ready then, because it's going to be a big one . . .' She held on to the back and pulled him up slowly. 'Hold very tight, because it's going to be really, really big . . .'

Fergus squealed excitedly, kicking his legs. 'Do it, Mumma. Do it!'

'Are you sure you're ready?' Frankie teased. 'Are you quite, quite sure?'

'What an adorable little boy!'

Frankie almost let go of the swing, she was so shocked to hear the woman's voice. The voice that had taunted her in nightmares all week, the voice she kept hearing in her head. *He's MY son. And I want him back!*

'Julia,' she said, her heart thumping up into her throat as she glanced round and saw her there, the return of the Bad Fairy. She swallowed hard and set Fergus swinging, not wanting him to pick up on her panic. *Oh God, oh God,* she thought anxiously. *What should I do? What should I DO?*

'We meet again,' Julia said, smiling broadly as if they were old friends. Had she followed them there from the flat? Frankie wondered with a lurch. How long had she been watching? Had she seen Fergus joggle against the swing just now, when he wasn't holding on?

'Hi,' Frankie said weakly, her heart fluttering like a dying butterfly.

'I take it my letter arrived safely?' Julia went on in a conversational tone. She was wearing cropped jeans and a bright-pink T-shirt, her wild spiralling hair pulled back under a navy headscarf. She looked radiant and Earth Mother-ish, her skin a healthy golden, her teeth white in her smile.

'Yes,' Frankie replied guardedly. 'It did.'

'Excellent.' Julia leaned against one of the swing posts as if settling in at a bar. 'And what did Craig have to say about the contents?'

What did Craig have to say? Absolutely nothing that could be repeated in a children's play area, Frankie thought to herself. 'He . . . he's still mulling it over,' she fudged.

'Ahh,' said Julia, her expression giving little away. 'Well, he needs to hurry up and reply,' she went on in a brisk, business-like manner. 'Because, obviously, if he won't even attempt mediation to resolve the issue, then I'm legally entitled to go to court and issue an application for a child arrangement order. Just saying!'

The words sent a seam of ice splitting Frankie's heart. Julia clearly hadn't wasted any time ascertaining her rights and the procedures she'd need to take. 'Right,' she replied dully.

Julia flashed her another toothy smile. 'Anyway. More importantly – hello, Fergus,' she cried, stepping closer to the swing and wiggling her fingers in a little wave. 'Remember me?'

Of course he doesn't remember you, Frankie wanted to snap. You left him before he could even sit up, let alone form his earliest memories. *Remember* you? He doesn't even know you exist!

Fergus was kicking his legs with exuberance, ignoring the interruption. 'Faster, Mumma!' he yelled imperiously. 'Do a rocket again!'

'Oka-a-a-ay,' Frankie replied. Maybe if she and Fergus just closed Julia right out, she would go away. 'To the moon, this time. Are you ready? Are you holding tight?'

'He calls you that?' Julia asked, arching an eyebrow. 'He thinks you're his mum?'

Frankie flinched, finding the other woman's presence ominous. What was she even doing there? If she thought Frankie was about to be manipulated into making introductions amidst the happy shrieks and laughter of the children's playground, turning Fergus's small world upside down with revelations, then she had another think coming. 'Yes,' she replied curtly, giving Fergus a push. *Yes, he calls me that. Because in his eyes, that's exactly who I am. All right?*

A flicker of emotion crossed Julia's face, before she strode a few steps further so that Fergus could see her better. 'Hey, Fergus,' she said in a wheedling sort of voice. 'Hey, buddy, I brought you a present.'

Frankie found herself gritting her teeth. Oh, really? You're going to bribe him now, are you? 'Julia, I'm not sure this is the time or—'

The word 'present' had caught Fergus's attention, though. 'Mumma, who is that lady?' he interrupted, trying to twist round in the swing.

'Sit still, darling, and hold on,' Frankie said at once, slowing the swing before he tried to fling himself bodily from it. Fergus was very keen on the concept of presents. It had been his birthday in April and he still liked to talk about the occasion months later, often wanting to leaf through the cards again and examine photos of himself wearing a party hat, tucking into Frankie's best effort at a Thomas the Tank Engine cake.

'This is Julia,' she added belatedly, in answer to his question. Oh God, she agonized as she lifted him down and the three of them moved a little way away, near the sandpit. Please let this be all right. Please don't let Julia smash his world to bits with one ill-judged, impetuous remark. Please don't let her try to snatch him away. She found herself glancing round to see if there were any mums she knew nearby, someone who could call the police for her, if Frankie had to give chase. If only Craig were here too, she despaired. At least they'd have safety in numbers then, a united show of defence!

'Well, look at you,' said Julia, crouching down and beaming at Fergus. She crooked a finger at him. 'Do you want your present? Come and say hello to me.'

Fergus didn't seem to like this idea, leaning against Frankie's legs and sliding a thumb into his mouth. He stared at the floor and shook his head, no, and Frankie crouched down too, putting a protective arm around his small warm body. *You can't win him over that easily, love.* 'He can be a bit shy sometimes with people he doesn't know,' she said.

If Julia noticed the barb, she chose not to react, instead dipping a hand into a large canvas tote bag and drawing out a gift wrapped in shiny green paper. 'Here you are,' she said coaxingly, holding it out.

Still Fergus didn't move. Frankie stroked his springy hair, finding herself checking out Julia's shoes to gauge how fast the woman might be able to run, if she did make a grab for him. Gold high-heeled sandals with wispy, insubstantial-looking straps. Okay. They were probably safe. 'Go on, darling, it's all right,' she told him. 'It's a present, for you!'

She dropped her voice to a pretend whisper. 'And don't forget to say . . .'

'Fank you,' he said obediently, stepping forward and taking the present. With a glance up at Frankie to check it was okay – yes, go on, you can open it – he tore apart the wrapping to reveal . . . 'A bear,' he said, with a noticeable lack of enthusiasm. Other children his age had bedrooms populated with whole jungles of cuddly toys, but Fergus had never been one for stuffed animals, preferring things with wheels that he could push around the floor, preferably crashing into one another.

'A teddy, how kind,' Frankie said politely. 'Well, we really should be going now, so—'

'What do you think you'll call him? Wait – is it a girl bear or a boy bear?' asked Julia, who seemed determined to engage with Fergus. She put a finger to her lips in an affected, wondering sort of way. 'Can you think of any cool names?'

Fergus lifted a shoulder in one of his doubtful shrugs, and Frankie could almost read the thoughts that were going around his head. *I dunno. Why's she asking me? She's the one who got it. I don't even like bears!*

Okay, time to wrap this up, Frankie thought. 'Maybe we should call him . . . Lunchtime! Because that's what time it is. Shall we go home now?'

Fergus giggled, rescued by her ridiculousness. 'Lunchtime isn't a *name*,' he scolded, leaning against her.

'Oh no? How about Ham Sandwich? Or Strawberry Yogurt?'

'No, Mumma! Those are silly names.'

Julia looked hurt, as if her present wasn't being taken seriously. But then she put on her big fake smile again and held her arms wide. 'How about a hug before you go? A cuddle? Do you want a cuddle?'

Fergus bit his lip and glanced at Frankie again. He was like this with Craig's Aunty Lindsey sometimes, who was always wanting to pinch his cheeks and hug him and kiss him, as if he were some kind of pet. 'You don't have to, if you don't want to,' Frankie said, still with her arm around him. Her thighs were starting to ache from her crouched position, but she paid them no heed. She would crouch like this all day if she had to.

'Come here and I'll tell you a secret,' Julia coaxed, with a funny smile on her face, making her eyes big and round. 'Do you want to hear a secret?'

Uh-oh. Frankie did *not* want Julia telling Fergus any secrets. No, thank you. 'Well, we're off now,' she said, rising and taking Fergus's hand, before wheeling him sharply around. 'Bye.'

'Oh, but I think he wants to know the secret,' Julia said, in an awful sing-songy voice, one that set Frankie's teeth on edge. She was trotting up behind them, heels clacking against the path, the smell of her sickly perfume making Frankie want to gag. 'Because it's a very cool secret!'

'Julia, just leave it,' Frankie warned, without breaking stride. Her hand was becoming clammy where she was gripping on to Fergus and she found herself wishing she'd brought the buggy with her, so she could bundle him into it and run. 'Another time maybe. Goodbye.'

'Well, I'm going to tell him anyway,' Julia said, all syrupy and sweet. 'Hey, you'll never guess what, Fergus.' She gave a fake little laugh that made Frankie want to scream. 'It's ever so funny because . . . well, because I'm your real mummy!'

Chapter Thirteen

Alison stood at the kitchen worktop and poured herself a gin and tonic. Ice cubes, a juicy slice of lime, a swizzle stick to mix it all together. She sipped the concoction thoughtfully, then added more gin. Nothing worse than a G&T without a bit of poke – that was her motto. Well, it wasn't, but maybe it should be.

Wandering out into the garden with her drink, she sat down on her old wooden Lutyens bench and wiggled her bare toes. It was a warm June evening, and the blooms on the peonies were gorgeously ripe and full. The sweet peas were romping up the bamboo wigwam, white and lilac and crimson, with their delicate notes of scent just reaching her. Further down the garden, the alliums stood to attention like a row of soldiers, their rounded starry heads a rich purple against the stone wall, while her luscious pink roses spilled over with fragrance. Alison took a long swig of gin, breathed in the beautiful surroundings and exhaled. Okay, then. Was she ready for this? Was she bold enough to dare?

That morning she'd been cutting the hair of Mo Marshall, who was seventy-five, wise and permanently cheerful, and Alison had found herself confessing how she'd been feeling a bit blue recently.

'Ah, Widow's Itch, that's what you've got,' Mo had said with a dirty cackle. She was having her hair washed at the time, and Alison, rinsing off the suds behind her, was glad that her client couldn't see the startled look on her face. 'You want to get back in the dating world, my girl. Have yourself a bit of fun.'

Widow's Itch? It sounded like some revolting sexually transmitted disease, but according to Mo, every bereaved woman experienced it at some point or another. 'Don't fight it, feel it,' she advised, wagging a finger as Alison rubbed in the conditioner. 'If you hear what I'm saying.'

Alison wasn't sure she wanted to hear what Mo was saying, but she was a firm believer in Business Rule Number One: the customer is always right. And so she did her best to make interested-sounding noises while Mo detailed the pros and cons of various matchmaking sites she'd sampled, and went on to provide her with a full list of tips and anecdotes when it came to modern-day dating. *This is not for me*, Alison assured herself, snipping and styling and blow-drying. *I'm just nodding and being polite here, that's all.* But then Mo had ended her little spiel by taking Alison's hand and saying earnestly, 'We all just want some companionship, at the end of the day, don't we? And a bit of a laugh and a cuddle to sweeten the evenings.'

The phrase resonated within Alison. Yes, actually, she found herself thinking. Mo was right: if Alison was honest with herself, she did want those things. But did she really have the nerve to venture out in search of them?

Come on, girl. You might as well have a look, at least. Check out the totty, said Mo in her head. You could almost hear that cackle of hers echoing around the garden.

Alison took a deep breath and switched on her laptop. Now, what was that website called, the one that Mo had told her about? Silver and Single, that was it. 'There's another called Grab-a-Granny, but I've heard a few dodgy things about it,' Mo had advised, wrinkling her nose. Grab-a-Granny indeed, Alison thought, eyes spinning heavenwards. Where was the dignity in that?

Silver and Single it was, then. Just to shut Mo up, if nothing else. 'Well, here goes,' she said aloud, and then for some reason she picked up her glass of gin and held it in the air. 'Cheers to you, Rich, wherever you are. Nobody will ever match up to you, my darling. But let's just see who else is out there.'

Then she typed in the name of the website and, suddenly feeling a bit trembly and giddy, clicked on the link.

Silver and Single . . . You're Never Too Old! Come on in, the water's lovely, read the introductory page, and Alison gave a little sniff because, actually, she didn't think of herself as 'old' in the slightest, and certainly didn't need a website to tell her as much. 'That's your first warning,' she said darkly. Any more patronizing nonsense and she'd switch the silly thing off and go indoors. Her finger hovered over a scarlet heart-shaped button that urged 'Join Us!' and, after a deep breath – *Got to be in it to win it!* Mo reminded her – she clicked again. She would merely *investigate* at this stage, she told herself. She would simply have a *look*. It didn't mean she actually had to do anything she didn't want to.

A form had come up, with lots of boxes to fill in. Name, age, gender, profession, height, colour of eyes . . .

She sniffed again. Did people really care about the height and eye colour of a prospective partner, then? Did they actually specify that they wanted tall, blue-eyed women or short, green-eyed men, as if they were ordering a model from a catalogue? It seemed very shallow and unimportant. She hoped that wasn't a sign of the sort of clientele Silver and Single attracted.

I am interested in Men__ Women__ Both__ (tick as applicable).

I am searching for Friend__ Partner__ Lover__ Soul-mate__ (tick as applicable).

'Goodness,' Alison murmured, feeling doubtful. Surely ticking 'Soulmate' was wildly optimistic and against all the odds? Still, optimism was good, she reminded herself, marking the box anyway. The next few questions had her stumped, though:

What is your idea of a good first date?
Please describe the person you'd ideally like to meet through this dating site.

Alison's fingers hung in mid-air above the keyboard, like a pianist about to launch into a concerto, but inspiration remained elusive. It had been well over forty years since she'd been on a first date, after all: fish and chips on the sea front with Rich, and then walking shyly home together hand-in-hand, wondering if he would try to kiss her outside her front door. She pictured herself in the yellow cotton dress she'd liked to wear back then, when her waist was small and the world seemed full of possibilities. It seemed now like something that had happened to another woman.

Dinner, she typed hesitantly in answer to the first question, then had second thoughts and deleted her reply. Because dinner would be full of pitfalls, she realized. And as someone who strongly disliked bad manners at the table – people chomping their food, anyone talking with their mouth full, those idiots who made such a performance of tasting their wine, like they were some kind of connoisseur – Alison was almost certainly going to find herself put off. Maybe dinner was not the best option. The cinema, then? A play? At least she wouldn't have to talk much, and there'd be less chance of disaster striking by her saying something daft, she reasoned. Then again, what if the date was more cultured than her and opted to see something highbrow and confusing? She'd end up feeling stupid, with nothing to say for herself. And what if the date was a perv who just wanted to take advantage of the dark surroundings to start fondling her thigh – or worse?

A walk on a summer's day, she typed instead. That sounded romantic, at least, didn't it? But heavens, what would she *wear*? Shorts and hiking boots? It wasn't exactly a sexy look, even with her hair and make-up done. Plus – more alarmingly – you got some real weirdos, didn't you, these days, who might attack her in the middle of nowhere, who might strangle her in a sunny meadow, dismember her on a remote part of the headland. She'd be found days later by dog walkers. Imagine Robyn's bewildered face when the police knocked on her door to tell her the news.

No. No walks. No dinner, cinema or theatre.

A drink in the pub and a good chat, she typed eventually and left it at that, before she could start worrying about how cheap and unadventurous this answer might make her look. Bugger it, she'd be here all night otherwise.

Okay, next question: the person she'd ideally like to meet. Her mind went completely blank as she tried to think. When she'd first considered the possibility of another relationship, she'd really only imagined someone sitting beside her, companionably watching telly with her (and *not* talking through all the dramatic bits). Someone who might say, 'Fancy a cup of tea, love?' every now and then or 'Why don't we try that new restaurant that's opened in town?' or 'Let's go for a rummage around the antiques market together'. Maybe this ideal person of hers could mow the lawn for her too, once in a while, sort the kitchen drain out. But she could hardly put that down on a dating site, could she? It wasn't exactly the most romantic line in the world. And just imagine the conversations that might follow!

'So, what attracted you to Alison in the first place?'

'Oh, it was the fact she was looking for a fella to fix her plumbing for her and put the kettle on. She sounded like my dream woman. How could anyone resist?'

Dear Lord, she'd have to come back to that later, she decided. Maybe once she'd had another gin and felt more inspired. Now then, next:

Describe yourself in a few sentences. What are the best things about you?

The best things about her? Help. She was good at cutting

hair . . . She had an encyclopaedic knowledge of every soap opera going . . . She . . . Oh, this was useless. Surely it wasn't supposed to be so hard to dredge up a few positive things about yourself?

Wait – she'd missed a bit, in brackets below the last question:

If you're not sure what to say here, ask a friend or loved one to list what's great about you. Don't be modest!

Alison felt her shoulders slump. She could ask Robyn, she supposed, but her daughter would seize upon the news that her stubbornly unsociable mother was daring to dip a toe in the dating pool ('Finally!' she imagined Robyn crying) and would never let her hear the end of it. *Any replies?* she'd ask, giggling like it was a big joke. *Any dates? Let's have a look at what's on offer – ooh, he's nice. What about him?*

No. The mortification of this little scenario had quite changed her mind about Silver and Single now. She just wasn't ready yet, after all. Mo would tease her and make chicken noises at her, but so be it. Nobody else had to know. Sometimes it was best to stay in the safety of your own comfort zone, wasn't it? And so what if that comfort zone felt as if it was becoming a tiny bit boring occasionally? So what if other people had more exciting lives? Alison knew her place and it was right here at home, managing perfectly well all by herself, just as she had done for the last thirty-three years.

She went in, switched on the television and sat there, doing her best to ignore the tiny part of her that felt disappointed.

Robyn still wasn't any the wiser as to what had happened to John's job, and why he had apparently lost it in such unceremonious fashion. She had brought up the subject of the 'redundancy' a couple of times, giving him the opportunity to correct her, and yet for whatever reason he had chosen not to tell her the truth. If anything, she could feel him edging away from her, looking for excuses not to be on his own with her, whenever possible. He'd even started going to bed after she did, staying up to watch films or late-night current-affairs programmes with his dad and then creeping up in the early hours, once he could be sure she was asleep.

Robyn didn't know what to do, how to start the conversation. How did you go about saying to your husband, *Look, I know you've been lying to me. I know you were sacked*, without getting tangled up in your own confessions of going behind his back with phone calls to his former secretary? Neither of them came out looking like an honest, trusting spouse in this scenario. And yet it was driving her crazy, his resistance to just being straight with her.

'Maybe we could have a chat later tonight,' she suggested

on Friday evening when, for once, the two of them were alone in the kitchen. Harry was having a very competitive game of badminton outside in the back garden with the children – 'You two against me, that's fair, seeing as I'm absolutely *not* going to give you an easy time of it,' he'd said – and Robyn had been bashing steaks with a rolling pin, when John walked in and began pulling open the drawers.

'What was that?' he asked distractedly, rifling through the contents. 'For heaven's sake, what do our kids *do* with all the chargers in this house?' he grumbled, slamming them all shut again in defeat.

'I said, we could have a chat tonight, just the two of us,' Robyn repeated. 'Maybe ask Harry to babysit, so that we could go out somewhere for a change. Because I think we need to—'

He cut her off before she could get any further. 'Ah. I said I'd go for a drink with Stephen – sorry,' he said, then spotted a charger plugged in by the kettle and attached his phone with a muttered 'At last'. And then he was hurrying out to join Harry and the kids – safety in numbers – and that seemed to be the end of the matter.

Except that later on in the evening, a good hour after John had changed his shirt and left the house in a waft of spicy aftershave, there was a knock at the front door. Robyn opened it to see – well, to see Stephen himself, of all people. *Sans* John. 'Oh!' she exclaimed, puzzled. 'Is John all right?'

He seemed surprised by the question. 'Er . . . far as I know?' he replied cagily. 'I was just popping round to see Dad actually, if he's around.'

'Right,' said Robyn, still holding on to the door, trying to make sense of this. 'It's just that John said he was meeting you this evening, so . . .'

There was only the tiniest twist of alarm on Stephen's face before his expression became smooth and guileless once more. He was a solicitor, used to thinking on his feet, trained in inscrutability. 'Um, yeah,' he said with a little laugh, raking a hand through his dark hair. 'He's in the pub with a couple of others. I just thought I'd swing by, see if Dad wanted to join us, that was all. If he's here?'

'Right,' said Robyn, not believing this for a second. She knew the three Mortimer brothers had all been heart-breakers in their youth, and this deft covering for one another was no doubt a reflex response, still there, deep in their blood. The stories they must have told to unsuspecting admirers, the tales they'd no doubt woven to protect each other. And now, unless she was completely mistaken, this was happening to her. Really, Stephen? she wanted to ask, eyeballing him. But how could she quiz him without sound-ing like a fishwife? 'Yes, come in, he's in the living room,' she managed to mumble after a few moments.

Having shown her brother-in-law inside, Robyn went and skulked in the kitchen, unable to bear the indignity of eavesdropping on whatever concocted excuse Stephen was giving Harry – *Don't let on, all right? Mum's the word* – and gripped her own fists tight, tight, tighter, as she wondered where John was and what the hell was going on. Did the rest of the family know what her husband was up to? Had she become a figure of pity amidst the Mortimers, excluded from the secret while they closed ranks against her?

No. She was getting paranoid. Jumping to wild, unfounded conclusions. All the same, she could feel John pulling away from the relationship, slipping out in his own direction alone, with no backward glance, no thought of inviting her along. Just like he'd slipped out tonight with a cover story that had proved to be full of holes almost immediately.

She shivered, gazing out into the garden where the shadows were thickening below the hedges, where the swing swayed childlessly in a ghostly breeze. She had married into the Mortimers, glad to see the back of those years as an only child, happy to be caught up as part of this large, friendly family. Except . . . as it transpired, you could still feel lonely amidst a crowd. You could still end up very much on your own, stranded on the sidelines, if it turned out the others wanted to put you there.

'Rob?' There was Stephen again, popping his head round the door, as she stood by the sink, silent as a doll. 'I'm off. Dad's staying in after all, so I'd better get back to the lads.

What's the betting it'll be my round?' He was smiling as if nothing was wrong, but she could see embarrassment and awkwardness in his smile. Apology even, because it was obvious then that John was meeting someone else, rather than waiting at a pub table for his brother's return.

'Sure,' she said, without smiling back. She felt as if her heart was splintering. Stephen had always been a great brother-in-law, full of funny gossipy stories, affectionate and teasing at all times, and a brilliant uncle to her children. But now he looked stiff and uncomfortable, as if he couldn't wait to leave. *Don't get me involved,* his body language was saying. Robyn swallowed, part of her wanting to interrogate him like one of his own cross-examinations. What did he know? What was going on? 'Okay. Have a good evening, then,' she said unhappily, in the end. 'Give my love to Ed.'

He came over and gave her an impulsive hug, and she breathed in his gorgeous cologne. 'I will, darling, thanks,' he said. 'Take care, yeah?'

And then he was gone, and she was closing the front door again, her mind crawling with awful thoughts. *Take care,* he'd said, like he was worried about her. Like she should be worried for herself. She cringed at the thought of Stephen going back to Eddie and announcing this new drama. *I was mortified!* she imagined him exclaiming. *What was I supposed to say? And what the hell is John up to, anyway?*

Canned laughter blared out into the subdued silence of

the house, as Harry put the TV on in the living room. Did *Harry* know John was up to something? she wondered miserably. Did Paula? She hadn't seen her sister-in-law since the anniversary party, in fact, which was odd – usually the two of them caught up fairly regularly for coffee, or a chat on the phone. Was she keeping her distance deliberately? Robyn fretted. If push came to shove, John was Paula's brother after all, just as he was Stephen's. She was pretty sure she knew where the family loyalties would lie.

More canned laughter came from the living room – HAHAHAHAHAHA – and the sound of Harry chuckling along, too. Robyn's heart raced with anxiety as she wondered if there was anyone she could talk to about this, anyone at all. Her mum – no. Having always made such a thing about the Mortimers and how much she loved being part of their big family, it would require a huge, mortifying loss of face for Robyn to confess that this same family might actually be closing ranks against her now.

In terms of finding out what had happened with John's job, the university probably wouldn't tell her anything she didn't already know, either; they would build a brick wall of confidentiality, if she tried poking around for any more information. Which meant that the only person who might be able to help was Beth Broadwood, the mum from school who'd let slip the news about John losing his job in the first place.

Oh God, thought Robyn miserably. It would be so humiliating, though, having to go to another woman – a woman she didn't even really know very well – in order to beg for some squalid little titbits about her husband. She wasn't so desperate as to stoop to that, was she?

HAHAHAHAHAHAHAHAHA went the television again, and Robyn sighed heavily into the quiet hallway.

Was she?

Chapter Fourteen

Bunny had been at the absolute end of her tether, that was the thing. She just couldn't stand it any longer. That was what she had told the police when they came to see her in the hospital, one male officer, one female, both stern-faced as they sat in the plastic chairs at her bedside and asked her question after question. 'I just wanted him to stop,' she had sobbed, engulfed by another wave of tears as she relived the moment all over again.

Funny word, 'tether'. It made her think of a greying piece of rope used to tie up a farm animal to prevent it from wandering off unchecked. Which was appropriate, really, when that was exactly how her marriage to Mark Roberts had been. All under his control; her the nervous sheep who knew her place, him the master who kept her there. Oh, he'd been charming at first, of course. *They always are,* said the fierce-but-kind female QC who had defended her in court. *When they want to be, that is.*

Mark had seemed like the perfect man when she met

him: charismatic and funny, handsome too, with his muscular physique and unusual grey eyes. He was a local councillor for the town and hugely popular in the area, after seeing off plans for a bypass that would have cut straight through school playing fields and woodland. Back then she'd been a size twelve, confident and happy, always laughing about something or other. 'What a lovely couple,' their friends had said. 'You two are made for each other!' And that was what she had thought too, right up until a fortnight before they got married, when Mark knocked her flying across the room.

It was the oldest story in the book. Tale as old as time, as her Disney-obsessed niece Chloe liked to sing. Because he was so desperately sorry, he had said, as she lay there winded on the floor, her head throbbing where it had smacked against the wall on the way down. Their eyes had met in a terrible moment of silence: herself stunned, Mark aghast, the room seemingly holding its breath. It would never happen again, he had assured her, gathering her into his arms. Please, would she forgive him? Could she give him another chance?

They were due to get married in two weeks and everything had been booked, arranged, paid for. A beautiful ivory dress hung in her mum's wardrobe, their friend Rhona was planning a meringue extravaganza for the cake, there were two boarding passes for their honeymoon flight to Sardinia already printed and in a safe place with an envelope of euros and the passports. And he was a local hero, a good person – everyone said so!

Of course none of these lines of argument validated staying with a man who had hit you, but they certainly weighed on her mind while Mark was prostrating himself before her with contrition. Whatever, she must have been an idiot because she had said yes, she would forgive him. Yes, she still wanted to marry him; and yes, she would give him another chance.

But then it happened again. And again. And within the space of a year he'd quite run out of chances, and they had both stopped being quite so shocked about his sudden violent tendencies. By then she had begun comfort-eating her way into a corner and didn't know how to get out.

It went on and on. She became fatter and fatter. And the bigger she became, the angrier his rages and the smaller she felt inside, until she eventually felt like nothing, a speck of dirt on the floor, insignificant and pathetic and weak. The laughter stopped. It was hard to look Mark in his charming, handsome face any more. His muscular body had stopped being something to lust after, becoming instead something to fear, to cower away from whenever he moved unexpectedly.

'I didn't mean to do it,' she had said brokenly to the police officers in the hospital, tears running down her swollen cheeks until they pooled damply in the bandages that cradled her smashed jaw. Except – if she was being honest – in the dark, wild heat of the moment, she *had* meant to do it, when he punched her face so hard they both heard a crack and one of her teeth fell out, shining and bloodied on the kitchen floor. Hell yes, she meant to do it all right, as she grabbed the kitchen knife with its natty red handle and plunged it into his side. A Kitchen Devil, it was called; she remembered thinking later that that was a good description of her own self at that very moment. A kitchen banshee, screaming insults back at him, her hands sodden with his splashing crimson blood. That jolt of satisfaction at seeing the shocked look on his face at what she'd done. *There. See how YOU like it.*

'He just kept on hitting me,' she'd explained, her voice so tiny that the police officer who was jotting down her words in a notepad had to lean closer to hear. 'I thought he was going to kill me this time.'

But he hadn't managed that at least. The neighbours must have heard her screaming because they'd called the police, although she couldn't remember any of that: the ambulance journey, his arrest, nothing. For six weeks she'd remained in hospital, being patched and stitched and splinted, off her head with strong painkillers most of the time, but safe from him at least. Safe from harm. Those six long weeks had passed, one after another, while she thought and she pondered and she made a few decisions. Meanwhile, pound by pound, the weight was already beginning to drop silently off her as she lay there recovering.

Afterwards there had been the court case, when he'd been sent to prison on charges of Grievous Bodily Harm and she'd been allowed to walk away free. Free of him, free to start again. Or so she thought. Except that people kept acting strangely around her. The local press – which had always fawned over Mark – seemed to have taken his side, portraying her as some kind of psycho, even hinting in their comment pieces that *she* should be the one in prison. Friends went quiet on her, scared no doubt that she had become the knife-wielding maniac of the news stories. Even her own family appeared repelled. Her mum was embarrassed about what the neighbours thought and didn't want to talk about it, whereas her sister-in-law went even further. 'I'm sorry,' her brother Stu had said awkwardly, when Bunny was newly out of hospital and had dredged up the energy to drop round, 'but Sonia's not happy about you seeing our Chlo any more. I'm really sorry.'

Another woman might have been permanently defeated by this. And in fairness, Bunny had gone home and wept copiously for the loss of her adored nine-year-old niece with her shining black hair and giggling fits. Bunny had been the most doting aunty to Chloe until then, always willing to play tea-parties or read stories or create Lego constructions together. She still had a card Chloe had made for her birthday one year – *Deere Arntie Raych, I love you xxx* – written in wavering, wonky letters, with a picture of two smiling stick-people holding hands ('That's me and you').

Eventually, when she had been cold-shouldered from all sides, she had felt a burst of defiance appear from out of nowhere; her old fighting spirit fighting back. She was not a bad person, whatever they thought. She deserved a second chance. And so she had packed up her pitifully small collection of belongings in order to make a new start, somewhere that nobody knew her. York, she decided, randomly jabbing a finger at her road atlas. It seemed as good a place as any.

York was beautiful and the people were friendly. She left Rachel behind and became Bunny, a name from happier times, and set about finding herself various cash-in-hand jobs – cleaning, bar work, waitressing – as well as a tiny flat to rent. She sorted out a divorce and took back her maiden name, then settled on her current job, which she enjoyed, working at Grains deli, a small café in town that specialized in healthy snacks and wholesome salads. Above all, she went on losing the weight, joining a Zumba class and walking to work, finding strategies to stop herself from slipping down to her bad old comfort-eating habits. Slowly but surely, strength began to bloom within her like a Yorkshire rose.

Then of course she had met Dave – sprinting to his rescue in the street, only for him eventually to rescue her right back, by being so trustworthy and good and kind, restoring her faith in the possibility of love, when she'd believed it to be gone forever. He'd asked her her name in the A&E department as he lay there, woolly-headed and drowsy, and misheard her reply. 'Bernie?' he'd said. 'What's that short for – Bernadette?'

She'd twinkled at him, arched an eyebrow. 'Bernie *is* usually short for Bernadette, yes,' she'd agreed, without correcting the misunderstanding. 'But my friends call me Bunny.'

'Bunny,' he'd repeated woozily, smiling up at her. He had a lovely smile. 'Hello there, Bunny. Do you come here often?'

Later, he'd introduced her to members of his family as 'Bernadette', but she always cried, 'Oh please, call me Bunny! Bernadette sounds too severe. I'm really *not* a severe sort of person.' And somehow she'd never quite managed to say, *By the way, Dave, my name isn't actually Bernadette at all. It's Rachel Roberts, but you probably shouldn't Google me, if you know what I mean.* It was easier to go along with the story, to spin a little fairy-tale of goodness around herself. Rachel Roberts was a torrid tragedy that had been someone else altogether.

Things like bank cards and post were slightly trickier to explain, sure, but Bunny arranged for any important mail to be forwarded to a PO box in town, swooping by and picking it up now and then. It wasn't as if she was lying, exactly, to Dave. More that she was edging around the truth, keeping certain things from him. Self-preservation, she saw it as, and who could blame her? Because she'd been kicked to rags down on the floor already, and it had been enough for one lifetime. Never again would she let a person hurt her like that; never again would she be the powerless, scared sheep on someone else's tether.

This had all been fine at first; a means of sealing that tender, bruised part of herself away from the rest of the world. But as she began to fall in love with Dave, and trust him, as she moved into his house and they took holidays together, and his mum dropped hints about Dave popping the question and making things 'official', Bunny had been feeling less confident concerning what she had omitted telling him about her life, about her. 'I'm not in any hurry to get married,' she said pre-emptively before Valentine's Day, terrified he was going to propose. That was the moment when she should have told him she'd been married once before, but something stopped her. Why jinx her relationship by letting the past sneak in and taint it? Why jeopardize the second chance she'd so painstakingly created for herself?

Back when she was a teenager, there'd been an advert in the local paper one week for a Saturday girl at the New Age shop in town. She'd rung up to find out more, only to be asked for her date of birth. 'The manager needs to study your star chart to see if you're suitable,' she was told. A few long moments later the judgement came. 'Sorry,' the woman on the phone said, 'but it's a no. We don't think you'd be right for the job.'

'Oh,' Bunny – Rachel, rather – had replied, taken aback by this unorthodox recruitment process. She'd gone on to get a Saturday job in a supermarket instead, where they were more interested in your numeracy skills and friendliness with customers, rather than your star sign, thankfully. It had niggled at her ever since, though, that brusque rejection, the lack of further explanation. What had the manager *seen* in her birth chart that had been so off-putting, she sometimes wondered. Had they known from her planetary alignments that she would turn out to be the sort of person who plunged a knife into a man in a desperate fight-or-die adrenalin rush?

She had spent eighteen months trying not to think about Mark Roberts, but after the Cotswold slimmers-group nightmare, he was back and lurking in her head like an evil spirit. *Is it true you stabbed your husband?* the man from the other evening repeated in Bunny's ear as she ate breakfast with Dave, as she folded their laundry, as he made them spaghetti carbonara for dinner, whistling and sloshing extra wine into the sauce. She didn't deserve such a lovely boyfriend, she thought as she listened to his breathing in bed at night, as he rolled over in his sleep and flung a loving arm across her. Oh, Dave. And he was going to find out the truth about her one day – he was certain to – and he would be so, so disappointed. He would look at her in shock, wounded by her betrayal, devastated by her double life.

It would only take one suspicious member of the Cotswold audience to think, *That was a bit weird. I wonder if . . . ?* and then begin hunting about on the Internet, for the walls to start crumbling. She could already imagine the tabloid headlines: *'Slimmer of the Year's Secret Shame.' 'Former Fattie's Hunger for Violence.' 'Slice Vegetables? I'd Rather—'*

All right, calm down. No need to get carried away, she told herself, as her imagination spiralled out of control. It felt as if her luck was trickling through her fingers, though. As if all the skeletons in her cupboard were scrambling to get out and catch up with her, their bones clicking and clacking like castanets. As if Rachel – poor old unhappy Rachel – was resurfacing once more, clawing her way back up into Bunny's nice new life, like it or not.

She didn't want that to happen. She had too much to lose – Dave and their home, his family, their friends, the tender shoots of happiness and hope that she had nurtured so carefully. The feeling that she was in the right place, with the right people, at last. She couldn't let it all slip from her grasp. She mustn't!

Not suitable, the manager at the New Age shop had said all those years ago. Bunny was starting to think she wasn't suitable for anything. She'd failed at marriage. She was failing at being a girlfriend. She was even starting to fail at being slim, because she kept tucking into wine-laced carbonara, when it was one of the most fattening dinners out there. So should she call the whole thing quits, bail out and just leave while the going was good? Or should she risk blowing any future chance of happiness here by revealing herself to Dave – her true, ugly, shameful self – before somebody else did?

Craig had been predictably livid when he heard about Frankie's encounter with Julia in the park, promptly ringing her solicitor and telling her that Julia could stuff her suggestions of mediation somewhere painful. Fergus, in contrast, took a while longer to respond to what had happened.

He was a deep thinker, Fergus, you could practically hear him tussling away with an idea sometimes, the cogs grinding. And, chatty as he was, with all his questions and observations and jokes, there were times when he nursed a worry to himself, when Frankie didn't have a clue what he was thinking. *What a funny lady,* she had exclaimed brightly on the way back from the park, but he hadn't really replied, just held her hand and walked beside her, jumping over cracks in the paving slabs, his blue trainers bright in the sunshine. Had he picked up on the peculiar tension between her and Julia? And what had his little-boy brain made of Julia's extraordinary parting shot – *I'm your real mummy?* Should Frankie raise the subject with him or pretend it had never happened?

It was only later on that evening that she saw any manifest-
ation of his feelings. Craig was bathing Fergus, and Frankie
was putting away clean vests and T-shirts in his drawers,
when she noticed that the teddy Julia had given Fergus had
been fiercely stuffed head-down into the toy-box. 'Oh dear,'
Frankie said as Fergus emerged pyjama-clad from the bathroom a few moments later, hair tousled and damp. 'Teddy's
stuck. Help! I can't get out,' she added in a growly-bear voice
for good measure, lifting one of the bear's legs and waggling
it around.

Fergus laughed, but only pushed harder at the teddy's
rounded bottom, wedging it further into the box. 'He's silly,'
he said scathingly and then flopped face-down onto his bed.
'Who was that lady?' he asked in a muffled voice.

Ah, the big question 'She . . . she's somebody Daddy used
to know,' Frankie replied carefully, smoothing a hand over his
springy wet curls, curls so similar to Julia's it made her heart
ache a little. Then she paused. Was it her place to say anything else here, or should she dodge the bullet and start
discussing which bedtime story they would read tonight
instead? 'Um . . .' she said, uncertainly. 'So anyway . . .'

She had hesitated too long, though. 'I don't like that
lady,' Fergus pronounced, his face still in the bedcovers. 'She
said she was my mummy. But *you* are my mummy!'

Oh, help – here they were, right at the very nub of it,
and she had no idea how to respond. Tell him the truth and

break his world into a hundred confusing pieces? Or fob him off, leave the facts to be tackled another day? Frankie quailed at having been put in such an impossible position. But then again, hadn't she put herself there, the very first time she let Fergus call her 'Mumma'? She thought of Julia's coolly enquiring eyebrow – *He calls you that?* – and took a deep breath.

'Well, you are *definitely* my boy,' she replied, heart thumping. Was this the right thing to say? Or was she making matters worse? 'So I'm pretty sure that makes me your mummy. Hooray!' she cheered, tickling his feet. 'Because I really like being your mummy. ESPECIALLY . . .' she added dramatically, 'when you let me choose the bedtime story.' She lay down next to him, so that her face was beside his, and put on a funny high-pitched voice. 'Oh, please let me choose the story tonight. Please please *please* let me choose the story tonight!'

Fergus started to giggle, because this was one of their running jokes. 'No, no, *no*,' he replied bossily, squirming to get off the bed. 'I am choosing the story. Because it is MY story,' he said, scurrying over to the bookcase. 'And I am choosing . . . THIS one!'

The dinosaur one again. Of course. 'Excellent choice,' Frankie said warmly, as he hopped back onto the bed and snuggled against her. She hugged him close and dropped a kiss on his head. 'My goodness me, I am the luckiest mummy that ever, ever lived,' she said, putting the book on her lap. 'And do you know why?'

'Why?' he asked, sliding his thumb into his mouth.

'Because you are the best boy that ever, ever lived. And actually . . .' She walked her fingers down his plump little pyjamaed thigh, and he giggled again in anticipation. 'You are also . . .' *Walk, walk, walk,* went her fingers. 'The. Most. Ticklish. Boy. Ever-ever-ever!'

And then he was squealing and breathless, and throwing himself around on the duvet – and she was allowing him to get far too worked up, frankly, considering it was nearly his bedtime and she still had the dinosaur book to get through first. She'd pay for it ten minutes later, she knew, when she was trying to get Fergus to sleep and he was still hyper and silly, but right then, his face split open with rich chuckles and yelps, she wanted to live in the moment forever, and never, ever leave.

She and Craig discussed the situation in low voices after Fergus had eventually calmed down and fallen asleep. The whole incident in the playground was starting to feel like a bad dream now, but Frankie's mind kept fixating on Julia's wide, almost manic smile, the threats she'd issued in that friendly-sounding voice, and she felt distinctly uneasy. She wished Craig hadn't been so impulsive about ringing Julia's solicitor and telling her to shove her meeting. Frankie knew already that Julia was not going to be a pushover.

'We've got to take her seriously,' she warned Craig. 'It's not like she'll fade away again into the background, just because we don't want her around. And Fergus is asking me really hard questions – I don't know how to answer him. Maybe . . .' She swallowed, because she'd been dreading this moment. 'Maybe he's old enough to sort of understand that he has two different mummies,' she said miserably. 'Maybe we should just . . . have the talk. Then do our best to reassure him.'

Craig shook his head. 'It's too confusing,' he said, drumming his fingers on the arm of his chair. He'd been in a grunge-band as a teenager and still played percussion on inanimate objects if he was thinking hard. 'And as soon as we tell him about Julia, then we'll have to let her into his life. Trust me, we don't want that to happen.'

'But . . .' Frankie felt conflicted. Just because Craig hated his ex, was it right to keep her completely away from Fergus? Was he acting in good faith for his son, or out of revenge? He had once loved Julia after all. She couldn't be that bad. Could she? 'The thing is, I don't think a court would actually refuse to let her see him, though,' she ventured. 'I mean . . . is that in his best interest?'

'Yes!' he cried. 'Because she is a terrible mother. We have proof – solid proof – that she was crap. The fact that she bailed out on him so early, and has been entirely off his radar ever since. You can't switch parenting on and off like that, out of some kind of whim.'

'I know, but—'

'Why are you taking her side?' Craig's face was accusing. 'You don't *know* her! She's bad news. I've a good mind to put a protection order on her, stop her coming anywhere near him or us.'

Frankie hesitated, doubtful that this would ever be granted. Doubtful that *that* would be in Fergus's best interest, either. Imagine him as a teenager, finding out he had another mother somewhere – his real, biological mother – and then them telling him that they'd legislated against Julia seeing him. It had been strange enough for her, hearing about Harry Mortimer, but at least she'd had the choice of going to find him. Denied this, Fergus might end up hating them. 'You can't stop her from wanting to be in his life,' she said quietly, 'when she gave birth to him. That's not going to happen.'

Craig's eyes were mutinous. 'We'll just see about that,' he replied.

Chapter Fifteen

'Goodness, you're *very* tense,' the woman said, pushing her knuckles into Paula's shoulder blades and grinding them around. 'Try to relax. Let yourself go limp. Deep breath out . . .'

It was late Saturday morning and Paula was lying on a massage table, cocooned in towels and anointed with rosemary-scented oil like a great big pink leg of lamb. A tense leg of lamb. Truth be told, she felt about as relaxed and limp as a tree trunk. She was here for her friend Nicky's birthday treat – girls' day in the spa! – but was finding it impossible to 'let herself go', despite the massaging woman's exhortations.

'And breathe in . . .' Pummel, pummel, grind, grind. It felt as if the woman was digging her elbows into Paula's knotted shoulders. 'And out. All the way out, that's it. Release the pressure. Release the tension.'

I'll give *you* pressure and tension in a minute, if you don't pipe down, Paula felt like saying. She'd been hoping that this forty-five-minute 'Back, Neck and Shoulder Miracle' might be conducted in silence, so that she could at least zone out for a while and stop worrying about her parents, but that now seemed unlikely. Should she pretend to be asleep? Maybe let out a little snore? She gave a deep, long sigh instead, and that seemed to please the massage woman.

'Good. Lovely. There we go,' she said tenderly, swishing her oiled hands up and down Paula's back. 'Much better.'

If only it were that simple, Paula thought to herself, face pressed into the towel-clad hole of the massage table. Because back in the real world, there had still been no word from her mum, other than the hotel's polite messages of rebuff. She and her dad were hoping that Jeanie might be on the return flight from Madeira tomorrow and that they could reconcile their differences, but . . . Well, Paula wasn't going to bet the house on it, put it that way.

Seeing how quickly your parents' marriage could go from apparent fifty-year bliss to hitting the buffers didn't half focus the mind on your own relationship, she found herself thinking worriedly. Could something similar ever happen to her and Matt? Were they strong enough to withstand a stress-test? She loved Matt with all her heart and was fairly sure the feeling was mutual, but with work and teenage sons and day-to-day domestic dramas, she sometimes felt they didn't make time for one another. They took each other for granted and muddled along through the weeks, without stopping to appreciate their marriage on the way. When was the last time they'd gone out on a date, for instance? When was the last time she'd thought to do anything romantic, act spontaneously? A relationship could drift into the sidelines if you didn't pay it enough attention. What if Matt was starting to feel stuck in a too-small world, as Harry had done?

'Now you're tensing up again,' the masseuse scolded her just then. 'Relax. Relax!'

Later on, after the back-pummeller had signalled the end of the session by clapping two tiny prayer bells together with a small ting (what was all *that* about, anyway?), Paula rolled her swimming costume back up and put on her complimentary towelling robe and slippers again, before shuffling out of the dimly lit room to meet her friends for lunch. Paula had been at secondary school with Nicky, as had two of the other friends, Emma and Fliss, and then there were Nicky's two sisters, Amy and Louise, which made them a table of six. They'd all just had treatments and so everyone was a bit slow-moving and dreamy as they sat down to eat.

Perhaps it was the 'Miracle' massage leaving her a bit light-headed, perhaps it was the sneaky glass of wine that Nicky insisted on them all having with their food, or perhaps it was seeing Nicky and her sisters looking so alike, with their spiralling red curls and their identical mannerisms. Something, anyway, prompted Paula to tell them her bombshell family news. 'Guess what: I found out the other week that I've got a sister,' she blurted out during a lull in conversation. 'A half-sister, rather. And none of us even knew she existed, not even my dad.'

That certainly got a reaction from her blissed-out friends, their glazed eyes snapping into focus at once. 'Wow! Bloody hell,' cried Nicky, spluttering on her drink in shock.

'Amazing!' exclaimed Amy, clapping her hands together.

'Oh my God!'

'What happened?'

'Does she live round here?'

To a woman, they were all so thrilled for her, leaning in, twittering excitedly. A new sister! How lovely – tell us everything!

'Well . . .' And then Paula felt slightly shamefaced for making her announcement in the first place, when there wasn't even that much to tell. 'Unfortunately we've sort of lost her again. She turned up at Mum and Dad's party and then vanished, and we don't know how to find her. To be honest, we don't really know anything much about her at all.'

Lost her? Vanished? The drama! The intrigue! Paula found herself blinking at their delight and wonder, their eager stream of questions. It occurred to her that this was the first time anyone had actually expressed a positive opinion about Frankie's existence, rather than it being this dirty little secret, a puncture wound to the Mortimer collective. She started explaining how badly her mum had taken the news, how the family had been rocked by the revelation, and how her dad had hit a brick wall in trying to track her down. Even nosy neighbour Lynne hadn't been able to help.

'Oh my God! This is so exciting. What a mystery! You've got to find her. There must be a way,' Nicky and the others cried out, lunches forgotten.

'Have you got a photo?' asked Emma, who still had towel-marks on her forehead, like a pinprick rash, from where she'd been pressed down into her massage table.

'Yeah, does she look like you?' Amy asked, before rolling her eyes at her so-similar sisters and adding, 'Because that is a curse and a blessing, believe me. Especially if everyone thinks you're, like, the oldest one when you're not.'

'She does look like me,' Paula replied, describing to them how she'd mistakenly thought Frankie was her, in the background of a photograph. 'In fact,' she added, reaching into the pocket of her robe and pulling out her phone, 'I can show you.' She pressed a few buttons. 'Here,' she said, passing it to Nicky.

'Oh, wow!' said Nicky, and then they were all crowding around to see, peering at the tiny lit screen and commenting, Gosh, yes, she *did* look like Paula. And yes, you could *definitely* tell they were sisters. What a surprise! What a bonus!

'I *know*,' Paula said, feeling rather overcome by their enthusiasm and excitement. 'It's so weird! After growing up with three brothers as well.'

'Wait a minute,' said Fliss, peering in for a closer look. Then she frowned. 'I've seen her somewhere before,' she said, forehead crinkling as she stared. She turned the phone slightly so that she could inspect the picture in a better light and nodded thoughtfully. 'Yes. Definitely. Now let me think. Where have I seen her before?'

A gasp went up around the table. 'Seriously?' asked Paula, leaning forward.

'Think, Fliss,' Nicky urged. 'Where have you seen her?'

Still frowning, Fliss shook her head. 'I can't put my finger on it,' she said, frustrated, and they all groaned. 'But I've got a good memory for a face,' she added. 'And I'm telling you: I've seen her. It'll come back to me.'

'I'm just off to meet Dave for a round of golf. I'll be back later, probably sometime this afternoon, unless we stop for a pint,' John said after lunch on Saturday, halfway out of the door.

'Right,' Robyn said tonelessly. Not that he noticed her lack of enthusiasm, or the fact that she hadn't called out to pass on her love to Dave, as she usually would. He was already gone, heaving his golf clubs into the boot of the car as if that was enough to convince anyone, before reversing out of the drive, then speeding away. Here we go again, she thought to herself. Going to play golf with Dave, indeed. Did *Dave* know about this, she wondered? Or would he, like Stephen, unwittingly blow John's cover by turning up at the door later on, his alibi unprepared?

Well, bugger it. If John wanted to sneak around, then so could she. In fact, she'd already started. After the other night, when she'd known full well he had lied about going out with Stephen, Robyn had taken the liberty of installing a tracking app on her phone and had linked it to John's. He had no idea that, any time she wanted, she could open the app and find out where he was. Like now, for instance, when, funnily enough, he didn't appear to be heading in the direction of the golf course at all. In fact, according to the little map on the screen of Robyn's phone, he was travelling in the opposite direction: up Fulford Road towards the city centre.

'Harry, would you mind keeping an eye on the kids for a while? I'm just popping out to the supermarket,' she called through to her father-in-law. *Two can play at this game, John*, she thought, grabbing her car keys. 'Kids, be good for your grandpa, okay? Text me if there are any problems. I won't be long.'

It was actually quite exciting starting up her engine and glancing down at the map to track John's progress. *Follow that car!* Well, okay, so perhaps 'exciting' was the wrong word, she corrected herself. Setting off in pursuit of her lying husband, in the hope of catching him out, was more what you'd call nerve-racking than exciting. Did she really want to know John's secrets?

Not particularly, she conceded, driving grimly out of their cul-de-sac. But she had reached the point where she couldn't *not* know any more. She was so desperate to have her suspicions proved wrong that stalking her husband this way had come to seem acceptable, rather than weird or creepy. Needs must. There would almost certainly be a good reason for John's subterfuge anyway, right? A perfectly normal, plausible reason. And she'd find this out by following him, and could then breathe a sigh of relief, chastise herself for letting her imagination run away with her and go home again. That was the plan. Who knew, they might even end up laughing about this one day!

According to her phone screen, John was still heading towards town. The app had promised discretion – *The one you are watching need never know you can see them!* its description had declared – and it reminded her of playing a spy game as a child, cat-and-mouse. He was parking in the Peel Street car park, she saw and hung back, circling the block a few times, waiting for him to leave again before she went in. *I'm onto you, John. I'm right behind you.*

His marker was now moving more slowly along Piccadilly towards the main shopping area, she saw. Having parked herself, a safe distance from his car, she broke into a jog to keep up with him, trotting over the river and getting caught up in the crowds of Saturday shoppers. John, where are you going? she thought as he cut down side streets and turned corners. Then the marker stopped again, this time on Stonegate. Had he gone into a shop? she wondered, hurrying that way. A café? A pub? Was he buying something nice for her as a surprise? Going for a job interview, even?

Her adrenalin was really racing as she scuttled up the road. She remembered playing 'Hunt the Thimble' at Brownies, where those in the know would call out to let you know how near or far you were from the hidden thimble. *Getting warmer . . . Warmer still . . . Cold again. Freezing! Ah . . . getting warmer again now. Warm. Hot! Really hot! Boiling boiling hot!*

The chant went up in her head as she drew closer and closer. *Warmer. Warmer still!* There was the marker flashing encouragingly on her screen in its same spot. *Hot. Hot!* She was almost there, one building away from him. She could hardly breathe with the anticipation. What was he doing? What was he *doing*?

The next building along was the Plant Café, a trendy vegetarian bistro, full of students and young people usually. Definitely not the sort of place where John 'Meat-and-Two-Veg' Mortimer would normally hang out. Definitely not the sort of place he'd be applying for a job, either. *Boiling boiling hot,* she thought grimly. This was it, the moment of revelation. Did she really want to know after all?

All right, deep breath. She had come this far, she had to at least *look,* she told herself, and edged gingerly towards the café window to peer inside.

Shit, there he was, taking a seat at a table, and she dodged back hurriedly so that he wouldn't see her. Okay, it was all right, he had his back to her, she saw, peeping around again. And there sitting opposite him was . . .

Her heart seemed to seize in panic. A groan of anguish escaped her lips. Oh, why had she come here, why had she looked? When she had known deep down, all along, that this was what she might discover? Of course he wasn't going for a job interview on a Saturday afternoon. Of course he wasn't out buying her surprise presents! 'You absolute shit,' she muttered under her breath, fists clenching by her side.

Because opposite John at the café table was a girl. A young woman, rather. A woman with pale, creamy skin and a long coppery plait and a piercing in her nose. She must have been half John's age, thought Robyn in dismay as the woman laughed at something John said, then leaned across the table to kiss him.

She swung her head away immediately – don't look, don't look – and walked blindly in the other direction, gulping for breath, a shot of adrenalin making her feel like she wanted to throw up; all her worst suspicions confirmed.

What a cliché. What a cheesy, naff old cliché – and yet it still hurt so badly. *Oh, John,* she thought in desolation, her heart shattering into tiny shocked pieces. *Tell me she isn't one of your students. Tell me that isn't why you got sacked!*

She broke into a run back towards the car park, her breath rasping. Playing golf with Dave, he'd said to her, bold as brass, but there he was with another woman, in public, in daylight, for the whole world to see. He'd lied and lied again. What other secrets was he keeping from her?

Chapter Sixteen

To say that Alison felt nervous on Saturday night was like saying the sea was wet. It was the first time in . . . well, months, possibly years actually, that she had been out of the house on a Saturday night for starters with make-up and heels on, rather than camping out in her usual spot on the sofa, telly blaring cosily, snacks at hand. As she approached the Old Bell, she couldn't help feeling a sudden pang as she thought about her Internet group of friends who'd all be watching *Casualty* without her.

Not like Alison to miss a show, they'd think. *Is she ill? Is she okay? Alison, are you there?* they would type in concern.

No, she was not there, she thought, with another flurry of jitters. She was here, out in the real world, and walking into a pub. She was stumbling a bit on the rarely worn high heels, wondering if she had put on too much eye make-up, wondering if she looked too old, too fat, too frumpy. Trying, nonetheless, to appear confident, yet approachable. Fun without being a maniac. Was such a combination even possible?

She had succumbed to the lure of the Silver and Single dating site, giving it a second go after her abortive first attempt. Yes, she had 'put herself out there', as Robyn liked to say, opened her inbox to a whole hoard of would-be suitors and marvelled at what a varied mix of people humanity had to offer. Tonight, she was meeting what appeared to be the pick of the bunch: Calum McRae, aged sixty-seven and a businessman from Leeds, according to his mini-biography.

I'm looking for a fun, confident lady who likes a laugh, his description had read and she'd thought at the time – Yep, that's me. Now, though, she didn't feel as if she fitted the bill when it came to any of those adjectives. She might be fun, confident and full of laughs at work, or in her own home, but out here, in this pub full of strangers, she felt scared and uncertain, as if she had nothing to say for herself any more. What a fraud she was! Coming here under false pretences! Maybe she should turn round and go home. Maybe her instincts for a quiet, simple life had been right all along.

He had sounded nice, though, Calum McRae, even if she suspected he might dye his hair, judging by the photo. At least he hadn't been too prescriptive, like some of the other men on the website, with their ridiculously specific wish-lists of requirements. *I'm looking for a lady aged between 62 and 65, must not be taller than 5' 8", slim (maximum size 12), clean, young-looking, attractive, financially independent, no plastic surgery,* one charmer had written. And to think people said romance was dead, Alison had thought witheringly, scrolling on past at once.

Having reached the bar, she glanced around in anticipation, wondering if she would recognize her date amidst all the other men in here. She and Calum had exchanged a few messages in order to arrange tonight's meeting, providing visual pointers for one another, so that they wouldn't be left stranded. *I'll be wearing a dark-green dress with a purple brooch,* she had written, after some thought. (She hoped that would do. What *did* one wear for one's first date in nearly fifty years anyway?)

Navy shirt and corduroy trousers, he had replied instantly, implying he wasn't having a similar wardrobe panic. Maybe he was just one of those supremely confident people who didn't really care about clothes. (Or maybe he was an old fart who bought his clothes from catalogues. Oh dear.)

It was a cool evening – disappointing for July, everyone had been moaning about it – but even so, she could feel a trickle of sweat between her shoulder blades as she continued to gaze about in search of a man matching that description. No. Nobody there. Was he even going to show up? she wondered in horror. She'd forgotten how terrifying it was, going on a first date, how vulnerable you made yourself. Well, never mind, she thought as she tried to catch the barmaid's eye. She was here now, she would have a drink on her own, if the worst came to the worst.

The bar was busy, with only one person working there and several customers already waiting. For some reason, Alison found herself thinking back to the very first date she'd ever had – a Saturday night at the pictures with Tom Naylor, back when she was sixteen years old – and wanted to blush as she remembered how they had cuddled experimentally in the darkness. (Gosh, yes! Tom Naylor, with his freckles and that cowlick of hair, and those rather adorable jug-ears. Now *he* had been a good kisser.) She bit her lip, wondering if there would be any cuddling tonight – and how she might feel if there were. How quickly was a sixty-something woman sup- posed to move on a date these days anyway?

'Alice! Is that you? Sorry I'm late,' came a booming voice from behind her, and she jumped, miles away, and turned to see a short, red-faced man with his hair every bit as badly coloured and cut as she'd dreaded from his photo, plus a paunch that threatened to send all the buttons of his shirt pinging off like small bullets. Welcome to Silver and Single, she thought, trying not to look dismayed.

'Alison,' she corrected him politely as he leaned in to kiss her cheek. 'And you must be Calum.' Disappointment cur- dled inside her. Calum McRae might well turn out to be the funniest, kindest, best person in the whole world, but on first impressions, she didn't fancy him one bit.

'Correct-a-mundo!' he said with a laugh, putting his elbow on the bar. 'Now, have you been served? What can I get you? It feels like a gin-and-tonic sort of evening to me, what do you say? Like gin, do you?'

'A gin and tonic sounds a great idea,' Alison replied faintly. Oh well. She'd make an effort, she told herself. They would have a drink and a chat, and she'd write the whole thing off as a bad idea from now on. *I tried it, it didn't work out,* she could say to Robyn next time her daughter started nagging her. In the meantime, she hoped nobody would see them here together and jump to any false conclusions. For some reason, she found herself imagining Jeanie Mortimer walking in, with that pitying look on her face. *It must be hard, Alison, when you can't find yourself a very attractive boyfriend.*

'Marvellous! Splendid!' cried Calum, interrupting her thoughts. 'Two gin and tonics here, please. Excuse me. I said, two gin and tonics over here!'

The barmaid, young, with dyed black hair and a raggedy little ponytail (she would suit a nice elfin crop so much better, with those hollow cheekbones, Alison couldn't help thinking), was already serving another customer further down the bar and shot Calum something of a poisonous look. 'Yeah, in a minute,' she said, rolling her eyes in annoyance.

'Young people, eh! Terrible service you get these days. Back when we were young, people took a pride in their work, didn't they, Alice – not to mention a pride in their appearance, as well. What is the world coming to, eh? My granddaughter, Olivia – she's sixteen and the silly girl's only gone and got her belly button pierced. I mean, it's disgusting, if you ask me. It's just not right. Nobody wants to see that, I tell her, but she doesn't listen. Have you got grandchildren yourself, Alice?'

'It's Alison,' said Alison again. 'And yes, I have. A girl and a boy.'

'Splendid! They keep us young, don't they? I've got six of the little scamps – my wife and I had three children and they've all cracked on with the parenting. My word, takes you back, doesn't it, all those milestones . . . walking and talking and first teeth, and what have you. Although Olivia, the eldest – her with the pierced belly button, this is – she's just done her – what do you call them – not O-levels these days, is it? My memory, honestly, I don't know what my name is half the time, I—'

'GCSEs?' Alison proffered helpfully, then smiled as the truculent barmaid appeared in front of them. 'Oh, hi. We'd like—'

'We'd like two gin and tonics, please, my good lady,' Calum said over her. 'Ice and a slice, that would be nice. Ha! GCSEs, that's the chap. Yes, so she's just taken those and . . .' He frowned, suddenly looking blank. 'What was I talking about?'

'I'm not quite sure,' Alison replied. 'Quite a few things all at once.'

'Was I? That sounds about right. My Nessie – Vanessa, my wife, God rest her soul – she used to say to me, *One topic at a time, Calum. I feel like I'm talking to six different people when I have a conversation with you!*' He gave a sheepish shrug, then produced a wallet from his pocket as the barmaid dumped their drinks on the bar and muttered a price. So he was a widower, Alison registered, wondering if he had actually talked his wife to death.

'Allow me. My treat! The first of many!' Calum cried exuberantly to Alison, fishing in his wallet and paying for the drinks. 'Now then. Shall we find a pew? Perch our derrières? Throw ourselves into conversational shenanigans?'

He was nervous, too, Alison realized as he blathered on and on, weaving through the pub tables until he found what he declared to be the perfect spot. And, daft as it may sound, recognizing his nerves gave her a boost of confidence in turn. After all, she was a hairdresser – she was an expert at putting people at their ease. 'Tell me about yourself,' she said gently as they sat down and the first silence of the evening threatened to announce itself. 'Do you work?'

'Still got the business ticking along, yes indeed,' he replied. 'It's a tweed mill, been in the family for generations. Although I've taken a bit of time off recently, handed on some responsibility to my son, after . . .' He broke off abruptly and licked his lips, a haunted expression flitting across his face. 'Well, my Nessie died and I've . . .' He swallowed hard.

Oh dear, thought Alison. He wasn't about to cry, was he? She felt bad now for her rather mean thought moments earlier.

'I've . . .' He took out a handkerchief and blew his nose. His eyes were suspiciously moist. 'Excuse me. I'm not really . . .' He was still wearing his wedding ring, she noticed. Was he even ready to start dating again? 'I'm not really coping very well,' he admitted eventually.

'Oh, Calum,' she said sympathetically, noticing how his jaw had clenched in an effort to control himself. 'I'm sorry. It's very hard, isn't it, when—'

'She was everything to me,' he said hoarsely, gripping his handkerchief, eyes bulging as he battled valorously with emotion. 'Everything, Alice.'

Alison patted his hand, not bothering to correct him again. 'How long ago did it happen?' she enquired kindly. 'If you don't mind me asking.'

'Two months,' he said, and she could see him reliving the pain, poor thing. The devastation at having been left behind, alone. With colossal effort, he brought himself back to the present and cleared his throat. 'I'll be straight with you, Alice, I just feel so damned lonely. I miss her so much. And I thought maybe going out with another lady might give me a bit of a lift, but . . .' He hung his head. 'Well. No offence to you, darling, you're very nice, but . . . but the thing is, you're not her.'

'No,' Alison agreed. 'I'm not.' She remembered how raw she had felt after Rich had died; she had been like an open wound. Two months in, she'd been barely functioning, let alone attempting to go on dates with other people.

'And maybe I just want her, still.'

'Yes. I think you probably do.' Alison sipped her drink, feeling a wave of what felt absurdly like relief. He wasn't interested in her. Which was fine, because she wasn't interested in him, either. Panic over, she thought. This date's going nowhere. With a bit of luck, she might even be back home in time to watch the last twenty minutes of *Casualty*.

Meanwhile, over in Madeira, Jeanie was having a very different sort of Saturday night. She had spent the day on an excursion to Funchal, admiring the old cobbled streets as well as the Botanic Gardens and the Cathedral. She'd made some new friends on the trip – Patsy and Kate, who were both divorced Lancastrians and 'on the market', as Patsy put it, waggling an eyebrow. Now the three of them had met for pre-dinner cocktails at the hotel, all clad in their finery. It was a beautiful evening, as ever – the air warm and perfumed from the yellow angel's trumpet flowers nearby, and Jeanie was wearing the new dangly earrings she'd bought herself in Funchal, as well her bright-pink dress. She was tanned, and feeling in good shape from all the swimming she'd been doing, and had just about stopped being startled whenever she caught a glimpse of her own reflection. The hotel stylist had given her a choppy, flicky new do, with some bright silvery highlights, which seemed to lift her whole face.

Maybe it was a combination of all these things that made Jeanie wave flirtatiously to Luis, the handsome waiter, when he walked by them that evening. 'Come and join us. Have a drink on us!' she called out.

'Ooh, she likes the young ones,' Patsy teased to Kate.

'Wouldn't kick him out of bed for eating biscuits,' Kate replied approvingly. 'Hello, darling, what's your name?' she called out as Luis approached their table.

He made a mock bow before them. 'Ladies, I am at your service,' he said, his dark eyes twinkling as his gaze turned from one woman to the next. He really was gorgeous, Jeanie thought, smiling goofily back at him. He really, really was.

'Luis, these are my friends, Patsy and Kate,' she said. 'And we would love to have your company this evening. Can we buy you a drink?'

'Truly, I am honoured,' he said, in that sexy broken English of his. Then he looked sorrowful. 'But I am on duty. No drinks for me, I'm afraid. Not yet, anyway.'

'Not *yet*?' Patsy repeated, arching an eyebrow. 'I think that means he might be up for one later, girls. What time do you clock off, love?'

'Not until eleven,' he said, looking at his watch and letting out a sigh – ahh! – that there was still so much of the evening left before then. He leaned forward to collect their empty glasses and Jeanie caught a whiff of his aftershave, pungent and spicy and manly. Gosh, he smelled good, she thought.

'Can I get you ladies anything else?' he asked, their glasses all gathered in.

'Well, not right now, but maybe later,' Jeanie heard herself say daringly. Showing off to impress her new friends, her sister Barbara would comment, no doubt in tones of disdain. She leaned forward, trying to give him her best sultry look. 'Maybe I'll see you back here at eleven.'

He smiled and she saw a dimple flash in his cheek. She was only having a bit of fun, obviously, only kidding around, because he was far too young for her, and a million times too good-looking to boot. But then he raised an eyebrow in a suggestive sort of way. 'Eleven o'clock it is,' he agreed.

They all watched his bum as he walked away, then the three women collapsed in giggles. 'Jeanie, you little devil,' Patsy gurgled. 'And there was me, thinking you were a nice well-brought-up sort of girl, too!'

'Are you really going to meet him?' Kate asked. 'Are you,

217

Jeanie? Look at her, Pats, she's totally going to. And good for you, kid! Good for you! Why not have a bit of fun on your holiday, eh?'

'What happens on holiday stays on holiday,' Patsy said, tapping her nose and winking. 'Am I right, or am I right?'

Jeanie had never been unfaithful in her life and was already starting to feel a bit uncertain about the whole idea. She'd only meant to have a drink with the man, but these two were carrying on as if she was about to throw caution to the winds and . . . well, throw her clothes to the winds as well. 'It's just a *drink*,' she cried indignantly, which only made them laugh even more.

'Yeah, we know. Course it is. A "drink",' said Kate meaningfully, making inverted commas with her fingers. 'We all love a good old "drink" now and then, don't we?'

'Ooh, yes. A long, slow "drink" with a sexy young man, you can't beat it,' sniggered Patsy.

'Honestly,' Jeanie spluttered. 'You two! Come on, let's go and have dinner. See if we can find a couple of nice chaps for you, while we're at it.'

Nothing's going to happen, she told herself as they wandered towards the restaurant, still laughing. Of *course* nothing would happen. It was ridiculous to even *think* so. She was a wife and mother – she was a *grandma*, for heaven's sake!

But even as these words were going through her head, she was aware of a new, light-hearted girlishness that ran in parallel with them. A wild sort of naughtiness, which had bubbled up, seemingly out of nowhere. She was miles from home, on a beautiful island; it was a warm summer's evening and there was just this sense of opportunity floating on the breeze, there for the taking. If she wanted it. *What happens on holiday stays on holiday,* Patsy had said. And if anything *did* happen . . . well, nobody needed to know, did they?

'Hello, yes, my name is Harry Mortimer. I believe my wife, Jeanie Mortimer, has been staying with you for the last two weeks. That's right. I'm just ringing to see . . . Well, to see if she's checked out today, basically. In case she'd like a lift back from the airport later on.'

It was Sunday morning and Harry had come over to Paula's house, where he was telephoning the hotel in Madeira. Too agitated to sit down, he was pacing around her kitchen, frowning as he listened to the response, a forgotten cup of coffee cooling on the table.

'She didn't come down to breakfast this morning? Does that mean she's already left?' He gazed over hopefully at Paula with the air of a man who could practically smell the return of normal life once more. Paula knew that her dad – having just spent a week with Dave, then a week with John – was itching to get back to his usual routine, with Jeanie there by his side. He was a creature of habit, he liked to have everything in its rightful place. Including his wife.

'Ahh. She hasn't checked out.' His face fell. 'What time would she have had to . . . ? Ten o'clock.' They both glanced at the clock on the wall, which said quite plainly that it was quarter to eleven. Paula sighed, knowing that there was no time difference between the two places, and felt her hopes slide away like an outgoing tide. It was now a whole fortnight since her mother had jetted off in an almighty huff and they still had heard barely a word from her. If she hadn't checked out yet, then the chances of her being on the return flight today did not look promising.

'Rightio,' said Harry heavily. 'I see. Thank you. If you could just tell her that Harry called again, then. Yes, she knows the number. Goodbye.'

'Oh, Dad,' said Paula, feeling helpless as he hung up. 'I don't know what to say. Maybe she's just overslept or . . .'

'Nope,' he said. You could see the hurt in his eyes, the disappointment crashing through him as he gave a despondent sigh and sank into a chair. 'The man said she hasn't even booked a return flight. You know how stubborn your mother is. She could sit this one out for weeks yet, mark my words.'

Paula had a horrible feeling he was right, but did her best to reassure him. 'She'll come back,' she said weakly. 'She has to! Being stubborn is one thing, but there comes a point when she has to face up to real life and get on that plane home.' She hoped so anyway. Her mum's wall of silence was beginning to feel like the Cold War. What was going on in her head?

'I don't know what she thinks she's proving, other than that she knows how to prolong a sulk,' Harry went on. 'And for what? I said sorry, it's not as if I can change the past and make Frankie disappear.' He gazed glumly out of the window. 'Not that I've heard from *her* again, either, before you ask. What a mess, honestly. What a sorry mess.'

Oscar, Paula's dachshund, seemed to detect the unhappiness in Harry's voice and trotted over to him to offer some supportive hand-licking. Paula watched her dad make a fuss of him, knowing how much he missed having a dog of his own. He and Jeanie had always had springer spaniels – bouncy, exuberant and loving – but when their last one, Charlie, had died just after Christmas, they'd taken the hard decision not to have another dog, what with Harry's bad back and Jeanie's bouts of sciatica, and the pair of them being that bit more tired in general these days.

Paula sat down beside him, trying to put herself in her mum's shoes, doing her best to imagine how she must be feeling by now, out in her self-imposed Madeiran exile. If this had been Paula and Matt, how would she have liked things to be resolved? With a big, romantic face-saving gesture at the very least, she realized. 'I think you're going to have to go out there, you know, Dad,' she said after a moment. 'Try and put this right together, face-to-face. Mum's upset, she's angry – and you know what she's like, she's proud, too. Perhaps too proud to come home without knowing what she's flying back to.' She patted his arm, feeling sorry for him. 'Shall I fetch the laptop so that we can have a look at flights out? See when you might be able to go?'

He nodded, looking resigned. 'I suppose so,' he agreed. 'If it means she'll come home, then yes. Let's give it a whirl. In the meantime . . .' He scratched his head and pulled a rueful face. 'I reckon John and Robyn have had their fill of me by now. Don't suppose you could put your old man up for a few nights, could you?'

Chapter Seventeen

It was two o'clock on Monday afternoon, the lunchtime rush was over and Bunny had nipped out to get some fresh air, in the hope that it would clear her head. Since the disaster that had been her Gloucestershire SlimmerYou talk, she had felt as if her composure was crumbling on a daily basis. Vivid memories of the man shouting at her would surface without warning when she was trying to serve a customer, leaving her distracted and forgetful, muddling up people's orders or accidentally overcharging them. 'Everything all right?' her boss Jasmine had asked, overhearing one customer complaining that she'd been given the wrong food, and then another that she'd been given the wrong change. Bunny had blushed scarlet and apologized in a fluster, but knew she'd have to pull her socks up if she wanted to avoid her manager's bad books.

Outside now, she marched past a tempting-looking bakery, deliberately not looking at the flaky sausage rolls in the window, or the traybakes and cream cakes. Since losing all the weight, she had developed a strategy towards food like that: she visualized a massive block of lard, and then imagined the sausage roll or cake or brownie tasting of the lard. It worked well enough to keep her walking on, most of the time, and today she headed resolutely instead towards Museum Gardens, clutching the takeaway salad that staff were allowed to have free for their lunch.

Museum Gardens was her favourite spot to take a break, with its riverside setting, medieval abbey ruins and flower-filled borders. Today, though, her phone started ringing before she had arrived there, and she stopped to answer it in the street. The caller was Margaret from SlimmerYou, according to the screen, and Bunny steeled herself in readiness. After Gloucestershire, she had vowed she wouldn't take on any more promotional work, but Margaret would wheedle and beg, she knew. Bunny would have to be firm this time, stick to her guns. 'Margaret, hi,' she said. 'How are you?'

'Well, to be honest, I'm a little bit concerned,' Margaret said without so much as a 'hello'. 'It sounds as if there was something of a to-do at your talk last week. I hope you're all right.'

Ah. So word had got back to head office. This put a different spin on things. Bunny swallowed, wondering if she could speak honestly to Margaret. She'd only met her once before – a commanding sort of person in her fifties – but she'd liked the other woman's crisp, practical manner. 'I'm fine,' she replied after a moment. 'Absolutely fine.'

'It did sound rather unpleasant,' Margaret went on. 'Is there anything you need to tell me?'

'Um . . .' Bunny hesitated. Sometimes when you kept a secret to yourself – a bad secret – it swelled up bigger and nastier, the longer you remained silent. Obviously she hadn't been able to tell Dave what had happened at the Cotswold village hall the other week, because that would have meant unrolling the full awful story for him. But maybe Margaret, another woman, would understand, if Bunny explained. 'The thing is . . .' she began, and then out it came. 'I was in an abusive relationship,' she said in a tiny voice, edging around the side of the shop into an alley so that nobody would hear her. 'And one day he was beating me. Quite badly. I thought I might die. And so I . . . I de-fended myself.'

'You stabbed him, is that right?' Margaret had always been very businesslike, but the brisk, matter-of-fact manner in which she asked the question quite took Bunny's breath away.

'Well . . . yes,' she replied after a moment. 'In self-defence. And I—'

'I see,' Margaret said. Clearly, for her to have asked the question in the first place, she'd already known that this was the answer, but she sounded horribly disapproving, as if her worst fears about Bunny had just been confirmed. 'And this man in the audience last week recognized you, and brought it to the attention of the entire gathering, I hear. One hundred and fifty-two people, might I add, according to Sally, the organizer.'

'Yes,' Bunny said humbly, wrapping her arms around herself. She was leaning against the brick wall of the building and could smell the ripe pong of a nearby dumpster. The air was muggy and fetid, but she was shivering all of a sudden.

'Right. Well, forgive me for stating the obvious, but this is not the sort of negative publicity we want associated with our brand, frankly,' said Margaret. She sounded positively cold now. Angry with Bunny. 'You should have told us these . . . these circumstances at the time of winning, because of this very eventuality. As it is, I'm afraid SlimmerYou no longer wants you to represent the company in further talks, or promotions of any kind. Our contract with you is hereby terminated, with immediate effect.'

Bunny let out a gulp. 'But, Margaret, I—'

'I'm sorry, but that's just how it is,' came the reply. 'It's a shame we have to part on these terms, but my job is to protect our brand. Let me know if you have any outstanding expenses to put through, otherwise . . . Well, otherwise this is goodbye.'

Bunny wanted to shout, to punch the wall behind her as

the call ended. This was so unfair! It wasn't so much the fact that Margaret had stopped her from doing any more talks – she didn't *want* to do any more stupid talks; she was done with the wretched talks! – it was that the other woman had taken her ex-boyfriend's side, just like the Gloucestershire press had, and – let's face it – even her own family, who'd made very little effort to see Bunny while she'd been in York. Margaret might be from an older generation and not exactly touchy-feely, but she'd left Bunny feeling as if she was the one to blame for what had happened.

Tears burned in her eyes at the injustice of it all. What, so she should have let Mark beat her to death on the kitchen floor, should she? She wasn't supposed to fight back and protect herself? Because some people definitely seemed to think that way. Her purse-lipped sister-in-law, who had banned her from seeing Chloe, her own niece, for one. And now Margaret, punishing Bunny by turfing her out of their slimming promotions, terrified of her diet programme becoming tainted by association. So much for understanding. So much for sisterhood!

Swallowing back a sob, Bunny tried to control her emotions, remembering that she needed to be back at work in half an hour, and that her customers did not want to see a blotchy face and red eyes when being served. But the strength had gone out of her, the willpower too, and so it was that she found herself trudging back towards the bakery, as if it was drawing her magnetically closer and she was powerless to resist. And yes, then she was buying a warm sausage roll and an oozy square of millionaire's shortbread for her lunch, just like Rachel used to do after a bad day, when she too had felt low and weakened. Who cared about calories? What was the point of trying to stay in shape when your past was tapping on your shoulder, catching you up?

Once back in the small staffroom above the café, she tucked into her diet-busting lunch, doing her best to savour each mouthful rather than shovel it down, like she wanted to. Bloody hell, it all tasted amazing. Bakery treats made her feel a million times better than a box of quinoa and grated carrot – just like the family-sized slabs of Dairy Milk and the huge cheesy pizzas always had done in the past. The very realization of this was enough to stop her short, though, and then her eyes jerked wide open again.

Was this another sign that her new life was slipping away from her? The dwindling willpower. The longing for something tasty, just to help her through the day. It was all horribly familiar. She mustn't let herself get drawn into that downward spiral again, she thought, brushing pastry flakes from her skirt and scrunching up the empty paper bag. She mustn't. Because she was stronger than that now, wasn't she?

'Bunny? Are you there? We're getting busy again downstairs,' came the voice of Jasmine just then.

'Coming,' called Bunny, throwing the crumpled bag into the bin. No more bakery binges, she told herself sternly. No more weeping in public. Rachel was gone – and good riddance to her. Bunny was absolutely not about to let her back.

Chapter Eighteen

Meanwhile, in Madeira, Jeanie was keeping a low profile. It was Monday evening now, almost forty-eight hours since the incident with Luis and she had barely left her bed in all that time. She wasn't sure she ever wanted to face the world again, in fact. Because boy, oh boy, had she made a fool of herself. A right royal fool.

In hindsight, she shouldn't have had that last cocktail on Saturday night. Or all that fizzy wine with dinner, or the round of Madeiran liqueurs afterwards. She'd been so jubilant at the prospect of staying on holiday for another week, though – maybe even longer! – that she just hadn't been able to say no. After dinner they'd ended up in the Hollywood bar, where the pianist played jazzy versions of show tunes, and she'd polished off another cocktail, urged on by Patsy and Kate. It was something sickly and lurid, with bobbing segments of orange and a glacé cherry, and it had tipped her from being drunk to . . . well, to being completely blotto, unfortunately. Uninhibited. Out of control.

She had a dim recollection of plonking herself down at the piano, when the resident pianist took a break, and calling 'Any requests?', before playing a stumbling rendition of 'Copacabana'. Possibly even some Neil Diamond as well. It was all rather hazy now, but she had the distinct feeling she might have been singing along, just to put the icing on the cake.

Oh, Jeanie, she had been saying to herself ever since, in the manner of a very disappointed great-aunt. *What were you* thinking?

She was thinking that she was young – that was what. She was thinking that she was young and free and naughty, that she was having the time of her life. There she was, far from Harry (the liar! the cheater! the betrayer!), far from her children and her neighbours and her friends. Miles and miles, in fact, from anyone who might judge her or give her a look, or put the brakes on her behaviour in any way.

Having slid from the piano stool at the pianist's return, she was laughing and bowing to nobody in particular just as Luis appeared, and any last shred of caution had been well and truly left behind. 'Here he is! Here's my handsome darling,' she called, hurrying back to her friends' table and patting the seat next to her coquettishly. 'Get that gorgeous little bottom over here immediately.' (It went without saying that remembering this made her want to curl up in a foetal position under the bedcovers and not emerge for several hundred years, if ever.)

Luis, of course, had been his usual charming self. 'But how can I refuse?' he had replied, sitting down. 'I am the lucky one today, yes?'

'Oh yes,' Jeanie said, sliding one hand daringly onto his thigh. (Cringe.) 'Your luck is well and truly in tonight, sweetheart.' (Double cringe.) She plucked the glacé cherry from her glass and held it teasingly in mid-air. 'Would you like to pop my cherry?' she'd giggled, before taking it in her teeth and offering her mouth to his. (Death by cringing.)

'Jeanie, you're such a legend!' Patsy whooped as Luis moved in towards her, his teeth carefully biting half of the cherry, his lips brushing against Jeanie's. My God, he smelled amazing. It took every ounce of Jeanie's restraint not to clamp her hands around his face so that he had to stay there, mouth pressed to hers even longer.

'Wooo! Get a room!' Kate sniggered, applauding as Luis broke free with a grin, having bitten suggestively through the cherry.

'Delicious,' he declared, licking his lips to the women's cheers.

The next slice of time was even more shadowy in Jeanie's memory. Patsy and Kate must have disappeared off to bed at some point – she couldn't remember this happening – but then she and Luis were left alone. Jeanie had never seduced a man before, not even Harry. She had always felt too prim and respectable for that sort of thing, and Harry's striped Marks and Spencer pyjamas were not exactly the signal for sparks of passion.

But that night, she felt different. She felt womanly; attractive and self-confident, with her new hairdo and her bright clothes and all the make-up she'd put on at the start of the evening. This was the new daring Jeanie, who said yes to everything, rather than *I probably shouldn't*. And it was this Jeanie who took Luis by the hand and said, 'Would you like to come up to my room for a nightcap?'

Looking back, she wasn't sure that Luis's English was good enough for him to even know what a nightcap *was*, but he certainly understood the subtext. 'If you are sure?' he queried doubtfully, ever the gentleman, before she'd said, 'Oh, I'm sure' and rose, swayingly, to her feet.

Oh, Jeanie. Jeanie, Jeanie, Jeanie. She barely remembered getting up to her room – had she lunged at him in the lift, tried to kiss him? – but somehow or other they had arrived on the seventh floor and she'd fumbled her door open, so that they were in her bedroom. The bed had been made up, as usual, by the chambermaids, and the curtains pulled shut against the night. 'So here we are,' Jeanie said, trying to act seductive as she sank down onto the bed. Again she patted the space beside her. 'Luis?'

He sat down and she took his hand. 'You are a very

handsome man,' she slurred. 'Much more handsome than Harry.' Damn it, she shouldn't have mentioned Harry. Why was she even thinking about Harry, when this was her big, wild moment?

'And you are also very beautiful,' he replied, smiling into her eyes. 'Although perhaps I should go now. It is late and . . .'

'Oh, come on,' she demurred, not wanting him to leave. 'I'm probably not your usual type of girl, but . . .' She stopped suddenly, aware of a churning inside her stomach. A bilious feeling, a rising nausea. Oh Lord, she thought. Oh *no*. 'I'm sorry, would you excuse me a moment,' she garbled, lurching from the bed and into the small spotless bathroom. She barely had time to close the door before she was retching and then throwing up over the toilet bowl, as back came all of her dinner and every last one of those cocktails. Even the bitten cherry pieces were there, bobbing in the slurry of sick.

Another wave of vomit erupted, so intense she could feel her eyes bulging in their sockets. Ugh, she thought deliriously, panting and resting her face on the toilet seat. Then came quite a lot of dry-retching until her throat ached. Her head was spinning, but her stomach seemed to have gone quiet at least. Better out than in, she heard her own mother's voice in her head, and she spat weakly into the bowl, feeling herself on the verge of tears, shivery and weak.

Mopping her mouth with toilet roll, she flushed away the foul-smelling evidence and rose shakily to her feet once more, clutching the side of the washbasin and staring blearily into the mirror. Dismay hit her like a brick in the face. Look at the state of her. Just look at that woman with the smudged glittery eyeshadow, with the silly choppy haircut that, let's face it, did not really suit her. As for the lurid pink dress, falling off one shoulder so wantonly, exposing her wrinkled old shoulder, why hadn't she noticed before how tacky it was? Mutton dressed as lamb, that was her.

A tear rolled down her cheek, taking a snaking black line of mascara with it. 'You stupid old woman,' she said to herself, and then had to turn her head away because she simply couldn't bear to look at her own pathetic reflection any more.

There was a gentle knock at the door. 'Jeanie. Are you all right?'

Had he heard her being sick? Probably. Her breath must stink. She sluiced water around her mouth, trembling with embarrassment. 'Sorry,' she mumbled eventually. 'I . . . I'm not feeling very well.'

A lightweight, that was what her boys had teased each other about being, when they were teenagers and one of them had too much to drink. It had been a running joke: which of them would throw up each Friday and Saturday night; John had even started a Chunder Chart at one point.

What would they say now, those lads of hers, if they could see their own mother like this, drunk and dishevelled, desperately trying to get the taste of vomit out of her mouth, a young barman waiting for her on the hotel bed? They would be horrified. Embarrassed of her. *God, Mum,* she imagined John saying, *what are you playing at?*

'Can I help?' Luis asked tentatively through the door. 'Or would you like me to go?'

Trying not to sob out loud, Jeanie shut her eyes, but the room was spinning and she had to jerk them open again before the nausea returned. 'I think you'd better go,' she said faintly. 'I'm so sorry. I'm really, really sorry.'

She was saying the words to Harry as well, of course, not that he could hear her. Not that he had any idea what his dreadful wife had been getting up to behind his back, either, thank goodness. She sank to the floor and sat there on the cold ceramic tiles, leaning against the bathtub until she heard Luis saying goodbye and that he hoped she felt better in the morning.

Then, when she was quite sure he had gone, she crawled through into the bedroom, clambered up onto the bed and fell asleep.

If she had felt bad the night before, then to wake the next morning, cold, hungover and tortured by fragments of memory replaying how badly she had behaved . . . well, that was a whole new level of awful. That was down there at the bottom of the dustbin, with all the potato peelings and stinking fish packets and bin juice.

Her mouth was dry and foul-tasting. Her head thumped abominably. Both her throat and her stomach hurt from all the retching. Worse than the physical complaints, though, was the feeling of hot and terrible shame that pressed down on her like a rock. She had brought Luis up here to her bedroom, meaning to seduce him, throwing herself at him like a randy old goat. And instead of being sophisticated and cosmopolitan, she had made a complete and utter show of herself. He had probably told all the other bar staff, and they'd no doubt had a good old laugh at her expense. Sad British granny, can't handle her drink, thinks she's a cougar – yeah, right!

And if she hadn't thrown up at that moment . . . if she hadn't pulled the plug on their prospective night of passion – what then? Would she really have gone through with it, really have slept with a man young enough to be her grandson?

Yes. She was pretty sure that the answer to that last question was Yes. After coming out to Madeira in a fury as well, having discovered that Harry had been similarly unfaithful all those years ago. So who was the better person now? Despite his carrying-on, despite this new daughter of his that Jeanie had been devastated by, she could not imagine Harry getting spectacularly drunk and enticing a twenty-something-year-old barmaid up to a hotel bedroom. A funereal dirge played in her head as she thought about what a hypocrite that made her.

A tear rolled down her cheek. She wanted to be at home right now, apron on, making a fish pie for dinner, Harry's favourite. She wanted to be deadheading the roses in her garden and ordering bulb catalogues for the autumn. Baking cakes with her grandchildren, listening to their funny stories and letting them lick the spoon when they thought she wasn't looking. She wanted to be out for a day-trip to Scarborough with Harry, holding hands along the prom. Chatting on the phone to Paula or one of her boys. She missed them all so desperately. Why had she ever thought that staying here on her own for so long was a good idea?

Sunday passed very quietly. She lurked in her room all day, ordering room service and avoiding the rest of the world. She couldn't bear the thought of the knowing looks she'd get, not just from the hotel staff, but from the other guests who had seen her in the restaurant and bar last night, playing 'Copacabana' at the piano – 'Join in with the chorus, everyone!'

Even now, on Monday, she wasn't sure she was ready to face life outside her own four walls again. How was she going to live down her Saturday-night antics? But equally, how could she go home and look her family in the eye?

★

'Paula? It's Fliss. Listen, I can't chat long because Rory's still potty-training and if I take my eye off him for, like, more than two minutes there could be a terrible poo incident at any moment. But, anyway, I was just ringing to say: I remembered.'

'You remembered?' Paula repeated uncertainly. She was in the middle of a house-viewing and held up an apologetic finger to the prospective vendor, before edging tactfully to the side of the spotless designer kitchen. (She loved this house already. She wanted, very much, to be able to sell this house with its generous garden and its gorgeous Victorian quirks, because a) she knew she could do it justice; and b) the commission alone would be enough to pay for a family skiing holiday at Christmas.) 'What did you remember?' she asked in a low voice.

'Where I saw that woman,' said Fliss excitedly. 'Your half-sister. It was in this article in the paper – the *Guardian*, I think. Big piece in the Saturday magazine a few months ago. I'm sure it was her. Rory!' she suddenly exclaimed, sounding panicked. 'I've got to go.'

'Okay, email me a link,' Paula said, just as the line went dead. Bugger! Then, for the benefit of the vendor who might be eavesdropping, she said into the phone, 'And they want to make an offer of one-point-two? Right, well, let's see if we can push them up to one-point-four. That house deserves the best price. I know we can get it.' Stuffing the phone back in her bag, she wheeled around with a bright smile. 'I'm sorry! Now where we? Did you say that these units are Shaker? They're so gorgeous, I love what you've done in here. And will you be taking these fab pendant lights when you move out, or would they come as part of the fixtures and fittings? Right you are. Let me make some notes.'

Ladling on the charm and schmoozing a potential customer had never been a problem for Paula, especially when she was in a beautiful property like this one. She had her technique down pat: gratify the owner by noticing the tiny personal touches about a place, lavish on the compliments at all opportunities, and spot potential in any under-used areas. But beneath the smile, positivity and charm offensive, her mind was working like the clappers now, replaying what Fliss had just said to her. Frankie had been in the *Guardian*? Was her half-sister famous or something? This was too intriguing for words!

It wasn't until Paula was back in her car, some forty minutes later, having enjoyed a thorough look around the property, followed by her full sales pitch and suggestion of a price, that she was able to check her phone once more. And there in her inbox, as requested, was a link that Fliss had found to the article, which had appeared last year. 'When Work Means It's Love-All' was the headline, and it featured three different stories about couples who'd met at the work-place. Including Frankie!

Paula let out a squeal and zoomed in on the picture of Frankie snuggling up to a smiling man who seemed vaguely familiar himself. Then the penny dropped. No! Was it really him? Yes! It *was* him – Craig Jacobs, the guy who wrote the 'Dad About the House' column!

'Oh my *God*,' Paula exclaimed aloud, poring over the text. And Frankie was his partner as well as being the illus-trator, it turned out. Wow – Paula loved that column! She read it every Sunday! And she loved the artwork, too: witty and bright and eye-catching. So Frankie did that? Amazing! Her sister was an artist!

Paula suddenly remembered that she was still sitting in her potential client's driveway, and quickly started the engine to make her departure. What a stroke of luck, though, she thought, speeding down the road in jubilation. And actually, she realized, having read Craig's column over the years, she already knew all sorts of things about Frankie's life. They had a little boy, didn't they? A really cute-sounding boy, who'd overcome some gruelling oper-ations and health problems; that was right. They lived in London, she seemed to remember, and had an idyllic work set-up together over the kitchen table, or something equally romantic, where they conjured up their delightfully charm-ing words and pictures each week.

241

Oh my goodness. This was so exciting! And Paula was *related* to her – how weird was that? Who would have thought? Now she just had to hope that Frankie was still interested in getting to know the Yorkshire side of her family. Because now that Paula had a means of getting in touch, she was most definitely going to use it.

Chapter Nineteen

'Tea?'

'Lovely,' said Robyn, sitting on Beth Broadwood's elegant grey sofa with her hands in her lap. It was Tuesday afternoon and she had succumbed to her own desperate curiosity. *Can we talk?* she had texted Beth, finding her number on a list of PTA members' contact details that one mum had helpfully pulled together some time ago. What the hell, Robyn had thought grimly. This was sure to be humiliating, but she was already way past the point of trying to avoid losing face. Besides, before she set about confronting her husband, she needed to have the facts. She needed to know just how angry with him she should be.

Sitting in a dusty-pink button-back armchair, Beth leaned forward to pour the tea. There were framed photos all around the room of her beautiful daughters with their neat plaits and wide smiles, and a large black-and-white print of Beth's wedding, where the bride and groom gazed into each other's eyes with complete adoration. Beth seemed to have the perfect life, Robyn thought miserably, unable to help comparing it to the current mess of her own.

'So,' said Beth pleasantly, passing her a cup and saucer. 'How are things?'

Robyn stirred her tea, fingers trembling on the spoon. Here we go. 'Things,' she replied in a rather strangled voice, 'have been better.' She attempted a smile, but it probably looked more like a grimace. Deep breath. Get it out. 'Listen, Beth, I hope you don't mind, but I've got something I need to ask you. I'm just going to get straight to the point. What do you know about John getting sacked from the university?'

Beth blanched at the direct question. 'Well . . .' she began carefully, pausing for just a fraction too long.

'It's all right, you can tell me,' Robyn assured her. 'I know it's something terrible. I know there's this woman he's been seeing on the sly. A very young woman, by the looks of things, too, maybe even a student. But I don't know the details.' She gritted her teeth, cringing to find herself in this predicament. She and Beth had once run a stall at the school Christmas fair together, and they'd exchanged chit-chat at university social events or in the school playground, but that had been their limit. Until now. 'I feel really embarrassed to be asking you, and I'm sorry if this makes you feel awkward or . . . or on the spot,' she went on. 'But John's been . . .' She swallowed, lowering her gaze. 'He's been lying to me about this, all along, and I just want to hear the truth now. How-ever awful it may be.'

Beth nodded gravely. She was a tall, rather horsey woman with a mid-length brown bob, pinned back with a clip. The sort who had been head girl once upon a time, no doubt, form captain, sports prefect. Maybe all of those things. But at least she was kind enough not to kick a person who was down, so she didn't pretend not to know what Robyn was talking about. 'Okay. Well, from what I can gather, there was something of a cheating scandal this summer in terms of the second-year exams,' she began slowly, and Robyn's ears pricked up, remembering having vaguely heard something about this herself. 'The students suspected of cheating were questioned, and allegations were made about John – namely, that he had supplied copies of the exam papers to one of the undergraduates, who went about selling them for a profit.'

Ka-boom. Robyn hadn't seen *that* coming. Give him his credit, her husband still knew how to surprise her. 'Oh God,' she croaked, twisting her hands together.

'The student in question is a rather attractive young woman called Naomi Ellis,' Beth went on, with an appre-hensive glance across at Robyn, as if she really didn't want to say the next part. Robyn, meanwhile, was torturing her-self with visions of the woman she'd seen in the café with John: that long coppery hair, the pierced nose, the creamy skin. Was that her, Naomi? 'And Naomi has complained to the university that . . . ah . . . that apparently John seduced her, promising her the exam paper if she would sleep with him – I'm sorry,' she added unhappily, seeing the agony on Robyn's face. 'Should I go on?'

Robyn nodded without speaking. Let's hear it, the full mortifying works, she thought. Give me the worst you've got.

'Then, before term ended, I gather her father turned up on campus, making threats against John, as well as alleging that his daughter had been taken advantage of, and demanding that she be allowed to continue the course,' Beth went on, with an apologetic grimace.

Robyn put her head in her hands. Great. A whole soap opera played out in public. She could just imagine how the gossip had gone whipping through the corridors and around the lecture theatres. *Have you heard? Oh my God, have you heard?* No wonder Gabrielle had sounded so peculiar on the phone.

'So it's a bit messy, really,' Beth said. To put it mildly. 'John has been . . . his contract has not been renewed, as you know, and as far as I can tell, the situation with Naomi, in regards to the uni, is ongoing.' She flushed suddenly, seeming to remember herself. 'Um. Whoops. It goes without saying that this is all confidential. I probably shouldn't have told you that last bit, but . . .'

'It's fine. I'm not exactly going to spread it around,'

Robyn replied dully. John, cheating. John, seducing a student. John, turfed out ignominiously. John, receiving threats from some furious, ranting dad. She wasn't sure which of it was worse. The whole saga was so horrifically tawdry from start to finish.

'I'm sorry,' Beth said again, biting her lip. 'That's all I know, I promise.' There was a moment of miserable silence while they both stared at their teacups, no doubt wishing to be elsewhere. 'Are you all right?' she asked after a few seconds. 'I mean, I'm sure you're not, but . . . Can I help at all? Can I do anything? If you want to talk, I'm a good listener.'

Robyn wasn't sure anyone could help her right now, unless they had discovered how to rewind time. 'Maybe you could murder my husband for me,' she replied, trying to make a joke, but the words just came out sounding really angry and bitter. Then she groaned and shook her head. 'Thank you,' she said. 'For being straight with me. But I guess I've got to work the next bit out all by myself. Somehow or other.'

Beth nodded. 'Okay,' she said, 'but I'm here if you need anything.' Her grey eyes were sincere and sympathetic. 'And by the way, I'm pretty good with a spade. If you *do* decide on the murder option and need a hand digging a shallow grave or anything . . .'

Robyn made a noise that was mostly laugh, but with some element of sob. She gulped down her very nice tea, blew her nose and tried to compose herself. 'Thank you,' she managed to say after a moment. 'You never know, I might just take you up on that.'

The conversation with Beth drummed around Robyn's ears for the next few hours – while she was picking up the children from school, while she was preparing dinner, while she somehow navigated her way through all the usual bathtime and bedtime routines. She gave it her best shot at acting completely normally, but inside she was shell-shocked and battle-weary; numb that all this had been going on in John's world and he'd deliberately kept her at arm's length the whole time. Her husband, the man she loved, and he'd been leading this sleazy double life without a single glimmer of guilt, as far as she could tell. She felt so bitterly disappointed in him. So let-down. How could a couple come back from this? Was it even possible?

By nine o'clock that evening the children were in bed, the dishwasher was taking care of the dinner plates, and John was stretched out on the sofa, his hair wet where he'd showered after a run. (*Had* he been for a run, though? she found herself wondering upstairs, paranoid that everything he told her was now a lie.) Robyn peered at her pale face in the bedroom mirror, putting on some lipstick and brushing her hair, wishing she didn't look quite so frightened. It was ridiculous, wasn't it, prettying yourself up when you were about to have a showdown with your husband, but these tiny things felt like the application of armour. *I am worth more*, she reminded her reflection. *I deserve better. He can't treat me like this and get away with it.*

'Glass of wine?' she called through to the living room, where John was still acting the part of everyday spouse with impressive aplomb.

'Love one,' he called back, swinging his bare feet up on the coffee table.

Me too, she thought darkly, sploshing cold Sauvignon Blanc into two glasses and knocking back half of hers in a single gulp. Dutch courage – bring it on. She topped up the glass, her insides clenching. If what Beth had said was true, then their whole way of life here was in jeopardy. But she really couldn't ignore the facts any more. Who could?

'I was wondering,' she began, walking into the living room and lowering herself into the armchair opposite her husband. 'Is there anything you would like to tell me, John? Anything that you need to get off your chest?'

He was laughing at something on his phone. 'God, have you seen this on Facebook, the dancing-dog video that's going round? Dad would love it.' He took the glass from her. 'Thanks. Sorry, what were you saying?'

Robyn gritted her teeth. Somehow the words seemed even harder to get out a second time. 'I was asking if you had anything to tell me,' she replied, and then her voice cracked with emotion. 'And if our marriage has ever meant anything to you, then you really need to tell me the truth this time.'

The laughter left his face, replaced by a wary expression. 'What do you mean?'

She held his gaze unhappily. 'Don't make me spell it out,' she said. 'I mean you getting sacked from work, the cheating, this Naomi woman . . .' Then all of the hurt and embarrassment and anxiety took hold of her, and her voice rose. 'What the hell is going on with you? Why did I have to hear this from another person? How do you think that made me feel?'

He swallowed, shifting uneasily in the chair. 'Well . . .'

'Did you think I wouldn't find out? Were you hoping to just get away with it?' The questions kept bursting from her with increasing shrillness as he sat there, head lowered, his expression worryingly blank. She thought of the children upstairs in their beds, their faces rosy and soft as they slept, and felt an ache inside that she was having to ask these things, that John had steered them onto such a narrow precipice. Why had he gone and lit this great big bonfire in the middle of his life, for everyone to witness? 'John! Talk to me!' she cried, unable to bear his silence. 'What happens now?'

He twisted his hands in his lap, his shoulders slumped. 'I . . .' he said, eventually, staring down at the carpet. 'The thing is, I love her. I'm sorry, but that's just how it is. I love her.'

Robyn, who'd been expecting a grovelling apology and the promise of John being able to put everything right, felt as if her breath had been snatched away from her. *'What?'* she replied.

'I love her,' he mumbled again, his eyes still fixed on the carpet as if it held the answers to everything, rather than a red-wine stain hidden under the rug and some waxy blobs left by a dripping Advent candle three Christmases ago.

Robyn could hardly believe what she was hearing. 'John, she must be half your age!' *Love?* Was he *serious?* 'She's practically a *child.* Are you sure this isn't just some mid-life crisis you're going through, some—'

'I've never felt like this before,' he said, not seeming to care how these words might bruise Robyn's heart. 'And she feels the same way. We're going to elope. We want to be together.'

Now he *had* to be kidding. 'She's *using* you!' Robyn told him, shock turning to disbelief. 'Can't you see that? She used you to cheat on the exams, and now she's using you as an excuse – John, that's not love. This is insane!' She stared at him, willing him to see the light, desperate for him to realize what an idiot he sounded. 'Hang on a minute – I thought she was the one who got you sacked anyway, telling tales, landing you in it? That's not exactly loyal, is it? How can you say you love her, after that?'

He shrugged. 'I'm sorry, Robyn. I should have told you

earlier. But . . . I can't help the way I feel. And it was my idea for her to blame me. '

'It was *your* idea?' Robyn blinked, trying to take this in. Had he really jettisoned everything – his family, his career – for this woman, in so cavalier a fashion? 'You're infatuated, John, that's all. Flattered that this girl has even looked twice at you. It's called a crush, a massive great crush – and fair enough, I saw her myself, she does look gorgeous—'

'What do you mean, you saw her yourself?' His head whipped round. 'How do you know about this anyway?'

She snorted. 'How I know is hardly the point,' she told him. 'The point is that all of this was going on and you didn't think to mention it to me. Me, your wife! Instead, you're carrying on with this . . . this *teenager*—'

'She's twenty-two.'

'Oh, twenty-*two*! That makes all the difference. Christ, John, will you just *listen* to yourself? Can you not hear how this sounds?' She shook her head, anger rising, but he merely shrugged again, seemingly unmoved.

'You might as well know, we've decided to head up to Edinburgh together for the summer – I was going to tell you,' he said quickly as Robyn gave a startled squawk. 'She's got some friends there, they said they'll put us up for the time being, just until we can get our own place.'

'John, stop,' Robyn said, putting up a hand. Was he having some kind of breakdown? 'Stop saying these . . .

these crazy things. You can't just . . . What about the kids? You seem to have forgotten them. Are you seriously saying you're just going to abandon—'

'We're in love,' he said again, with the simplicity of a drunk, or somebody brainwashed, who wouldn't listen to reason.

'She's stringing you along, more like,' Robyn cried, still reeling from the turn the conversation had taken. Love? Elopement? Edinburgh? He couldn't mean it, could he? He couldn't genuinely think this was a good idea, to move all the way up to Scotland with his twenty-two-year-old crush? Staying with some of her mates, it would be like regressing to student years: tie-dyed Indian throws hiding naff old furniture; awaiting your turn to use the shower in the morning; bitching about who had finished the milk. She shook her head, trying to assimilate the image, but found it impossible. 'I think you're making a big mistake here,' she told him, voice shaking.

Her words simply rolled off him. 'I'm sorry,' he said once more. 'It's all happened really quickly, I've been trying to find the right time to tell you, but . . .'

'But guess what, there isn't a right time to tell your wife that you've been sacked, you're having an affair with a student and you're leaving her and your children while you hop over the border to set up a love-nest. Strange, that. You would have thought it would be so easy, too.' Her sarcasm gave way to rage suddenly, sheer boiling rage that John could do this, wreck everything on such a stupid, selfish whim, and that she was a mere afterthought. 'And your brothers know all about it, I'm guessing,' she added, remembering his lying alibis of recent days. Her cheeks burned with the humiliation. 'Does everyone else know, then? Been having a good old laugh behind my back? God, John!' Her voice rose to a shout. 'Come *on*! Do you really think this is a good idea? I mean, seriously? Genuinely?'

He sat in silence for a moment and she felt a brief flare of hope that he was about to come to his senses at last, see reason and apologize. But then he rose to his feet. 'I'm sorry,' he said again. 'I can see you're upset. But I know how I feel. And I've been given a chance at something amazing, with Naomi. I'd be mad to turn it down.'

Robyn's mouth fell open, but nothing came out. She seemed to have run out of words, used up all her arguments.

'So I'm just going to go, okay?' he said, somewhat apprehensively. 'And then we can talk in a week or so. Decide what we're going to do about the kids, and everything.'

Oh, now he mentions the kids. Now that he's about to walk out the door, he finally thinks about the kids, Robyn fumed. How dare he treat them – and her – like non-priorities? How *dare* he? 'I can't listen to this any longer,' she said shakily. 'You go and live out your deluded little fantasy in Edinburgh, if you must. But do me a favour and don't bother crawling back here when it all ends in tears.' She stared at him, hating him, but still desperately hoping that he would change his mind.

He didn't, though. He merely gave her a sorrowful look, raised his hands in an *All right – calm down!* sort of gesture and walked out of the room. Then, as she sat there, dumb-founded, she heard the front door close and she knew that he'd walked out of the house, too.

He'd come back, Robyn said fiercely to herself as his car started up outside. Of course he would. This was his home, this was his family, this was where he belonged!

Her heart started banging as panic set in. But what if he didn't? she thought fearfully. What if he *didn't* come back, what if he genuinely meant all those crazy things he'd said and their marriage was over? Her breath rasped shallow and fast, her head began to ache with all the terrible questions that were swirling there. Was it really the end? How was she going to explain this to the children? How ever would she cope?

Mum, what would you do? Frankie thought that evening, washing up the dinner things as a quiet, anxious mood set-tled upon her. She and Craig had been to see their solicitor today, who had strongly advised mediation as a first step, but Craig seemed adamant that he wouldn't go along with anything Julia wanted, claiming that he'd rather go straight to court to settle the issue. Frankie, who disagreed with him, had been left feeling helpless, as if her opinion counted for nothing.

Her mum had always been so brilliant at talking through a thorny problem, she remembered with a pang: listening carefully and weighing up the balance, before offering practical suggestions and advice. Sure, Frankie had friends she could talk to about the Julia situation, but they were Craig's friends too, and it would have felt disloyal, confessing her private thoughts to them. She had her stepdad, Gareth, but he was living out his retirement in Spain and always seemed to be in some bar or other when she called, the sports channel blaring in the background. Plus, his advice tended to be 'Chin up, love, it'll be all right', which, although cheering, wasn't exactly specific.

This was the downside of having a small family, she mused, rinsing a saucepan: not enough people to turn to in a crisis. *You always wanted a brother or a sister, didn't you?* her mum had written in that final letter, and Frankie thought guiltily again of her dad, Harry Mortimer, and those four mystery half-siblings, who might hate her now. She still hadn't managed to write any kind of letter herself, what with all the drama of Julia's arrival. *Oh, hi there, Mortimer gang, I'm Frankie. Christ, it's a nightmare when someone bursts into your happy family unannounced and stirs everything up, isn't it? Sorry, guys. Any advice, by the way?*

Scrubbing at the burned-on cheesy sauce bits around the rim of the lasagne dish, she thought about Julia and Fergus and Craig, and the seemingly impossible tangle they were in. What would her mum have said about it, had she still been around to advise? Frankie had the strong feeling she'd have been more generous to Julia, for starters. Kathy had been a staunch supporter of women in general – when Frankie was growing up, there was always a steady stream of her female friends dropping by for tea and sympathy, and sometimes even a place to stay when the going got tough. If Kathy was alive now, Frankie was sure she wouldn't have been so quick to cast Julia as the villain of the piece; she'd have responded with compassion rather than fear. 'Poor woman,' Frankie could imagine her saying. 'Sounds like she's had a rough time. Why does Craig think he has to punish her for it? Why can't he give her a break?'

Why indeed? Frankie thought, putting the dish upside down on the draining board. In her position, her mum might even have gone behind Craig's back, telephoned Julia, tried to sort it out, woman-to-woman. Knowing Kathy, she'd have talked her round as well; they'd have come up with a plan that suited everyone, before popping open a bottle of wine and drinking to the future. But Frankie was not so bold and brave as her mother had been. Was she?

She washed up the last saucepan and gave the salad bowl a rinse, still thinking. She could hear Fergus giggling hysterically from the bathroom where Craig was giving him a bath, and felt her heart soften for them both. She remembered one of the first columns Craig had ever written about Fergus, which had essentially been a love-letter, a promise: *I will never let you down, son,* he had written. *I am on your side, fighting your corner, come what may.*

She knew, at heart, that this was why he was puffing up like a cobra whenever Julia's name was mentioned, because of his deep-rooted instinct to protect his child, to keep him safe. Craig was a good person, he believed he was doing the right thing here – but somehow his actions were coming across as aggressive rather than kind. Whatever happened next in this saga, however she and Craig negotiated with Julia, they had to keep remembering that this was about Fergus, the small, exuberant person they all adored. They had to act out of love, in other words, rather than from misguided vengeance or rivalry. But could she make Craig see this, before they found themselves trading insults in a courtroom and making everything a hundred times worse? Or was he too blinded by his own convictions to listen?

Chapter Twenty

When Work Means It's Love-All

Craig Jacobs, 41, and Frankie Carlyle, 34, are the real-life couple behind the hugely successful 'Dad About the House' column – a genuine happy-ever-after tale that has captured the hearts of readers everywhere. The pair of them live in west London with Craig's young son Fergus, the co-star of the columns. So how did the story begin?

FRANKIE: *As a freelance artist, it's rare that I get to meet the writers whose work I illustrate, but in Craig's case I felt as if I knew him from the first few paragraphs. There's something so honest about his work, and his writing is so witty and moving, that I very quickly gained a sense of the real person behind the page and found myself eagerly awaiting the latest instalment of his column. Like the rest of the country, I was willing him and Fergus on, cheering every achievement – as well as sympathizing through each setback. Then came the newspaper's Christmas party, and I couldn't help crossing the room to introduce myself. I think my* *opening gambit to him was something really cheesy like 'I'm such a fan of your work', which I now realize he gets a lot, but once I introduced myself and we began talking, it turned out that he was a fan of my work, too. And—*

Harry was blinking as if he couldn't take in any more of the words on Paula's iPad screen. 'And it's really her?' he said faintly, his eyes full of tears. 'She's . . . the same Frankie?'

'Well, you tell me,' Paula said. 'I mean, I've only seen photos of her. You're the one who actually met her.'

They were sitting in the airport car park, his suitcase in the back of Paula's car, a printed boarding pass and his passport in a plastic wallet by his feet. At long last Harry Mortimer was ready to catch his flight to Madeira and, without wanting to sound unkind, it had not come a moment too soon for his long-suffering daughter. Much as Paula loved her dad, he was not the easiest of house-guests, she had discovered. It hadn't once occurred to him, for instance, to fill the dishwasher or clean up after himself – well, until Paula blew her top the night before, that was. 'No wonder Mum has extended her holiday several times over!' she'd snapped, having come home after a long day's work to find the house a tip and the clean, wet laundry still in the washing machine, where it had been all day, Harry not having thought to hang it out. 'Dad, if you're going to make things work with Mum, you could do worse than mucking in a bit around the house, you know.'

They'd made up soon enough – Paula had a quick temper and had apologized for her outburst almost immediately, and then he'd apologized too, quite humbly, for his domestic failings. All the same, she'd been so exasperated that she'd quite forgotten to show him the *Guardian* article featuring Frankie that Fliss had sent her – until now, the next day. Having arrived at the airport with time to spare before Harry could check in, Paula had belatedly remembered, and looked up the feature on her iPad for him to see.

'My goodness me,' he said, biting his lip. He gave a shaky little laugh. 'This is very strange. Reading about my own daughter on a website. Seeing her, almost for the first time, as a grown woman. A successful woman, too.' He blinked several times more, seemingly overcome.

'I know,' said Paula. 'I did some Googling, and she's done all kinds of other work as well – greetings cards and stuff, it's all really good. She's talented.' Hopefully not *too* talented that she wouldn't want to know provincial estate agent Paula, she had found herself thinking the night before, as she pored over Frankie's online portfolio. Was it awful that she had felt the tiniest stabbings of envy, the faintest prickles of inferiority? 'Obviously gets it from her mum,' she joked, nudging Harry in the hope of lightening the mood, and was rewarded by a small smile from him.

Then she hesitated before adding, 'I guess the big question now is: do you want me to try and get in touch with her while you're away? I mean . . . *I'd* like to, but Mum was pretty clear about how she felt. I don't want to tread on any toes, if you'd rather not go there.'

Harry was still staring at the picture of Frankie onscreen. She looked happy and pretty, as if life had been good to her over the years. As if she'd done just fine without the Mortimers, thank you very much. For all Paula knew, she already had a whole melange of siblings and cousins and other relatives anyway, possibly all high-fliers in London, like her.

'I *would* like to see her again,' Harry replied. 'And don't you worry about your mum. I'm going to sort everything out on that front.' He glanced at his watch. 'Talking of which, I'd better make tracks.' He handed the iPad back to Paula after one last glance. 'Thanks, lovey,' he said. 'Thanks for finding her. And for being so understanding.' His eyes were still a bit moist as he smiled fondly at her. 'A brand-new daughter is all very exciting, but my golly, I'm glad I've already got a daughter like you. Aren't I the lucky one?'

That evening, at around the same time that Harry's plane touched down, rather bumpily, in Funchal, Alison was making a similarly hopeful, if slightly apprehensive journey of her own, past the golf course and over the River Nidd into Knaresborough. Despite her previous dating disaster, she had decided to give Silver and Single one more chance, just to prove that she wasn't a quitter; and so here she was now, singing along to Glen Campbell on the radio as she headed towards the car park. Moments later, she reversed into a space and took a last critical check of herself in the rear-view mirror. Was this the face of a woman about to be swept off her feet, about to capture a new man's heart?

Well, her hair looked good, for starters: shiny and bouncy after a wash and blow-dry, plus some of her favourite finishing spray, which smelled almost as nice as perfume, in Alison's opinion. Her make-up still appeared dewy and she had bothered to use lip-liner for once, so as to avoid her lipstick bleeding out into the lines around her mouth. Meanwhile her eyelids gleamed with a frosted caramel eyeshadow that really accentuated her hazel eyes. Not bad, in short, even if she said so herself.

And okay, so driving here instead of getting the bus over meant that she wouldn't be able to drink more than one small glass of wine to keep the nerves at bay, but it also meant that she could escape quickly, if need be. So she was all set. Now she just needed to get out of the car and meet this hunk of burning love that Silver and Single had sent her way. Hopefully there would be cartoon hearts flashing in her eyes within minutes.

Tonight's date was called Alastair Kirk. He was sixty-two (a younger man!), a retired veterinary surgeon and, with a bit of luck, would be so interesting and amusing and handsome that the evening would fly by. (Alastair and Alison – come on, they even sounded good as a couple. She'd already planned to make a joke of saying, 'You can call me Al', like the Paul Simon song, as an ice-breaker. Hopefully he would get the reference and find her witty rather than weird. Hmm. Maybe she wouldn't mention it after all.)

She got out of the car, tugged her dress down where it had stuck to her legs and set off. Even if Alastair Kirk didn't turn out to be Mr Wonderful, she hoped the evening would be worth missing her favourite TV quiz for, at least. Second time lucky?

He was waiting at a table in the pub for her with a glass of red wine and noticed her immediately, standing up with a little wave. First impressions: quite handsome, tall and slim with neat hair, well cut. He was clearly attentive, punctual and friendly, she thought, crossing the room towards him, a nervous smile plastered in place. All good things about a man. But then as they introduced each other and he went to buy her a drink, she noticed that he seemed to have brought several full carrier bags with him, clustered by the foot of the table. Had he been shopping prior to meeting her? she wondered, frowning and taking a surreptitious look. One bag appeared to be full of clothes, she saw. Another was stuffed with tins of food, and a third contained a variety of objects: a pair of knackered old trainers, a book, a folder of papers and . . . was that a toothbrush sticking out?

Not shopping, then, she thought, disconcerted and biting her lip. He appeared to have brought along a collection of belongings with him. She glanced over to the bar, where he was making the barmaid laugh about something. He seemed charming enough, but did he actually have any-where to live? she wondered. He wasn't hoping to cadge a bed at her place when the night came to a close, was he?

'Excuse the bags!' he cried in a jovial voice, as he returned with her glass of wine, presumably noticing her staring quizzically at them. He was well spoken and well presented too, clean-shaven, with a smart striped shirt and dark trousers, cufflinks glinting at his wrists. 'I'm between houses at the moment, camping out with friends. I appreci-ate this makes me look rather like a vagrant, but it's just a temporary setback. Not a down-and-out just yet, ha!'

'Ahh,' Alison said, smiling politely. 'That must be frustrat-ing. When will you be able to move into your new place?'

'It's rather a long story,' he replied, sitting down opposite her, 'and something of a tedious one, unfortunately. In a nut-shell: blame the ex-wife!' He gave a loud laugh that didn't sound remotely genuine, and Alison heard a warning bell jangle in her head. Oh dear. No home, an ongoing feud with his ex . . . First impressions could be misleading, sure, but she had a strong feeling that here was another man who was not at all ready to be out in the dating world, when there was clearly so much baggage in his life. And no, she didn't mean the three very full Morrisons bags slumped against his ankles. (Honestly, though, why were these men so desperate to get back out there? Why couldn't they wait thirty or so years, like she had? At this rate, she would be waiting another thirty before she met anyone remotely suitable.)

At least the food was meant to be good here, she consoled herself, studying the menu. Now, what to choose – haddock or scampi? Steak? Ooh – someone on the next table had a burger, which looked nice and juicy, she noticed. Although burgers could be very messy to eat, couldn't they? She didn't want to be getting ketchup all over her fingers and embarrassing herself. Forget the burger.

'Is that your phone ringing?' Alastair asked after a moment.

'Sorry, what?' she asked, lost in her thoughts. 'My phone! Yes. Thank you, it is.' She reached down and took it from her bag – Robyn, she saw on the screen. With an apologetic grimace at her daughter's name, she sent the call to voicemail, not wanting Robyn to know what she was doing. *You're on a date? Cool!* she imagined the response, practically breathless with enthusiasm. *How's it going? Is he nice-looking? Text me a sneaky photo!*

Alastair was watching her as she put the phone away. 'I

saw that look,' he commented. 'Don't tell me – that's your ex ringing up. Mine always picks the worst moment too.'

Ah, there she was – the ex, popping up at the table once again. Come on, love, pull up a chair if you're going to be with us for the whole evening, Alison thought, trying not to show her irritation. 'Actually my ex is dead,' she said, turning back to the menu. 'It was a long time ago,' she added quickly, in case she'd made him feel awkward. People always felt they had to say sorry when you told them your other half had died, and then they'd give you that sad, worried face, and you could tell they were wondering if you were about to burst into tears.

He nodded. 'I wish my ex was dead,' was all he muttered, though. Which was pretty much the most unsympathetic and mean-spirited reaction she'd ever experienced in all the years since Rich's death. And to think she'd just been worrying about him feeling uncomfortable!

Her phone was ringing again – Robyn once more, she saw. Alison might not get out much, but even she knew that taking a call while you were on a dinner date was bad manners. However, it wasn't as if the man opposite her had exactly displayed exemplary dating etiquette himself so far. He probably wouldn't even notice if she answered her phone. Besides, Robyn wouldn't call twice like this if it wasn't important. Maybe even an emergency. The one time her daughter came to her with a problem, rather than the Mortimers, and Alison was ignoring her!

'Excuse me,' she said. 'It's my daughter. I just need to . . . Hello, love,' she said, accepting the call. 'Everything okay?'

'Oh, *there* you are! Is everything all right with your land-line? I've been calling it and calling it and it just rang out. I was starting to get worried. Where are you?' Robyn sounded highly strung, her voice squeaky, the words tumbling out in a rush.

'I'm fine, I'm . . . I'm out,' Alison said, turning slightly away from Alastair, in the hope of being discreet. 'Are you all right? You sound a bit fraught.'

'I'm . . . Oh God, Mum. You'll never believe it. John's been acting really weird for ages, and last night I plucked up the courage to ask him about it and . . .' Alison pressed the phone to her ear as Robyn started gulping, her speech being taken over by sobs.

'Darling, slow down. Take a breath and tell me again,' she urged, feeling alarmed. Robyn had always been the most self-possessed child, not one given to histrionics and melodrama, and that was how she'd stayed as an adult, too. Alison couldn't even remember the last time she'd heard her daughter cry.

'He's . . . he's left me. Gone off with some student to . . .' A hiccup. 'To *Edinburgh*. He says he's in love! I just feel so humiliated, Mum. So let down. I kept thinking he was joking, but he's actually gone. And she's twenty-*two*!'

Alison could hardly take this in. 'Oh my goodness!' she cried, her hand flying to her mouth. 'I can't believe it. What a shock for you.' Her head spun and she glanced over at Alastair, feeling bad, but knowing that she couldn't possibly refuse Robyn in her hour of need. 'Listen, I'm coming over, all right? So sit tight and I'll be with you as soon as I can.' She hung up, about to apologize and explain, but Alastair had clearly been listening, because his face was like thunder.

'What?' he cried indignantly. 'You're going? I've just bought you a drink – three quid, that cost me!'

Alison was not a rude person, but this was an emergency. 'I'm really sorry,' she told him, getting to her feet, 'but my daughter's . . . Well, something awful has happened and she needs me. So—'

'Well, that's just fucking great,' snarled Alastair and there was something about the way his demeanour had changed, so completely, into sheer fury that took her aback. No, more than that. It made her want to leave very fast, run possibly and jump in her car.

'I'm sorry,' she repeated, edging away, noticing anxiously how his hands had curled into fists. She rummaged in her purse and slapped a few coins on the table. 'But it was nice to meet you anyway.' Er, no, on balance, it really wasn't. 'And good luck with the house situation. Bye!'

And then she was weaving her way out of there, casting a quick glance over her shoulder to make sure she wasn't being followed – luckily not; it would have been a bit cumbersome for him, with all those bags, she imagined. Nonetheless, she found herself breaking into a jog as she left the pub, arriving red-faced and out of breath at her car minutes later. She'd never been so relieved to hurl herself in there, lock the door and start the engine. The road to romance did not start here, after all.

Bloody hell! Another deadbeat! A totally charmless loser to boot this time, who was probably already ringing up Silver and Single to complain about her bailing out, demanding that she be taken off the books for wasting his time. Well, and so be it, Alison thought, as she put her foot down and set off towards her heartbroken, weeping daughter. She would cancel her account there anyway, after the two dreadful dates she'd had through the website. From now on, she was done with romance, absolutely done with it. It was far better to stay on her own than waste an evening on any more chumps.

Besides, by the sound of things, Robyn was done with romance too, done with that cheating husband of hers and needed her mother right now. So it was just as well Alison wouldn't be indulging in any more gallivanting around with these idiot men. Because Robyn came first – and she always would.

★

As luck would have it, Jeanie was already down in the hotel reception when Harry made his entrance that evening. After a few quiet days, lying low about the place, she was waiting at the desk in order to let Bernardo, the manager, know that she planned to leave Madeira on the Sunday flight. It was finally time to go home, she had decided, and face the music. Pop the bubble and return to real life, tail between her legs. If Bernardo ever got off the phone, that was. He put a hand up to indicate he had noticed her standing there, and made an apologetic *just-a-moment* sort of a face, but didn't seem in any hurry to wind up the call.

Jeanie leaned against the cool marble counter, listening to Bernardo's acquiescent, polite voice, hearing the sound of the lift bell ding-dinging as it reached the ground floor and the tinkling of the ornate fountain that splashed behind her. Her mind drifted to thoughts of dinner later on – perhaps she would brave it down to the restaurant tonight, rather than hiding away in her room again; exchange a brisk *please-don't-talk-to-me* smile with Luis, to show that she was over the experience and not looking to repeat it, and then tuck into a pleasant meal, gazing out at the sunset, knowing that the countdown to her departure had begun.

All of this was going through her head as she stood and waited; and afterwards she couldn't have told you what prompted her to turn round at that precise moment – some sixth sense perhaps, making the hairs on the back of her neck stand on end – but turn she did, just in time to see Harry, her Harry, striding through the main doors.

Her breath caught in her throat and she blinked twice, quite overcome at the sight of him there in the hotel. For a moment, she thought she must be imagining things – that he was some kind of mirage, with his wheely suitcase and that rather battered Panama hat he liked to wear in warmer countries, the one she'd always teased him about. But no, it was really him – as tall and straight-backed as ever, glancing around for a single moment, before orienting himself and striding towards the reception desk. Towards her.

'Harry!' she cried joyfully, making a beeline for him, her shoes clacking as she crossed the floor. 'Oh, Harry!'

He saw her and his face changed from trepidation to relief, all the way into a smile. 'Hello there, stranger!' he cried as she rushed up to him, and then his arms were around her, tight and strong, and there was the most enormous lump in her throat. 'Jeanie,' he said, sounding every bit as emotional as she felt. It was the longest time they'd been apart in fifty years and she was only just realizing now how much she had missed him. 'I'm sorry,' he said.

'I'm sorry too,' she said, her voice catching. Would she ever be able to tell him how sorry she was? She pressed her face into his cotton shirt, breathing in the familiar smell of his cologne, and felt unbearably happy and sad and wrung-out all at once. What a strange few weeks it had been. What an abrupt turn her life had taken, the day of the party, and then afterwards, in the airport – a turn away from him, a striking-out on her own into the sunshine and into all kinds of trouble. 'I'm sorry,' she repeated, disentangling herself and stepping back. The whole scene in the airport where she'd forbidden him to come with her seemed like a strange, vivid dream now. She felt a different person from the woman who had shouted at him and marched off without a backward glance. 'I overreacted, I didn't know how to handle the news.'

'And I let you down,' he said, taking her hands. 'I let you down and I wasn't a good husband. You had every right to be angry with me. I hope, in time, you can forgive me.'

She couldn't stop looking at his face. His dear, kind face. There was a flicker-reel of images running through her head: all the good times they'd shared, all the happy moments. He hadn't been a good husband back when he'd had his fling, but then she hadn't been a good wife lately, either. How could she not forgive him, now that she knew how easy it was to be tempted? Would *he* ever forgive *her*, if he knew what she'd been up to moreover? 'We'll get through this,' she said staunchly, her heart pounding. 'We can work it all out together.' They had both made mistakes, she thought, as she flung herself into his arms again, but she knew now, as plainly as she knew her own name, that this was where she belonged, with Harry.

'Yes,' he said. 'We will.'

Jeanie led him towards the reception desk, where Bernardo had at last finished his phone call and was gazing expectantly at her. 'Bernardo, this is my husband, Harry,' she said; her two worlds colliding. 'Is it all right if he stays with me until . . .' She glanced back at Harry. 'Maybe Sunday?' she asked, feeling almost coy in making the suggestion. 'I was thinking maybe we could go home on Sunday.'

Harry nodded and squeezed her hand again. 'Perfect,' he said. 'We'll go home on Sunday.'

Bernardo's face was wreathed in smiles. 'But of course!' he cried, delightedly. 'It would be our pleasure to have you both staying with us. Perhaps I could book you a table for dinner tonight as well?'

Jeanie felt her own smile waver for just a single moment as she considered the possibility of Luis seeing them both later on, maybe even giving her a meaningful look across the restaurant, a telltale raised eyebrow or, worse, a disparaging smirk. Well, if he did, she'd just have to deal with the consequences, she thought; accept it as the price she had to pay. She had made her own bed, as her mother used to say, and she would lie in it. With Harry, not Luis.

'Yes, please,' she replied. 'A table for two would be lovely.'

Chapter Twenty-One

It was midday on Friday, and Frankie and Craig were walking down the street towards Fergus's playgroup. Now the princely age of four, he would be starting at the local infant school come September, and this was the final day of term for the playgroup and therefore the last ever session that Fergus and his cohort would attend. To mark the occasion, all the parents had been invited to share a special celebration lunch with their offspring – their 'graduation', the staff were calling it, tongue-in-cheek. The children were apparently making their own graduation hats out of colourful paper that morning, which they would all be wearing as the parents arrived. Frankie was already feeling tearful at the prospect. She was going to miss, terribly, these easy-going playgroup mornings, where Fergus made things and played and sang songs with his friends, where he'd had so much fun. Next stop: school, where he'd be squeezed into a uniform like all the other boys and girls, where he'd have to sit still and pay attention, where the playing would be measured into educational boxes that the teachers needed to tick off.

She found herself sniffling as they rounded the corner and walked the last few steps towards the church hall where the playgroup was based. 'I feel so emotional!' she cried with a little laugh, putting a hand to her heart. 'I can't believe this chapter in his life is about to end. I'm not sure I'm ready for it yet.' She'd grown so fond of the staff there – substitute mothers, all of them – and the other mums of the children as well; she was going to have to readjust to the new world of infant school almost as much as Fergus would.

Before Craig could answer, though, his phone rang and he pulled it from his pocket. 'Oh – I'd better take this,' he said, glancing at the screen. 'It's Lloyd.'

The name meant nothing to Frankie for a moment, too caught up in her sentimental feelings. Lloyd? Ah, their solicitor, she realized and wrinkled her nose, the mood puncturing at once. She had been twitchy and apprehensive ever since they'd gone to meet him, when Craig had effectively commanded that the dogs of war be unleashed on Julia. What would Julia's answering salvo be?

'Hi, yes, fine thank you,' Craig said, as they reached the railings that surrounded the little yard at the front of the hall. There was a painted hopscotch on the paving slabs, a small raised bed in which had been planted sunflowers and runner beans, and a colourful shed that housed all sorts of trikes and scooters. 'You're kidding me,' he said suddenly, stopping dead on the pavement. A muscle twitched in his jaw. 'Well, that's just *ridiculous*. What the hell?'

Uh-oh. Frankie felt her spirits sink as she hesitated there beside him. This didn't sound good. Whatever shot Julia had fired, it had certainly hit its intended target.

'Hi, Frankie!' came a voice behind her and she turned to see Pippa and Aisling, two of the mums she knew, walking up the road towards them, both looking a bit pink-eyed with wobbly smiles. 'Big day. Hope you've remembered your tissues!' said Pippa, pretending to dab at her eyes.

'I've got a whole packet,' Frankie confessed, patting her shoulder bag, just as Craig said tersely, 'I don't care how she feels, frankly. I couldn't care less. Yeah, well, she can sue me then. Bring it on.'

Pippa and Alice turned, startled, at the sound of Craig's angry voice, then glanced back to Frankie. They looked embarrassed and also slightly uncertain, unused to seeing Craig as anything other than his usual charming, friendly self.

'Drama at work,' Frankie said with a little laugh, the lie coming from nowhere. Her face burned with the awkwardness of the moment, and she found herself wishing the two of them would move on quickly, before Craig said anything else. He, meanwhile, seemed oblivious, still scowling into the middle distance.

'We'll see you in there,' said Aisling tactfully, as she and Pippa scuttled off.

'Right. Well, can you email me the correspondence, please, so that I can read it?' Craig said. His hand curled around an iron spike at the top of the railings, gripping it as if he would like to wrench it from the ground and stab it into Julia's heart. His eye fell on Frankie, waiting patiently there, and then he blinked as if he'd forgotten about her and Fergus and the playgroup graduation. 'Listen, I've got to go, but I'll call you back later. Thanks. Yeah, okay.' He hung up. 'That fucking bitch, you'll never guess.'

'Can it wait?' Frankie pleaded, seeing Marie, the playgroup leader, appearing at the doorway of the hall with a bright smile and a beckoning wave.

'We're about to start!' she called.

'Just coming!' Frankie called back. She took Craig's arm and steered him towards the steps up to the hall. 'Let's just enjoy Fergus's last—'

'She wants me to stop writing the column,' Craig said, thunder-faced, not seeming to hear.

'Day at play . . . What?'

'She says it could damage Fergus in future years. Says it's wrong to have him in the public eye, that it's intrusive and unfair, that he could be teased or bullied for it at school . . .'

'No!'

'She says – and so does her solicitor – that it's an example of my bad parenting, my lack of respect for his privacy. I mean, for fuck's sake!' They had entered the building now and he punched the wall angrily. Marie, a few steps ahead of them in the corridor, wheeled round in alarm.

'Sorry,' Frankie said hastily. 'Sorry, Marie. We've just had some bad news.' Her head was spinning with Julia's bloodying counter-attack, the seriousness of the hit. By dangling a sword over Craig's 'Dad About the House' column, she was not only threatening to derail his career at its peak, but was also putting their finances in jeopardy, seeing as it was the biggest source of income for them both. As for claiming to question Craig's parenting, in the name of Fergus's welfare . . . that was particularly mean. A real blow to the heart.

'Oh dear.' Marie was plump and kindly, a grandmother of seven, with vibrant hennaed hair and paint-spattered jeans. 'Is there anything I can do to help? Do you need to leave?'

'No, we're fine,' Frankie replied firmly, trying to smile and look normal. She was not about to let Julia spoil Fergus's last day here. 'We don't want to miss this. Do we, Craig?'

'No,' he agreed after a moment, his jaw still clenched, his whole body seeming to bristle with tension. There was no doubt about it, Julia was really upping the stakes. *You don't want to talk about this like reasonable adults? You want to rubbish me in a court? Fine,* Frankie imagined the other woman thinking. *I can give as good as I get, you know. Just watch me.*

Trying to shake these thoughts away, Frankie took Craig's hand and they followed Marie through the double doors into the main hall. The children were sitting cross-legged in a big circle on the floor, all wearing their colourful hats with beaming smiles, and there was a buzz of excitement in the air. Frankie felt a surge of emotion as she spotted Fergus wearing a bright-orange hat and waving at them, looking so proud and happy. Her throat tightened as she looked around the room at the gaudy paintings up on the wall, the Wendy house standing empty for once, the boxes of toys and musical instruments now put away for the summer. It was almost over, his time of belonging here, being part of this place. It was coming to an end, just like the happy, carefree family existence she'd enjoyed with him and Craig until now. Everything was changing beyond her control.

They sat down with the other parents on the rows of little chairs that ran along the side of the wall, and Frankie gave Fergus a tiny secret wave with the tips of her fingers, twinkling her eyes at him. 'Should get a thousand words' copy out of this,' Craig had said earlier, only half-joking, as they'd left the flat. It was his catchphrase, one shared with every other journalist; always looking for the story. Fergus's first tooth? A column. First steps? A column. First words, and funny habits, and comic misunderstandings – all captured lovingly in print, there on a digital file somewhere for evermore.

Each piece had been written out of affection, no question, but every now and then Frankie had found herself nagged by the worry that the Fergus of the future might not appreciate having his life mined for copy in this way. A prickly teenage Fergus, for instance, might resent his potty-training antics being recorded for posterity online, leaving him vulnerable to being teased by his peers. Similarly, a job-seeking Fergus might not be thrilled that a prospective employer's Internet search of his name could reveal the story about his floor-punching tantrum in the Asda baked-goods aisle, or his brief obsession with random women's breasts, which compelled him to comment on them with the authoritative air of a connoisseur ('That lady got BIG boobies. BIG!').

Periodically Frankie had voiced her concerns to Craig, who'd admitted wishing he'd given Fergus a pseudonym from the start, rather than using his real (and fairly unusual) name. 'But it's no worse than all those parents who document everything on Facebook, is it?' he'd reasoned. 'Everyone does it, it's just life.'

And yet now here was Julia, sanctimoniously holding up her moral mirror in order to shine a light on Craig's writing and question it in the interests of Fergus, far more loudly and publicly than Frankie had ever done. Did that make her a better woman than Frankie? Shouldn't Frankie have tried harder to make this same point?

'Hello, everyone, and welcome to our very special leavers' celebration,' said Chimoa, Marie's second-in-command, just then. 'Okay, then, children, are we all ready?' she asked, clapping her hands. She was perched on a small wooden chair and pretended to be blown backwards by the raucous cheer that went up. 'Excellent! Parents and carers, are we all ready?'

'Yes!' replied Frankie along with all the other adults, apart from Craig, who made a tutting noise as he read something on his phone – whatever Lloyd had just emailed him, presumably. She elbowed him, not wanting Fergus to be overshadowed. 'Craig!' she hissed.

The children started singing their goodbye song, their sweet, high voices wavering in and out of tune adorably and Frankie fumbled for a tissue, as tears misted her eyes. Look at Fergus forgetting the words as he grinned over at them both, that orange paper hat perched at such a jaunty angle on his curls. After this song the children would be collecting their 'graduation' certificates and memory books from the staff, before sitting down for a final picnic lunch together, of cheese sandwiches and crisps and apple slices. Then they would be saying goodbye and leaving this place for the very last time.

Frankie had never been good when it came to dealing with change. Aged six, she'd apparently lain on the floor, weeping and trying to clutch at the carpet, the day she and her mum moved house, practically needing to be dragged over the threshold. Aged eleven, she had refused to speak to Gareth for three whole weeks when her mum started seeing him, so resistant was she to any upsetting of the status quo. As an adult, she hung on to old knackered items of clothing if they reminded her of happy days, even if she had no intention of ever wearing them again. The same went for ancient sketchpads, favourite (broken) pens, her mother's tarnished jewellery . . .

She tried to concentrate on the song, to really be present in the moment, but her thoughts were being pulled in all directions. For someone who disliked change, she was coming up against it again and again this summer, she thought, ambushed by one surprise after another. Change kept sending her down new paths she didn't want to take, forcing her into situations she'd rather avoid, jostling her out of her comfortable, cosy existence and leaving her in this wilderness of doubt and uncertainty. What with the disastrous encounter with the Mortimers and the no-holds-barred battle with Julia, she was beginning to wonder where she'd end up by the time the first autumn leaves were on the trees. When would life start to feel more normal again?

Up in the North, Robyn was lying on her sofa staring up at the ceiling. Life did not exactly feel normal for her, either. It was her day off and usually she'd have a list of at least ten things to be getting on with. Today, however, she simply did not have the energy for cleaning or supermarket shopping or changing bed-sheets. All she wanted to do was lie down and let the world carry on around her.

She hadn't had a single word from John since he'd left two days ago, presumably for Edinburgh with his nubile young girlfriend in search of his thrill-seeking new life. 'Dad's gone on holiday,' she'd managed to say brightly to the children over breakfast the following morning, to which Sam had frowned and asked, 'Without *us*?', shortly followed by Daisy's 'But that's not fair!' They'd both sounded so offended and cross that Robyn might well have laughed at their indignation. If she hadn't felt like bursting into tears, that was.

Of course all four of them were supposed to be going on holiday together, to Portugal for a week in August, the flights and villa booked long ago. Would John have got over his mid-life meltdown and come home by then, apologetic and humble? she wondered in anguish. Would she even *want* to splash about in the kidney-shaped, azure-blue pool with him, after his devastating, life-tipped-upside-down betrayal? Or would there just be three of them getting on the plane together, one ghostly seat remaining empty on the flight out? She imagined the Herculean tasks of trying to be jolly and holiday-ish all on her own, of having to find the villa (and drive the hire car!) by herself and then be responsible for everything else: the security, the food, the day-trips, the fun. She imagined the subdued evenings once the children were in bed and she was alone: drinking her way through bottles of local rosé and slapping mosquitoes from her legs, while listening to the families in neighbouring villas laughing and enjoying themselves. Holiday? Right now it felt as if it would be more like a punishment than a week to savour.

She rolled over on the sofa into a more comfortable position and tried to motivate herself to venture into the kitchen to make lunch. The spirit was willing – not to mention hungry – but the flesh was weak. Too weak to move off the sofa and cut slices of bread, even though her stomach had been rumbling plaintively for the last twenty minutes. Starving seemed like the easier option. Starving, or waiting for her mum to come back from work and make her something, anyway. Which was admittedly kind of tragic, but that was what her life had apparently become now – heartbreak causing her to regress to being a helpless child again, the girl who just wanted her mummy to make everything better.

Alison had answered her distress call on Wednesday night, driving over all dressed up for some reason (which, in hindsight, was odd, although Robyn had been so upset, she hadn't got round to asking why), and she'd been tending to her ever since. She had listened to Robyn sob out the whole humiliating story, then had poured her a glass of wine and run her a hot bath, giving her a series of mini pep-talks throughout the remains of the evening.

'You'll get through this,' she said, finding Robyn a pair of clean pyjamas. 'You're stronger than you think,' she said, warming milk in a pan for hot chocolate. 'We're survivors, you and me,' she said, as they sat together on the sofa, Robyn rosy-skinned from the bath, sipping her chocolate like an obedient little girl.

Robyn did not feel like a survivor, though. She felt as if she'd been dropped from a great height and was still lying stunned on the ground below: battered and broken and concussed. Reeling with the pain of John's betrayal. She would never have cheated on him, never, but he had gone, just like that. Left her for this other woman half his age. This is really happening, she kept thinking in a daze. It's not a dream or a film I'm watching, this is my *life*. So what do I do now?

Alison had stayed on Thursday night too, making her famous shepherd's pie for dinner, reading Daisy's bedtime story and teaching Sam card tricks before his bath, and this morning she'd gone off to work, promising to be back again tonight with provisions for the weekend. 'You don't have to, Mum,' Robyn had said weakly, feeling she had to put up some kind of resistance, if only for the sake of her pride. (Not too much resistance, though, obviously, in case her mum withdrew the offer.)

'I know I don't,' Alison had replied. 'But I want to. Text me if you'd like anything in particular picking up. And don't you even think about doing any housework. I can get stuck into that over the weekend.'

Thank goodness for mums who came to the rescue when the chips were down. Especially as Alison could well end up being Robyn's last relative standing, now that John had left. Without her husband, the Mortimers might already have squeezed Robyn out of their inner circle, she thought miserably, rescinded her membership from the clan. She hadn't just married John, after all, she had married the whole family, but now she tormented herself with visions of being shunned by her in-laws, dropped off the invitation list for Jeanie's birthday tea parties, scissored out of the photos. It made her heart ache. Losing John would mean losing so much more besides.

Paula read the text – *Love is in the air!* – and smiled at the accompanying photo: a selfie of her parents, shoulders together as they beamed into the camera, holding cocktails with paper umbrellas. Her mum's face was a deep mahogany, while her dad's nose had turned a bit pink; skin shades that told the story of their stand-off separation. But they were smiling at least, she thought, and comfortable in each other's presence again. *Enjoying our second honeymoon – better late than never!* Harry had written in a second text, along with several thumbs-up emojis. *We'll be back on Sunday.*

She forwarded the texts to her brothers, just in case they didn't know this good news for themselves, then gazed out at the river, the sun sparkling on it in gold flashes as one of the tourist cruisers went chugging beneath Lendal Bridge. It was her lunch-hour and she'd managed to nab a bench down by the water, wanting somewhere more private than the office to make a personal call. It was silly, but her heart was thumping as she pulled out the scrap of paper where she'd jotted down the number. Constance Albright, Artists' Agent, the website had said, detailing a list of the various illustrators, painters and fine artists represented. And there was Frankie, along with a mini-portfolio and biography: bold, humorous artwork, and details of her successes. A range of greetings cards. Prints of zoo animals against bright backgrounds. A couple of children's picture books, as well as the column with her partner, Craig, which had been running for almost four years. There was also a beautiful black-and-white photograph of her where she'd been positioned side-on, looking over her shoulder slightly with an arch, *I-see-you* sort of half-smile. She looked friendly, good fun, Paula had thought, gazing at the warmth of her half-sister's eyes, the gorgeous wide mouth that looked as if it might open at any moment in a laugh. She appeared to be the sort of sister, in other words, that Paula had always hankered after.

'Constance Albright speaking, how may I help you?' came the voice down the phone when Paula finally plucked up the courage to dial.

'Hi. Um. Bit of a strange request,' she confessed, 'but I'm ringing about one of your artists – Frankie Carlyle.'

'Oh yes? After a commission, are you?' was the reply.

'Not exactly,' Paula replied. 'It's a personal matter. I wondered if there was a way of getting in touch with her directly, an email address or . . .'

'Ah. No, I'm afraid not.' Constance Albright sounded curtly disapproving at the question – and fair enough, Paula supposed; she had to protect the privacy of her clients. 'I can't give out that sort of information. If you want to leave your contact details with me, I can pass them on to her, but—'

'Okay, yes, sorry,' Paula said, accidentally interrupting, in her haste not to be seen as a stalker or random weirdo. 'It's a bit of an odd situation. I'm . . . I'm Frankie's sister. But she doesn't even know I exist, so . . .' She tailed off, feeling as if she was getting this all wrong.

'Frankie doesn't have a sister,' the woman replied tartly. She was sounding more suspicious by the minute. 'I'm afraid I'm very busy right now. If you want to send an email, kindly do so via the main agency address, it's on the website.'

'Wait,' Paula blurted out, sensing that Constance was about to hang up. 'I know it sounds weird and you might not believe me. But please could you give her a message, at least, from me? Say it's Paula from York, Harry Mortimer's daughter, and that I would love to make contact with her. If you've got a pen, I'll give you my number.'

Even the *mm-hmm* noises Constance Albright made, as she took down Paula's details, sounded as if she didn't trust this unorthodox caller for a minute, but Paula persevered. Whether Constance passed on the message or not, she had tried at least. She'd stretched out a hand across the miles between them. 'Thank you,' she said, before hanging up and wondering if her message and number were already being balled up and thrown into the nearest bin.

Her phone bleeped with two new texts moments later and she almost dropped it, fumbling to see if by some miracle this was Frankie contacting her already – *Oh my goodness! Paula! Are you really who I think you are?* – but the beeps were only the slightly more earthly replies from Dave and then Stephen, one after another, having seen the photo of their parents. *Great. Nice one.*

Nothing from John, but then he was always a bit crap about texting and communicating in general. She would send the picture to Robyn instead, who was much better at such things, she decided, but just then her phone rang, causing her to have palpitations all over again. But it was only a work call – a new customer wanting a valuation. 'No problem at all,' said Paula, switching back into professional mode and perking up when she heard the rather prestigious address of the property. 'That would be my pleasure. Now let me just check my diary . . .'

Chapter Twenty-Two

If the last few days had been a struggle for Robyn, the weekend seemed to move things up a gear, in terms of doom and despair. Usually weekends meant socializing, either with the rest of the Mortimers or, for the children, sporting fixtures or parties with school friends and other such fun stuff. Unfortunately, fun felt pretty low on the agenda for Robyn now – added to which, the calendar was unusually empty. It was almost the end of term – one week to go – and all the sports clubs had finished for the summer, so she didn't even have the distraction of a cricket match for Sam, or a dance class for Daisy, to chip away the hours.

'So, what *are* you going to do then?' asked Alison after breakfast, sorting through her hairdressing kit on the kitchen table. She was going to have to leave in twenty minutes, she'd said, in order to work some magic on a bride's hair over in Harrogate, and was paranoid about leaving any of her equipment behind. 'Heated rollers,' she muttered to herself. 'Tongs. Grips. Vines . . . Daisy, have you been playing with my hair vines?'

It was childish of her, she knew, but Robyn couldn't help feeling a bit peevish that her mum was leaving when she still felt so low, when the day stretched ahead with such empty desolation. 'Dunno,' she replied. Still in her pyjamas, she was fuggy and ripe, compared to her blow-dried, fully made-up mother, which made her feel even worse. 'I haven't got anything *to* do, either, seeing as the Mortimers are all cold-shouldering me,' she said, noting, as she did so, how whiny she sounded, but unable to prevent herself from sliding into self-pity. 'Can you believe, none of them have bothered getting in touch to see if I'm all right? I mean . . . They've totally closed ranks against me. It's like they've rejected me overnight.'

'Oh, Robyn, come on, now,' Alison scolded, still rummaging through her kit. 'Of course they haven't. Give them a chance. Do they even know about—Ah, thank you!' she said as Daisy appeared just then, rhinestones sparkling amidst her hair, thanks to all the beaded accessories she'd swiped from her grandma's collection. 'Little monkey,' she said, wagging her finger, before unwinding them all again.

Robyn waited until her daughter had skipped away once more, before continuing with her moan. 'And it's Luke's birthday next week – Paula's eldest – and nobody's mentioned any kind of celebratory party tea to me. I think I've just been uninvited. I'm totally off the guest list. Dropped like a hot brick!'

'Robyn.' Alison zipped up her bag and stood there, palms flat on the kitchen table, looking stern. 'Listen to me. You can cope with this two ways: you can feel sorry for yourself, and blame other people and become all bitter and resentful—'

'Charming!' God, this was really not helping.

'Or you can roll your sleeves up and get on with life. You can say: Okay, this bad thing has happened to me, but I'm not going to lie down in defeat. I'm not going to submit. I know it's hard – believe me, I remember – but being on your own is not the end of the world. See it as an opportunity; a beginning, rather than an ending. Don't forget, once the children know what has happened, they'll be counting on you to get all three of you through this. So—'

'All right! All right!' Robyn cried, rolling her eyes. *Don't forget*, indeed. Like she could just *forget*! When she was absolutely dreading having to tell Sam and Daisy about John! 'No need to lecture me.' Was her mother *trying* to make her feel worse than she already did?

'Because when your dad died, I didn't have a choice,' Alison said, warming to her theme. 'It was out of my control. Much as I wanted to give up and stay in bed crying for the rest of my life, I had to keep going for the sake of both of us. Whereas—'

'Yes, but Dad couldn't *help* dying,' Robyn pointed out. 'It wasn't like he deliberately left you in the lurch, unlike John.'

Her mum stiffened for a moment, then she pursed her lips and hoisted her bag onto her shoulder. 'All I'm saying,' she went on quietly, a wounded expression on her face, 'is that you mustn't give up. This is your chance to follow your own dreams again, to start thinking about the life *you* want, rather than living around your husband.'

Robyn had had enough of being lectured. An acrid coil of nastiness was untwisting inside her, putting words in her mouth. 'Says you, who's never dared do anything,' she replied scornfully before she could stop herself. 'Says you, who never goes out, who doesn't have a life, who's too scared to seek out any kind of relationship that doesn't involve cutting someone's hair and asking them about their holidays. What about *your* holidays, eh? What about *your* dreams? Don't preach at me, when you're too cowardly to do anything new!'

As soon as she had finished saying all of these terrible things, Robyn would have given anything to spool them back inside again. There was a dreadful shocked silence when Alison looked like she'd been slapped. She opened her mouth as if she was about to retaliate in defence, then clamped it shut again and wheeled round on the spot. 'I've got to go,' she said, in a tight voice that didn't sound like her at all.

Robyn felt as if she might just have nominated herself as the worst daughter in the world. 'Mum, I'm sorry,' she started saying, following her from the room, as Alison walked briskly towards the front door. 'I didn't mean to – Mum!'

But Alison was already out of the house and marching up the path to her car, nose in the air. Robyn stood in the doorway, pulling her dressing gown around her, knowing that she'd been cruel, knowing that she'd been unfair. When her mum had been such a rock to her, as well; when she'd comforted and supported Robyn through the worst few days of her life. *And this is how you thank me,* Alison's body language seemed to say, hurt and stiff, as she got into the car with a slam of the door, then reversed out of the drive. *Why do I bother?*

Robyn pushed the door closed with a soft click, feeling ashamed and guilty and mean. Catching sight of herself in the hall mirror – bed-hair all over the place, complexion sallow where she'd hardly left the house in the last twenty-four hours, a splotch of coffee on her pyjama top – her instinct was to turn away quickly, but she forced herself to look, to take it all in.

Okay, she thought, eyeing her reflection. This is as bad as it gets for you. This is as low as you're going to sink. From now on, the only way is up. Starting with heading up those stairs and having a shower, you stinking old slattern. Then you can work out how you're going to apologize.

'You all right, Mum?' There was Sam, looking over the banister at her. She hadn't just said all that aloud, had she?

'I'm fine, sweetheart,' she assured him with a shaky smile. 'I'm going to have a wash and get dressed, and then let's think of something fun to do today, you, me and Daze, all right?'

'There's that new Marvel film out,' he said immediately, brightening. 'We could go and watch that together.'

'With popcorn!' added Daisy, appearing beside her brother with a hopeful look on her face. She had ears like a bat, particularly when it came to the matter of potential treats.

A film and popcorn, thought Robyn, trudging up the stairs towards them. Sitting in the darkness while super-heroes slugged it out on a big screen, with explosions and special effects, and at least ninety minutes when she knew the children wouldn't be asking difficult questions about when John was coming back. Surely even she could manage that. 'Sounds like a plan to me,' she replied, gratified to hear their cheers in response.

There. The day might be saved after all. And maybe she could pick up something nice for her mum in town too, by way of making amends. She wandered into the bathroom, feeling a tiny bit more positive about the world, just as Sam said, 'Oh – wait, though.'

'What?'

'I just remembered: Dad said he wanted to see that film as well,' he replied. 'Should we wait until he's back before we go?'

'When *will* he be back anyway?' Daisy asked in the next breath.

And there it was again, the rising tide of uncertainty that kept threatening to pull her under. She gritted her teeth, wondering how long she could keep fobbing them off with vague answers. 'Let's go and see the film anyway,' she replied eventually, then turned back with another smile, hoping it wasn't too obviously fake. 'And then if he—*When* he's back, if he still wants to see it, we can all go again!'

'YES!' cried Daisy, punching the air exuberantly, although Sam looked less convinced by her answer. He narrowed his eyes a little, looking straight at Robyn with a frown of doubt. He wasn't buying it, she thought in panic. He knew something was going on. And sooner or later he was going to seek her out, alone, and ask some blunt questions, to which she'd have to provide some honest answers without completely breaking his heart.

But not right now. Not while she was unwashed and smarting, after the exchange with her mum, not when she hadn't prepared how to tell him. She escaped into the bathroom and turned on the shower, knowing that it was only a matter of time.

Bunny had taken to looking at maps recently. Wales. Cornwall. The Highlands. She scrolled through them on her phone screen, zooming in to city centres and around towns, thinking: This one? Here? Maybe that one? while waiting for some impulse within her to ring like a struck bell. Hoping for a signal – a premonition, a good feeling, anything – that would guide her next move. She'd even considered London, with its warren of roads and districts and communities. Everyone could have a fresh start in London, right?

It wasn't working out for her in York any more, that was for sure. Ever since the horrible, shouting man in Gloucestershire, she'd felt as if she was on borrowed time. She was hiding behind her lies, hiding behind Dave, using whatever she could find as a shield to protect herself. It made her think of history lessons at school: imagining wooden fortresses in old battles, the boom of gunpowder, the clamour of dying men. And there she was, crouching behind her increasingly flimsy shield, the hot, thick stink of sulphur and mud and metal in the air; too scared to let anyone see her real self.

With every day that passed, she felt as if the new life she'd built for herself here as Bunny was under threat of collapse. She'd begun eating sweets in secret, stashing bags of them in her knicker drawer or handbag. She'd bailed out of her last two gym sessions with excuses about coming down with a cold and feeling lethargic. And it was becoming harder to resist temptation, to walk past chip shops without diving in for a hot salty bagful, to stop herself hacking off great lumps of cheese to post into her mouth while cooking, to recognize when she was full and put her cutlery down.

Go away, Rachel. Go away, spineless weak Rachel. You can't come back.

This wasn't a sustainable way to live. In hindsight, she should have come clean with Dave right from the start, told him: This is me, take me or leave me. This is what you're getting into, if you want to be with me. Here's what you should know.

But now it was too late to have that conversation. Telling him the truth now, because she was worried she'd be caught out, was weak and would only make everything worse. So she'd slip away from him instead, she had decided: write a brief note of apology, get in her car and take off somewhere new. Start over. Try and get it right next time. He seemed distracted by the news he'd had about John that morning, she figured. He'd get over her soon enough.

Dave deserved better than her anyway. Look at him, how delighted he was that his parents seemed to have sorted out their differences and were coming home together from

Madeira, the second honeymoon finally completed! He believed in true love and sailing off into the sunset with someone, and it was only right that he should find an uncomplicated woman who could give him everything he wanted from life, a woman free from baggage and police interviews and prison-contained ex-husbands.

And so, while Dave went off to the airport on Sunday to welcome home the second-honeymooners, Bunny looked around the quiet house one last time, took a deep resigned breath and decided to make her move. She didn't have much to pack – a sports bag or two of clothes, a few pieces of jewellery, the card from Chloe, her make-up and toiletries. Her cardboard doppelgänger could stay, she decided scornfully, folding the huge, sad figure in half and treading it down, before stuffing it into the recycling box.

Dave, you're the loveliest man in the world and the best thing that ever happened to me, she wrote on a piece of paper, feeling tears starting to gather in her eyes at the thought of him coming back and finding her gone:

But the truth is, you're too good for me – and if you knew what I'd done, you'd probably think the same, too. Someone better is out there for you, someone worthy of you. I hope you're happy together. But I'm going now and you won't see me again. I'm sorry to let you down. Love—

She started to form the B for Bunny, but it felt like one last lie to him, when she was trying to be honest. She thought about writing 'Me' instead, but then realized that signing off 'Love Me' might sound like a command, rather than a closure. A big kiss – that would have to do. Her brain felt too strange and sad and churned up to deliberate over the details any longer.

Bags in the car, she posted her door keys through the letter-box, hearing them drop to the mat there, but then was paralysed with doubt and second thoughts. Was she making the right decision? Was it too late for her to change her mind? Oh, talk about pathetic, she couldn't even do a bunk properly, she thought miserably to herself, turning on her heel and getting into her car just as the rain began. And where was she going to go? She didn't even have a plan in place. This was the most shambolic running-away attempt ever. Hopeless! Just like she was hopeless at everything.

Tears leaked from her eyes as she started driving towards the ring-road, the wipers flicking back and forth as the rain hammered down, deciding on impulse that she'd head north and just see where she got to. Despite today's thunderstorm, it was summer; there would be jobs going at hotels and bars in every big city or tourist place, she figured. Something cash-in-hand, where she wouldn't need a reference, somewhere bustling and busy where she wouldn't be asked too many difficult questions. And if the job turned out to be boring and repetitive, and if whichever cheap place she found to stay was grotty and grimy, then she'd just have to suck it up, because it would be her own stupid fault and all she deserved anyway.

Oh God, she thought, suddenly despairing at the enormity of yet another new start when she already felt so worthless. Could she do it? Was it even worth trying?

By the time she'd reached the ring-road, the rain was really coming down in sheets: water drumming on the car roof and spraying against the windscreen, great wide pools already appearing on the tarmac. Inside the car she was still crying, the tears coursing down her cheeks, despite her efforts to dash them away on her sleeve. And then, maybe it was the wet road, or this brief lapse in concentration, maybe it was even her having given up and no longer caring, but suddenly her wheels went skidding beneath her and the car swerved across the next lane. There was the sound of urgent hooting and, with a thud of alarm, she saw that another car was barrelling down towards her. Horns blared. Rain thundered. She hauled at the steering wheel, she pumped at the brake, she heard herself giving a scream of fright.

And then everything went black.

Chapter Twenty-Three

So here she was again, Paula thought, walking through the car park towards the entrance of the terminal. Round Two of 'Airport Cross Your Fingers' – although this time, at least, she was pretty sure Jeanie would actually be on the flight home, accompanied by Harry, seeing as they'd both already texted her that morning to say they had checked in and were on their way. Paula wasn't one to tempt fate, but it seemed as if the stand-off between her parents might finally be over, and she was looking forward to putting the turbulent events of recent weeks firmly behind them. Not that the saga was completely resolved, mind, what with the Frankie situation still ongoing, but one thing at a time, eh?

The airport was busy as she entered, with people queuing back from the check-in counters and harassed-looking staff attempting to direct them. Over in the Arrivals area, Paula spotted Dave already waiting there, checking the screen for information, takeaway coffee cup in hand. 'Hi,' she said, going over and giving him a hug. 'Long time no see. How are you? We must sort out a pub night sometime, I feel like I haven't caught up with you properly for ages.'

'I know, same,' said Dave. 'Although I take it you've heard about John, have you? I'm not sure he'll be coming to any family get-togethers in the near future. Sounds like he's lost the plot.'

'John? What do you mean?' asked Paula. She'd never had a reply from her text to him the other day, come to think of it. 'What's going on?'

Dave looked pained. He had a big, pink face, Dave, just verging on being a bit moon-shaped, and it sagged now, as he filled her in on the news. 'Uggh, it's really awful. Stephen went round the other night to see John and he wasn't there – but apparently John had told Robyn that he was out with *him*, Stephen, I mean. So Robyn was confused and Steve had to make up an excuse on the spot, just in case this was John organizing some big secret surprise for Robyn or something . . .'

'I'm guessing it was *not* a big, secret surprise for Robyn,' Paula put in, heart sinking. 'Not a nice one anyway.'

'No. Because when Stephen actually caught up with him on the phone last night, John told him he's been having a fling with this woman – she's twenty-*two*, can you believe it, one of his students, and they've both gone off to Edinburgh!'

'Edinburgh? What the hell . . . ?' Paula stared at him in shock. 'And she's twenty-two? You're kidding me.'

'God, I wish I was. Stephen's gone up there now, got the train this morning; he's hoping to talk some sense into John. Get him to come home and face up to his responsibilities.'

'And apologize to his poor bloody wife,' Paula finished, stunned by this news. She thought of Robyn's sweet, shy face and felt a terrible stab of guilt that she hadn't got round to calling her recently. Robyn was devoted to John! She absolutely worshipped the ground he walked on. Her whole world must have fallen apart in the last week. 'Bloody hell, Dave, I can't believe this.' She shook her head. 'What's got into him?'

'Search me,' said Dave grimly. 'Horrible, isn't it? I only heard about it myself today.' He pulled a face. 'First Dad, now John – it's like the family's falling apart this summer.'

'Don't say that,' Paula replied automatically. She hated the thought of the family fragmenting and breaking down. She never wanted that to happen! 'Look, their flight's landed,' she said, seeing that the screen nearest them had updated. 'I guess today isn't the day to tell Mum and Dad about John, do you agree? We can save that little bombshell at least until they've had a chance to unpack.'

'Definitely,' Dave said. 'Mum's going to go *nuts*. We definitely need to get her out of the airport before we break the news, otherwise she'll be straight on the next flight to Edinburgh to dish out one of her special bollockings.'

Paula snorted. 'Sounds about right,' she said. 'Hey, by

the way,' she added, remembering her own recent discoveries, 'do you want to see some more pictures of our mystery sister?' She rummaged in her bag to retrieve her tablet and flicked it on. 'I didn't tell you, did I, but my friend Fliss recognized her, and I've found a way to get in touch.' She told him the story, then showed him Frankie's website and some of her artwork samples. 'I've left a message with her agent, but I haven't heard anything back yet. I hope we didn't put her off last time. She sounds great.'

'Bloody hell, she's good, isn't she?' Dave said, flipping through the pictures of her work. 'Living in London with a journalist . . . Christ, she'll be disappointed when she finds out how boring us lot are,' he joked.

'Speak for yourself!' Paula retorted, pretending to be offended, and then they both laughed, but it sounded hollow to her ears. *The family's falling apart this summer,* Dave had said, and with her parents having so recently faltered, and now John breaking away, that left her, as the next-eldest, feeling responsible for pulling them all back together. She hoped she wouldn't be making things worse now by getting in touch with their half-sister.

A few minutes later she looked up to see her mum and dad coming through the Arrivals door, tanned and smiling and – yes! – holding hands. 'Oh, wow: here they are. That was quick!' she cried, stuffing her iPad back in her bag and feeling a surge of relief at the sight of them.

'Over here!' Dave called, waving an arm above his head.

'Look how brown Mum is,' Paula exclaimed. 'Whoa, and check out that hairdo,' she added in a lower voice. She'd noticed that something had happened to her mother's hair in the selfie picture her dad had texted, but hadn't been able to make out the full effect until now. Was it unkind to say that it was a really bad haircut? This wasn't Mum going through some crisis of her own, was it?

Paula hastily rearranged her features into a smile as her parents looked round and caught sight of them there. 'Hi,' she cried. 'Welcome back!'

'Oh, darling,' Jeanie said, hurrying over and throwing her arms around her. She was wearing a new perfume, one Paula didn't recognize, with a pastel-pink top and pale cropped trousers that showed off her tan. It was almost like hugging a stranger for a moment, somebody else's mum. Except for the fact that then Jeanie was clucking apologetically about ignoring her on the phone all those times.

'Oh, Mum,' Paula said in response, assuring her that it didn't matter and there was no harm done. 'Did you have a lovely holiday, though?' she asked, trying to move on to something cheerier. 'The longest holiday ever!'

Jeanie looked rather sheepish, but managed a smile at least. 'It had its moments,' she said, 'and was mostly wonderful. Even more wonderful when your dad turned up out of the blue, obviously.'

'Welcome back, Dad,' said Dave, hugging him. 'You look well. Want a hand with your bags?'

'Thanks, son,' Harry said. 'We've had a smashing few days.'

'Glad to hear it,' Dave replied. 'Hang on,' he said, as his phone started ringing, 'I'll just take this.'

'Mum, do you want me to carry anything?' Paula asked. 'Blimey, are you sure you've got enough duty-free there?'

'I couldn't resist picking up a few things for the kiddies,' Jeanie confessed, opening the carrier bag to reveal Toblerones, a science kit, some cool-looking headphones. 'And there's your favourite perfume somewhere in there as well, plus . . .'

'*What?*' Dave said just then into the phone in such a shocked voice that they all looked over at him. 'Oh God. Is she okay?'

Paula had a bad feeling inside as she saw how the colour was blanching from his face. 'No, her name's Bernadette,' Dave said, passing a hand across his face. His mouth seemed to buckle and he leaned heavily against a pillar for support. 'Bunny for short . . . Is it definitely her? What's the car registration?' His body sagged. 'Right. Yes. That is her.'

'What's going on?' Jeanie asked Paula in concern. 'Is he all right?'

'I don't know,' Paula replied, still watching her brother's

face. His eyes were glassy as if he was being told something terrible, and she felt her own stomach bottom out in alarm.

'Right,' he said, swallowing hard and nodding, seemingly oblivious to the others staring at him. 'Okay. I'll come over straight away. Oh God. Okay, thanks.' He hung up, looking dazed and kind of queasy. 'I've got to go,' he said. 'That was the police. Bunny . . . she's been in an accident.'

Once Dave had left, practically sprinting in his haste, Paula and her parents headed for the car park in subdued silence. Dave hadn't been able to give them any more details other than that Bunny was in hospital, following a car crash, but it had sounded serious. Paula loaded the suitcases into the boot of her car, feeling worried for vibrant, smiling Bunny and for poor Dave too, who was so besotted with her. Yet another crisis to hit the family!

When would it end? she thought, gripping the steering wheel as she drove her parents home. What else would be flung at them? Paula felt, more strongly than ever, that she had to step up and try to get things straight again, to be there for whoever needed her. Jeanie being away for so long had made her realize just how much her mum did for the family; how she was the glue that held them together. From now on, Paula was determined to share some of that responsibility, not least to give her mum a bit of a break.

'Here we are,' she said, parking outside her parents'

house a while later. 'Now listen, don't go worrying about Dave and Bunny, okay? I'll keep on top of the situation and let you know anything I hear. You just unpack and have a rest, get the kettle on. Oh – I should have thought to pick up some milk for you—'

'No need,' her dad said, heaving his case out of the boot. 'I went and bought a few bits and pieces earlier in the week. Ran the Hoover round as well. What?' he laughed, seeing Paula and Jeanie both staring at him in surprise. 'Nothing wrong with a man wanting to look after his wife and home, is there?'

'Nothing wrong at all,' Paula said, blinking at this unexpected turn of events. Sure, she'd been a bit sharp with him about tidying up after himself while he'd been staying with her, she supposed, and she'd ticked him off for not thinking about Jeanie, but . . . Well. This was a turn-up for the books.

Harry twinkled his eyes at her. 'Our daughter put me straight on a few things,' he told Jeanie. 'And I'm going to do more around the house to help from now on, you just wait. I might even make you a cheese omelette for your tea.'

'Whoa,' said Paula, who wasn't aware that he'd so much as cracked an egg before. 'Steady on there. Are you sure about this, Dad?'

'Your Luke's been giving me a few tips,' he replied. 'Proper good cook, that lad is, isn't he? I texted him while I was away, asked him for something to cook that even an old fella like me might be able to manage, and he sent me back a recipe. Not just women's work, Grandad, he said to me. That put me in my place.'

'Well, I never,' Jeanie said faintly, smiling at Paula, who raised her eyebrows comically in return. 'Sounds like I owe your Luke a few favours for all this. Tell him I'll be over with a *very* nice present from my holiday soon, all right?' She hugged Paula and gave her a kiss on the cheek. 'Ooh, I missed you, love. It's good to be back. And thanks for every-thing. What would I do without you?'

Paula saw them inside and got back into the car, smiling to herself that her own son had been feminist enough to set his grandad straight on matters of equality. Maybe she and Matt were better parents than they gave themselves credit for. She was just about to drive off home, to tell them that Harry seemed to be a changed man, when the news about John hit her all over again and the smile abruptly left her face. Oh God, yes, another drama she had yet to get to the bottom of. On impulse, she pulled out her phone and fired off a text to him: *Just heard about your pathetic mid-life crisis. For fuck's sake, John!! Get over yourself and come home. P*

He'd be angry, of course, to get a message like that from his little sister, when he was the type of brother who thought he knew the answers to everything, but she didn't care as she pressed Send. Because she was angry, too, and because he deserved it, frankly. Then she found Robyn's number on her phone and hit Call.

'Hey! It's me, Paula. I've just heard about John,' she said when her sister-in-law picked up. It was only then that it occurred to her – too late, of course – that Robyn might be the sort of person who preferred to get on stoically with being dumped, who might not appreciate being called up to discuss the situation, but by then Paula's words were already spilling out, and backtracking was no longer an option. 'God, Robyn! What a complete and utter twat he is. I'm so sorry to be related to such a total idiot. How are you? Are the kids okay? Do you want some company or . . .'

She heard a sniff from the other end and cringed that she might just blunderingly have made matters worse. 'Are you all right? Is this a bad time to ring? If you don't feel like talking about it, I'll understand. I just wanted to commiserate, to see how you are.' She bit her lip. 'But if you'd rather do this some other time—'

'No.' The word was a gulp, and then Paula heard Robyn sniff again and blow her nose. 'Sorry. I'm . . . I'm coping really well, as you can tell,' she said self-deprecatingly, but you could hear the wobble in her voice. 'No, I'm not,' she went on. 'I'm not coping very well at all. But thank you. Thank you for ringing.'

'Oh, Robyn.' Paula leaned back against the car seat. 'I would have rung before if I'd known. Dave only just told me, I didn't have a clue. What a moron John is, honestly. I can't believe it.' Perhaps it was time to stop slagging him off, she thought belatedly. She wasn't sure such an approach was all that helpful, especially if Robyn hoped they might get back together at some point. 'But look, if you want me to come over any time – or help with the kids – or, you know, listen or chat, or I can take you out for gallons of wine . . .'

Robyn's voice had gone all small and trembly when she spoke again, as if she was about to cry. 'I'm so glad you rang,' she said. 'I thought . . . I was worried . . .' Her pitch seemed to rise with every word. 'I was worried I wouldn't be part of the family any more.'

Paula's mouth swung open. 'Robyn, no! Of course you're part of the family! Oh my God, don't ever think that. You can't get rid of us that easily.' Goodness, Robyn sounded so distressed at the prospect – it hadn't even occurred to Paula that they would drop her, just because John had. 'Oh, love,' she went on. 'Were you really worrying about that? Please don't. We all think you're great, and that John's an arsehole for doing this. I swear. Not that Mum and Dad know yet, they've only just got back from Madeira – but Dave's horrified, and Stephen's actually up in Edinburgh now, trying to talk some sense into John. He felt awful, by the way, about basically lying to your face the other day, according to Dave. He didn't have a clue what was going on when he turned up at yours and you told him

what John had said, about them supposedly being out . . .
Bless him, he thought John might be planning a nice surprise for you and he didn't want to wreck it, so—'

She heard Robyn give a sob.

'Oh, darling,' Paula said wretchedly. 'I'm *so* sorry. I
really am.'

'Thank you,' Robyn gulped. 'Thank you for ringing and
telling me all of that. It means a lot to me. I haven't managed to break it to the kids yet, I don't know what I'm going
to say, but . . . but I'm glad nobody is blaming me or—'

'*Blaming* you? Not a bit of it. Of course we're not.' Blaming Robyn, indeed! There was only one person Paula was
blaming in this whole saga and it definitely wasn't her sister-
in-law. 'Now, listen,' she said, deciding to steer the subject
away. 'Something else I've just heard – and as a fully paid-up
member of the family, you'll want to know this, too: Dave
got a call, like an hour ago, saying that Bunny's been in
some sort of accident and is in hospital. I haven't got the full
details yet – I'll pass on anything I hear from him – but
maybe the two of us could go and see her at some point.
We sisters-in-law have got to stick together, right?'

'Oh, gosh,' said Robyn, sounding startled. 'I hope she's all
right. Yes – keep me posted, and let's do that. Poor Bunny.'

'I know. Sounded bad. I thought Dave was going to keel
over, he looked so queasy on the phone. Anyway,' she said,
noticing the time, 'I'd better go, but I'll text you when I hear

any news and we can sort something out, okay? And you take care in the meantime. Go and punch some cushions or something. Take the garden shears to John's favourite shirt, at the very least.'

'Don't tempt me,' said Robyn with one last sniffle. 'Thanks, Paula.'

'Any time,' said Paula, starting the engine.

'Bunny? Can you hear me, love? Bunny, it's me, Dave.'

Bunny felt as if she were swimming up through a great thick darkness, unable to see where she was going. There was a voice from somewhere above her, a voice she recognized, but she couldn't quite reach it, couldn't quite register.

'You're in the hospital, darling. I'm right here with you. You're going to be okay. Bunny?'

Her throat felt very sore as if she'd been screaming. Had she been screaming? Everything felt vague and blurred. Her head was pounding and she ached, but in a drifty sort of way. As if it wasn't actually real. What *was* real, anyway?

'The police said you were out near Skelton, heading north. With bags of stuff in the boot. Where were you going, love? Was it one of your slimming talks? Only you didn't tell me you were going off for another one. Bun?'

Groggily she managed to open her eyes a crack, to see Dave peering anxiously at her. Everything seemed very white around him, white and bright, and she blinked, feeling disorientated. His hair was wet, she noticed, and then she remembered the rain. Drumming against the windscreen. Hammering on the roof. She'd been in the car, that's right, she thought blearily. Driving the car through the rain. But where was she now?

'Hello,' Dave said softly, leaning closer. He smelled of coffee and his eyes were red, as if he'd been crying. 'Hey. Oh, love. I've been so worried.'

'Dave,' she croaked, the fog in her head clearing a little. She'd been leaving him, she remembered with a guilty start. She'd packed up her bags, written a note, posted the keys back through the front door. But . . . What had happened? How had he found her? Everything was shifting around in her memory, blurring and slippery when she tried to focus. Was this a dream or something?

'You're in hospital, you've had a car accident,' Dave said. His face seemed to be zooming in and out of focus, it was making her head spin. 'No bones are broken, thank goodness, but the doctors think you're concussed.' He gave a tiny smile. 'You've been saying all sorts in your sleep, you know. "I never meant to kill him," you were mumbling a few minutes ago. You must have had a right old bump on your head,' he added, squeezing her hand gently. 'The other driver was absolutely fine, by the way. The cars are a bit of a mess, but you haven't killed anybody.' He stroked a finger tenderly down the side of her face, then raised a teasing eyebrow.

'Unless there's anything in your past that you want to tell me, that is . . .'

Tears leaked out of Bunny's eyes as the words sank into her consciousness, like tiny knives. *Unless there was anything in her past that she wanted to tell him.* Oh God. Where should she start? She could almost laugh, if it wasn't so spectacularly awful. If only he knew . . .

'Hey,' he said gently. 'Come on, it's okay.'

She tried to shake her head, but it hurt. 'It's not okay,' she whimpered. 'It's not.'

'I know this must all seem a bit weird, Bun, but—'

A sob burst from her throat. 'That's not even my name,' she cried, closing her eyes so that she didn't have to look at him any more. Her head was thumping now and she experienced a sudden vivid flash of memory: her wheels skidding on the road, a navy-blue Toyota coming towards her, a scream of terror and then the impact of collision, being thrown back in her seat. But she hadn't killed anybody, according to Dave. So that made it two people she hadn't quite despatched, then. She was building up rather a collection.

There was a pause. 'The police did say something about your name,' he replied, sounding worried. 'Something about the car being registered to a different person – Rachel, was it? But . . .'

It was all unravelling now; her carefully wrapped secrets

splitting and falling apart. 'Look me up,' she wept, her face in the pillow, knowing she was already found out and it was too late. 'Rachel Roberts from Danforth Cross. Google me and then you'll know. Or rather . . .' The sobs threatened to overwhelm her. 'Or rather, then you won't *want* to know any more.'

'Bunny! I mean – Rachel. Of course I'll want to know. What do you mean?'

She dared to open her eyes again, but Dave's bewildered face staring back at her was enough to break her heart. 'Just Google me when you get home,' she said unhappily. 'I'll understand if . . . if you're not interested when you know the truth.'

'I'll always be interested!' he cried. 'I love you!' He squeezed her hand again. 'Look, you've had a shock, you've banged your head, you're not yourself. Come on, stop worrying about . . . whatever it is, and just rest now, okay? Don't distress yourself. Whatever it is, we'll sort it out, all right? We'll sort it out together.'

Bunny no longer had the energy to speak. Tears rolled silently down her face into the damp pillowcase. She wished his words could possibly be true, but at the same time she knew this might well be the last time she ever saw him.

Then came the sound of footsteps, a swish as the curtain was pulled back and she smelled a light floral perfume. 'How are we doing in here? I thought I heard voices,' said a woman.

A nurse, Bunny guessed, her mind still groggy. 'Are you waking up there, love? Rachel? That *is* her name, isn't it?'

'Yeah,' said Dave after a moment. 'That's her name. Um.' She could hear him getting to his feet. 'I'll leave you to it. She's a bit upset,' he said in a low voice to the nurse. Then he patted Bunny's arm gently and leaned over to kiss her forehead. 'Don't you worry,' he told her. 'It's all going to be okay. I promise.'

Bunny sighed as he left and the nurse began fastening a blood-pressure cuff to her arm. Oh, Dave, she thought wretchedly. Good, kind, loving David Mortimer. Hadn't anyone ever told him: you shouldn't make a promise you couldn't keep?

Chapter Twenty-Four

Dad About the House: The Mummy Returns

Bedtime stories! One of the nicest slices of a parent's day: your child all cuddly and sleepy and pyjama-clad, the book propped cosily between you so that you can pore over the pictures together. Plus – let's not beat about the bush – that joyful anticipation of liberation, the knowledge that you're almost off-duty for the evening and there's a bottle of wine with your name on it waiting in the fridge, to be opened just as soon as the lights go out. But along with all that, bedtime stories can lead to some strange questions, too; questions that steer you into unexpected conversations.

'Why is the stepmother always bad?' asked Fergus last night. We've borrowed a book of fairy-tales from the library and have been reading them a lot recently. And he's right – the stepmother of fairy-tales is always frightening or murderous or vengeful. Beware the stepmother with her poisoned apple and magic mirror! Mind she doesn't send you

off with a woodcutter, instructed to put you to a violent death in the depths of the dark forest!

'That's a very good question,' I replied – which, as you may know yourself, is every parent's quick-let-me-think-up-a-decent-answer response. And then I was stuck. Because . . . well, not to put too fine a point on it, sometimes in real life the stepmothers are actually the heroes who come riding to the rescue and make everything better, aren't they? If you ask me, it's the actual mothers you've got to watch out for.

Before you start getting het up and thinking: Excuse me, I'm an actual mother and I'm certainly not murderous or frightening, thank you very much – I'm really only thinking of one person here. Fergus's biological mother, in fact. Yes, readers, she's back. With a thunderclap and some horror-movie music, and possibly a magic mirror of her own, she has returned to our lives. A happy reunion? Not exactly. Turns out that, just like all the most evil fairy-tale villains, she's hell-bent on shaking things up for the worse.

'So what do you think?' Craig asked impatiently.

Sitting in front of his laptop screen, Frankie blinked. She'd only read halfway down the page so far and wasn't sure she wanted to continue, guessing that there was worse to come. 'This is a joke, right?' she asked weakly. It *had* to be a joke, she thought, seeking confirmation in his face. Craig's columns were usually warm and funny observations about family life, the sort that left you feeling uplifted. Vindictive and spiteful attacks had never been a feature of his writing before.

He seemed surprised at the question, though. 'Er . . . no,' he replied. 'It's not a joke.'

'But you can't . . . Surely you don't want to have this in print,' Frankie said uneasily, fearing as she spoke the words that oh yes, actually he did. 'I mean, it's all a bit . . . airing dirty laundry in public. Don't you think?'

'Exactly,' Craig said, sounding pleased.

'And given that she's already said how unhappy she is that you're doing the column at all—'

'Then my column is a clear and definitive two-fingers up to what she wants,' Craig replied. 'Yes. As intended.'

Frankie sighed. 'Craig, I don't think there's any need to be so combative about this,' she began saying, just as Fergus pelted into the room clutching a plastic dinosaur in each hand. He grabbed the oven glove from the radiator, wrapped it around his neck like a scarf and ran out again. It was Monday morning and their first day without any child-care until September; give it fifteen minutes and he would be saying he was bored and had nothing to do. In the mean-time, Frankie needed to talk her partner down from his hostile high-horse position. 'I can't see Vicki going along with this, either,' she said, citing the name of his editor as back-up. 'Or the readers. Please, Craig. Write something nice. Don't use this as a means of stoking the fire.'

Her phone started ringing, just as Fergus charged back into the room, still wearing the oven glove, then flopped down dramatically onto the floor and announced, 'I'm *bored*.'

'Dad will play with you,' Frankie told him, seeing her agent's name onscreen and feeling a pinprick of guilt that she wasn't doing any work. 'Hi, Constance,' she said, leaving the room before anyone tried to stop her. If Constance was ringing up to check on how Frankie was progressing with the dragon sketches, she was just going to have to lie, she decided with a grimace. And then stay up all night to catch up on herself. 'How are you? Good weekend?'

'I'm very well, thank you, darling,' said Constance. Constance was quite possibly the most glamorous person Frankie had ever met. She had silver-grey hair, cropped very close to her head, and liked to drape herself in jewel-coloured velvet pashminas and statement necklaces. If you didn't notice her for her dress sense, you would know her for her loud cut-glass voice, and her habit of saying exactly what she thought, whether you wanted to hear it or not. 'Now then, I'm ringing because I had rather a strange call on Friday afternoon,' she went on in her usual theatrical style. 'Probably some lunatic – we do get our fair share of them – but I thought I'd run it past you, all the same.'

'Okay,' said Frankie, going into her and Craig's bedroom and closing the door. This sounded intriguing. She'd had one man ringing up before, very keen for Frankie to paint nude pictures of him ('Tasteful, like!' he'd said apparently, as if that made all the difference), and another woman who'd wanted Frankie to paint her lurcher, which turned out to be dead, and stuffed, with the creepiest I'm-watching-you glass eyes. 'I'm bracing myself. Fire away.'

'Well,' said Constance, 'like I said, to be taken with a pinch of salt. And probably ignored. But anyway I feel obliged to pass it on, because the woman did sound quite sincere. Her name is – wait a moment – Paula Brent, and she said to tell you she was Harry Mortimer's daughter. And that she was your . . .' Constance gave a short bark of a laugh. 'Well, actually, darling, she was quite insistent that she was your sister, too.'

'Oh my God,' said Frankie, feeling shivers travelling up and down the length of her body. *Harry Mortimer's daughter. Your sister.*

'I know – I mean, rest assured, I did say to her: Frankie does not *have* a sister, but—'

'No, wait, Constance; the thing is, I do,' said Frankie, gathering herself and blinking several times. 'Apparently I do.'

'You do?' For once, her garrulous agent sounded lost for words. 'Goodness me. So when you say "Apparently", you mean . . . ?'

'I've only recently found out. Quite a surprise,' Frankie

said wryly. 'But she *phoned* – oh, I'm so pleased to hear that. Did she leave a number or anything?'

'Yes, she did, I wrote it down. Gosh, I'm glad I didn't just throw this away now,' Constance exclaimed. 'I nearly did, to be honest, because I thought it was one of those silly prank things . . . Where did I put it? Ah yes. Have you got a pen?'

'Yes,' said Frankie, grabbing an eyeliner from her dressing table and an old envelope that she'd been using as a bookmark. 'I'm ready.'

She could feel herself filling with delighted anticipation as she took down the number. With all the palaver around the unexpected appearance of Julia lately, Frankie had been feeling somewhat pessimistic about her dad and the disastrous episode up in York. She'd written the whole thing off, pretty much, as a mistake, a turn she shouldn't have taken, and it had faded to the back of her mind. And yet here was a woman called Paula – her actual half-sister – who had somehow tracked her down to Constance, and wanted to get in touch. Did that mean that Harry, her dad, felt the same way? Was this an olive branch from the Mortimers, the start of something new?

She tried to keep her feelings in check. There was a chance, of course, that this Paula was ringing to warn her off, to say: stay away from my dad, you're not welcome in our family. But if that was the case, would she really be ringing Constance and introducing herself as Frankie's sister? No. Surely not.

'Zero . . . four . . .' said Constance, coming to the end of the number.

There was a lump in Frankie's throat as she finished writing; she felt happy and excited, dazed even. 'Thank you!' she said, staring at the numbers on the paper and underlining the name *Paula* with a flourish. The start of a whole new conversation. *You always wanted a brother or a sister, didn't you?* she heard her mum say in her head. Oh, and she *had*. She had! 'Thank you very much.'

'My pleasure,' Constance replied. 'I must say, I'm quite intrigued. You'll have to tell me all about it next time we meet up. But in the meantime . . . How are those dragons?'

Gah. Frankie should have known that, even with sisterly revelations and bombshells, Constance wouldn't let her get away without checking in on her work. 'Um . . .' she said. 'The dragons are coming together. I'll have something to show you before long.' Just as soon as I've worked out what to say to my new sister, she thought, hanging up and beaming at her reflection.

'Talk to you soon, Paula,' she said into the quiet air, trying to tamp down the excitement sparking up inside her. Because it might all come to nothing, she reminded herself sternly. It might be a closed door, rather than an open one. But then again, it might be wonderful. A really lovely new connection to be made. 'Here's hoping,' she murmured, crossing her fingers as she went to tell Craig.

Up in Harrogate, Alison was in the spotless kitchen of a new client, snipping the ends off her wet hair, the blades of her scissors flashing in the sunshine. It was a warm bright day outside and her client – Molly – had made her a really delicious coffee with properly frothed milk, but even so, Alison felt distracted and ill at ease. She hadn't spoken to Robyn since her daughter's little outburst on Saturday morning, keeping herself busy instead, first with her bridal-hair appointment immediately afterwards, and then knuckling down to a thorough cleaning session at home later in the afternoon. That evening, she'd sat on the sofa for five straight hours, catching up on all the programmes she'd missed while staying at her daughter's, but annoyingly it had been difficult to concentrate. Try as she might, she couldn't stop herself thinking about the look on Robyn's face as she'd spat all those cruel words out, tearing into Alison as if she felt nothing but disdain for her.

Says you, who's never dared do anything, she had sneered, pointing an angry finger. Her face had actually twisted, distorted with contempt. *Says you, who never goes out, who doesn't have a life, who's too scared to seek out any kind of relationship. Don't preach at me, when you're too cowardly to do anything new!*

The sentences had cut Alison to the quick, had dug into her like barbs that were impossible to remove. Her own daughter calling her a coward, jeering at her as if she was nothing. It had hurt. Really hurt. When she *did* have a full and busy life, with work and her telly-lover Internet friends. When she *had* been going out recently as well, thank you very much, on her two terrible dates! So what did Robyn know about anything?

Oh, there had been apologetic messages ever since, on Alison's voicemail, and texts too, telling her that she hadn't meant it, she was so sorry. Fed up with the incessant beeping of her phone, Alison had eventually texted back with a brief: *It's okay, don't worry about it* – but it was not okay, whatever she might say, and they both knew it. A line had been crossed. A slap had been dealt. And however much Robyn might wish she could take the words back, they were out there now, and there could be no unsaying of them.

The worst thing was, Alison recognized herself in her daughter's ugly description. However much she disliked the idea of being a coward, she knew, deep down, that Robyn had a point. And this recognition had remained lodged in her head the entire weekend, buzzing around her thoughts like a demented bluebottle, even when she tried to distract herself by sorting out the shed or immersing herself in a good film. *My daughter thinks I'm a coward,* she kept thinking miserably. *And I am.*

But anyway. It was a new day now, a new week, and here she was, cutting the hair of Molly, who was in her late fifties at a guess and who seemed very pleasant, wearing a navy blouse with a seagull print, and who had gleaming chequered lino in her kitchen and a posh coffee machine. The last thing Alison wanted was to spread her dark mood around and infect another person, especially a new client whom she was supposed to be impressing. Had she even spoken in the last five minutes? No. Gloom had swallowed her up for too long now, and she needed to bring out her inner perky.

'Got anything nice on this week?' she asked chattily, pulling strands down on either side of the woman's face to check she had matched the lengths correctly. Perhaps the left was just a fraction shorter than the right, she decided, straightening up.

'Well . . .' Alison saw Molly's expression change. 'Actually this week is always a bit of a strange one for me,' she said, wrinkling her nose. 'Which is partly why I decided to get a haircut, you know, to give myself a bit of a lift. It's the anniversary of my son's death, so . . .'

'Oh my goodness,' Alison said, sympathy flaring inside her. Her fingers hovered uselessly behind the woman's head; she didn't know whether to resume snipping or not. 'I'm so sorry. How awful.'

'It was eight years ago now,' Molly said, her voice flat.

'Meningitis; he was only twenty-six. The nicest kid you can imagine. Just started a new job as a chef over in Leeds, and he had everything going for him – lovely girlfriend, smashing little flat.'

'Oh dear,' said Alison wretchedly, measuring a length of Molly's hair between her fingers. Snip, snip, snip. 'The world can be so cruel sometimes.'

'You're not wrong,' said Molly, as soft tufts of hair fell to the floor around her. 'The thing is, I know I'll be fine again next week – well, as fine as you ever can be, that is. I've dealt with the grief, I've come to terms with the fact that he's gone. It's just this one week of the year, it always gets to me. Makes me feel fragile.' She gave a rueful-sounding sigh. 'Sorry, love. You don't want to hear me feeling sorry for myself, do you? I bet you're wishing you'd never asked me now!'

'No, you're fine, no need to apologize,' Alison told her. There was a lump in her throat suddenly – a pang of sympathy for the woman, and the resonance that came from having suffered a similar loss. Her instinct was to steer the subject round to more cheerful subjects, to move away from bereavement and its lingering effects, but in her head Robyn was still glaring and pointing that finger, calling her a coward. So instead she found herself blurting out, 'And I know exactly what you mean.' She swallowed, feeling the colour rise to her cheeks, as the words came tripping off her tongue. 'I always have a wobble myself at the beginning of March – that was when my husband died. Even longer ago than your son, but it still brings everything back. I'll turn the page on my calendar and there it is, that ache of grief again.'

'It's tough, losing someone,' Molly agreed. 'Even though we all know nothing lasts forever, it still doesn't make it any easier.' She paused as Alison came round to measure her hair once more, a strand in each hand, looking left and right to gauge the lengths. 'Had he been ill for a long time, your husband, or was it a sudden thing? Not that either way is any better, mind.'

'He . . .' Alison felt herself closing up as she always did whenever the subject of Rich was raised. In all these years she'd hardly spoken about him, let alone confided in anyone what, exactly, had happened in his last moments. Not a single other person in Yorkshire knew the facts surrounding his death, because she'd been so paranoid about Robyn ever finding out. 'Um,' she said, resuming snipping, 'it was sudden. Very sudden. He—'

She broke off in anguish and Molly reached a hand round and patted her arm soothingly. 'It's okay,' she said. 'You don't have to tell me if you don't want to. Forget I asked.'

Normally, of course, this was where Alison would accept the escape route with gratitude, where she would lapse into silence with perhaps a mumbled 'I don't really like talking about it' as her defence card. Nobody ever questioned that statement, they withdrew immediately and the subject would be tactfully changed. But today for some reason – perhaps due to Molly's calm, kind presence, or perhaps Robyn's words still smarting beneath the surface – Alison felt a shift inside her, an unlocking sensation. And then she was stunned to hear her own voice saying, 'Actually, it was suicide. Completely out of the blue. I've never really got over it.'

'Oh, Alison,' said Molly, a hand flying up to her mouth. 'I'm sorry. That must have been terrible.'

'It was, it really was. I found him one morning and—' She broke off because she had remembered, belatedly, that it was Alison's rather gossipy client, Tina, who'd given Molly Alison's number in the first place; they were friends, and if Tina got to hear about Alison's misfortunes, it would be all over town within seconds. 'Listen, please don't tell anyone,' she begged fearfully. 'My own daughter doesn't even know how her dad died. I would hate for word to get around.'

'Goodness, of course I won't tell anyone,' Molly said. 'You can trust me, I promise.'

'Nobody here knows – I've never talked about it before. I don't know why I've started pouring my heart out to you, when we've only just met.' Alison's hands shook on the scissors and she had to take a deep breath and a mouthful of coffee to compose herself. 'Sorry,' she said, embarrassed. What must this woman think of her?

'Honestly, it's fine,' Molly assured her again. 'These things can take a while to work themselves to the surface. I didn't cry for two weeks after my Scott died; I was completely numb. Then this woman knocked on the door, delivering some flowers, and I found myself breaking down on her. Poor thing, she looked terrified, having this random lunatic sobbing on the front doorstep. Made *me* feel a lot better, but I doubt it was mutual.'

'Can you tip your head forward for me?' Alison said just then, and Molly bent at the neck obligingly. 'Maybe I should have got it out of my system at the time, but . . . Well, I was trying to pick up the pieces and protect my daughter, and keeping going seemed like the best way to cope.'

'Whatever gets you through,' agreed Molly. 'Still, it's good if you're feeling able to talk about what happened now, even if it's just to me. I could give you the number of the counsellor I went to see, if you want. I found that really helped – just getting everything off my chest to a stranger, who sat there and listened, who didn't judge me or tell me to pull myself together. Honestly, it was very cathartic.'

Alison had been rather dubious about counselling in the past; she'd grown up as part of a generation where you toughed things out and got on with life, rather than indulging in anything more emotional. It was on the tip of her tongue to say: no, thank you, she would be fine, she didn't need help. But *was* she fine? she thought despondently in the next moment. Because maybe it would do her good to release the whole terrible story out into somebody's quiet consulting room. To say it out loud, at last, to unburden the details from where they'd lain like a heavy, damp blanket on her for so many years. Even better, to have someone say, 'It wasn't your fault' in reply, which was really all she had ever wanted to hear.

'Thank you,' she said after a moment. Maybe this was the universe telling her that her old coping mechanisms were no longer fit for purpose, she thought to herself; a sign that she should stop being such a coward, as Robyn had accused her. Maybe this wise new client of hers was offering a means of conquering those old demons and getting her life back in order. 'Sounds good to me,' she heard herself saying, as she snipped a neat line against Molly's pale neck. 'I'll give that a try.'

Chapter Twenty-Five

'Knock, knock, you've got visitors,' Paula said, pulling back the floor-length curtain and slipping through to Bunny's bedside. 'How are you feeling?'

'We've brought you some magazines and chocolate,' Robyn added, following her in and setting the carrier bag down carefully at the end of the bed. She was trying not to wince at the sight of her sister-in-law's bashed-up face, but it was not a pretty sight.

'Hi,' croaked Bunny in a small voice. There was a large bandage around her head and a surgical dressing taped to one cheek, her eyes were puffy and red and there was a sore-looking red graze on her chin. Normally she was gorgeous, Bunny, with her blonde hair carefully styled and her make-up beautifully applied, but today there wasn't so much as a lick of mascara on her lashes, and her hair lay clumpy and tousled against the pillow. She reminded Robyn of a broken doll, lying there so still and quiet, the white sheets pulled up almost to her chin. 'Thank you.'

'Poor you, what a nightmare,' Paula said, perching in a plastic chair by the bed. 'Mum and Dad send their love, by the way. They're back home and haven't argued once yet, apparently, so I think it's happy days Chez Mortimer again – touch wood. But enough about them, how are you?'

'Did Dave . . . Is he here?' Bunny asked.

'Um . . . no,' said Robyn, glancing round as if he might appear from behind the curtain. 'I mean, he didn't come in with us, no, but he might be on his way,' she added, as the other woman's face crumpled.

'He texted everyone last night to let us know how you were doing,' Paula said. 'He's told your boss at the café as well, by the way, so don't worry about that. Have you got to stay in here long?'

'I'm not sure,' Bunny replied, but in such a subdued voice she almost sounded as if she didn't care either way. 'Did Dave say . . . anything else?'

'Just that he'd been in to see you and that you felt pretty crap, but that it could have been worse,' Paula replied. 'Has he been back today?'

'No,' said Bunny, and Robyn saw, to her dismay, that tears were forming in Bunny's eyes. 'I don't know if he will.'

'I'm sure he will!' Paula cried in surprise. 'He doesn't get off until five-thirty usually, does he? We're only here this early because my four o'clock viewing cancelled on me at the last minute and my boss said I didn't have to come back in. Luke's been roped into looking after Robyn's kids, so we thought we'd pop on over.'

Bunny blinked at the barrage of information delivered in one single breath. 'Thank you,' she said listlessly.

'It's amazing the power you have over a fifteen-year-old boy when he's got a birthday coming up,' Paula joked. 'Which reminds me – I'm doing the birthday tea for him at our place this time: Sunday, three o'clock. Mum's actually agreed to hand over the responsibility for party teas to me from now on, so I'm going all out to make this first one a goodie. Obviously *everyone*'s invited,' she said, with a meaningful glance at Robyn. 'And don't worry, it won't be me doing all the baking, so nobody will end up with food poisoning. Mum's still doing the big cake, but Matt reckons he can knock up some sausage rolls, Joe's on scone duty and actually Luke himself is such a good cook, he's dead keen to get involved and show off his skills. My job is to buy all the ingredients and wash up afterwards. So there's something to get yourself better for,' she told Bunny.

Bunny said nothing, but a tear trickled from her eye into the pillow. 'Hey,' said Robyn gently, plucking a tissue from a box on the side. 'Come on, now. You'll feel better soon.'

Bunny sniffled. 'I might not be able to go to the party,' she said mournfully. 'Because Dave—' A sob engulfed her, and Paula and Robyn exchanged concerned glances.

'What's Dave gone and done?' Paula asked. 'Honestly!

These bloody brothers of mine, they're all as bad as each other. Do I need to have a word? Cross *him* off my Christmas list and all?'

'Should I get the nurse?' Robyn asked, wondering if Bunny's tears were due to the pain of her injuries rather than emotional goings-on. 'How about a drink of water?'

But Bunny shook her head miserably, declining all options, until the other two women felt quite useless. It must be the concussion making her so upset, Robyn thought, biting her lip and hoping their visit hadn't in fact made Bunny feel worse.

'Sorry,' spluttered Bunny eventually, pressing a tissue into one eye, then the other. 'I'm . . . I'm sorry. Will you tell him that for me? Will you tell him that I said sorry?'

'Yes, of course,' Paula said, puzzled. 'But don't worry, I'm sure you haven't done anything to be sorry *for.*'

Bunny shuddered, her eyes dark and haunted-looking. 'But I have,' she insisted tonelessly. And then she turned away and wouldn't say any more.

Life could change so fast, thought Robyn later on, once she'd picked up Sam and Daisy from Paula's and was driving them home. The last time she'd seen Bunny, she'd been the vibrant, fun-loving girl, giving it her all on a dance floor – and now today she was whimpering and despairing in a hospital bed, barely able to stop crying. One ill-timed spin of her front wheels, and her spirit seemed to have been as badly wrecked as the bonnet of her car.

'I hope she'll be all right,' Paula had said worriedly when they came out of the hospital. 'You hear such scary things about head injuries and brain damage, don't you? She seemed all over the place.'

'It must have been shock too,' Robyn said, although she had been similarly alarmed by Bunny's fragility. 'And I bet they've got her on really powerful painkillers – they can make you over-emotional. It was all that stuff about Dave that took me by surprise, though; I'd always thought those two were rock-solid.' Like me and John, she thought dully. Which went to show how little anyone really knew about someone else's relationship.

'Same,' Paula had mused. 'But Bunny obviously doesn't.' She hugged Robyn goodbye. 'You okay, by the way? Sorry, we didn't get much of a chance to talk about you. How are you doing?'

'Hanging in there by the skin of my teeth,' replied Robyn grimly, having made it through the weekend and now a day's work, albeit with enormous effort. Stephen had dropped in the other evening with a massive bunch of flowers for her, and his commiserations. He'd done his best in Edinburgh, he'd told her, but John was still firmly convinced he was in love with this student, and that was that. *I'm sorry, darling,* he'd said, hugging Robyn. *What can I say –*

he doesn't deserve you. She'd been so touched by his kindness, she'd nearly burst into tears on him.

'Well, you know I've got your back,' Paula told her now. 'So you just keep on hanging in there and ring me any time you want to chat. And I'll see you soon, yeah? For Luke's party?'

'Yeah,' Robyn replied. 'Thanks. We'll be there.'

With a last goodbye, she set off, driving home extra-carefully with Bunny in mind; keeping well under the speed limit, checking her mirrors with exaggerated deliberation. You never knew when an accident might happen – when a freak skid would send you flying, when a loving husband would walk out of your life. However hard you tried to keep your world safe, there was just this unknown random element that could topple you without warning. As she parked up and let the kids into the house, it struck her that the really crucial thing was to make the most of what you had while it was still there – and not to allow bad feeling to fester between loved ones.

And so, just as soon as she'd put the oven on and slid two supermarket pizzas inside (look, she was going to start cooking from scratch properly again soon, all right? Definitely next week), she dialled her mum's number for what felt like the hundredth time since Saturday. If Alison was getting sick of her calls, then so be it, but Robyn felt more determined than ever to put things right between them. Not really expecting her mum to pick up, she had a speech prepared for the voicemail regardless, about how important family was, and how much she valued Alison, as well as apologizing again for what she'd said. Which meant that she was taken by surprise when, after three rings, she heard her mother's voice in her ear. 'Hi, love.'

'Mum, hi!' Robyn said, all of her planned eloquence immediately deserting her. 'How are you?'

'I'm fine,' Alison replied. 'How are you?'

'I'm okay,' she said, 'but, Mum, listen, I was ringing to say that I really don't want to fall out with you, and I'm truly sorry. The advice you gave me the other day was spot-on and you were only being kind, I shouldn't have spoken to you like that.'

'I don't want to fall out, either,' Alison told her. 'But I've been doing a lot of thinking. What you said to me . . . I found the comments hard to take. They got to me. But perhaps that was because there was an element of truth in them. And perhaps I needed to hear it.' A small sigh came down the line. 'Sometimes you just have to take the medicine, don't you, however nasty it tastes.'

'I shouldn't have upset you, though,' Robyn replied wretchedly. 'I could have said those things in a far nicer way, rather than beating you over the head with them.'

'True,' Alison agreed. 'But the fact is: you spoke from the heart. I *have* been a coward, you were right. I've not really dealt with my feelings very well, I've not been brave. And maybe I just needed a kick up the backside to realize that. After talking to you and a client I had today, it's made me decide: I'm going to do my best to change.'

'You don't have to change!' Robyn cried, feeling more guilty than ever. For all the times she'd wished her mum would leave the safe confines of her comfort zone, she didn't want it to be like this – with Robyn forcibly tipping her out. 'Not if you don't want to, Mum!'

There was a pause where Robyn pulled a bag of salad from the fridge and automatically dropped a handful of leaves onto four plates, before remembering that John wasn't there for dinner any more. When would she get used to that?

'I think I want to change,' Alison said quietly in the next moment. 'I want to get out there and . . . have another try. Say yes to a few things again, rather than no all the time.' She gave a little laugh. 'Believe it or not, when you called me last Wednesday, the reason I wasn't at home was because . . . well, I was actually on a date. So, you know, I'm not past it just yet.'

'Mum!' Robyn could hardly believe what she was hearing. She felt quite lost for words – for a whole two seconds anyway, before the questions came gushing forth. 'So did it go well? Did you like him?' Then reality dawned on her and she choked on a cry. 'Oh God. And I interrupted it! I'm so sorry. Did you abandon him?'

'Yes, I bloody did, and I've never been so glad to make an excuse and leave,' Alison told her. 'Honestly, he was awful. Absolutely awful. Two dates I've been on, and they've both been terrible. The good guys were all snapped up decades ago, it seems.'

Two dates! She was a dark horse. 'Well, you know what they say,' Robyn replied encouragingly. 'Third time lucky, Mum. There'll be a real-life prince for you next time, I bet.'

'Hmm, I'm not so sure there's going to be a next time,' Alison replied. 'But never mind. Chalk it up to experience.'

'Forget men for the time being, then,' Robyn said. 'And let me take you out one night – to the cinema or for dinner, or . . . whatever you want to do. My treat for you rescuing me last week and being so kind and lovely when I needed you.'

'Oh, now,' said Alison, but she sounded pleased and didn't argue, for once. 'That would be very nice. Thank you.'

'You're welcome,' Robyn said, glad that the two of them seemed to be back on their usual footing once more. 'Anyway, I need to be brave too,' she went on, eyeing the fourth plate she'd accidentally set out, before tipping the salad leaves back in the bag and returning the plate to its shelf on the dresser. 'I need to start living again, without John – to sort myself out, just like you were saying the other day. I've got to get my head around the fact that he might not come back, that there'll just be the three of us for the foreseeable future. So maybe we could make a pact together, that we're both going to do our best to nail this life-business, somehow or other. Okay?'

'You're on,' said Alison, sounding much more positive. 'Now, enough pep-talking, it's nearly time for my favourite TV programme – I'm joking! Not really. I'm going to leave the telly off tonight, pour myself a glass of wine and make a plan of action. The bold new Alison Tremayne starts here! How about you?'

'I'm in,' said Robyn. 'The independent new Robyn Mortimer is just waiting to come out of hiding too, I'm sure. And we'll meet up soon to compare how go-getting and invincible we are, yeah?' She peered through the oven door to see that the cheese on top of the pizzas was bubbling and just starting to brown. Perfect. 'I'd better go. Bye, Mum. Love you.'

'Bye, darling. Thanks for ringing. Love you, too.'

A plan of action, thought Robyn, cutting the pizzas into slices and bellowing for the children to come and wash their hands. Options to ponder over, decisions to make, worlds to conquer. She could put out feelers in her old department, she supposed: brush up her CV, get on the phone and see what work she could drum up. The thought of calling the shots again, taking control in this way, was daunting but at the same time kind of exciting.

No more sitting around waiting for John to come home,

no more needing to be rescued by another person, she told herself staunchly. She was Robyn Mortimer, and she was perfectly capable of rescuing herself.

Lying in her hospital bed, Bunny kept having woozy flash-backs to the last time she'd been similarly indisposed, when Mark Roberts had punched the living daylights out of her and done his best to break every bone in her body. Back then, of course, she'd been glad to stay within the safety of the hospital where he couldn't get her; back then she'd drifted in and out of painkiller-fuelled delirium, grateful for the novelty of being cared for. This time, though, she felt imprisoned; trapped by her own bad luck, with the added misery of wondering if Dave was ever going to forgive her for her deceit. If things had been different, she'd have been in a new town by now, setting out the parameters of a whole new life for herself. Unfortunately she was going to have to stay right here and face the music of her old one instead.

She'd felt so embarrassed when Paula and Robyn had turned up earlier that afternoon, all concerned faces and kind comments, she'd hardly been able to look them in the eye. How much did they know? What had Dave said? Did he hate her? Did they? Too befuddled by the drugs, too scared to ask outright, she'd had to try and read between the lines of what they'd said, but that had proved less than satisfactory. From what she could gather, Dave hadn't told his sister any of the drama that lay behind her secrets – which gave absolutely no clues as to his feelings on the subject.

And now it was six o'clock and the ward was filling with visitors; you could hear them arriving either side of the privacy curtains, fussing over their loved ones, bringing cups of tea and exchanging small items of news. The woman in the bed to the left – Elsie, Bunny thought she was called – was telling some uninterested-sounding bloke about the cottage pie they'd been served for lunch, while the woman on her right was speaking in what might have been Polish, very fast and animatedly, to a friend. Meanwhile, in Bunny's cubicle all that could be heard was the ringing No-Dave silence. Was he going to strand her there in her own miserable company all evening, punish her by abandonment? He must have gone home and Googled her last night, as she'd instructed him to, and discovered everything. Now that he was wise to what she'd done, he clearly didn't want to know her any more, just as she'd predicted. It felt awful. Even though she'd originally tried to leave, saying that he deserved better and she wasn't good enough for him – the fact that he now seemed to be agreeing with her seemed a much harder pill to swallow.

After he'd said goodbye the night before, she'd had her phone ready beside her for hours afterwards, braced for a text or a call, some word that would tell her Dave's response.

But no word had come. Her phone remained resolutely silent. And then this morning she'd woken up and reached for it, only to realize in dismay that at some point it had gone stone dead, with no means of recharging. She couldn't even text Dave a tentative hello, let alone anything more exploratory. Short of passing her brief message to him via Paula, she was just going to have to wait for him to make contact – if he even chose to, that was.

'As for the peas, they were straight out of a tin. And ruddy disgusting they were, too!' exploded Elsie from the left just then. 'I said to the nurse: I'm not eating those. You'd have to *pay* me to eat those!' (It was true, Bunny had heard her scathing refusal with her own ears. The entire ward had.)

'Oh dear,' said her visitor, who sounded practically comatose with boredom by now.

Elsie went on to describe the insult that had been the treacle sponge pudding ('with the runniest custard – like water it was, and I'm not exaggerating!') while Bunny's thoughts turned to the possible whereabouts of her phone charger, which had last been seen in the boot of her car, stuffed into one of her bags. She wondered what had become of it, as well as the rest of her things, for that matter – not to mention what had happened to the car itself. One of the paramedics had brought her handbag in for her when they'd arrived in A&E, but that was the sole possession she had at the moment. If Dave was really angry with her, might he have destroyed the rest of her stuff? Dumped the lot of it in the nearest skip? How could she go creeping back for her clothes and make-up when he probably wanted nothing more to do with her? With her car a write-off and barely one hundred pounds in her account, she wouldn't be able to get very far now. What was she going to do?

'All right there, pet, let's have a quick look at you,' said a nurse just then, whisking through the curtain with a portable blood-pressure monitor. 'How are you feeling this evening?'

Like my heart is breaking and I've got nowhere to turn. 'Still a bit weird,' Bunny confessed, shuffling up into a sitting position.

'Don't we all, my darling,' replied the nurse. She was in her forties, broad-shouldered and freckly, her auburn ponytail swinging as she bent over Bunny to slide the blood-pressure cuff up her forearm. 'But in your case, at least you've got an excuse, with that bumped head of yours. How are you managing with the pain?'

'It's okay,' Bunny said because, despite the dull throbbing of her temples, that was really the least of her worries. 'Has anybody phoned for me?' she asked.

'Phoned for you? Not that I know of, but I've only just started my shift. I can find out for you once I've finished here.' She pumped up the cuff until Bunny's arm was squeezed tight, then examined the reading. 'That's looking better,' she said, giving Bunny a quizzical once-over. 'And your colour's coming back too, that's another good sign.' She jotted a few things down on her file and smiled. 'You'll be out of here in no time, don't you fret.'

Bunny tried to smile back, but didn't have the heart to say that actually getting out of here, and having to figure out what the hell she was going to do with herself, was *exactly* what she was fretting about. 'Thanks,' she mumbled.

'I'll leave you to it for—Oh!' The nurse stepped back as another person came through the curtain. 'Excuse me,' she said, edging around him and out again.

'Dave!' cried Bunny, weak with relief at the sight of him walking towards the bed, still with one cycle clip around his trouser leg, his hair tufting up slightly, as it did every night when he got in and removed his bike helmet. She felt a wash of trepidation to see him, tempered with relief and maybe even hope. 'You came back.'

'Of course I came back,' he said, sounding bemused. 'You can't get rid of me that easily.' He sat down beside her and took her hands. 'How are you today? You don't look as peaky as you did last night.'

Bunny blinked at him, confused. He *had* actually read the stuff about her, hadn't he? Because he was acting as if nothing had happened. 'I'm okay,' she replied cautiously. Was this some kind of trick? 'So . . . do you know?' she blurted out, unable to help herself. 'What I did, I mean. Did you look me up, like I said to?'

He nodded, his face impassive for a moment. Then he turned to her, his eyes sad. 'I wish you'd told me before, about all of that. And about your name, and everything. I've been telling everyone your name's Bernadette. I felt a right idiot when the police rang yesterday, saying you were called Rachel. Why didn't you set me straight?'

Bunny thought dejectedly of the way the local press had sensationalized the story, of her own family reacting with such horror, of how Margaret hadn't been able to get rid of her quickly enough. It had just been easier, at the start, to pretend and conceal, to bury Rachel somewhere deep down inside her. 'I just . . . I didn't want what happened then to be the biggest thing about me,' she replied. 'I didn't want to put you off. I didn't want you to flinch every time I picked up a knife to chop vegetables, or for you to doubt me, or look at me in a different way.' She could feel those tears again, gathering at the corners of her eyes. 'I was just trying to put the past behind me and start again. And when you misunderstood my name that first time . . .' She bit her lip. 'Look, we'd only just met, I didn't know that I was going to fall in love with you and move in. And after a while it was too hard to go back and correct you. That's all. I'm sorry. I was scared I would ruin everything.' A small, miserable laugh escaped her throat. 'Turns out I managed that, anyway.'

There was silence for a moment, interrupted by Elsie's loud voice from the left. 'Well, you know what my bowels are like,' she was saying dourly.

'Yes, love,' her visitor replied with a distinct lack of enthusiasm. 'Yes, I do.'

Dave was still so het up he hadn't noticed the conversation on the other side of the curtain. 'But it's not like you did anything to be ashamed of,' he said in confusion. 'He attacked you – and you defended yourself. As would anybody, in that situation. What you did, it was just self-preservation, wasn't it?'

'Yes,' Bunny replied. 'Although . . .' She sighed, feeling the pounding in her head increase. 'Dave, I've got to be honest with you, I did really hate him by then,' she added in a low voice.

'I'm not surprised you did. I bloody hate him as well,' Dave said passionately. 'In fact, I've a good mind to find out which prison he's currently languishing in and—'

It had suddenly gone very quiet in the beds on either side, Bunny realized, and she took his hand to silence him, wary of the furious eavesdropping that was almost certainly taking place. 'Sshh,' she said. 'Maybe this isn't the most private place to discuss it.'

He clasped her hand between both of his. 'I'm so sorry

you had to go through all of that, anyway,' he said quietly. 'It sounds absolutely horrendous. And I understand why you wanted a new start. But you can talk to me, you know, love. About anything at all. I'm on your side – always will be.'

She had been so certain that Dave would reject her, like everybody else, that his calm, kind acceptance was hard to get her head around. 'You're on my side,' she repeated dumbly, wondering if she had somehow misunderstood.

'Yes! One hundred per cent.' He shook his head, as if baffled that this needed confirmation. 'Bun, when I got home and saw the note you'd left, and realized that you'd actually planned to go, just like that, without any forwarding address . . . I was gutted that you could have done such a thing. Because the thought of losing you like that – of you just *vanishing* and me not being able to find you . . .' His mouth pressed together momentarily, his expression stricken. 'I don't know what I'd have done. I'd have been broken without you. I mean it.'

'Sorry,' she croaked, feeling a lump in her throat. Her departure had, at the time, seemed like the kindest move, long-term, but now she just felt cruel for the way she'd gone about it.

'I was almost glad that you'd been prevented from getting very far – no, not *glad*,' he said, correcting himself. 'Relieved, at least, that you hadn't completely gone.' He gazed beseechingly at her. 'Please, don't ever do that to me again. I couldn't bear it if you just went like that. I'm not saying you have to stay with me forever – although I really hope you'll want to – but at least tell me, next time you're dumping me and moving out.'

This last was said in a jokey sort of way, but all the same, Bunny knew he was serious. 'I promise,' she replied, just as the nurse popped her head around the curtain.

'Phone calls!' she cried. 'You were asking me if anyone had phoned – and I've just found a whole list of messages scribbled down on our desk, which clearly nobody has passed on to you. I'm so sorry.'

'You haven't been getting my messages?' Dave asked, and Bunny shook her head.

'So there are – let me see – six messages here from Dave Mortimer.'

Bunny made a choking sound as Dave told the nurse, 'That's me. There should be another five or six on your phone,' he added to Bunny.

'Which is unhelpfully dead,' she replied.

'Oh dear!' said the nurse. 'Well, I'm sorry to both of you then. Someone on the morning shift must have jotted them down – and then a folder was left on top of the pad and . . . Anyway, you're all caught up now at least. I'll leave you in peace.'

Dave looked over at Bunny as the curtain swished shut once more. 'You must have been thinking all sorts,' he said.

'I was,' replied Bunny, which was pretty much the under-statement of the year. 'I was kind of assuming you didn't want to know.'

'Well, that's where you're wrong,' he said firmly. 'I absolutely do want to know. And I love you every bit as much as I did before this all happened. So there.'

Maybe it was the extra-strength painkillers making her feel strange, but it was as if a hard, granite lump inside Bunny was loosening its bonds, turning soft and liquid, draining away. Hope burst within her. 'Do you really—' she began, but all of a sudden Dave was getting off his seat and kneeling down on the hospital floor.

'Bunny, also known as Rachel,' he began.

'Dave!' she squeaked, hardly able to believe what was happening.

'Would you make me the happiest man in Yorkshire and do me the honour of becoming my wife?'

'Dave!' she yelped again. 'Are you . . . are you actually serious?'

'Oh my God, listen, Derek,' she heard Elsie saying in hushed tones on the other side of the curtain.

'I have never been more serious,' Dave pronounced. 'Will you marry me?'

Once again, tears were glistening in Bunny's eyes, but these were good tears. Happy tears. 'Yes,' she managed to say. 'Oh yes!'

'Did you hear that? She said yes!' Elsie cried, in a shame-lessly unsubtle way, but Bunny didn't care. In fact, she didn't care about anything other than Dave leaning over and kissing her so tenderly, so lovingly, that she never wanted him to stop.

Chapter Twenty-Six

Paula was having a good day. She'd just shown a very keen couple around an extremely nice townhouse a stone's throw from the Minster and was confident they'd be after a second viewing, if not making an offer, within forty-eight hours. The property was one of those rare unicorn-like beasts in York – a Georgian property that had been beautifully restored, with no ongoing chain – the sort that you could move into immediately and feel completely at home in. The keys still jangling in her pocket (she'd take them back to the office tomorrow), she was now following a white-uniformed waitress and her mother downstairs to the lower lounge at Betty's, where they had arranged to meet for tea and a catch-up. Yes, she was sloping off work an hour early, again. No, she didn't feel the slightest twinge of guilt about this transgression.

'Well, I cannot *believe* what your brother's been up to,' Jeanie said, the moment they'd ordered, cosily ensconced at a table for two, amidst the wood panelling and softly glowing wall-lamps. They were seated next to a boisterous family with three young children, who had just been to the Viking museum and were insistent on wearing their helmets at the table. 'John, I mean – obviously. The shame of it! The brass neck of him! Phoning me from Edinburgh last night, telling me he's in love with this . . . this *girl*! "For goodness' sake," I told him, "will you get over yourself and stop being such a complete and utter nitwit?" '

'Is that what you said?' Paula asked, trying not to snigger at the thought of John having to contend with one of Jeanie's legendary dressing-downs over the phone. Even when you were in your forties, there was something kind of satisfying about your parents slagging off one of your siblings so reproachfully, especially when this particular brother had always been the self-professed Golden Boy. She was reminded of her own sons, who always loved it when the other one got in trouble. 'Am *I* being good, Mum?' the smug cry would go up. It was on the tip of her tongue to say the same words now, but she managed to restrain herself.

'Yes, I jolly well did say that to him. Worse, actually, because I'd had a sherry and I was a bit emotional. What does he think he's playing at, though? A dirty old man, that's what he is, going off with a young girl like that. It's disgusting!' Her lips trembled suddenly. 'And how dare he jeopardize things with my grandchildren? I mean, he's my son, my eldest child, and of course I love the absolute bones of him, but for him to do this . . . to behave in such a way . . . This is not how your father and I brought him up. "I'm ashamed of you," I told him. "You're not the son I thought you were." '

Jeanie was looking quite distressed and Paula felt bad for having smirked moments earlier. 'It's grim,' she agreed. 'It's not just the fact of her being so young, it's that John could treat Robyn and the kids so shabbily. What's he playing at?'

'I know. Poor Robyn!' cried Jeanie. 'I don't know what to do, whether to go round there or not. Robyn might not want anything more to do with our family.'

'I think she does,' Paula replied. 'I think she'd appreciate it, if you popped round. In fact she was worried that we would all cut her off, or something – you know, drop her, just like John did.'

'She said that? No!' Jeanie said, looking aghast. 'Where did she get that idea from? Oh – thank you,' she said, as the waitress appeared just then with their tea tray. 'Lovely. Gosh, I did miss my tea while I was away. It's not the same, is it, tea on holiday? Not as good as the real thing.'

They busied themselves pouring drinks and adding milk, then Paula braced herself to wheel out the big question. 'How's it going with you and Dad, then?' she asked, picking an almond off the top of her warm Fat Rascal scone and posting it into her mouth. 'How are you finding the return back to normal life? Tell me he's done the dishes a few times. Made you another cheese omelette, even?'

Jeanie gave a small smile as she buttered her teacake. 'Breakfast in bed, the other morning,' she replied. 'Honestly, I don't know what you said to him, but he's become very helpful around the place. As for the two of us . . . well, we're getting there. We've talked about –' she hesitated, as if she couldn't quite bring herself to say the words – 'his affair, and this woman who claims to be his daughter . . .'

'I'm pretty sure she is, Mum,' Paula said gently.

'And we're just trying to get on with things now. There are only so many times you can hear your husband yapping plaintively on about how sorry he is, before it gets right on your wick. So I've said okay and never mind, and all the rest of it. But the thing is, Paula . . .'

The children at the next table were now whacking each other on their helmets with plastic Viking swords, and Paula had to lean in closer to hear. 'Yes?' she asked apprehensively, cutting her scone in half.

'The thing is . . .' Jeanie repeated, putting a hand up to her face suddenly, as if in shame. 'You're going to think me a terrible person now. But the truth is, I didn't behave very well on holiday myself.'

'STOP THAT THIS MINUTE,' the woman on the next table hissed just then, snatching swords off her children and shoving them out of reach. (Paula always rather loved seeing unruly children and harassed parents out in public; it never failed to make her feel better about her own mothering skills, or lack of.) Then Jeanie's words percolated through the clamour.

'What do you mean?' Paula asked. 'What did you *do*?' she went on, when no reply came. 'Mum?'

Jeanie sighed. 'I had a lot of fun, put it like that,' she said, sipping her tea. 'Perhaps . . .' Her hand trembled as she set the cup down. 'Perhaps rather too much fun.'

Uh-oh. Paula wasn't sure she liked the sound of this. Please say that her mum wasn't about to confess to having indulged in rampant sex all around Madeira. 'When you say "too much fun",' she began delicately, her mind now thoroughly boggled, 'you're not saying . . . Mum, you didn't have a fling yourself, did you?'

There was an awful moment of silence before Jeanie slowly shook her head. 'No. Not exactly. But I wanted to,' she admitted, her voice low. 'And I might have done, if . . .' She looked agonized. 'If the man in question hadn't been too much of a gentleman.'

'Oh, Mum,' said Paula, half-appalled, half-enthralled. 'But you didn't, so—'

'I drank too much, I acted like a silly schoolgirl, I had this ridiculous makeover, which doesn't even suit me,' Jeanie said despondently, flicking her fingers at the ends of her hair.

'So what? You were on holiday! Give yourself a break,'

Paula cried. 'And your hair will grow back anyway, if you're not keen.' It was on the tip of her tongue to lean forward conspiratorially, as she would have done with a friend, and ask if the gentleman in question had been hot, until she remembered her dad's mournful face of recent weeks. 'I take it Dad doesn't know about this,' she said instead.

Jeanie turned pale beneath her tan. 'Goodness, no, and I'm not planning to tell him either. This is strictly between you and me. I just wanted to get it off my chest – to confess my wickedness. I hope you don't mind. Honestly, nothing happened, except for me making a fool of myself. Being a silly old woman.'

'You're not a silly old woman,' Paula said. 'Look, we've all done daft things we regret. It's just part of being human.' Now she felt sorry for her mum, whose lip was wobbling. 'Don't worry,' she said, patting her hand. 'Honestly, Mum. And you know I can keep a secret.'

'Thank you, darling. Anyway, this is why I can't be too angry with your dad any more,' Jeanie said with a sigh. 'Because I know what it is to be tempted. And it's easier than you think.' She pulled a guilty face and nibbled a small piece of teacake, the very image of the contrite wife. It didn't last long, though. Because then her eyes glittered and the contrition was gone again. 'It *was* really fun, though, flirting with a handsome man who wasn't your father,' she confided, leaning forward. 'Just a little bit anyway.'

'Mum!'

'I did feel naughty. Because I'd never done it before! And it made me feel very womanly. Very minxy. My goodness, I was a different person, I can tell you.'

'Mum!' Paula cried again, almost choking on her scone. 'Please! I'm not sure I want to hear this.' Minxy indeed. What had got into her?

'Sorry,' Jeanie said, although she didn't look that sorry, to be fair. 'I'll be doing all my flirting with your dad from now on, don't worry. But . . . do you think I'm awful? And if so, do you think you can forgive me for it?'

Paula looked at her mahogany-tanned, choppy-haired mother and smiled. 'You're not awful,' she assured her. 'And as far as I'm concerned, there's nothing to forgive.' Then she tapped her nose. 'Mum's the word.'

The conversation turned, thankfully, to more cheering subjects: first, to the fact that Bunny was coming out of hospital later that day and, even better, that she and Dave were going to get married in the spring. 'A wedding to look forward to, isn't it lovely?' Jeanie cried, clapping her hands together happily. Then they discussed the details of Luke's birthday tea, due to be held in two days' time, and whether Paula was *sure* she didn't mind having it at her house this time. (Yes, Paula was sure. Her mum had been an admirable captain of the Good Ship Mortimer for decades, but now it was Paula's turn to step up to the wheel.)

All this talk of parties reminded Paula that she still hadn't got very far with her present-buying for Luke. There was something about working in the city centre and having all the shops on her doorstep that meant she rather took them for granted, always ending up in a panicked last-minute rush before birthdays and Christmas.

Luckily, just as she and her mum parted ways, full of tea and scones, Paula's phone flashed up a message from Matt: a photo of him posing with an electric guitar in the music shop. *Present idea?* read the caption.

She smiled to herself. That husband of hers was a mind-reader sometimes. *Perfect,* she typed back. Then, because her mum's words about flirting were still echoing around her head, and because she had been struck by a rush of warmth for Matt, she sent another message immediately afterwards. *The present idea's not bad, either,* she typed with a winking-face emoji.

Her phone rang in the next second. 'Shall I buy it, then? I mean . . . it's a bit more than our budget, but he'll love it,' Matt said. Then, with a rather sheepish air, he added, 'I quite love it as well. Had a little go at "Stairway to Heaven" in the shop, I think the guy was impressed.'

'I'm amazed he hasn't asked you to be in his band,' Paula said, rolling her eyes. The keys to the property she'd viewed earlier jingled in her pocket as she walked along, and suddenly the most outrageous idea popped into her head. Maybe her mum wasn't the only one who could be a minx. 'Hey, so you're in town too,' she said thoughtfully, remembering the thick, soft carpet in the living room of the gorgeous Georgian townhouse. Shag-pile by name . . . 'Don't suppose you fancy doing something a little bit naughty, do you?'

'With you, always,' he replied at once. 'What are we talking?'

'You buy that guitar,' she told him, knowing how easily he could be sidetracked, 'and then come and meet me.' She gave him the address of the house, her fingers winding around the keys in her pocket. Now who was being awful? She could get sacked for this, if anyone found out. Ah, sod it. Sometimes you had to bend the rules for a bit of fun.

He gave a whistle. 'Paula Brent, I never thought I'd see the day,' he said. 'You want me to serenade you in a posh empty house – is that what you're saying?'

'Something way filthier than that,' she replied. She lowered her voice, making it breathily suggestive. 'Hurry up now. I'll be waiting.' Then she quickened her step, feeling positively devilish. Oh my goodness. Was she really going to do this? Yes, she blooming well was.

Barely had she put the phone back in her bag, however, than it rang again. 'Don't tell me,' she said, answering it with a laugh in her voice, 'you've gone and bought yourself one as well.'

There was a pause, and then an unfamiliar voice spoke – a voice that wasn't Matt at all. 'Um . . . Is that Paula's phone?'

Shit, and that was probably a client, and now she'd made a right tit of herself, she realized in the next moment. Not very professional. 'Sorry, yes, this is Paula speaking,' she said, trying to sound more sensible and businesslike.

'Paula, hi,' said the woman on the other end of the line. 'This is Frankie.'

Chapter Twenty-Seven

'Oh, wow, Frankie, hello!' came Paula's voice, sounding very northern and very excited. 'God, I'm so sorry I answered the phone like that. I thought you were my husband, about to go crazy in a music shop. But it's you. Hello! Sorry for babbling! I don't seem to be able to stop!'

Frankie laughed at the torrent of words pouring into her ear. Craig was giving Fergus his tea in the kitchen, and she'd seized the moment to escape into the bedroom with her phone. 'That's all right,' she said, suddenly feeling rather shy, now that a connection had been made. 'It's not your typical phone call, I realize. Is this a good time by the way?'

'Aargh,' came the response. 'Do you know, Frankie, I am actually on my way somewhere, so I'm going to walk and talk. Sorry if you hear any puffing and panting, I'm not the most athletic person in the world. But anyway! You got my message – thank you so much for ringing back. Your agent sounded dead suspicious of me, she must have thought I was a right weirdo.'

'She was a bit surprised,' Frankie agreed with another laugh. There was something so warm and friendly about the way Paula spoke, it instantly banished all the nerves that had been swirling about inside her. 'How did you track me down anyway? I've been trying to write a letter to Harry, introduce myself properly, but I couldn't find the words. I couldn't believe it when Constance said you'd rung.'

'Well, I found you on the video we got made for the party,' Paula explained. Frankie could hear traffic behind her voice, then the pinging of a pedestrian crossing. 'And do you know – we really look alike, us two! I saw you on the screen and thought it was me. Then I showed my friend and she recognized you from a magazine article, and then I just did some sleuthing and found your agent's number.' Now it was her turn to sound shy all of a sudden. 'I hope you don't mind me practically stalking you. I wasn't sure how I felt about you turning up at first, but as soon as I saw you, it was like recognizing myself and I got a bit over-excited. I've got three brothers, see – no sister. Until now.'

'I've never had a sister before, either,' Frankie said. 'Or a brother, come to that.'

'Well, you've got three great big ugly ones now, unlucky for you,' Paula told her, and they both laughed. 'No, they're all right, most of the time. Listen, though, I'm going to have to go in a minute – my husband's on his way to meet me and, um . . .' She trailed off for some reason.

'It's fine,' Frankie said quickly. 'We can chat properly another time. And meet up! If you want to?'

'I would love that,' Paula said. 'Can you believe it, I'm forty-two and I've never been to London before. Not that I'm inviting myself down or anything,' she added hastily.

'You're welcome at ours any time,' Frankie told her at once. 'Look, I know you've got to go, but just before we say goodbye – I hope I haven't caused massive problems for your family. It really wasn't my intention. I had absolutely no idea it was your parents' anniversary party, or I'd never have blundered in like that. Are they . . . I mean, is everything okay?'

'Er . . .' There was a short pause. 'I'm not gonna lie, it was a massive shock,' came the candid reply. 'To all of us. But I've just seen Mum for a catch-up and yeah, she's getting used to the idea.'

'Good,' Frankie said. 'And your dad? How does he feel?' Her breath caught in her lungs while she waited for the response.

'He's one hundred per cent chuffed,' Paula said. 'Well, apart from the bit when Mum threatened to leave him, and all the rest of it – but even then, he was telling me he wanted to meet you, and how fab your mum was. He didn't mention that to *my* mum, obviously, but . . . long story. So anyway, you're fine by us. And don't worry about turning up, like you did. I'm not sure a letter would have been any better. You've got guts – that's a good thing!'

'Thank you,' Frankie said, and it was as if a weight she hadn't even known was there had been lifted from her shoulders. 'That's really—'

But Paula was laughing. 'Oh God, here he comes,' she said. 'My husband, I mean. He's practically sprinting up the road with this enormous box . . . what a chump he is, honestly. Listen, I'd better go. So bloody lovely to speak to you, though! I'm just made up, really I am. And we'll speak again soon, yeah?'

'Yeah,' agreed Frankie. 'Lovely to talk to you, too. Bye, Paula.'

She ended the call and flopped back on the bed, beaming up at the ceiling. Oh my goodness. What a gift of a conversation. What an absolute win! She had a sister, who looked like her, and sounded so nice and funny and friendly. She had a dad, who wanted to meet her, and who still spoke fondly of her mum – as well as three older brothers into the bargain. This whole extra helping of family that she hadn't gone looking for, that had just come her way. Maybe her mum had been right to break cover with her letter, after all. And maybe, despite her fears, Frankie hadn't ruined her chances with the Mortimers, either.

The door burst open just then and in rushed Fergus, with tomato sauce all round his mouth. 'I had bersketti,' he said happily, his word for spaghetti, which Frankie always found completely endearing.

'I can see,' she laughed. 'Whoa – not on the bed, with those mucky chops, tomato-boy. Let's go and clean you up.' She jumped off to grab him, then scooped him up and twirled him around. 'Oh, the world's a good place, isn't it, Ferg?' she said, feeling insanely cheerful all of a sudden.

'Yes, Mumma,' he agreed. Then, as she stopped twirling, 'Again! Again!'

Paula's words sang around Frankie's head for the whole evening, and even the next morning she could feel a joyful spring in her step, a new positivity about facing the day. *You've got guts,* Paula had said warmly – admiringly, even! – and every time Frankie thought about this, she felt as if a genetic connection was twanging gently between her and her mother. Kathy had always been the gutsy one, going out on a limb if she felt strongly about a cause, a firm believer in doing the right thing, even if you were afraid. Maybe Frankie was more like her mum than she'd dared hope after all.

Silly, wasn't it, how you could be so pleased by another person's throwaway compliment? Sometimes that was all it took to set the tone of the day, though. Because not only did Frankie make an effort and stand at the hob, stirring a pan of creamy porridge for everyone's breakfast first thing, but then she decided to get on top of the mound of recycling that had been neglected in recent weeks. 'Ferg, come and help me with the paper,' she called, dragging the wicker basket out from the side of the sofa, where they dumped old newspapers and letters and other assorted pieces of paper. She didn't even get cross when, in a fit of mischief, he plunged both hands into the pile and threw a load of it into the air, yelling, 'It's snowing!'

Maybe it was some quirk of fate, some little test for this new-found gutsiness of hers, but it just so happened that as she was picking up all the many receipts and old envelopes and other scraps now littered about the carpet, her gaze snagged on some handwritten numbers on one particular piece, and then she realized she was staring at Julia's contact details, left the first time she'd appeared at the flat. Craig must have discarded the paper into the basket in a *we-won't-be-wanting-THIS* sort of gesture.

Coincidence? Or Fate intervening? Who could say, but Frankie found herself thoughtfully tucking the paper into the back pocket of her denim skirt all the same. Just in case it was needed.

The Julia situation was still bubbling away beneath the surface, needless to say. Despite Frankie's protestations, Craig had sent his spiteful mother-bashing column to his editor, Vicki, who had promptly phoned him in concern. 'You know we can't print this,' she'd said. 'Come on, Craig, she's a real person, we don't want a lawsuit on our hands.'

So that was that particular disaster avoided, thank goodness, and Craig had written something charming instead about how he and Fergus had made biscuits together, and how Fergus hadn't wanted to eat the one he'd made shaped like a train, and how they were going to enjoy watching it grow mouldy over the weeks, in the hope that it would end up as blue as Thomas the Tank Engine. But Frankie knew that all those nasty words about his ex were still there, inside her partner – and if they hadn't made it into print this time, then they could very well end up being shouted at her in person across a courtroom. Which was not something to look forward to, either.

Get in touch when you want to discuss this like an adult, Julia had said, or something along those lines, when she'd first rocked up at the flat. And yet nobody had really behaved like an adult since then, opting instead for juvenile point-scoring and petulant name-calling. Craig might not want to speak to his ex, but maybe she could, Frankie thought, remembering the phone number in her pocket. If she was gutsy enough. Was she?

'Just going to take the recycling down,' she called, having loaded up the council-provided bag, without a huge amount of help from Fergus. Then, on impulse, she grabbed her phone too, her mind racing. Should she? Well, could she really make things any worse? she wondered as she lugged the bag down to the ground-floor communal bins. She'd felt so sidelined by Craig throughout this process, so un-consulted, when he hadn't once asked her opinion. And yet, from her position as onlooker, she couldn't help thinking he was making an absolute pig's ear of it all.

Down in the courtyard, she dumped the recycling into the correct bins, then stood there in the sunshine, trying to decide what to do. Sod it, she thought after a few moments. Yesterday with Paula had gone well – it had proved that when women just got on with stuff together, you could sort anything out. And so, before she could change her mind again, she walked away from the stinking bins, perched on a low brick wall and dialled Julia's number. *You've got guts,* she reminded herself. *That's a good thing!*

'Hello?' she heard after the third ring.

It was weirdly similar to yesterday's call, really – Frank-ie's heart in her mouth, her palms suddenly clammy, hoping she was doing the right thing by phoning. 'Julia, this is Frankie,' she said politely. 'I was wondering if maybe the two of us could meet up and talk.'

Julia gave a low chuckle. 'Interesting,' she replied, sound-ing amused as she dragged out the syllables. 'I take it Craig doesn't know about this?'

'Um . . . no,' Frankie admitted.

'Even better. Ooh, this will sound good, won't it – even his girlfriend is plotting against him. Bad luck, Craig!'

Frankie found herself gritting her teeth. What was it

about this woman and her ability to put words in your mouth, words that you did not want spoken for you? 'It's not—' she began defensively, but Julia was speaking over her.

'I'm only messing with you. Yeah, sure we could meet. You're good cop, I take it, going to offer me a sweetener, while he grunts and growls, as bad cop?'

Again Frankie cringed at how tacky this sounded – and how near the knuckle it actually was, too. She assumed Julia was teasing her, but the subject of Fergus felt too precarious to be teased over. 'Look, I only want to talk—' she began, before being interrupted a second time.

'I know. I'm kidding. Well, I think I am, anyway. So, where are we meeting? I'd invite you to mine, but I'm staying with a mate in Highbury and it's a bit of a shit-hole, to say the least. But we can hook up somewhere in Upper Street, maybe? If you're paying, that is. You practically need to sell a limb to buy yourself a latte in some of those places.'

Was she reading too much into this or did Julia sound kind of manic? Frankie thought in alarm, already wondering what she was letting herself in for. 'Okay,' she said, trying to keep her cool. 'How about Barney's at midday?'

'I will see you there,' said Julia.

With a click, the line went dead and Frankie stuffed the phone back in her pocket, a queasy sensation curdling her stomach, along with the fervent hope that she hadn't just set herself up for an almighty own-goal.

'I've got to go and see Constance,' she lied to Craig, on re-entering the flat. 'I'm going to head out soon, if that's okay. I'll just put on a bit of slap and change this top.' Her heart was thumping as he nodded absent-mindedly, her fingers clumsy as she sorted through the hangers in the wardrobe to find something nice to wear. Lying to Craig, meeting Julia behind his back – she was playing with fire, she knew it. But sometimes you just had to take a risk, right?

That's my girl, said Kathy in her head, as Frankie slipped a short-sleeved apple-print blouse over her head and spritzed perfume on her neck and wrists. She was doing this for Fergus, she told herself firmly, walking through the sunny streets to the Tube station a short while later. Which was why she was determined not to screw it up.

That said, she almost bottled out of their meeting when she emerged from Highbury and Islington Tube station and made the short walk towards Barney's Café. It seemed insane, all of a sudden, that she was behaving in such a cloak-and-dagger manner, being so underhand. She was jeopardizing her entire relationship here – and not just with Craig, because with Craig came Fergus. She was totally laying herself on the line, and for what? Because a half-sister she'd never actually met made a passing remark about her being gutsy? Was she really that impressionable that another person's opinion could cause her to act with such recklessness?

Oh Lord. Put it that way, and she wanted to screech to a halt right there on the pavement, put her hands up and say *Whoa!* Just a minute. What the hell?

But some dogged instinct drove her on nonetheless, step after step, until she was pushing open the door of the café and gazing around, adrenalin racing through her veins. Fight or flight, fight or flight . . . Wait. Julia wasn't even there. She let out her breath in anticlimax and made her way over to the counter.

The café was moody, with dark-painted walls and framed posters of classic album covers, but there was a cosy feel about the place too, due to the soft, bashed-up old sofas and mismatched chairs. The man behind the counter wore dungarees and cool glasses and was reading *The Collected Plays of Brecht* while perched on a three-legged stool. He seemed irritated to be interrupted by Frankie ordering an Earl Grey tea.

She retreated to a dingy corner with her mug, feeling increasingly agitated with every minute that ticked by. Five past twelve. Ten past twelve. Was Julia even going to show, after all this? Would it be just another of her mind-games? But then at quarter-past twelve, in she sauntered at last. True to form, she ordered a macchiato at the counter and said, 'She's paying', with a dismissive jerk of the thumb at Frankie. Which was one way to call the shots, Frankie thought wryly, getting out her purse.

'So, this is a lovely surprise,' Julia drawled, sitting down at Frankie's table and somehow managing to make her words sound as if she meant the complete opposite. She was wearing really dark burgundy lipstick and had swept her curly hair back into an impressively tight bun, with a long black pinafore, white short-sleeved stretchy top and a pair of gold trainers to complete the look. 'Secret meetings, eh? Well, well, well. Interesting relationship dynamic you and my ex have got going on there, then. What else are you up to that he doesn't know about?'

Frankie ignored the jibe. 'I just wanted to see you, woman-to-woman,' she began, trying to keep her cool. 'And I guess what I want more than anything is to assure you that, growing up, Fergus has had nothing but love.'

'My Fergus, you mean,' Julia put in, wagging a finger. 'My son.'

'Your son,' Frankie agreed. 'He's a really happy kid, his enthusiasm and love of life know no bounds. He's growing up into such a lovely boy.'

'Yep,' Julia said irritably, as if Frankie was telling her something she already knew. She ripped open two sugar packets and stirred them into her coffee. 'And?'

'Craig's been a great dad,' Frankie went on, even though she could feel her nerve starting to falter. 'And I've done my best too, to make every day a good one for Fergus, to teach him, to help him, to make him laugh.'

'Right.' Julia eyed her over the mug. 'And you're telling me this . . . why? To make me feel bad for not having been there? Or am I meant to be bowled over by gratitude?'

God, she didn't half know which buttons to press, Frankie thought, feeling her skin prickling. Look at her sitting there, sneering so contemptuously, when Frankie was just trying to make things better, to open up a new, more civil communication channel. 'I'm telling you because I absolutely love that boy,' she replied steadily. 'And because I just want what's best for him.'

'Right,' said Julia again. Her nostrils flared as she breathed out crossly and her eyes were hard. 'I get it. And now I'm guessing you're going to say that what's best for him is to stay right where he is, with dear, devoted Craig and kind, loving Frankie and—'

'No,' Frankie interrupted, trying to keep her voice even, despite the fact that Julia was clearly doing her damnedest to rile her. 'I wasn't going to say that. I think Fergus *should* see you. Of course he should. You're his mum.'

'You don't have to tell me that, love,' said Julia, but Frankie could tell she hadn't been expecting the comment. 'So what are you suggesting?' she asked after a moment.

Now they were getting to it. 'I guess I'm interested in what your ideal resolution to all of this is,' Frankie replied slowly. 'Genuine question. What would you like to happen?

When you turned up at the flat that first time – what were you hoping for?'

Julia actually looked taken aback to be asked, but then, a split-second later, her eyes resumed their narrowing, as if she suspected Frankie of laying some kind of trap. 'Well, to have Fergus back, of course,' she replied warily. 'To have my son.'

'To have him full-time: that's what you want, is it?' Frankie asked, clarifying. 'That's what you've instructed your solicitor?'

Again, that mistrustful side-eye, that are-you-for-real? glance. 'Sure,' Julia said. 'I mean, the way I see it, Craig's had him for four years without me getting a look-in. Fair's fair.'

She wasn't thinking of Fergus as an actual person in his own right at this point, that was the crucial thing, Frankie realized. For Julia, he was still an object to be tussled over, a bargaining chip. 'You know he's got a place at Saint Helena's primary,' Frankie said carefully. 'That's just round the corner from us. He starts in September.'

'Saint Helena's? What's that, some religious school?' Julia shook her head. 'No way. No kid of mine is being brought up religious.'

'It's not religious,' Frankie said mildly. 'It's just an ordinary state primary school where all his friends are going. It seems really great, actually.'

'Yeah, well,' Julia said, and Frankie could tell – she *knew* –

that Julia had not even considered the subject of schooling, or how that would happen. 'I could sort something out.'

'You've got a bedroom for him, have you?' Frankie went on in the same mild tone, remembering Julia's words earlier about dossing with a mate in their 'shit-hole' of a flat. 'And you'll be able to fit work in around looking after him, and taking him to hospital appointments, and all the rest of it? He still has to have check-ups, if you didn't know, seeing as he was so poorly when he was little. Where is it you work, again?'

Julia scowled as if she realized where Frankie was going. 'Look, if you're trying to make out that I'm some kind of unfit mother, just because I don't have a job or a house right now—'

'I'm not,' said Frankie quickly, 'I'm honestly not. But the court will look at your circumstances and—'

'Well, they can sod off and all, then, because he's still *my* son, and nothing can top a mother's love. Nothing.' Julia was getting angry and, if Frankie wasn't careful, she'd be flouncing off out of the café and this conversation would be over, her chance blown. 'And I'm not the one writing about every detail of Fergus's life in a national newspaper for the world to see, either. I'm not the one who's taking away his privacy every bloody week!'

Touché, thought Frankie, lowering her eyes. 'I know he's your son. I'd never deny you that,' she said after a moment, trying to calm things down. 'I swear, I'm not trying to get at you. It's just . . . there's a lot to think about. Fergus is such a brilliant kid, and of course you should be part of his life, of course you two should have a relationship, but it's a big deal. The court would look at what's best for him – and how settled and happy he is right now – and—'

'I can't be bothered with this,' Julia said, pushing her chair back with a squawk and getting to her feet. 'I cannot be bothered.'

Frankie was losing her, she thought in dismay. 'He still has massive tantrums sometimes, you know,' she found herself blurting out. 'His shoes cost a bloody fortune. He wets the bed if he has a nightmare.'

'Right, so you're trying to put me off my own kid. That's nice. That's charming. Whatever.' Julia began walking away, her back stiff and haughty, and the encounter seemed to be slipping through Frankie's fingers.

'I just want you to know, that's all,' Frankie yelled out across the café, and several people in there stopped what they were doing to stare. 'It's not that easy! Sometimes it's the best thing ever, but sometimes it's really hard work!'

Julia wheeled round, eyes like gimlets. 'Fuck you. He's my child.'

Now everyone was staring at them. The guy in dungarees behind the counter even bookmarked his Brecht in order to pay full attention, just as Julia stormed out, letting the door crash shut behind her. Frankie put her hot, red face in her hands and wished she could rewind the entire morning so that none of this had happened.

Shit. She had blown it. She had made the situation a million times worse, not only for her, but for Craig and Fergus, too. And now Julia might step things up and fight harder than ever for Fergus, and Frankie wouldn't be a mum any more. The thought made her nauseous. Her pulse throbbed where adrenalin was pinballing around her system, and dismay crashed through her. How could she have been so stupid, so impulsive? How could she have staked everything she held dearest on this one foolhardy throw of the dice?

Chapter Twenty-Eight

'Victoria? It's Robyn Mortimer. How are you?' Today was officially Bite-the-Bullet day, Robyn had decided. Following the cheerleading *we-can-do-this* conversation with her mum, she had dug out a contact number for her old boss, the inimitable Professor Victoria Tomlinson, former Sydneysider-turned-Yorkshirewoman. Now, seizing a quiet moment in her lunch-break at school, she had apprehensively punched the number into her phone.

'Robyn *Mortimer*! Good to hear from you, darl. I'm very well and lying on a sun-lounger in Tuscany, thank you very much. How are you?'

'Oh! You're on holiday? I'm so sorry – this can totally wait until you get back then,' Robyn gabbled, not wanting to irk the one person whose good books she needed to access. She'd walked to the top of the school playing field so as to get some privacy, and made an *oh-no-you-don't* gesture at a couple of Year Ten girls who were sloping that way, cigarette packs in hand. It would be the end of term on Friday and she felt as if the entire school, staff and kids alike, was easing towards the finish line, rules and regulations gladly discarded in their collective wake.

'Rubbish! I'm only lying here turning walnut – in terms of colour *and* wrinkles, I should add, ha!' said Victoria. She sounded as if she might have had one or two Aperol Spritzes too, Robyn thought, although perhaps that was just her holiday mood seeping down the line. 'So how are things? Life treating you well?'

'Ah . . .' Victoria had never been a person you could bull-shit, whether it was about lab results, student grades or matters of the heart. 'Actually, no,' Robyn replied frankly, leaning against the wire fencing and pretending to be scanning the horizon for rule-breaking teenagers. 'Let's just say things have been better. John and I . . . well, you might have heard, actually. He's run away to Scotland with a former student. Which is . . .' She tried to find a polite way of ending the sentence, until she remembered who she was talking to, 'well, it's completely shit, basically.'

'Oh, mate. I did hear a little bird squawking about some terrible goings-on. What a prick, eh? What a bastard.'

'Yes,' said Robyn, 'but I wasn't ringing to talk about him, I was ringing to—'

'Do you remember I went through it myself? Shitty ball-ache of a husband doing the dirty on me, the most horrendous dragged-out divorce in the history of all-time marriage disasters?' Victoria gave a snort down the phone.

Robyn did have a vague memory, now that Victoria mentioned it, of when she'd first started work in the department, and hearing a story about Victoria going down to one of the labs and smashing up loads of equipment. She'd written it off as a college myth at the time, but maybe the two were connected. 'Grim times,' she replied with feeling.

'I'll say. But hey, please tell me you've taken some revenge on the bastard. You have, haven't you? It's the only satisfying, fun thing about the whole rotten, stinking business.'

'Um . . . well . . .' said Robyn, not wanting to sound like the weedy sort of person who would just catatonically accept a husband's atrocious behaviour as their lot, even though that was pretty much how she'd gone about it so far. 'Not exactly.'

'I sent my ex-husband an envelope of scrambled egg through the post every day for a whole month, because I knew the smell of egg made him vomit,' Victoria went on, hooting at the memory. 'He went mad, of course – oh, he was *livid* about it, but did that stop me? Bollocks, did it. Anyway, enough about that. He's lost most of his hair since then – ha! – and I'm now married to the most divine woman on the planet, so we're all square.'

Robyn could hear laughter in the background, and intuited that the most divine woman on the planet might well be on the next sun-lounger to Victoria. 'Good!' she said. 'Sounds like a happy ending to me. Anyway, I was just ringing – and honestly, this can wait until you're back – but—'

'You were ringing to see if there was any work that might be going for you at the uni?' Victoria guessed. 'Oh, mate, I would love to have you back on the team! Let me think . . . Well, Alfonso has just taken a sabbatical at the moment, so there's potentially some kind of vacancy there. We've got a maternity leave coming up as well, so . . . Exciting! Let me see what strings I can pull when I'm back in Blighty.'

'Oh!' Robyn felt excited, too. She had hardly dared get her hopes up, but it really did sound as if there might be a way back for her. 'Thank you, that would be amazing. I can update my CV and send it over or—'

'You don't need to update your CV, I know how talented and fabulous you are,' Victoria told her. 'Look, I'm back in August, why don't we hook up then and talk through what we'd both like from the arrangement? I'm sure we can make it work between us, all right? Cool. Good to have you back. Hey, and listen: don't forget the scrambled eggs. That will be a key part of your interview, by the way – you telling me how you wreaked your terrible revenge on the ass-wipe. Got it?'

Robyn laughed again. Victoria was definitely a bit worse for wear. She hoped her old boss would actually remember the work part of this conversation when she sobered up. 'Sadly, I don't have the address of his new love-nest, so the scrambled-egg option is out of the question,' she replied, deadpan, pointing a warning finger at a Year Nine and miming to her that she needed to unroll the top of her school skirt, which she had gathered up so that it was more like a school belt. 'But I'll do my best,' she added, not wanting Victoria to think she'd gone soft.

'You'd better. And you have a great summer, now. Ciao!'

'Bye,' said Robyn, hanging up. Then she marvelled for a few glorious seconds that there might still be this small pocket of the universe where she belonged, where she was respected, where she was told she was fabulous. A place where she didn't have to police smoking and snogging students, where she didn't have to nag on about skirt lengths and too much flicky eye make-up. But in the meantime . . . 'Sasha Higginbotham, will you pull that skirt down to its proper length, please,' she bellowed, striding back down towards the school building as the bell rang for afternoon lessons.

Later on, having finished work, Robyn was walking to pick up Sam and Daisy from school, bracing herself for part two of Bite the Bullet day: telling them the truth about where John really was. While negotiating with Victoria – if she could even *use* the word 'negotiating' – had been gratifyingly straightforward, she suspected that this next challenge was going to be a whole lot harder. The thought of her

children's bewildered, sad little faces turned up questioningly to hers as they tried to fathom why – *why?* – their dad
had done such a thing was enough to break her heart clean
in two. What were you even supposed to *say* in this situation? Were there any words in the lexicon that could make
this remotely okay to an eleven-year-old and a nine-year-old?
She suspected not.

Her phone started ringing as she walked through the
primary-school gates and she gave a little start as John's
office number came up on her screen. Oh my goodness.
What was he doing, back at work? How long had he been in
town? Turning hot and cold all over, she jabbed the button
to pick up. 'Hello?'

'Robyn? It's Gabby here. From the engineering faculty.'

'Oh,' said Robyn, deflating all over again. Of course it
wasn't John. He was living the life of Riley up in Edinburgh
and probably hadn't even thought about her – or work – since
he'd left. 'Hello. Is everything all right?' she remembered to
say in the next moment. It was probably something tedious
concerning John's dismissal, she thought glumly, wandering
through to the juniors' playground.

'Yes,' replied Gabby. 'We had a message from John the
other day with his new postal address, for any mail to be
sent on to him,' she went on, 'and I've just had a call from a
Professor – Tomlinson? – asking me to urgently pass the
address on to you. Something about . . .' Her voice was

becoming more doubtful by the second. 'Ah, I might have got this wrong, but . . . scrambled egg?'

Robyn let out a snort of laughter as she pieced all of this together. What was Victoria like? 'Thank you,' she managed to say. 'Don't worry, that makes perfect sense. If you could just email me those details, that would be very helpful. You've got my email address, haven't you? Great. Thanks very much.'

She gave another snigger of amusement as she reached the edge of the playground, imagining John's face if she really did send him an envelope full of scrambled egg. It was actually kind of tempting.

'Hi, how are you?' She hadn't noticed Beth Broadwood walking up next to her. 'You look – dare I say it? – more like your usual self. How's it going?'

Robyn was still smirking. 'I know this might sound childish,' she said, 'but I've just been given John's new address. And I was wondering . . . if you were a gorgeous young twenty-two-year-old shacked up with a much older man, what would you be most horrified to see arriving in the post for him?'

Beth didn't reply immediately and for a moment Robyn thought she hadn't picked up on her meaning. But then Beth raised a mischievous eyebrow. 'Adult nappies?' she suggested. 'Haemorrhoid cream?'

'Hair-loss treatment?' Robyn added, lips twitching.

'Oh, you could have a bit of fun with this,' Beth said, giggling. 'You could really go to town. Wouldn't it be awful if somebody signed him up to all these junk-mailing lists for – I don't know – pensioner holidays or hearing aids . . .'

Robyn heard herself making a gurgling sound. 'Or gave his details to the local Jehovah's Witnesses, saying he wanted to be saved . . .'

'Yes, and needed an urgent baptism,' said Beth. 'That would be a real shame.'

The two of them collapsed into giggles, leaning against each other. 'The possibilities are endless,' said Robyn, feeling more cheerful than she had for a long time.

'Decisions, decisions,' agreed Beth with a grin. 'Well, keep me posted,' she added as the children started pouring out of the school. 'Hey, let's go out for a drink sometime in the holidays – you can tell me all about it then.'

'I'd love that,' said Robyn, feeling a small glow of pleasure. With every conversation that she'd had with Beth, she'd come to like the woman more each time. Was it cheesy to say that she felt as if she might just have made a new friend?

Here came Sam and Daisy now anyway, both smiling as they ran towards her, and she felt a churn of anxiety inside, that she was about to really shake their happy worlds with what she had to say back at home. But she wouldn't let them down, she thought, crouching a little so that she could hug them both, one on each side. She had all these great women around her who were going to help her survive this ordeal – her mum and Paula, Victoria and Beth – and she would make damn sure that her children came through it with her as best she could manage, too.

'Alison? Is that you?'

Alison, her hand on her car door, turned at the voice. She'd popped over to see Robyn after work, and had ended up staying for dinner because Robyn had just broken the news about John to the children and emotions were running high. Sam had been silent and unhappy, while Daisy had spouted anguished tears of sorrow. It had been a wrench to leave, frankly, despite Robyn's assurances that she could cope.

'Jeanie!' she said now, blinking in surprise as she saw Robyn's mother-in-law approaching along the pavement from where she'd parked, a duty-free bag in hand. Jeanie looked very brown, she noticed, although what had she done to her hair? Someone had given her a very bad cut that didn't suit her in the slightest. 'Hello, it's been ages,' she added politely, feeling a complete hypocrite, seeing as this was entirely down to her. 'How are you?'

'I'm fine, but . . .' Jeanie grimaced. 'Goodness, I'm very sad about what's happened with John and Robyn, as I'm sure you are. I couldn't believe it.' She shook her head. 'Words fail me.'

'I know,' said Alison tightly. Talk about awkward, she thought, as Jeanie came to a standstill beside her. Because Robyn was her daughter, who'd been very badly let down by Jeanie's son, and there was no getting away from that. If Jeanie dared started trying to defend John in any way, or twist things around so that she blamed Robyn at all, then . . .

'Poor Robyn, how *is* she?' Jeanie asked, cutting into Alison's thoughts. 'Honestly, I could wring John's neck, I really could. I've never been so disappointed in one of my own children. I feel absolutely dreadful about the whole thing – and me being out of the country as well, while it happened.'

To be fair, she did look pretty wretched about it. Not least because of the terrible haircut. 'Robyn's bearing up,' Alison replied guardedly, wondering if Jeanie was here to report back to John. 'Doing the best she can. She broke the news to Sam and Daisy tonight, which sounded pretty upsetting.'

'Oh dear.' Was that actually a *tear* in Jeanie's eye? 'The poor little loves. I brought them some presents from my holiday, but it's going to take more than that, isn't it? Bless them.'

'I'm sure they'll be glad of a distraction – they'll be really pleased to see you,' Alison said, softening slightly towards the other woman. Anyone who was kind to her grandchildren was okay by her, after all, and she knew how fond Robyn was of Jeanie, too. She was relieved that the Mortimers seemed to be sticking by Robyn, moreover, despite her daughter's initial fears. 'How was your holiday, by the way?' she added, noticing a plane flying above their heads. 'Did you have a lovely time?'

'Well . . .' To Alison's surprise, Jeanie looked uncharacteristically bashful. Embarrassed, even. 'Yes, but it's probably a good thing that I'm back home,' she said rather cryptically, lowering her voice, as one of Robyn's neighbours cycled past them. 'Back home, and acting my age again, too.'

Alison wasn't sure what to say for a moment. Gosh, was that Jeanie Mortimer being vulnerable? She couldn't remember ever seeing her unsure of herself like this before. 'Age is just a number,' she reminded her kindly. This was what she told all her clients who came to her, doubtful and lacking in confidence. 'Who wants to act their age, anyway? Not me.'

Jeanie gave her a rueful smile and then her face cleared, an idea seemingly occurring to her. 'Oh – Alison. I've just thought. You're a hairdresser, aren't you? I don't suppose you could do me a huge favour and sort this mess out for me sometime, could you?' She tugged at a strand of her hair. 'This is what I mean about acting my age . . . I went and booked myself in for a makeover at the hotel, thinking I was a spring chicken, when . . .' She rolled her eyes. 'Turns out I'm mutton after all.'

'You're not mutton!' Alison told her, tutting. She hated that word and the way it made women feel. 'And of course

I can change the style for you. Let me find my diary and see when I'm free.'

'Thank you,' Jeanie said, as Alison pulled out her appointment notebook and began rifling through. 'I'm too embarrassed to go to my usual stylist, because I know they'll tell me off for it. Deluded fool that I am.'

'Hey, we all do foolish things,' Alison said. Goodness me, so the woman was fallible after all, she thought, startled. Whenever Alison had seen Jeanie previously, she'd always been organizing a buffet or in charge of the teapot, the hostess with the mostest, running the show. And as such, Alison had held her up as – well, not the enemy exactly, but certainly somebody better than her, somebody with a richer, fuller life than herself. A person to be envied.

In actual fact, she was just a woman who loved her grandchildren to bits, who was fretting about her son's bad behaviour *and* happened to be sporting an unfortunate haircut into the bargain. Your average human being, in other words. 'Listen, I'll tell you about my dreadful blind dates when I'm doing your hair – that'll cheer you up,' she added, rolling her eyes. 'Then we'll see who's the deluded one. Now, how about Thursday morning? I could fit you in then.'

'Thursday morning would be perfect,' Jeanie said thankfully. 'Blind dates, eh? How exciting! A hairdo rescue *and* some good stories. I might not be going back to my salon at this rate.'

Alison smiled at her, thinking that she really had got this woman all wrong. Completely wrong. 'Even better news,' she found herself saying. 'There's a big fat family discount for you.'

Family, she repeated to herself, as Jeanie smiled back and they agreed on a time. It felt as if a door had opened and Alison had just walked on through.

Chapter Twenty-Nine

Frankie had barely got inside the flat, following her disastrous encounter with Julia, when Craig appeared in the hall, asking in a strange, tight voice where she'd been. And then she could tell immediately that she'd been rumbled, that he knew *exactly* where she'd been.

Thank goodness Fergus was there, charging down to greet her in his usual manner, by hurling himself at her legs while he shouted 'Mumma!' in the most flatteringly joyful way. Because of this, she was able to bend over to make a fuss of him for a brief few moments, her heart pounding as she cast about for how best to reply to Craig without sending him into a towering rage. It seemed, in fact, as if she'd been tiptoeing around him for days now – weeks – trying to keep him from exploding on her. Was this what it had been like for Julia? she wondered, taking her shoes off and allowing her hair to swing down and hide her face while she wrangled with her thoughts. She wanted the old Craig back, she thought to herself. The relaxed, easy-going Craig who'd made her feel happy rather than on edge.

'Hi,' she said coolly, straightening up, Fergus still clutching at her hand and trying to tell her about a pigeon he'd seen out of the window. She met Craig's gaze squarely, noticing how clenched his jaw was. Oh God. Julia *had* told him, she realized, her heart sinking. Just look at the wounded betrayal in his eyes. 'Everything all right here?'

'I asked you where you'd been,' he repeated, 'because I had a very strange text while you were out.' He pulled his phone out of his back pocket and read aloud: '*Sending your girlfriend to meet me because you're too scared? Lame!*' Then he looked across at Frankie; no need to say anything more.

'I . . .' Frankie felt lost for words at the intensity of his gaze. (Damn Julia, she thought crossly. Why did she insist on making herself so hard to like? When Frankie had only been trying to help matters, too.) 'I thought it was a good idea,' she replied weakly after a moment.

'You thought,' he repeated, 'that it was a good idea.' He folded his arms across his chest, his expression cold, and Frankie's self-defence mechanism kicked right on in.

'Yes, I did,' she replied hotly. 'Because by refusing to speak to her or go through mediation, you've completely driven her to this position. You've put her totally on the offensive – and no wonder. It should have been you going to talk to her like an adult, face-to-face, not me. And you should have done it right from the start!'

Fergus pressed himself against her leg, burrowing into her. 'Mumma,' he said plaintively.

'You don't *know* her,' Craig snapped.

'So you keep telling me! Which is why I wanted to see her, because she has a right to be heard. Because at the end of the day, she is—' She suddenly became aware of Fergus right there, hot against her thigh, saying, 'Mumma, *Mumma*' at her, and she stopped to scoop him up. 'This isn't the right moment,' she said, holding him in her arms. 'Yes, lovely, it's all right,' she told him quietly.

'You shouldn't have gone,' Craig rebuked her, not seeming to hear. 'I'm handling this, I know what I'm doing. And I don't need—'

'But, Craig, your way of "handling this" seems to mean goading and antagonizing her,' she retaliated, the words bursting out of her. 'Not to mention sidelining me at every opportunity, refusing to discuss anything, making me feel like my opinion and input are completely worthless and irrelevant.' She glared at him. 'And I'm fed up with it!'

Fergus promptly dissolved into noisy sobs – of shock, probably, because she never usually raised her voice – and she stroked his hair and patted him soothingly. 'It's okay, poppet. Nobody's cross with you. Come on, let's go in the living room and get the building blocks out,' she said, before Craig could come back at her and make things any worse.

He followed her in there a few minutes later, when she'd upended the box of wooden bricks and she and Fergus were sorting through them on the rug, calm restored. 'For what it's worth,' Frankie went on, putting green bricks in a pile for Fergus, 'I don't think Julia's remotely prepared for what motherhood entails, or has properly thought it through. But I do think she's got a right to be taken seriously, and a right to start again with . . .' She indicated Fergus with her eyebrows, not wanting to alert him to the fact that he was under discussion. 'And *he* has that right, too. What we need to do is make that as good a relationship as possible, for his sake. If, in years to come, he finds out you've denied him that, he might never forgive you.'

It was quite the longest speech she'd made to Craig on the matter, but Fergus seemed unimpressed by all of this talking, and even less so by the fact that his father was standing there doing nothing, when he could be helping with something important. 'I am looking,' he said grandly, 'for red bricks, Daddy.'

Craig knelt down beside them and began obediently picking out all the red ones. 'Sorry,' he said in a gruff voice after a few moments.

'You made Mumma sad,' Fergus said accusingly, before Frankie could reply. He leaned against her possessively, patting her knee with a plump hand while giving Craig an extremely disapproving look. 'And then *I* was sad.'

Frankie felt her heart quiver with love for her loyal, sensitive boy, whose face was most definitely saying *Team Mumma all the way*. She was so choked up that she couldn't actually speak for a moment.

'Sorry, mate,' said Craig, contrite and shovelling a pile of red bricks over to him by way of apology. 'No one's going to do any more shouting.'

'Well, good!' said Fergus in such a grown-up-sounding way that Frankie had to struggle not to laugh. Then he frowned in concentration as he started stacking red bricks on top of each other. 'Now blue ones,' he ordered, and they both fell to his command like grovelling minions.

'Blue ones coming right up,' Frankie assured him.

A fragile truce was maintained for the rest of the day. She and Craig were polite to one another in the presence of Fergus, but Frankie could feel a tension between them, the air still ringing with words unsaid. She had never really stood up to Craig like that before, had never called him out so bluntly on his behaviour. Partly, of course, because their relationship had always been so accordant in the past that she hadn't needed to stand her ground and argue in such a way. They'd only really ever disagreed on small things – which film to watch on Netflix, whose turn it was to load the dishwasher –

issues that nobody could get too heated about. By sticking her head above the parapet this time, by making it clear her feelings were at odds with his, Frankie couldn't help wondering how the dynamic between them would be affected. One thing she knew for sure, though, was that there would be no turning back. The bottle had been well and truly unstoppered, the genie long since escaped.

Craig seemed thoughtful and preoccupied. He left his laptop off for the rest of the afternoon and took Fergus out to the high street, returning with a bag of picture books from the library, as well as an expensive-looking bottle of Merlot and some nice food for dinner. Frankie, meanwhile, took the chance to catch up on some work admin, but found it difficult to concentrate. It was as if they were both acting out parts that they'd usually be able to play without any effort, and yet today seemed unnatural and forced.

Later on, after they'd eaten and once Fergus had settled down to sleep, Craig turned to Frankie and asked, 'Glass of wine?' in a way that could only be the precursor to A Serious Chat. The Chat of Doom, she thought with a flutter of nerves.

'Sure,' she replied, trying to keep her cool. Here we go, she thought, hearing him in the kitchen. Any minute now she was going to get his full, unfiltered reaction to her earlier criticism, and this time she wouldn't have Fergus to act as a buffer. She had the horrible feeling it would be another case of Craig digging in his heels and refusing to see any angle other than his own.

He came and sat down next to her on the sofa, setting their drinks on the table in front of them. Just by the way he was sitting – slightly forward, hands clasped loosely between his legs – she could tell that he was tense. And then he looked at her sidelong and launched his opening salvo. 'I think I might give up the column.'

'Wow,' she said, taken aback. Kill the golden goose? She had not been expecting that. 'Seriously?'

He nodded. 'With Fergus starting school in a couple of months, maybe it's a good time.' He swilled his wine gently in the glass, the overhead light catching in the dark-red ripples. 'I've been thinking about it for a while,' he admitted. 'You've raised the subject before, obviously, and our friend Julia has brought things to a head more recently.' He sighed heavily, staring down into his glass. 'I hate to say it, but yeah, it's probably the right thing.' Another sideways glance her way. 'How would you feel about it, though? I mean, it's income for you too, and I know you've got other bits and pieces of work, but . . .'

He didn't need to spell out the 'but'. *But . . . it's your biggest earner. But . . . it's guaranteed money every week. But . . . it's been our joint project for years now and will mean the end of an era.* Still, at least he was asking her opinion on the matter, she realized.

'I think now might be a good time, yes,' Frankie replied, choosing her words carefully. 'I would hate Ferg ever to feel weird about it, if teachers or parents at the school recognize the name and put two and two together. And we've got to draw the line somewhere.' She hesitated, remembering Julia's barb about the column, how the other woman had condemned the weekly piece as a cynical money-making exercise at Fergus's expense. Frankie hoped Craig's change of heart would seem like a gracious climb-down on that front at least, an admission that yes, she was being listened to. 'Anyway, I'm going to sort out my dragon pitch any day now, and you've got all these other feature ideas,' she went on, bracingly. 'We can manage. We're more than just one-trick ponies, right?'

He nodded. 'Absolutely,' he agreed.

They both sipped their wine, rather self-consciously – which was a shame, because it was really fruity and delicious, the sort you could enjoy quaffing in big gulps – and then Craig went on. 'Look, what you were saying earlier, about being sidelined and me not listening . . . I'm sorry. I can see why you'd feel that way, when I've gone bull-dozing ahead each time.' He hung his head. 'I've not handled this terribly well, have I? Panic and smash things, that seems to have been my strategy, in hindsight.'

She managed a small smile. 'I wouldn't say you've been your most diplomatic, no,' she replied, then took a deep breath. 'I get where you're coming from though. I don't want to lose Fergus, either. Because, selfishly, then I won't be a mum any more. And I love being his mum. I couldn't bear it if that was taken away from me.' Her voice wobbled dangerously and she did her best to swallow down her emotion. 'You're always going to be Fergus's dad, but for me . . . For me, the stakes are high in a different way.' She closed her mouth abruptly, not wanting to risk getting into a whole other conversation about babies now, when they'd never explicitly discussed this before. If that was ever to be an option – as she hoped one day it would be – then it had to come from love, not merely as a knee-jerk reaction to Craig's nightmare ex.

'Anyway,' she went on, turning the stem of the wine glass between her fingers and trying to compose herself, 'I know you feel strongly about Julia, and I can tell there's a whole stew of resentment and anger simmering inside you. Fair enough. I'd probably react the same way, in your position. But we can't just close her out and hope she'll go away. Because she means business.'

He gave a rueful nod. 'I didn't want to break the spell, that was the thing,' he admitted after a moment. 'I didn't want Fergus to know the facts because I thought it would be too hard on him, too confusing. But you're right – we can't keep it from him forever. We can be straightforward about the whole biological situation, without it changing how he feels about you.'

'I hope so,' Frankie said.

'And as for Julia . . .' He sighed again. 'You know, given the choice, I'd rather she had stayed away forever. Although I can see, for Fergus, that would have left this hole in his life, even if he isn't aware of it now. So I guess we talk to her, like you said. Go back to Plan A and get round a table with her, see if we can thrash something out.'

'As long as we introduce Fergus to the idea of her gently, and really manage it at first, so that we're there too and it's gradual . . . I'm sure it will be good for everyone in the long term,' Frankie said. She risked a glance at Craig and saw that he was nodding, finally seeming to be considering the situation like a rational person, rather than through a filter of rage. 'Today, talking to Julia, I was trying to get her to see the real picture of looking after a child – the practicalities, the difficulties – not to put her off, but to enlighten her.' Now it was her turn to sigh. 'Although I think I just ended up annoying her, because she flounced out, not wanting to listen.'

She cringed, half-expecting Craig to chastise her again for what she'd done, but then he said, 'She's not an easy person,' and it was as if they were on the same side again.

'No,' she agreed, remembering Julia's hostility, her chippiness, the way she'd marched off as soon as the conversation took a turn she didn't like.

Craig reached out and took Frankie's hand. 'Sorry I had a go at you. You're the last person in the world I want to fall out with.'

'Same,' she replied. 'Let's see this one through together. No more secrets.'

'And no more sidelining.' He squeezed her fingers and it felt as if the two of them were clicking back into place at last, allies and equals once more.

'Deal,' she said, squeezing back.

Chapter Thirty

A few weeks passed by, and July's muggy nights and thunder-storms gave way to a sunny, pleasant August, with long, golden days. Since her go-getting conversation with Robyn, Alison hadn't wasted any time in packing them full of action. The first and scariest thing she did was to book herself in to see the counsellor whom her client Molly had recommended, not sure whether to be pleased or horrified when told that the counsellor had a cancellation available the following week.

Having duly taken the train over to Leeds for her appointment, Alison tracked down the counsellor's address to the upper floors of a beauty salon just off Kirkgate, where she was shown into a bright, comfortable office space. A middle-aged woman with a calm voice and compassionate eyes introduced herself as Emily, then said simply, 'So, Alison. Tell me a bit about why you're here.' The next thing she knew, she'd poured out the whole tragic story of Rich's death, sparing nothing, and tears were dripping down her chin as she brought alive all the heartache once more. The shock, the pain, the blame. She'd never been able to say goodbye, she hadn't been able to help him in time. She'd cut herself off from so many people, she'd built up all these walls because of her guilty feelings, the sense that she had failed her husband so badly.

'I've never really talked about this before,' Alison sobbed at the end, completely overwrought. 'Because I never wanted my daughter to know. He was her hero. She'd be so upset.'

'You don't have to tell your daughter,' Emily said, in her steady, wise voice. 'The important thing is that you've told *someone*, that you're not keeping these feelings locked up inside you any more. That's what matters.'

Alison had been crying too much to reply, other than to nod, and Emily leaned forward with a box of tissues. 'It wasn't your fault, Alison,' she said kindly. 'You know that, don't you? It really wasn't. You mustn't blame yourself.'

And there it was – the lifting of guilt at last, a chink of light pushing through the suffocating darkness. *It wasn't your fault.* How she'd longed to hear those words, to receive their absolution. 'Thank you,' she managed to say in a quavering voice, replaying them again in her head. *It wasn't your fault.* Then the two of them had just talked, and Alison had felt calmer and calmer, until to her great surprise Emily told her that the hour was almost up and their appointment was over.

'Come back next week and tell me about something you're really looking forward to in the future,' she said, as Alison thanked her and dabbed at her eyes, 'and think about one small way in which you can physically let go of your grief. It might be sorting through old photographs, or putting away possessions that hold sad memories. It might be simply trying to reset the way you think about your late husband each time, so that your angle is "We had some lovely times together" rather than "How I desperately miss him". Even if it's just one tiny change you make, I want to know.'

Alison had thought about this all the way home, sitting still and quiet in the train carriage as she was rocked along the track. Something to look forward to: well, Robyn had invited her to come on holiday to Portugal with her and the children, taking John's place, which would be lovely. She hadn't been much of a holidayer in the past – going away on her own made her feel lonelier than if she'd stayed at home, and she worried about the house being left empty. But she'd already mentioned it to her neighbours, Liz and Vince, and they'd fallen over themselves to assure her that they'd keep an eye on the place. Seeing as Liz had been newly promoted to sergeant in the police force, Alison was pretty sure that she could rely on her.

Another thing she was looking forward to – to her great surprise! – was meeting up with Jeanie and her knitting group again. For when she'd cut the other woman's hair a fortnight earlier, they had fallen into easy, friendly conversation, and it had turned out that the two of them were like-minded about all sorts of things, not least how wonderful their grandchildren were. Alison had never had a problem chatting with her clients – you couldn't be a hairdresser and *not* be good at talking to other people – but this particular cut and blow-dry was punctuated with laughter and all sorts of shared confidences, more than she'd been expecting. And at the end, Jeanie had said, 'Alison, I don't suppose you're a knitter, are you? Because you would love the girls – and token fella! – in the knitting group that I go to every other Thursday. I promise they're not a bunch of old farts; they're really good company. If you ever fancy joining us, you'd be very welcome.'

Not all that long ago Alison would have said no, out of habit, just like she'd said no to every other similar invitation. Thursday evenings? No, she couldn't possibly. She'd miss *EastEnders* and that reality show she liked! But to her surprise, she found herself saying yes, okay – and then enjoying one of the giggliest, most entertaining evenings she'd had in a long while, despite the fact that her knitting skills were pretty awful. 'Some of us are only here for the cake and gossip, don't worry,' one of the women assured her with a cackle. 'Not to mention the gin.'

So yes, she was definitely looking forward to seeing them again. The evening had actually been better than watching telly. As for Emily's instructions about doing something to let go of the grief in a physical way . . . Well, Alison had had an idea about that, too.

Once back at the house, she went straight through to the garage, where Rich's car had been standing since the day she'd moved in – undriven, unappreciated, unused. If you didn't count her sitting in it every now and then and having a little cry, that was.

Glancing around the garage, she realized – for the first time, really, if she was honest – that the space there was pretty decent. That if she sold the car, and got rid of all the boxes of junk lining the walls, she could easily slap on a few coats of emulsion and maybe put a proper warm carpet down over the concrete floor, to cheer it up a bit. With better lighting – maybe even some windows – this could become a usable extra room in the house: an office, per-haps, for sorting out her paperwork, or a sewing room, where she could spread out her fabrics and leave her machine rigged up in one place, rather than having to clear the dining table every time she wanted to make something. She could even put a treadmill in here, use it as a little gym space to keep herself fit, she thought, her eyes widening at the possibilities; at all these productive, energetic new ver-sions of herself that had come strolling into her imagination. In fact the more she thought about it, the more she decided that the garage was absolutely wasted on this old car, however sentimental she might feel about it.

And at the end of the day the Jensen *was* only a car: pieces of metal, tyres, mechanics. It wasn't Rich, and it wasn't going to bring him back. The truth of the matter was that having it under her roof just made her feel sad. 'We had some lovely times together,' she said, using the words Emily had given her, with one hand on the bonnet. 'But now it's time for us to go our separate ways.' She waited for the pang to hit her, as it had done in the past whenever Robyn had gone on at her about selling. This time it was more of a twinge, though. She could live with a twinge.

Having made the decision, she acted quickly, contacting the next day a local dealer who specialized in classic cars. Serendipitously, it turned out she'd been cutting his daughter-in-law's hair for years, and so she knew he wasn't about to stitch her up. Indeed, once he saw the car himself and had taken it for a test run, he offered Alison such a good price that she thought she might pass out with shock. A lump sum like that would mean she could retire a bit earlier, if she felt like it, she realized in a daze. It would mean she could help out Robyn financially too, if things became tricky following her marriage breakdown. And bugger it, she could even treat herself to a new runaround, seeing as the ancient Honda Jazz she drove had been so temperamental last winter.

'You're on,' she'd said, shaking his hand and not feeling

the slightest ache of guilt or sadness as he drove the car away. Quite the contrary, actually – she stood there in the empty space of the garage and could almost feel the air trembling with expectation. Whatever Fate offers me next, I'm going to take it, she found herself thinking with a smile on her face. I'm going to say yes.

Fate, like Alison herself, did not muck about, in this instance. Later that evening, she was tackling her accounts at the kitchen table when a notification flashed in the bottom right corner of the laptop screen, letting her know that she had a new friend request on Facebook.

Alison didn't have much time for Facebook, truth be told: the whole thing seemed like one never-ending parade of people showing off about some achievement or other. 'Bully for you,' she found herself muttering sardonically whenever she bothered to look at her timeline, wading through the stream of information that, more often than not, only served to make her feel inadequate. Clicking through now, to see who had sent the friend request, she found it hard to muster up any real enthusiasm; it would almost certainly be a client or maybe someone she'd been at school with in Bournemouth, about whom she hadn't thought for fifty years. Yeah, whatever. She would accept the request, like she always did, without it really meaning anything.

But then she saw the name there in her notifications list

and found herself gasping aloud and peering closer, in a classic double-take. Thomas Naylor? Gosh. It couldn't be, could it?

She squinted at the small photograph onscreen beside his name, before putting on her reading glasses to make absolutely sure. Thomas Naylor! It *was* him, her very first boyfriend – she recognized him immediately, despite the salt-and-pepper hair he now sported at the temples, because there was his dear wide smile, those laughing grey eyes and yes, the same cute jug-ears he'd had as a teenager. 'Well, I never,' she murmured, feeling a blush surging in her cheeks. He'd sent her a message, she noticed, and she opened it, heart pounding:

Dear Ali,

Has it really been forty-eight years? I don't know where the time goes. I was listening to the radio the other day – one of those 'Golden Oldies' shows, you know – and our song came on. ('Our what?' you're probably thinking. 'Who is this old codger anyway?') Well, I'm talking about 'Without You' by Nilsson, and suddenly there I was, back in Queen's Park with you, and a young man of seventeen again.

Alison had to blink a few times, because she was finding all of this hard to process. Queen's Park, with Tom

Naylor. Warm spring days, daffodils and cherry blossom, and 'Without You' – their song – playing from every café radio and car stereo for weeks on end. Of course she remembered it. Of course she remembered him.

Ali Brealey, I thought to myself. Whatever happened to that lovely Ali Brealey? So I had a little look – had to get my grandson to help me, to be honest, he's much better at these Internet things than me – and here you are; or, rather, here's Ali Tremayne, as I see you are nowadays.

Well, Ali Tremayne, I hope you've had a good life. I hope the world's been kind to you! And if you're listening to the radio one day and 'Without You' comes on, I hope you'll remember me as fondly as I remember you.

Love from your old pal Tom

Alison realized that she'd put a hand up to her heart. Her mouth had fallen open, like a trapdoor swinging. Tom Naylor, the one who'd got away! He'd joined the navy and they'd split up (oh, the buckets she had wept!) and then, by the time he came back, she was going out with Rich and the two of them were talking about setting up home together and moving to the Midlands for Rich's new job. Tom Naylor, though. Oh my. Was he still in Bournemouth? Was he married? Was this her reward from the universe for selling Rich's car, at long last?

Third time lucky, Mum, Robyn teased in her head and she rolled her eyes. 'Ridiculous,' she muttered under her breath, but she was smiling all the same and reading through his message again. Oh, but she'd been so desperately in love with him, back in the day. How she'd idolized that boy! No doubt he had been married for*ever* by now, though, she reminded herself sternly. He'd probably be madly devoted to his beautiful wife – he'd mentioned a grandson, hadn't he? A whole gang of jug-eared kids as well then, she bet. The good ones were always married.

Still, was she going to accept his friend request? Of course she blooming well was. And was she going to write back to him? You bet. And were those actually butterflies flipping and flapping in her stomach, a giddy feeling as if she'd just been on the waltzers at a fairground? Yes. Yes, it was. Who would have thought?

Fired up by nostalgia, she typed back a message immediately:

Dear Tom,

Goodness me, yes, of course I remember you. I am delighted to be reminded of you! How lovely to hear from you, after all these years.

Life has been pretty good to me on the whole, barring a few shocks along the way. I am widowed, but have a lovely daughter, Robyn, and two wonderful grandchildren, and live in Harrogate. I run my own business empire . . . well, I'm a self-employed mobile hairdresser, anyway. Same difference!

How about you? Tell me more. Are you still in Bournemouth? Are you happy? I still hear from Deborah Grayling sometimes – do you remember, my best friend with the blonde bob who worked in the tea rooms. She's in Poole these days, running a little gift shop.

She paused and then backspaced through the lines about Deborah, frowning and thinking he might not want to hear a load of old woman's gossip. Then she remembered the vow she and Robyn had made each other about being brave – the pact she'd made with Fate, too, about saying yes, and dared herself to up the ante. Well, why not? If this was the universe presenting her with an opportunity, then the least she could do was make it clear she was interested:

Funnily enough, I was thinking about you (fondly!) the other week when I went on a blind date. I was quite nervous about the whole thing, as I felt horribly out of practice, but then, for some reason, I found myself remembering our first date at the cinema – and it reminded me how much fun dating could be, with the right person. Sadly, this recent date was a complete disaster – very much NOT the right person! – but never mind!!

Oh dear, did that make her sound desperate? Frivolous? She bit her lip while she read it all back through, trying to imagine what his wife would think, if she saw it. Maybe it *was* a bit flirty, on second thoughts. She deleted the whole paragraph, not wanting to give the wrong impression.

Then a thought occurred to her. Now that they were Facebook friends, she should be able to see his profile and timeline anyway. Leaving her message as a draft, she clicked on his image and his details came up, along with a gorgeous big photo of him, handsome and smiling, with a small child perched on his shoulders.

Let's have a look then, she thought, scanning busily for details. He was living in Nottingham these days, she read – so that answered the Bournemouth question, although he'd left several comments about 'The Cherries', which was the nick-name for the Bournemouth football club, so clearly he hadn't abandoned his roots completely. What else? A nice picture of a grandson graduating, with Tom looking proud to bursting beside him, one hand clapping the young man's shoulder. Some pictures from last Christmas: various excited-looking small children in a living room with a big tree all lit up. Photos of a black Labrador in woodland. Somebody – his daughter, maybe? – celebrating her fortieth birthday. No sign of a wife, though, thought Alison, her interest piqued as she scrolled further down. And further. And further still. No sign of a wife at all. Which was interesting.

She went back to her half-written message and read it all through once more. Then she added:

I would love to know how you are, and what you've been up to all these years. And if you're ever up in Harrogate, do come and say hello!
   Love Alison

There, that would do. She pressed Send before she was tempted to tinker any more and sat there, a smile spreading on her face as she thought about him reading her message, a hundred miles or so away. Tom Naylor, eh? Tom Naylor! Was life about to take an interesting turn? she wondered, going to pour herself a drink. If Tom Naylor was involved, she really hoped so.

Across in York, Bunny-also-known-as-Rachel was feeling as if she too might finally be emerging from under a dark cloud, with the possibility of sunlit uplands straight ahead. Ever since she'd come out of hospital, patched up, recovered and with a socking great engagement ring sparkling on her left hand, she'd felt a different woman. Safe. Accepted. No more pretending. No more secrets. There was a whole new spring in her step.

Now that life felt more secure, she'd spent some time thinking long and hard about what she might want to do next. Although she'd been unceremoniously ditched by SlimmerYou, she still felt proud of the talks she'd done for them and knew she'd inspired other dieters each time. And so she'd taken the plunge and booked the local village hall for an hour-long slot on Wednesday evenings for her very own weight-watching club, planning to incorporate all the tips and advice she'd picked up, as well as the encourage-ment and support she knew she could offer her members. Jasmine, her boss at the café, had let her put an ad in the window, and Dave had helped her design and print hun-dreds of fliers advertising her idea, and her membership was gradually increasing as, week after week, word of mouth began to spread. For the first time Bunny felt as if she'd found her place, her people; she knew what they were going through and could help them along the way. She wasn't charging very much – just enough to cover the cost of the hall, really – but as far as she was concerned, if she could encourage other people to transform into fitter, happier ver-sions of themselves, then that was worth more than money.

'My name's Rachel Halliday, and I'm the proof that you can turn your life around,' she said at the beginning of every meeting, and she meant every word.

That was another thing, too – she was reclaiming her name, so that it no longer felt like that of a victim. She was happy for those closest to her to carry on calling her Bunny, but there would be no more hiding away from the rest of the world in a different guise, she had decided. Why should she? She had done nothing to be ashamed of. In fact she was proud to be a survivor, proud of her own inner strength.

As well as working at the café and running her weight-watching club, she was busying herself by looking into college courses available nearby. Floristry, perhaps – she liked the thought of that – or she'd found one where you could learn how to become a personal trainer, which would also be pretty cool. Maybe she'd do both, just for the hell of it, and be a garland-weaving fitness ninja.

Added to those things, there was the wedding to plan with Dave, which was the most fun of all. Having shied away from commitment for so long, suddenly she couldn't wait to marry him, now that everything was out in the open. Telling him her secrets had been like presenting him with her soft, vulnerable underbelly, but he hadn't wavered or let her down, not for a minute. If anything, his love was like a protective wrapping around her, healing old hurts, making her feel safe, happy and adored. Rachel Mortimer sounded lovely, too, didn't it? A whole new reinvention to come.

In a rush of enthusiasm, they'd gone ahead and booked the Register Office for a Saturday in early spring. Theirs was to be a small do – 'Well, as small as you can get, with all the Mortimers,' Dave acknowledged wryly – but she was really hoping that her mum and brother would want to join them for the occasion. Coming up to Yorkshire had been a way of cutting herself free from the past, but she'd cut herself off from her own family, too, in the process, bar the odd birthday and Christmas card to say that she was okay. Now that her life here was moving to a more permanent footing, she felt she might dare bring her two worlds together at last, build a few bridges. You might not like the past, but you could come to terms with it, she had realized. You could eye it dispassionately and see how far you had travelled. Besides, they would be happy for her, she was sure. Happy enough, maybe, even to permit her niece Chloe to be a bridesmaid, she hoped.

'Things are looking up for me,' she'd written in 'Save the Date' cards to them both recently. 'I feel as if I've been given this wonderful new start up in York, and I'm so happy. I'd absolutely love it if you could celebrate our Big Day with us. Perhaps we could get together before Christmas too, so that you can meet Dave? He's a really great person.'

A blank page, a second chance, a whole new chapter, Bunny thought, as she went about her day, feeling a distinct sense of optimism. Whatever this next chapter might contain, she had a feeling it could be her best one yet.

Chapter Thirty-One

The tinsel was swaying in the breeze from the heaters, the buffet had been well picked over, and the aunts were jigging tipsily to Slade amidst the flashing lights of the dance floor. It was the Mortimers' pre-Christmas knees-up at the village hall, and everyone had come along. There was John, glancing awkwardly across the room at Robyn and his children, while struggling through a conversation with one of his uncles. There was Alison, hooting with laughter in a corner with Jeanie and her other knitting-group pals, having made firm friends of them all. And there too was Frankie, up for the weekend for the first time – well, the second, if you included the fateful anniversary-party incident – with the rest of the immediate family under strict instructions to make her feel welcome, a part of the clan.

Paula and Frankie had already met once by now; and it was remarkable, Paula thought, how well you could feel you knew someone after just two encounters and a lot of phone calls. Geography and travelling distances meant that theirs wouldn't be a popping-round-for-coffee sort of relationship, before you even factored in the added complications of children and work and other commitments, but they'd managed a weekend together so far, with Paula venturing down to London in the autumn, feeling excited, if a little apprehensive, about the situation. After all, there were so many things that could wrong – and her in a strange city, far from home, too. But Frankie had been waiting for her at King's Cross station when the train pulled in and, after the briefest of hesitations, the two women had thrown their arms around each other. Following a huge breathless squeeze, they drew apart a fraction, to marvel laughingly at the similarities between their own faces; and then basically didn't stop talking for the next forty-eight hours, until it was time for Paula to go home again. And oh, having a sister was just *lovely*, Paula thought that whole weekend, and again and again afterwards, whenever they spoke on the phone or texted. You got to your forties and you thought life didn't really hold any surprises for you, but it did, and they could be unexpectedly wonderful. What a delight this one was turning out to be!

Harry, too, had made the same journey south to see his younger daughter on a separate occasion in September, returning with a dazed smile of happiness on his face. It turned out that he and Frankie were both keen cricket fans, and she'd pulled a few strings with a sports-journalist friend of Craig's to get them tickets to see Yorkshire playing

Surrey at the Oval. They'd had a lovely time, even though Harry almost had heart failure every time he was told the price of a drink. Jeanie had been somewhat tight-lipped about the whole excursion, choosing to stay at home, no doubt to rattle through a few thunderous concertos on the piano, but she had agreed to let him go at least, rather than brandishing a rolling pin as she blocked the front door, so that was something. One step at a time.

Today Frankie had the slightly more onerous task of meeting the rest of the Mortimers all at once on their home turf, God help her. This meant not only being introduced to her three half-brothers and their partners and families, as well as Matt, Luke and Joe, but also, of course, the one encounter about which they were all ever-so-slightly terrified: meeting Jeanie.

'It'll be fine, Mum, she's dead nice,' Paula had assured her mother earlier that week, when Jeanie had called round, ostensibly to help make plans for the party, but really to have a little wobble to her daughter about the whole thing. 'I know it's a bit weird for you – the thought of Frankie being there – but she's really easy-going and friendly. And there'll be so many other people around, you can just stay out of her way if you don't feel able to speak to her.'

'Mmm,' had been all that Jeanie had to say on the matter, before changing the subject.

Still, here was Frankie now, having been under the same

roof as Jeanie for at least twenty minutes, with not a single raised word or finger pointed in her direction. Okay, so neither of them had actually broken the ice and spoken to one another – Jeanie might well not even have *looked* at Frankie yet, come to think of it – but it was early days, Paula reminded herself, cutting slices of cake and putting them onto plates. She glanced over at Frankie, who was currently talking to Stephen and Eddie on the other side of the room. She was wearing this gorgeous silky blouse, as blue as a gas-flame, dark jeans and boots, with her hair loose around her shoulders, and was laughing at one of Stephen's stories. Paula grabbed pieces of cake for them all and went over to join the conversation.

'Have some sustenance,' she said, distributing plates. 'Mum's legendary chocolate-and-hazelnut meringue extravaganza: calorific joy on a fork. How are you doing, Frankie?' she added. 'Hopefully not too swamped by the noisy northern contingent.'

Frankie smiled. 'I'm good! Everyone's been so lovely. I think I've spoken to almost the whole family now – wow, and this cake looks incredible. Thank you. Oh, by the way.' She wrestled one-handedly with a shoulder bag and pulled out a square-shaped present wrapped in red paper. 'Happy belated birthday,' she said. 'Sorry it's a bit late. I would have posted this, but it's kind of fragile. Hope you like it.'

'Thank you!' Paula cried, in delight. Frankie had already

sent her a birthday card at the start of the month; she hadn't been expecting anything else. 'That's so kind. Just you coming here was present enough for me, honestly – not that I'm about to give this back now, mind,' she joked.

She set about unwrapping the gift at once, wondering if it might be some kind of picture from her talented half-sister. She'd seen enough of Frankie's artwork while staying with her – humorous pen-and-ink cartoons, some bright, zingy stylized dragon prints, plus various painted canvases hanging around the flat – for the hope to flicker up inside her that this present might be one of her pieces. Then she pulled off the paper to find . . .

'Oh! It's Oscar!' A really beautiful little painting of her dog, looking his most handsome and adorable. Somehow, without ever having met him, Frankie had captured the exact twinkle in her dachshund's eye, his mischievous, beady gaze. 'How did you . . . ? Oh my goodness. I love it!'

'That's so cute!' cried Stephen, peering to have a look. 'He's got his *just-nicked-a-sausage* glint and everything.'

'It's brilliant,' Eddie agreed.

Luke, Paula's eldest, was nearby and turned to see what everyone was exclaiming about. 'Whoa!' he laughed, seeing the picture. 'That is so cool. Did you, like, actually paint this yourself, Frankie?'

Frankie was smiling and blushing. 'Yes, I did,' she replied with a laugh. 'I'm glad you like it,' she said to Paula. 'I must confess I did ask Matt for help, and he emailed me a load of photos. I hope you don't think that's horribly sneaky of me.'

'Not at all! This is gorgeous, thank you so much.' Paula hugged her and then beamed at the painting all over again. What a special, unique gift, with such thought behind it. Was it shallow of her to see 'great presents' as another reason why she loved having a sister? Oh, well. Call her shallow, then. 'Matt, look!' she called, holding up the picture as he came over from the makeshift bar, a wonky Santa hat perched on his head.

'Aha! I love it when a plan comes together,' he replied with a grin. 'We've been plotting, haven't we, Frank? Plotting and scheming.' He inspected the painting with an approving nod. 'Isn't that great? It's him to a tee. Watch out, Frankie, the boys will have you commissioned to do the hamster next.'

'Hey, all commissions gratefully accepted,' laughed Frankie. 'Us self-employed types never say no. Bring on the hamster, I say!'

Paula hugged her and then gave Matt a squeeze too, for his part in the whole subterfuge. 'Good work, you two,' she said happily, leaning against him and feeling rather sickeningly contented that today was going so well. What was more, far from thinking Frankie sneaky, she loved that they'd both gone behind her back together, for her sake. They'd definitely risen a few rungs in her Christmas-present list now; she'd have to find some extra-special gifts for them in return. Maybe even that electric guitar Matt had been hinting about, ever since they bought one for Luke. As well as some industrial-strength earplugs for herself, of course.

Paula went to put the painting in a safe place in the kitchen (there was always at least one calamitous drink spillage at a Mortimer gathering), and set about handing around pieces of cake to the rest of the family, making sure she found an extra-large piece for her husband. Goodness, she felt happy, she realized suddenly, thinking of the painting again and feeling quite overcome with her own good fortune. Here they were, all her favourite people in the same place, celebrating and dancing and laughing together. A proper family. Sure, a slightly different-shaped family these days from where they'd been six months ago, but who was to say there was anything wrong with that? The Mortimers had survived all the various crises that had hit them this year, and had evolved into something stronger. Maybe even something better. Oh, and right on cue, here came the opening bars of her favourite Christmas song. 'Come on, you know you want to,' she said, grabbing Matt's hand with a laugh and pulling him onto the dance floor.

'How are the kids?' Across the room, John had finally plucked up the courage to approach Robyn, having shuffled about awkwardly on the sidelines until now. Unfortunately –

for him, anyway – his romantic dreams of shacking up in the Edinburgh love-nest with a girl half his age had abruptly collapsed when she dumped him, and he'd slunk home to York, tail between his legs, crest well and truly fallen. That was two months ago and, having slept in his parents' spare room for a few weeks on returning, he was now sharing a flat in Heslington with some random postgrad students while he looked for a job. Regrets? He had a few, as the old song went.

'Why don't you ask them yourself?' Robyn replied. Despite her complicated feelings of anger and betrayal, she couldn't help feeling a tiny twinge of pity for John as well, these days. Bearded and kind of shabby around the edges, he appeared a diminished figure since his return to the city, his swagger all gone. 'Robyn, I've been a fool, I'm so sorry,' he had said the first time they saw each other, and from the expectant expression on his face it was obvious that he was hoping for the welcoming arms of forgiveness, a return to their old partnership together. *We could give it another shot, yeah?* his eyes had pleaded.

But she just couldn't afford him complete absolution, she'd decided. He'd let her down so badly that she would never be able to trust him with her heart in the same way. However sorry he might be acting now, to let him back into her life would mean ushering in a side-helping of doubt at the same time, and who wanted to live with that? *The kids will be glad you're back* had been the most generous thing she could bring herself to say.

Since then, the two of them had seen each other fairly frequently, but for practical, civil reasons rather than social ones: parents' evenings at the children's schools, and doorstep exchanges when he had been looking after Sam and Daisy for an afternoon or night. It was a detached, disjointed arrangement, born of necessity, but it still felt unnatural.

'They're fine,' she added now, softening a little at his pinched face. 'Sam did well in his exams last week, and Daisy has made a new best friend at Brownies. But I'm sure they'll tell you all about it, if they manage to peel themselves away from Joe's game.' She indicated her head to where they were clustered around Paula's younger son, who was showing them something on his phone. 'At least I hope it's a game,' she added jokingly.

There was a small pause. 'And how are you?' he asked next.

He seemed so humble these days, it kept taking her by surprise. It was like talking to a stranger, a reduced version of the man she'd been married to, and it was hard to know how to reply. How was she? She was pretty bloody well, actually, thanks for asking, John. Coming to the end of her first term back at the university, having loved every minute of it: the lectures, the research, the camaraderie. There was even talk of her jetting off to San Francisco in the spring for a conference on Genetic and Protein Engineering, which sounded amazing. All of this while juggling Sam's first term at secondary school, managing to put dinner on the table every night and keeping on top of the laundry. It was busy, sure, but at least that left her with barely a minute in which to miss her ex-husband. More importantly, it was incredibly satisfying, as if her life had rich new seams running through it, full of interest and opportunity.

Perhaps it would be rubbing John's nose in it to articulate all of this to him in detail, though. 'Fine, thanks,' she said blandly instead. 'You?'

He started talking about a job he was hoping to go for, in a big car plant out of town; there was some old contact he had there, apparently, which he hoped might mean they could circumnavigate his lack of a good reference from the university and his exile of shame. She tuned out, nodding politely while trying not to laugh at the way her mum was letting rip on the dance floor with the knitting-group divas and John's aunts. Look at that woman go, she thought admiringly. Alison was a changed person these days, joining a Pilates class as well as hanging out with her new knitting mates ('They are just the *best* women!' she had cried to Robyn in delight) and whizzing about in her snazzy new Golf. Not only that, but she'd also recently met up with Tom, her very first love, from way back when, and he was still, apparently, the greatest kisser she had ever met. Wasn't life oddly circular sometimes? All these big loops that you found yourself on unexpectedly, repetitions and echoes of past events in new forms. Whichever direction her mum's future might take, no one could deny that Alison had blossomed remarkably in recent months. 'This is my third age, according to my pal Mo,' she'd said down the phone to Robyn the other night. 'Sixty-five is the new twenty-five, she reckons. And heavens, it's fun!'

'So yeah, fingers crossed,' John finished now, and Robyn jerked back to attention because he was looking at her as if waiting for an answer.

'Fingers crossed,' she agreed heartily. And despite having fantasized previously about John dying horribly of some disgusting venereal disease, alone and preferably in a ditch, with rats gnawing at his sweating, pox-ridden body, she was clearly far more mature about everything nowadays, because she actually did want him to find a new job and get himself together, if only for the sake of the children. No, for his own sake, too, she corrected herself more generously, so that he could regain his confidence and move on.

'Do you think you and Dad might . . . get back together?' Sam had asked when John had returned to the city, and the hope in his voice had almost been enough to drive a wedge through Robyn's heart. Of course he wanted his dad back home, and for the four of them to carry on as if nothing had happened; Daisy had asked something very similar too. And sure, once upon a time Robyn probably would have forgiven him and done her best to reassemble a happy family for the sake of everyone else; to keep up appearances as much as anything.

But she was done with faking it these days, and so she had had to dredge up all her courage and tell them the truth as gently as possible. No, Mum and Dad weren't getting back together. They were still going to be friends (which was stretching said truth, admittedly) and they still loved Sam and Daisy very, very much, but they were going to live in different houses from now on. It would be fine, honestly; she would make sure of that. They were all going to be absolutely fine.

And they were, by and large. Robyn's heart had been in her mouth when Sam had gone off for his first week at secondary school in his too-big blazer and shiny new shoes, but he had settled in quickly, discovered he loved chemistry (a boy after her own heart) and had been invited along to the basketball-club try-out sessions by the PE teacher. Robyn swore he seemed to be standing taller lately too, as if he was finally appreciating his own height. As for Daisy, she had exhausted her love of insects at long last, and had now moved on to a fascination with the solar system and space exploration. For her birthday a few weeks earlier, they had trekked down the motorway to the National Space Centre in Leicester and it had been, apparently, 'the best day of my *life*'.

Robyn was taking that as a pat on the back, a sign that

she was getting through this okay. Yes, Daisy and Sam still missed John being home; that was understandable. She'd never tell him as much, but she missed him too, every now and then – the companionship of marriage, at least. Still, her world had expanded in other areas, which felt like compensation. She'd been out for drinks with Beth Broadwood and some of the other mums from school, for instance, and they'd had a really great laugh. Plus Victoria, her boss, had talked her into joining the Divorcee Club, which was apparently a hand-picked selection of excellent women who were always up for a night out. Or a Saturday brunch, if the kids were with their dads and the weekend was looming emptily ahead. Or, hell, just a coffee sometimes, if anyone needed a friend to talk to. 'Count me in,' Robyn had told Victoria. 'To all of it.'

As well as that, she had realized that splitting up with your husband did not have to mean being shunned by his family, as she'd dreaded – once a Mortimer, always a Mortimer, Jeanie had assured her. Both Jeanie and Paula had been brilliant in terms of childcare and making sure Robyn and the children were still invited along to things, and other family kindnesses. Also, she, Paula and Bunny had started going jogging together every week, and Daisy was wildly excited about being a bridesmaid for Bunny and Dave, along with Bunny's niece Chloe. You could say Robyn had lost a set of in-laws and gained some friends instead.

'Will you excuse me a mo,' she said to John, noticing Bunny across the room now and giving her a little wave. Robyn had received a text from her last night, saying she'd passed the final part of her personal-trainer course, and she wanted to go and congratulate her with a hug, as well as book herself in as a client. And why not? Family had to stick together, in Robyn's opinion. 'Talk to you soon,' she said, already walking away. Then she smiled and hurried over to her sister-in-law. 'Hey there, you qualified fitness guru, you,' she called out. 'What brilliant news – well done!'

Chapter Thirty-Two

Frankie was enjoying herself hugely. So this was what it felt like to belong to a big, friendly family, with siblings and cousins and partners, she thought repeatedly, as her new relatives came up and introduced themselves, as she smiled at the teasing and in-jokes that bounced between them. There was this whole network of shared memories, this history that connected them all, with every allegiance, spat and happiness a valid part of the chain. And now she was a link in it, too.

She'd already been won over by Paula, and Matt had turned out to be as good-natured and lovable in person as he'd been in their secret pre-birthday correspondence. (She'd pretended to Paula that she wanted to ask his advice about trees, on behalf of a friend; Paula clearly hadn't suspected a thing.) Dave and Bunny were absolutely adorable, so visibly in love that they'd held hands almost the entire time, and were both super-friendly and welcoming, immediately inviting her, Craig and Fergus along to their wedding in the spring. She wasn't entirely sure what had happened between John and his wife (ex-wife?) Robyn, but they were both very pleasant, individually, to her, as were Stephen and his partner Eddie. As it turned out, Stephen was a solicitor specializing in family law and had been interested to hear about the Julia saga. 'Any further problems, ring me,' he'd said, handing her his card. Then he'd grinned. 'Or just ring for a chat too, obviously. I can do big-brotherly advice as well as the legal stuff.'

'Big-brotherly advice,' Eddie scoffed, rolling his eyes up to the ceiling. 'Spot the youngest child who's thrilled to be an older sibling all of a sudden,' he added teasingly. 'Don't let him start bossing you around now, Frankie. He's been longing for this moment, his whole life!'

Frankie had laughed at Stephen's indignant face. 'I don't mind at all,' she assured them. 'I'm thrilled, too, to have some big brothers and a sister, after being an only child forever. And thank you,' she added, tucking the card in her purse.

The only person who hadn't come over and chatted to her was the matriarch herself, Jeanie, but that was understandable, Frankie thought, eyeing her across the room as she briskly stacked empty plates and stooped to pick up a fallen wine glass. That was fine. Harry assured her that he was 'working on it', which was all Frankie could hope for, really.

Good old Harry. Her dad! They'd had such a great time together at the cricket back in September, it had felt really easy and companionable. He'd been lovely to Craig and

439

Fergus, insisting on making them all toad-in-the-hole and mash for dinner one night – his speciality, apparently. He was trying to learn a new dish every month, he'd explained: 'Turns out you *can* teach an old dog new tricks.' What was especially nice for Frankie was the fact that he was one of the few people in her life who'd known her mother as a young woman, and who could tell her funny stories about impetuous, rule-breaking Kathy, which felt like bonus prizes to Frankie. They'd already arranged for Harry to come down again and stay for a couple of days in the New Year, and she was looking forward to it very much. 'Anything you need in the meantime,' he'd told her, 'you just ask me, okay? You've got thirty-four years' worth of favours stored up with the Bank of Dad, after all. Ask away!'

Closer to home, things were settling down a bit, following the tumultuous summer they'd had. Fergus had started school and was exhausted half the time – on the second day he'd been horrified that he was expected to don his uniform and head off to the reception class once more ('What, I have to go *again*?' he'd asked in scandalized tones) – but he was now in the swing of things and seemed to be looking forward to the nativity play at the end of term, judging by the way he was singing Christmas songs around the flat at any opportunity. It was odd, having him out all day, though; the place felt weirdly quiet and empty without him, but the flipside was that she and Craig were getting so much more work done, with the extra free time, that they were almost too busy to notice.

Craig had told the newspaper that he wanted to end his parenting column, and had gone out on a high with a truly lovely final piece about looking forward to the future. He'd signed off by thanking the readers sincerely for the tremendous support he'd received from them ever since he'd begun writing about being a dad and as a result, he had been all over social media the day the piece was published. 'You're trending!' his editor had texted him excitedly, and Craig had received many heartfelt messages from the public wishing the family well. Since then they'd both found other strands of work to compensate for the demise of the column: Frankie had been commissioned to design some cards and stationery with her dragon illustrations and, having enjoyed painting Paula's little dog, had also decided to venture into the lucrative world of pet portraits. She'd advertised her services online, setting herself up as an Etsy seller, and had already had a gratifyingly enthusiastic response.

As for Craig, among other things he had successfully pitched an idea for a new magazine column called 'Dear Dad', a variation on the agony-uncle idea, where he dispensed fatherly wisdom to all those in need. So far he had covered topics as far-ranging as testicular-cancer checks, the best way to wallpaper a room and handling toddler meltdowns, and was thoroughly enjoying the variety. Even more excitingly, he'd been courted by a publisher, who'd approached him about writing a non-fiction book on modern fatherhood. Flattered by the praise and enthusiasm of the editor and dazzled by the financial offer that had been made, Craig felt his star was on the rise and had wasted no time in getting stuck into the opening chapters.

He seemed much happier in general, thank goodness – back to his old genial self, now that things with Julia were gradually figuring themselves out. The three of them had met up a number of times, in the presence of Julia's solicitor, to establish a way forward, and so far they'd managed to avoid going to court and having any official judgments made. Or bawling at one another across the table, either, which felt like progress.

Craig wanted to introduce Julia gradually to Fergus, one step at a time, and she, thankfully, had eventually agreed. They had managed the process carefully and sensitively, first by Craig and Frankie showing Fergus the baby photos he'd never seen ('So, you know how babies come out of ladies' tummies? Well, you came out of THIS lady's tummy – look, here she is, with a big tummy, and you're inside. Then – pop! – here you are. That's Mummy Julia, remember we saw her in the playground that day?') and doing their best to answer his questions. Then they'd invited Julia round to the flat a couple of times, so that she could play trains with him (lucky woman) and read him stories, taking everything at Fergus's pace.

Bless him, despite their angst and dread beforehand, he'd been totally cool about the whole situation – '*Lots* of people at school have extra mummies and daddies,' he'd said grandly – and Julia appeared to be trying her hardest too, markedly humbler and more acquiescent than she'd seemed on first arrival. She'd found herself a part-time job in a vegan café and was renting a small flat in Acton, not too far away, and had just started picking Fergus up from school one afternoon a week and giving him his tea. Most importantly, she had calmed right down, dropping her aggression and being more cooperative. She'd even confessed to Frankie how stressful she'd found motherhood initially, how scared she'd been that she wasn't a natural, but how determined she was to put things right now. She was seeing a therapist and working through her problems, and Frankie could tell that, although she was still troubled, Julia was doing her best. At times she found herself actually liking the other woman, especially her sparky sense of humour. She could understand why Craig had loved her all those years ago.

'I have a daddy and two mummies now,' Frankie had overheard Fergus loftily telling his friend Preena in the park the other day. 'One is Mumma and she's my favourite, but Mummy Julia is funny and has hair like me.'

'We're just achingly modern,' Frankie had laughed to

Preena's mum, rolling her eyes, but she felt proud of how far they'd come. If this year had taught her anything, it was that families could be resilient, could flex and bend to accommodate new additions or work around a problem. Was any family normal, deep down? Hers certainly wasn't, but she felt as if she and Craig were far stronger together, now that they'd weathered this storm side by side. Plus she felt part of something bigger these days, ever since she'd met the Mortimers. She had a dad and a sister, both of whom she adored, three brothers too, who all seemed great, and it felt as if there were whole new layers of safety net beneath her, ready to catch her if she needed support.

And who was to say what the future held, in terms of family, anyway? Because just yesterday she and Craig had gone to view some office space nearby that was up for rental, with the plan to give Frankie in particular more room to spread out, workwise. But as she looked around the whitewashed studio and made financial calculations in her head, another idea altogether had come to her. 'You know . . . for what this would cost us in terms of rent, on top of the existing mortgage payments for the flat, we could actually look at buying a bigger place to live instead,' she said in a low voice, conscious of the estate agent lurking discreetly in the background. 'Somewhere with a small office and maybe even a garden, if we put all our savings into the pot. What do you think?'

Craig had nodded, thinking it through. 'I'd really like that,' he said. 'Somewhere that's ours, somewhere permanent. Maybe with an extra room . . .'

'Oh yes, good idea, for when Harry or Paula comes down to stay,' she'd replied, but he'd looked awkward – shy, almost – and she realized that she'd misunderstood, that he was actually thinking about something quite different. Was he? 'Do you mean . . . what are you saying?' she asked, not wanting to get ahead of herself. They still hadn't quite had the conversation about babies, if that was where Craig was going; she'd been waiting for the dust to settle following Julia's arrival, but couldn't deny the subject had been on her mind.

'I'm saying . . .' He seemed uncharacteristically reticent. 'I think I'm saying that I'd like us to have a baby together. Expand the family. What do you think?'

So she'd been right. And what *did* she think? 'Wow,' she said, taken aback, trying to marshal a response.

'When you said to me you were worried about losing Fergus, and how that would mean you were no longer a mum . . . it broke my heart. Because you're the best mum,' he went on. 'A wonderful mum. And think about it: a little brother or sister for Ferg, an extra member of the family – the chance for you to pass on your seriously excellent genes to another human being. I mean, come on. What sort of idiot wouldn't want *that*?'

He grinned at her and it was all she could do not to grab him by the shirt collar and attempt some baby-making right there and then. She leaned in to kiss him instead, her heart filling with happiness. 'Well, this idiot isn't about to turn you down,' she said, smiling. 'Okay then, you're on: let's make some huge lifetime commitments together. As many as possible. Count me in for the long haul.'

Frankie was interrupted from her misty-eyed reverie just then by a tap on her arm. 'Hello,' said a voice, and Frankie jumped as she realized that Jeanie was standing next to her, lips pursed as if she meant business. *Oh, Christ – here we go.* She'd had nightmares about this moment.

'Hi,' she said politely, casting around to see if Paula or Harry had noticed her predicament, but neither of them was looking her way. 'Um.' She swallowed. 'Thanks so much for letting me come here today. I really appreciate it.'

Jeanie gave a curt little nod, her eyes giving nothing away. 'I was wondering . . .' she said in the next moment, and Frankie held her breath, imagining all the different ways this sentence could end, every single one of them unspeakably awful. 'The painting you did for Paula,' Jeanie went on. 'It's very good. Very good indeed. Matt said you did it all from photographs.'

'Yes, that's right,' Frankie replied cautiously. Okay, so of all the imaginary conversations she had played out in her head with her father's wife, it was fair to say that none of them had started like this.

'Well.' Jeanie still hadn't quite managed to look at her properly yet, her gaze fixed on the middle distance between them. 'I was wondering,' she began again, and then she *did* look at Frankie and, to Frankie's surprise, actually seemed kind of nervous. 'Do you ... Might you ... take a new commission? For Harry's Christmas present? Only our last dog died a year ago, and I know Harry still misses him very badly.' Her lips twisted together slightly, and Frankie had the impression that it wasn't only Harry who missed the dog. 'If I got some photographs together, do you think you could – I mean, I'm sure you're very busy, but ... ?'

'I would love to,' Frankie told her warmly, a lump in her throat. 'Of course I will. What sort of dog was he?'

'A springer spaniel. Charlie, we called him, and oh, he was a proper Charlie, if you know what I mean!' She was animated suddenly as she remembered him, the stiffness temporarily leaving her features and her eyes becoming far-away. Frankie guessed she was tramping through a forest somewhere with a bouncy dog, his nose to the ground, his tail beating with happiness. 'We always had springers, they're such smashing dogs. But with us getting on, we weren't sure we could cope with one any more.' She folded her arms across her chest and looked down, as if worried that she had said too much, made herself vulnerable in the face of the enemy. 'Anyway.'

'Well, I'll absolutely paint you a picture of Charlie,' Frankie replied, trying to recalibrate her workload as she said the words. There was only a fortnight to go before Christmas, and she already had quite a lot to get through before then, but there was no way she was about to turn down this offer from Jeanie, even if it meant having to work through the night in order to finish. 'He sounds brilliant – it would be my pleasure. Paula has all my details, so just as soon as you can get those pictures to me, I'll make a start,' she promised.

Jeanie smiled. A rather suspicious, grudging sort of smile, admittedly, but all the same to Frankie it felt like the bright summer sun coming out, right there, on that grey December day, heralding a truce. 'Lovely,' said Jeanie, before coming over all brisk and businesslike in the next second. 'Right! Well, if you'll excuse me, I'd better get the kettle on. Time to sober up Harry's sisters, before they fall over on the dance floor. Tea won't make itself!' She was about to bustle away again, but hesitated on the verge of departure as if something had just occurred to her. 'Would you like a cup, love?' she added after a moment.

It was the smallest of gestures, just the tiniest of things, and yet it felt so much bigger than the mere offer of a drink. 'I'd love one, please,' said Frankie, smiling back at Jeanie.

There! Was that the world applauding? Was that the ice finally cracking and thawing, a new rosy dawn on the horizon? Why, yes – yes, it was, and at that moment it seemed as if the whole family felt it, and were celebrating in their own way.

Across the room, Dave and Bunny were kissing under a sprig of mistletoe. Robyn and her children were making up a silly dance routine together and laughing breathlessly. Paula gave a squeak as she glanced at a text from the office, saying that a client had just put in a huge offer on one of her vendors' houses, and threw her arms around Matt. Stephen and Eddie started a conga with some of the aunts. Even John went to join in.

And Jeanie said to Frankie, 'Right you are then' and marched off to the kitchen, looking oddly pleased with herself.

Seeing all of this, Harry Mortimer winked across at his younger daughter and decided it was definitely time to pop open some celebratory champagne.

Acknowledgements

Love and thanks to Lizzy Kremer, Caroline Hogg, Anna Bond, Mel Four, Stuart Dwyer, Kate Tolley, Sarah Arratoon and the whole Pan Mac team. You're all superstars.

Thanks to Amanda Crutchley who patiently talked me through family law, and to Janette Pearson for answering my piano-related questions – any mistakes within the novel are most definitely my own.

Cocktails all round for the SWANs, my funny, clever, brilliant author colleagues – it's always such a pleasure to see you.

All the love to Martin, Hannah, Tom and Holly for being the best people I know.

And thanks to you for picking up this book. I really hope you enjoyed it.

Find out more
about Lucy and her books at
www.lucydiamond.co.uk

Or say hello at her Facebook page
www.facebook.com/LucyDiamondAuthor